ALSO BY ANNIE PROULX

Heart Songs and Other Stories

Postcards

The Shipping News

Accordion Crimes

Close Range

THAT OLD ACE IN THE HOLE

A Novel

Annie Proulx

SCRIBNER

New York London Toronto
Sydney Singapore

SCRIBNER
1230 Avenue of the Americas
New York, NY 10020

For information about special discounts for bulk purchases,
please contact Simon & Schuster Special Sales:
1-800-465-6798 or business@simonandschuster.com

Manufactured in the United States of America

1   3   5   7   9   10   8   6   4   2

Library of Congress Cataloging-in-Publication Data
is available.

ISBN 0-7432-4092-8

This book is for Jon and Gail

Muffy and Geoff

Morgan

Gillis

and for

Doug and Cathy

with the hope that all their chickens

will be prairie chickens

CONTENTS

ACKNOWLEDGMENTS ix

1. Global Pork Rind 1
2. Art Plastic 20
3. On the Road Again 36
4. The Evil Fat Boy 48
5. No Room in Cowboy Rose 65
6. Sheriff Hugh Dough 74
7. *The Rural Compendium* 91
8. Pioneer Fronk 108
9. The Busted Star 124
10. Old Dog 156
11. Tater Crouch 178
12. Rope Butt 207
13. Habakuk's Luck 229
14. The Young Couple 244
15. Abel and Cain 259
16. Curiosity Killed the Cat 286

CONTENTS

17. The Devil's Hatband   289

18. Just a Few Questions   298

19. The Sheriff's Office   306

20. Everything's O.K. So Far   313

21. Triple Cross   334

22. Ribeye Writes   356

23. Rich Orlando   364

24. Violet's Night on the Town   378

25. Top Sales   390

26. Brother Mesquite   408

27. Trip to Denver   419

28. Used but Not Abused   440

29. Ribeye Cluke's Office   446

30. Quick Change   453

31. Mrs. Betty Doak   472

32. Ace in the Hole   484

33. Failure   499

34. Barbwire   509

ACKNOWLEDGMENTS

So many people in the Texas and Oklahoma panhandles helped me with information about the past history of the region and their present lives on the high plains that it is impossible to thank them all. Not everything I heard and saw was used—that would have meant a book in encyclopedic size—but I was sorry not to be able to include it all.

Special thanks to Cathy and Doug Ricketts of Lipscomb, Texas, who gave invaluable help, showing me everything from old bison wallows to abandoned houses, sharing their friends, accompanying me to cattle auctions and other regional events. Their deep knowledge of the panhandle and their love for the high prairie country was infectious. Cathy, in particular, eased the research task by arranging meetings with dozens of men and women, knowledgeable in their fields, and made arrangements for the BBC crew covering some of the research for this book.

Cesa Espinoza, the archival specialist at the Panhandle-Plains Museum in Canyon, Texas, was most helpful in finding windmill material for me. The curator of the No Man's Land Museum in Goodwell,

ACKNOWLEDGMENTS

Oklahoma, suggested many books on the region's history. Thanks to Arlene Paschel at Five Star Equipment in Spearman, Texas, for her explanations of irrigation equipment and techniques; to Robert of an oil rig makeover crew, who let me use his cell phone when I got a flat tire from a sagebrush stob in the middle of nowhere; and thanks to Doug Ricketts, who left his furniture workshop and changed that flat. Thanks to Oscar and Sandy Drake, who owned and ran the Waca grain elevator for thirty-six years and who keep the famous crow's barbwire nest from 1930s dust bowl days in their garage. Oscar's anvil collection, from tiny dentists' anvils to enormous cone anvils, is the work history of the panhandle crammed into one room. Thanks, too, to Mike Ladd, Sandy Drake's son, wheat farmer and Peace Corps volunteer, for his comments on contemporary panhandle agriculture.

Naturalist Bob Rogers, of both the Texas Parks and Wildlife Department and Cloud Shadow Pigeons, was an enthusiastic guide through prairie dog towns and burrowing owl sites, and I thank him for his commentary on the woolybucket tree, his one-man front yard forest and miniature nature preserve, and his devoted work in the Canadian area of the panhandle in encouraging the conservation of the prairie landscape and its natural history.

Laura van Campenhout of De Geus, my publisher in the Netherlands, helped with Dutch windmill phrases. Phyllis Randolph, the director of the Cimarron Heritage Center Museum in Boise City, Oklahoma,

ACKNOWLEDGMENTS

showed me that museum's fascinating collection and Santa Fe Trail exhibit. Thanks to organic farmer and ranch restorer Clarence Yanke and his artist wife, Marilyn, of Yanke Farms in Sunray, fighting the good fight. Robin Mitchell of Canadian's Mitchell Ranch and her grandfather, Gober Mitchell, introduced me to the world of racing quarter horses and showed me an extraordinary day at the 6666 Ranch in Guthrie, Texas, and another good morning at their spring branding. Thanks, too, to Glenn Blodgett, DVM, of the 6666, for a look at the inner workings of a great breeding ranch. Phil Sell of Perryton Equity gave me a bottom-to-top tour of his Farnsworth grain elevator, especially memorable the ride to the top in the creaking wire cage.

Larry McMurtry of Booked Up in Archer City, Texas, supplied me with out-of-print books on panhandle history, geography and ways. Clint Swift helped with information on economic and corporate hog production. I spent pleasant hours at the forge of Lee Reeves—knifemaker, farrier, blacksmith extraordinaire—in Shattuck, Oklahoma. There was a happy afternoon with fiddle player Frankie McWhorter for a bit of prairie music and talk.

Special thanks to Darryl Birkenfeld of Stratford and Cactus, Texas, for a view of the invisible world of Mexican labor in the panhandle and for his broad knowledge of and comments on the rural high plains economy and moral geography. Watercolorist Phyllis Ballew of Shattuck, Oklahoma, one of the movers and

ACKNOWLEDGMENTS

shakers in establishing the wonderful windmill museum in that town, was most helpful, as was banker Clinton Davis, also of Shattuck, with his remarks on contemporary panhandle development and decline, and his knowledge of the turn-of-the-century local business of raising broomcorn.

District Manager C. E. Williams of Panhandle Ground Water Conservation District No. 3 made useful comments on the agricultural use of the Ogallala aquifer. Thanks to Don and Jo anne Malone for a detailed tour and explanation of oil and gas pumping stations and their maintenance. Thanks to Louis A. Rodriques of Canadian, Texas, parrot fancier and heavy metal enthusiast, as well as rig manager for the Unit Drilling Company, for his tour and explanation of a big, clean rig. Special thanks to Mike McKinney of Merex Oil Company, for a lucid and clear explanation of the technique of floodwater recovery of oil. Gene Purcell of Higgins, Texas, haymaker, wearer of the greasy black hat, makes the best lunches for miles around and there is always stimulating conversation at his funky café, the inspirational spark for the Old Dog. Thanks also to rancher Donnie Johnson, retiree Wesley Heesch and feed salesman Bruce Eakins for their lively opinions of the way things are going in the agricultural panhandle. Artist Ruth Erikson of Canadian was good company at an Oklahoma cockfight.

Mark W. Lang of the Cabot carbon black plant in Pampa, Texas, provided an explanation and tour of a very complicated business which I could not fit into

ACKNOWLEDGMENTS

this story except in fleeting references. Retired Park Service Ranger Ed Day gave a fine exhibition of flint knapping (deleted in the final version) and a detailed tour of Alibates flint quarries near Lake Meredith. Asa and Fannie Jones and Phyllis Anderson, keepers and curators of the Kenton Museum in Kenton, Oklahoma, provided hospitality and information on dozens of curious artifacts. And, also in Kenton, thanks to Ina Labrier and her daughter Jane Apple, two women who do the work of ten, and to Bob Apple for a visit to the ruins of the old 101 ranch buildings. Photographer Stuart Klipper introduced me to Brown Paper Pete. Last but not least, thanks to Mickey and Penny Province of Lipscomb for their help and kindness, and to Trey Webb of Flap-Air Helicopter Service, who, in the air, helps gather livestock, inspect pipeline, control predators, manage game and photograph the panhandle.

That about does it.

THAT OLD ACE
IN THE HOLE

Alle molens vangen wind

1

GLOBAL PORK RIND

In late March Bob Dollar, a young, curly-headed man of twenty-five with the broad face of a cat, pale innocent eyes fringed with sooty lashes, drove east along Texas State Highway 15 in the panhandle, down from Denver the day before, over the Raton Pass and through the dead volcano country of northeast New Mexico to the Oklahoma pistol barrel, then a wrong turn north and wasted hours before he regained the way. It was a roaring spring morning with green in the sky, the air spiced with sand sagebrush and aromatic sumac. NPR faded from the radio in a string of announcements of corporate supporters, replaced by a Christian station that alternated pabulum preaching and punchy music. He switched to shit-kicker airwaves and listened to songs about staying home, going home, being home and the errors of leaving home.

The road ran along a railroad track. He thought the bend of the rails unutterably sad, those cold and gleaming strips of metal turning away into the distance made him think of the morning he was left on Uncle Tam's doorstep listening for the inside clatter of coffee pot and cups although there had been no train nor tracks there. He did not know how the rails had gotten into his head as symbols of sadness.

Gradually the ancient thrill of moving against the horizon into the great yellow distance heated him, for even fenced and cut with roads the overwhelming presence of grassland persisted, though nothing of the original prairie remained. It was all flat expanse and wide sky. Two coyotes looking for afterbirths trotted through a pasture to the east, moving through fluid grass, the sun backlighting their fur in such a way that they appeared to have silver linings. Irrigated circles of winter wheat, dotted with stocker calves, grew on land as level as a runway. In other fields tractors lashed tails of dust. He noticed the habit of slower drivers to pull into the breakdown lane—here called the "courtesy lane"—and wave him on.

Ahead cities loomed, but as he came close the sky-scrapers, mosques and spires metamorphosed into grain elevators, water towers and storage bins. The elevators were the tallest buildings on the plains, symmetrical, their thrusting shapes seeming to entrap kinetic energy. After a while Bob noticed their verti-cal rhythm, for they rose up regularly every five or ten miles in trackside towns. Most were concrete cylinders, some brick or tile, but at many sidings the old wood elevators, peeling and shabby, still stood, some surfaced with asbestos shingles, a few with rusted metal loosened by the wind. Rectilinear streets joined at ninety-degree angles. Every town had a motto: "The Town Where No One Wears a Frown"; "The Richest Land and the Finest People"; "10,000 Friendly People and One or Two Old Grumps." He passed the Kar-Vu Drive-In, a midtown plywood Jesus, dead cows by the side of the road, legs stiff as two-by-fours, waiting for the renderer's truck. There were nodding pump jacks and pivot irrigation rigs (one still decked out in Christmas lights) to the left and right, condensation tanks and complex assemblies of pipes and gauges, though such was the size of the landscape and their random placement that they seemed metal trinkets strewn by a vast and careless hand. Orange-and-yellow signs marked the existence of underground pipelines, for beneath the fields and pastures lay an invisible world of pipes, cables, boreholes, pumps and extraction devices, forming, with the surface fences and roads, a monstrous three-dimensional grid. This grid extended into the sky through contrails and invisible satellite transmissions. At the edge of fields he noticed brightly painted V-8 diesel engines (most converted to natural gas), pumping up water from the Ogallala aquifer below. And he passed scores of anonymous, low, grey buildings with enormous fans at their ends set back from the road and surrounded by chain-link fence. From the air these guarded hog farms resembled strange grand pianos with six or ten white keys, the trapezoid shape of the body the effluent lagoon in the rear.

Still, all of these machines and wire and metal buildings seemed ephemeral. He knew he was on prairie, what had once been part of the enormous North American grassland extending from Canada to Mexico, showing its thousand faces to successions of travelers who described it in contradictory ways: under gritty spring wind the grass blew sidewise, figured with bluets and anemones, pussytoes and Johnny-jump-ups, alive with birds and antelope; in midsummer, away from the overgrazed trail margins, they traveled through groin-high grass rolling in waves; those on the trail in late summer saw dry, useless desert studded with horse-crippling cactus. Few, except working cowboys, ventured onto the plains in winter when stinging northers swept snow across it. Where once the howling of wolves was heard, now sounded the howl of tires.

Bob Dollar had no idea he was driving into a region of immeasurable natural complexity that some believed abused beyond saving. He saw only what others had seen—the bigness, pump jacks nodding pterodactyl heads, road alligators cast off from the big semi tires. Every few miles a red-tailed hawk marked its hunting boundary. The edges of the road were misty with purple-flowered wild mustard whose rank scent embittered the air. He said to the rearview mirror, "some flat-ass place." Though it seemed he was not so much in a place as confronting the raw material of human use.

A white van turned out of a side road in front of him and he narrowed his eyes; he knew white vans were favored by the criminally insane and escaped convicts, that the bad drivers of the world gravitated to them. The van sped away, exceeding the speed limit, and faded out of sight. There appeared, far ahead, on the other side of the road, a wambling black dot that resolved into a bicyclist. A trick of the heated air magnified the bicycle, which appeared thirty feet high and shivered as though constructed of aspic. He passed another hawk on a telephone pole.

The great prairie dog cities of the short-grass plains which once covered hundreds of square miles were gone, but some old-fashioned red-tails continued to hunt as their ancestors, in flat-shouldered soar, turning methodically in the air above the prairie, yellow eyes watching for the shiver of grass. Many more had taken up modern ways and sat atop convenient poles and posts waiting for vehicles to clip rabbits and prairie dogs. They retrieved the carrion with the insolent matter-of-factness of a housewife carelessly slinging a package of chops into her shopping cart. Such a hawk, a bit of fur stuck to the side of its beak, watched the bicyclist pumping along west. As the machine moved slowly through the focus of those amber eyes the bird lost interest; the bicycle had no future in the hawk world; more rewarding were trucks on the paved highways, grilles spattered with blood, weaving pickups that aimed for jacks and snakes as though directed by the superior will on a telephone pole.

The bicyclist, reduced to human size, and Bob Dollar, in his sedan, drew abreast; the bicyclist saw a red-flushed face, Bob had a glimpse of a stringy leg and a gold chain, then the bicycle descended a dip in the road. Alone on the highway again Bob squinted at a wadded quilt of cloud crawling over the sky. There unrolled beside the Saturn the level land, every inch put to use for crops, oil, gas, cattle, service towns. The ranches were set far back from the main road, and now and then he passed an abandoned house, weather-burned, surrounded by broken cottonwoods. In the fallen windmills and collapsed outbuildings he saw the country's fractured past scattered about like the pencils on the desk of a draughtsman who has gone to lunch. The ancestors of the place hovered over the bits and pieces of their finished lives. He did not notice the prairie dog that raced out of the road-side weeds into his path and the tires bumped slightly as he hit it. A female red-tail lifted into the air. It was the break she had been waiting for.

Bob Dollar was a stranger in the double-panhandle country north of the Canadian River. He had held two jobs in the five years since he had graduated from Horace Greeley Junior University, a hybrid institution housed in a cinder-block building at the edge of an onion field off Interstate 70 east of Denver. He had expected enlightenment at Horace Greeley, hoped to find an interest that would lead to an absorbing career, but that did not happen and his old doubts about what he should do for a career persisted. He thought a wider educational scope would help and so applied to the state university, but even with a modest scholarship offer (he had a large vocabulary, good reading habits and exemplary grades), there wasn't enough money for him to go.

Armed with his computer printout diploma from Horace Greeley he found it difficult to land what he thought of as "a good position," and, finally, rather than work in Uncle Tam's shop, took a minimum-wage job as inventory clerk for Platte River Lightbulb Supply.

After thirty months of toil with boxes and broken glass and miniscule annual raises he had had an unfortunate experience with the company's president, Mrs. Eudora Giddins, widow of Millrace Giddins who had founded the company. He was fired. And he was glad, for he did not want life to be a kind of fidgety waiting among lightbulbs, as for a report card. He wanted to aim at a high mark on a distant wall. If time had to pass, let it pass with meaning. He wanted direction and reward.

There followed five months of job hunting before he was hired on as a location man for Global Pork Rind, headquarters in Tokyo and Chicago, with a field office in Denver. He was assigned to the Texas-Oklahoma panhandle territory and sent out on his first trip for the company.

The day before he left, Mr. Cluke's secretary, Lucille, had flashed him a red smile and waved him into the office. Mr. Ribeye Cluke, the regional operations manager, got up from behind his glass-topped desk, the gleaming surface like a small lake, said "Bob, we don't have many friends down there in the panhandles except for one or two of the smarter politicians, and because of this situation we have to go about our business pretty quietly. I want you to be as circumspect as possible—do you know what that word 'circumspect' means?" His watery eyes washed over Bob. His large hand rose and smoothed the coarse mustache that Bob thought resembled a strip of porcupine. His shoulders sloped so steeply that from behind it looked as though his head was balanced on an arch.

"Yes sir. Keep a low profile."

Mr. Cluke picked up a can of shaving cream from the top of the filing cabinet and shook it. From a drawer in his desk he removed an arrangement of braces, straps and fittings and put it over his head so that part rested on his shoulders, and another part that was a large disk against his breast. He tugged at the disk and it opened out on a telescoping arm, becoming a mirror. He applied the shaving cream to his heavy cheeks and, with a straight razor which he took from his pencil jar, unfolded it and began to shave, skirting the borders of the mustache.

"Well, that's good, Bob. Last fellow we thought could scout for us believed it meant something that happened to him in the hospital when he was a baby. So he was no use. But you're smart, Bob, smart as a dollar, ha-ha."

"Ha-ha," laughed Bob, who had increased his word

power since the age of nine with *The Child's Illustrated Dictionary* given him by his uncle Tam. But his laughter was subdued, for he knew nothing of hogs beyond the fact that they were, mysteriously, the source of bacon.

"In other words, Bob, don't let the folks down there know that you are looking for sites for hog facilities or they will prevaricate and try to take us to the cleaners, they will carry on with letters to various editors, every kind of meanness and so forth, as they have been brainwashed by the Sierra Club to think that hog facilities are bad, even the folks who love baby back ribs, even the ones hunting jobs. But I will tell you something. The panhandle region is perfect for hog operations—plenty of room, low population, nice long dry seasons, good water. There is no reason why the Texas panhandle can't produce seventy-five percent of the world's pork. That's our aim. Bob, I notice you are wearing brown oxford shoes."

"Yes sir." He turned one foot a little, pleased with the waxy glint from the Cole Haan shoe which retailed at $300 plus, but which his uncle Tambourine Bapp had fished from a donation box left at the loading dock of his thrift shop on the outer banks of Colfax Avenue.

Uncle Tam had raised him. He was a slender, short man with vivid, water-blue eyes, the same eyes as Bob and his mother and the rest of the Bapp clan. Thick greying hair swept back from a square brow.

His quick chicken steps and darting hand movements irritated some people. Bob had been a little afraid of him the first week or two because his left ear rode half an inch higher than the right, giving him a crazy, tilted look, but slowly he yielded to Tam's kindness and sincere interest in him. His uncle's cropped ear was the result of a childhood injury when his sister Harp cut off the fleshy top with a pair of scissors as punishment for playing with her precious Barbie doll.

"He wasn't playing! He was *hanging* her," she had sobbed.

When he was eight, Bob's parents had brought him to the thrift shop doorstep very early in the morning, told him to sit there next to a box of dog-eared romance novels.

"Now when Uncle Tam gets up and starts slamming things around inside, you knock on the door. You're going to stay with him. We've got to run now or we'll miss the plane. Quick hug goodbye," said his mother. His father, waiting in the sedan, raised his hand briskly and saluted. Years later Bob thought it might have been the break the old man was waiting for.

At first his uncle claimed it wasn't abandonment. They were in the kitchen at the table, Uncle Tam having his Saturday coffee break.

"I *told* Viola and Adam to bring you over. The plan was for you to stay with me until they got back from Alaska. After they got their cabin built they were coming back to get you and you were all going to live in Alaska. You staying here was a temporary thing. We just don't know what happened. Viola called only one time to say they had found some land, but she never said exactly where and there's no record of it. The pilot that flew them to wherever they went left Alaska and went to Mississippi where he got into dusting crops. By the time we traced him it was useless. He'd crashed in a cotton field and suffered brain damage. Couldn't even remember his own name. Anything could have happened to your mother and father—grizzly bear, amnesia. Alaska's a big place. I don't for one minute think they abandoned you." He tapped his fingers on the table, impatient with his own words which sounded stupid and inadequate to him. It was not possible for two grown people to disappear as had Adam and Viola.

"Well, what did they do to make a living," Bob asked, hoping for a clue to his own direction. All he was sure about was that he hadn't been important enough to take along. He taught himself not to care that he was so uninteresting that his parents dropped him on a doorstep and never bothered to write or call. "I mean, what was my dad, an engineer, or a computer guy or what?"

"Well, your mother painted neckties. You know the one I've got of the *Titanic* sinking? That's one of hers. I would say that's my dearest possession. It'll be yours someday, Bob. As for your dad, that's a little hard to say. He was always taking tests to see what he should do with his life—aptitude tests. Don't get me wrong. He was a nice guy, a really nice guy, but a little unfocused. He never could settle on anything. He had about a hundred jobs before they went to Alaska. And there something happened to them that I'm sure they couldn't help. We don't know what. I spent a fortune in phone calls. Your uncle Xylo went out there for two months and turned up absolutely nothing except the name of that pilot. Put ads in the papers. Nobody knew anything, not the police, not our family, not a single person in Alaska ever heard of them. So I'd say you had bad luck with your folks disappearing, losing the chance to get raised in Alaska—instead getting brought up by a crazy unrich uncle with a junk shop." He arched his back and twisted his head, fidgeted with a loose thread on the cuff of his knit shirt. "I suppose the only thing I'd like to impress on you, Bob, is a sense of responsibility. Viola never had it, and for sure Adam didn't. If you take on a project then, dammit, see it through to the end. Let your word mean something. It just about broke my heart to see the way you'd run to the mailbox every day expecting to find a letter from Alaska. Adam and Viola were not what I'd call responsible."

"It was lucky in a way," said Bob. The lucky part was Uncle Tam. He read stories to Bob every night, asked his opinion on the weather, on the doneness of boiled corn, foraged through the junk shop detritus for things that might interest. Bob Dollar couldn't imagine what his life would have been like in the household of Uncle Xylo whose wife, Siobhan, was an impassioned clog dancer and who ran an astrology business out of their front living room in Pickens, Nebraska. She had a neon sign over the front door with a beckoning hand under the words "Psychic Readings."

"I guess it wasn't easy bringing up somebody else's kid," he mumbled. The bedtime reading had welded him to Uncle Tam and to stories. From the first night in the little apartment when Uncle Tam had turned a page and said the words "Part One: The Old Buccaneer," Bob had become a sucker for stories told. He slid into imaginary worlds, passive, listening, his mouth agape, a hard listener for whatever tale unfolded.

"Ah, you were an easy kid. Except for the library fines. You were always a nice kid, you always pitched in and helped. I never had to worry about phone calls from the cops, drugs, stolen cars, minimart holdups. The only headache you gave me was when you started hanging around with that heavy guy, Orlando the Freak. He was a wrong one. I'm not surprised he ended up in the pen. I'm thankful you're not there with him."

"It's not like he committed armed robbery or something. It was only computer hacking."

"Yeah? If you think diverting all the operating funds of the Colorado U.S. Forest Service to a Nevada bordello was 'just computer hacking,' I have news for you." He stretched and fiddled with his cuff, looked at his watch. "It's almost eleven. I've got to get back to the shop."

In the early years Bob often felt he was in fragments, in many small parts that did not join, an internal sack of wood chips. One chip was that old life with his parents, another the years with Uncle Tam and Wayne "Bromo" Redpoll, then just Uncle Tam. Another part was Orlando and Fever and weird movies, then the lightbulb time and Mrs. Giddins asking him to massage her feet and her fury when he drew back, gagging, from the stink of clammy nylon. It was true that Bob had always pitched in and helped with dishes and cooking and house chores, largely because he was so ashamed of Uncle Tam's withering poverty which somehow seemed less if everything was clean and squared up. He would rearrange the books in the bookcases by size and color and Bromo Redpoll, his uncle's business partner, would say, "Don't be such an old lady."

Uncle Tam doted on Bob Dollar but had little to offer as proof of affection beyond solicitous attention and gifts of relatively choice treasures from the thrift shop, including the recent brown oxfords.

"Bob! These look like your size, ten double E. Try em on. In a bag of stuff from some Cherry Creek fat cat. Probably the maid dropped them off."

"They're great. Now all I need is a sports coat." In fact the shoes looked odd with Bob's jeans and T-shirt.

"We got no sports coats you'd be caught dead in, but there is a real nice car coat, suede with shearling lining. Like new, and almost your size. Car coats are kind of old-fashioned now, but it could be useful. You never know. The thing is, it's a kind of—kind of a tan. Come back in the shop and have a look-see."

The car coat was tight across the shoulders and the sleeves somewhat short, but there was no denying, despite the lemony color of a bad dye lot, that it was a well-made garment. He lived in dread that on the street someday the previous owner would recognize the coat and make scathing remarks. It had happened twice in school, once when he wore an argyle sweater, once with a knitted cap, the name CHARLES spelled out on the cuff. He had tried to ink the letters out with a marker but they showed plainly enough. Eventually a large black beret with cigarette burn holes turned up and he wore it for years, telling himself some Frenchman had visited Denver and abandoned it there.

"Now, Bob," said Mr. Cluke, slapping his cheeks with a manly heather aftershave lotion, "you cannot go down to Texas wearing brown oxfords. Take my word for it. I've spent enough time down there to know a pair of brown oxfords can set you back with those people. Despite oilmen trigged out in suits, and wealthy wheat growers with diamond rings, the figure of respect in Texas is still the cattleman and the cattleman wants to look like a cowboy. It wouldn't hurt for you to get a pair of dress slacks and some long-sleeved shirts. But for sure you have got to get yourself a decent pair of cowboy boots and wear them. You don't need to wear the hat or western shirts, but you got to wear the boots."

"Yes sir," said Bob, seeing the logic of it.

"And Bob, here's a list of the qualities that I want you to look for—on the q.t.—in that country. Look for your smaller cow outfits and farms, not the great big ones or the ranches with four hundred oil wells. Look for areas where everybody is grey-headed. Older. People that age just want to live quiet and not get involved in a cause or fight city hall. That's the kind of population we want. Find out the names of local people who run things—bankers, church folks—get on their good side. Keep your eyes and ears open for farmers whose kids went off to school and those kids are not coming back unless somebody puts a gun to their heads. Read the obits for rural property owners who just died and their offspring are thinking 'show me the money' so they can get back to Kansas City or Key West or other fleshpots of their choice.

"And here's another thing. You will have to have a cover story because you can't go down there and say you're scouting for Global Pork Rind. Some people would be openly hostile. You will be there off and on for several months at a time, so you will have to think up a story to explain your presence. The fellow we had before told people he was a reporter for a national magazine working on a panhandle story—

that was supposed to let him get into every kind of corner and let him ask pertinent questions. You know what 'pertinent' means, don't you?"

"Yes sir. Pertaining to, or related in some way to a topic."

"Very good, I imagine you did well in school. That fellow I mentioned thought it had something to do with hair implants. Anyway, he thought that was a good cover story and expected doors to open to him like butter."

"What magazine did that fellow say he was working for, sir? Doing the profile for?"

"Well, he did not pick *Texas Monthly,* thinking the local populace might have heard of it. And of course it would have been folly to name *Cockfight Weekly* or *Ranch News.* I believe he said *Vogue.* He thought he would be safe with that one in the panhandle."

"And it didn't work for him?"

"No, no. It didn't." Ribeye Cluke's little finger swept a speck of shaving cream from his earlobe. "You will have to think of something else. I would stay away from the magazine idea, myself. But you'll think of something. Now, Bob, it's perfectly fine to stay in a motel for a few days until you get your bearings, but your best bet is to rent a room with someone in the area. Find some old lady or elderly couple with plenty of relatives. That way you'll get a beeline on what's happening. You'll get the lowdown. Now you just scour the properties north of the"—he consulted the map on the wall—"the Canadian River. Scour them good! Whenever you find a property that looks right and the owner is willing, you let me know and I'll send our Money Offer Person down. We've set up a subsidiary company to buy the parcels and then deed them over to Global. The residents do not know a hog farm is coming in until the bulldozers start constructing the waste lagoon. Later, when you've gained experience, when you've proved your value to Global Pork Rind, you can act as your own Money Offer Person, though generally we like to send a woman, mention a sum to the oldsters right on the spot. There's an advantage to that. Another thing, don't stay in one place, after a month or so switch to another town. And so forth. That fellow I mentioned? He picked Mobeetie, so if I were you that's not where I'd go. He made people suspicious. He got into trouble.

"Lucille here has made up a packet of maps and brochures, county profiles for you, and there's your corporate credit card—and you bet there's a limit on it, Bob. We need your signature on this card. Here you go then and I'll just wish you good luck. Report back to me by mail every week. And I don't mean that damn e-mail. I won't touch that. Get a post office box. Write to me at home and I'll respond from same so your postmaster down there doesn't see Global Pork Rind on the envelope and start putting five and five together. I'll see that the company newsletters are sent to you in a plain brown wrapper. Can't be too careful. Use a pay phone if there is an emergency."

"Yes sir."

"And remember, the thing that's *really* important is that—that we—that we do what we do."

Bob left with the feeling that Ribeye Cluke was somehow deceiving him.

That night he took his uncle Tam to a celebratory dinner at a famous Inuit-Japanese-Irish steak house where they poured melted Jersey butter from quart pitchers, where the baked potatoes, decorated with tiny umbrellas, were the size of footballs and the steaks so thick they could only be cut with samurai swords. His uncle winced at the menu prices, then overpraised the food, a sure sign he was homesick for Chickee's place down the block from his shop where he could enjoy a plate of fried gizzards or catfish hot pot. But it seemed his thoughts had gone in a different direction, for out on the sidewalk he belched and said, "I've been thinking of getting into vegetables. Becoming a vegetarian. Meat's too damn expensive. Oh. Wait a minute. Before I forget. Wayne sent you something. And there's a little thing from me." His uncle thrust two flat parcels at Bob. "Don't open them until you get there," he said.

"Bromo! I didn't even know you were in touch with him anymore."

"Yeah. I am. We are. Whatever."

2

ART PLASTIC

At the time Bob's parents had dropped him off on the doorstep, Uncle Tam had had a roommate, Wayne Redpoll, with glary eyes and a rubbery mug, his features arranged around a nose so beaked that it made his eyes unmemorable. His brown hair was crinkled and violent, springing with energy. In the mornings before ten o'clock when the shop opened, he lounged around without a shirt doing crossword puzzles, tapping the pencil against his discolored teeth. His chest was strange, the nipples almost under his armpits. He was not good at the puzzles, too impatient for them, and after a few minutes would go his own way, filling in the blanks with any old word, right or wrong. Bob disliked him mildly and it was partly to vanquish him at crosswords that he began to study *The Child's Illustrated Dictionary* which Uncle Tam had fished out of a box and handed to him, saying, "Happy congratulations on this great Wednesday morning." By the time he was twelve he could do the Tuesday *New York Times* puzzle with a pen in less than twenty minutes, but Thursday and Friday took many hours with pencil as the clues were sly and presumed

20

knowledge of cultural events in the dim past. All kinds of words streamed through his mind—ocelot, strabismus, plat du jour, archipelago, bemusement, vapor, mesa, sitar, boutique. Wayne tried to counter Bob's skill by dredging up odd crossword information and explaining it to him as though that were the point of the puzzles: that crosswords had been invented in 1913 by a Liverpool newspaperman, that in 1924 they became a national craze. He generally pooh-poohed the *New York Times* puzzles, which, he said, were child's play—a meaningful look at Bob—compared to the evil puzzles of the British, particularly those with cryptic clues constructed by the old masters, Torquemada, Ximenes and Azed. But this persiflage did him no good. He did not have the knack and Bob did.

Wayne Redpoll had come by the nickname "Bromo" after a night of heavy drinking not long after Bob Dollar arrived on the doorstep. He moaned with a hangover, drank black coffee to restore balance, said, "Goddamn, I'm going for a walk to clear my head," ended at Chickee's place down the street where he ordered a Bromo-Seltzer to settle his queasy gut. He swallowed the gassy mixture and within seconds puked on the counter.

He had a habit of holding his words behind his teeth, only letting them escape through the narrowest possible opening of his jaws, which gave his conversation a constricted sibilance. He had many dislikes. He hated the "drink milk" campaign that showed celebrities holding empty glasses of milk, their upper lips white with the stuff as though they drank like tapirs. Hijackers aside, he loathed flying, especially the attendants' merry commands to pull down the window shades so other passengers could watch grade-Z American movies. He refused to lower his shade, saying that the only pleasure in flying was the chance to look at the landscape from thirty-five thousand feet. Once he had been put off the plane in Kansas City for daring to argue about it. Tam had driven hundreds of miles to pick him up and listened all the way back to Bromo's rant about the horrible streets he had walked through while waiting. Phrases offered to the grief-stricken, such as "time heals all wounds" and "the day will come when you reach closure" irritated him, and there were times when he sat silent, seeming half-buried in some sediment of sorrow.

"Closure? When someone beloved dies there is no 'closure.'"

He disliked television programs featuring tornado chasers squealing "Big one! Big one!" and despised the rat-infested warrens of the Internet, riddled with misinformation and chicanery. He did not like old foreign movies where, when people parted, one stood in the middle of the road and waved. He thought people with cell phones should be immolated along with those who overcooked pasta. Calendars, especially the scenic types with their glowing views of a world without telephone lines, rusting cars or burger stands, enraged him, but he despised the kittens, motorcycles, famous women and jazz musicians of the special-interest calendars as well.

"Why not photographs of feral cats? Why not diseases?" he said furiously. Wal-Mart trucks on the highway received his curses and perfumed women in elevators invited his acid comment that they smelled of animal musk glands. For years he had been writing an essay entitled "This Land Is NOT Your Land."

Even though they did not get along, Bromo had opened a charge account for Bob at the local bookshop where he was allowed to buy one book every two weeks. Bob's longing for the books had overcome his dislike of any obligation to Bromo.

When donation boxes came to the shop's doorstep he offered scathing criticism of the contents. Once a strange garment arrived in a box stamped OUTDOOR GRILL DELUXE. It was an enormous vest made of an unidentified fur, coarse, long and brownish grey. It smelled of old smoke and mothballs.

"A beast!" cried Bromo in mock horror, backing away from it. "Good God, that's something from the sixties, some mountain commune garment. Feel in the pockets, Tam, see if there's any drugs."

The pockets were empty. Bromo disliked the vest, which reminded him of paisley skirts, peace signs, girls doctoring their children with coltsfoot and yarrow; he was particularly irked at being unable to identify the fur. At last he could stand it no longer, wrapped the vest up, took it to the Denver Natural History Museum.

"Pass the macaroni, Bob," said Uncle Tam that evening. Then, to Bromo, "Aren't you going to tell us what they said at the museum?"

"You really want to know?"

"Of course I want to know. It's a very unusual fur."

Bromo snorted. "You can say that again. It's also highly illegal. It is grizzly bear fur."

"Oh no," said Uncle Tam who was an ardent environmentalist with lifetime subscriptions to *Audubon*, *High Country News*, *Mother Nature*, *Wildlife of the Rockies* and *Colorado Wildlife*.

There followed a long discussion—argument—about what to do with "the Beast," as Bromo persisted in calling it. In the end it got a spotlighted solo place on a table with a sign reading UNIQUE BEAR-SKIN VEST and a price tag of $200.

The two men were housemates and business partners and, Bob wondered a few years later, if perhaps not something more, for there was in their relationship an odd intimacy that went beyond household or business matters. Yet he had never seen any affectionate glances or touching between them. Each man had his own bedroom at opposite ends of the upstairs hall. But neither did they ever bring women to the house. It was a poor bachelor establishment (though tidy and well-dusted), for the partners made very little money. In the end Bob decided that the sexual gears of both men (and perhaps his own) were engaged in neutral, except for one peculiar and inexplicable memory of Bromo Redpoll in Santa Fe sitting on the hotel shoeshine throne for the third time in one day, an expression on his face that nine-year-old Bob could only character-ize as "adult," while a Mexican boy snapped his rag over a glossy wingtip. When Bob was older he grasped the sexual content of that expression and he had a word for it—concupiscence—for he had seen it on his own face, though not in longing for a shoeshine boy, but for the sluts of Front Range High, as distant to him as calendar photographs. He imagined himself with a sultry, curly-headed, dimpled girl, but it had not worked out that way. Bob was not tall but by some stroke of genetic luck he was well-proportioned with smooth musculature, a hard little ass and boxy shoul-ders. As Bob matured, the unbidden thought had come to Tam that the boy was, as Wayne might say, "a casserole."

There were no dimpled girls with curly hair at Front Range High and in his junior year he had been picked out by a big, unclean girl with a muddy com-plexion, Marisa Berdstraw, who wore lipstick of a dark red color that made her teeth glow beaver yel-low. She had quickly inveigled him into a sexual servitude with all the declarations and trappings of professed love but none of the reality. This meant going steady, studying together, a Friday or Saturday night movie, a sex grapple on Sunday mornings when her parents, both with mottled, rough faces, were at church. He did what she said and she had a pattern of events and behavior worked out in her mind. She would call up in the evening.

"What ya doin?"

"Studying for a social studies test."

"I got a test too. In Diagonals. But I'm not studyin for it. It's more like a quiz."

Diagonals was an experimental course that darted tangentially from subject to subject as classroom discussion ranged. It had started off as a geology unit, veered to Esperanto, slid to the court of Louis XVI, on to the Whiskey Rebellion, the Oklahoma land rush, then to fractals, to oil tanker construction and, most recently, to mathematical calculation with an abacus.

"Only three more days till Sunday," she said archly.

"Yeah."

"Are you glad?"

"Glad about what? That there's three more days?"

"That it's *only* three more days."

"Sure."

But he wasn't that glad. The encounters in her gritty sheets, awash in her strong body odors, left him restless and disappointed. He wanted a few things to be different. But Marisa did have a hearty laugh and a certain sense of humor, though based on pain and accident. He had only once brought her to the apartment. She made it clear that she thought the apartment a cramped hole and Uncle Tam something of an idiot, nice but quite dumb.

"He's vague, you know? Not with it, is he?"

It was neither sorrow nor relief that he felt when she told him they had to break up.

"I'm not going with you anymore," she said. "There's another guy."

Soon enough he learned the other guy was Kevin Alk, a nearsighted math freak with an acned face and greasy hair that held the tracks of his comb.

"Good luck," he said politely, but privately his thought was that Marisa and Kevin Alk deserved each other. As for himself, Marisa's interest in him and then her lack of interest pointed up how unimportant he was to her. Only Uncle Tam counted some value in him, but what that value was Bob didn't know. Nothing more than kinship he supposed and maybe a sense of obligation to his lost sister.

The apartment had a particular smell, an effluvium that came up from the shop below—dust-choked carving, musty upholstery, the bitter out-gas of celluloid and Bakelite, the maritime odor of ancient fish glue. The stairway up from the shop was narrow and crooked, the walls papered with some odd 1940s pattern of yellow trellis hung with red teapots. Upstairs, at the midpoint of the hall's length, hung engravings and pictures that had come in with loads of junk and taken Uncle Tam's fancy. One showed fifty great rivers of the earth arranged as dangling strings and graded as to length, and the opposing corner illustrated a crush of mountain peaks, lined up from the smallest to the greatest, giving the impression of a fabulous and terrific range that existed nowhere in reality. Yet for years Bob believed that in some distant land hundreds of inverted ice-cream cone mountains gave way to an immeasurable plain cut by fifty rivers running parallel to each other.

"It's not a real place," said Bromo Redpoll. "You dunce. It's only for the sake of comparison."

The shop dealt in a wide variety of American junk but its specialty was plastic, and their mutual interest in resin and polymer objects joined the two men as twinned cherries on the stem. Uncle Tam could talk plastic manufacturing for hours, and had signed up for a course in chemistry the better to understand the complex processes.

There was a room in the shop—the best room—where nothing was for sale to the ordinary customer. A sign on the door said

ART PLASTIC
By Appointment Only

"One day," Uncle Tam said, "probably not in our lifetime, but maybe in yours, Bob, people will collect plastic objects from the twentieth century as art, like now they are going after wooden grain cradles and windmill weights. This will be worth a fortune," he said, waving grandly at the shelves and cases of Lucite bracelets, acrylic vases, Bakelite radios, polyethylene water pitchers. On floor pedestals, as if sculptures, stood plastic washing-machine agitators, black and white. The partners' scavenging hunts ranged from outlying yard sales to periodic rakes through the shops of Antique Row on Broadway where they foraged for baby rattles, ancient billiard balls, even celluloid bibs from nuns' old-style habits.

Within specialties there are often subsets of rarer specialties, and so it was with Bromo Redpoll and Tam Bapp. Bromo had collected a dozen phenol parasol handles with fancy metal bands. Tam sought out the British urea resin from the 1920s known as Beetleware—the forerunner of melamine. Silicone, polyurethane, epoxy were what they wanted but never would they buy anything for more than a few dollars. A side specialty was Bakelite jewelry from the 1920s. When Uncle Tam discovered, in the bottom of an old box of magazines, a Bakelite catalog from early in the century, both considered it a great find.

There were dozens of dolls and toys in the Art Plastic room but Bob preferred the Cleopatra Manicure Box to any of them, a striking red-and-black Art Deco box packed inside with plastic-handled files and emery boards and a few bottles of nail varnish dried to black powder. He pretended Cleopatra had actually owned it and the vials of dark dust were poisons.

The highlight of the week came on Sunday evenings when the *Antiques Roadshow* aired. Uncle Tam locked the shop at 4:30, even when customers stood beseechingly at the door as he hung up the Closed sign. The partners' devotion to the program was extreme and they had evolved certain rituals.

The coffee table was cleared of magazines and bills that had accumulated during the week. Their notebooks and pens were set out. The drinks, according to season and affordable ingredients, were to be made in the jazz-age silver penguin shaker—drinks containing coconut milk were esteemed, but coconut milk was expensive and it usually came down to a six-pack of Bud split between them. The food was peanut butter sandwiches, or carrot sticks and cheap cheese, or, if they were flush, buffalo wings or cardboard containers of tripe stew from Chickee's place.

Plastics rarely made it onto the *Antiques Roadshow* but when they did both men were beside themselves and scribbled in their notebooks. When a podgy Baltimore man displayed his pristine, bright red ABS Olivetti typewriter and red slip-on case from the 1960s they stamped their feet in jealousy and shouted angrily when the "expert" put a paltry value of a hundred dollars on it. Uncle Tam said that if he had the money, he would fly to Baltimore and make the man an offer, though the airfare, of course, would bump the cost into the stratosphere. In the end he resigned himself to a fruitless Denver search for a match of the beautiful instrument.

The *Antiques Roadshow* could have gone on for hours; they would have remained leaning forward in happy anticipation, assigning values before the experts could speak, eating the carrot sticks which curved as they dried. At the end of the program they were both restless and Bromo went into the Art Plastic room to dust and wipe. They talked about making the big discovery that would put them over the top, and, very often, filled with enthusiasm, they headed out for the evening flea markets, coming home at midnight with boxes of worthless oddities. The closest they came to the big time was a yellowed journal kept by one A. Jackson which Tam thought might be Andrew Jackson. But in the pages the loving references (which gradually cooled) to "Mr. Jackson" dulled their expectations as they puzzled out that "A." was Amelia Jackson of Poultney, Vermont, one in the grand parade of emigrants from New England to the gold fields of California in 1850. The diary— simple observations of weather and dust and miles traversed—ended abruptly at the Independence Rock stopover. Amelia Jackson wrote:

Mr. Jackson has concluded to break from this wagon train in company with several other men who cannot agree with our guide, Mr. Murk. I am to stay with the wagon and we will meet in San Francisco if Our Savior wills it. The men will undertake a short cut to the gold fields. I cannot think this the best plan. I would give a very great deal to be at home with mother and father and my dear sisters, in peace and harmony and with PLENTY of water in the cistern.

They managed to sell the journal for a few hundred dollars to the Pioneer Historical Library in Independence, Missouri, and Bromo said sourly that if it had been an *Andrew* Jackson journal they could have retired.

As the years went on Bob noticed that Bromo Red-poll was less keen on the antiques program than his uncle. He was increasingly derisive about Tiffany lamp shades and old journals. He would get up halfway through the hour, say "Call me if the Kenos come on" and go into the kitchen to poke through the refrigerator, for the only part of the show that seemed to interest him now was the appearance of the Keno twins from New York, experts on American furniture. Bob thought the Kenos looked like animated wax-works but their clothes were fascinating. The word "natty" came to him. They were natty dressers as no one in Denver was nor could be.

Finally, the year Bob graduated from high school, the partnership ended on a Sunday night following the program. Bromo had spent most of the hour in the kitchen making Peanut Butter Dreams, but with one ear turned toward the living room in case Tam called "Keno alert!" At the very end it had come and he rushed in to see an exquisite highboy that had set the television twins' hands trembling. Bromo watched, utterly rapt, the wooden spoon with its gob of batter in his hand. As the carousel music surged up and the credits rolled he sat on the sofa beside Tam and said, "We've got to talk." He put the spoon on the coffee table, heedless of the batter sliding onto the table. Then he looked up and saw Bob watching them both.

"Here, Bob, will you finish making the cookies? I've got to talk to Tam."

Bob, shooting a glance at his uncle who nodded, went into the kitchen, ostentatiously closing the swing door. He could hear Bromo's voice growling on and on in some kind of low-key manifesto. He was curious but could not make out what they were saying, even when he stood with his ear on the door. Once in a while Uncle Tam would ask a question and off Bromo would go again, long, rolling breakers of speech, saying more than Bob had heard him say in eight years. When the cookies were done he put some on a plate and brought them in but the moment he pushed the door open they both shut up, watched him put the plate down, said thank you and waited until he left before starting to talk again. He took a handful of warm cookies for himself and went up to his room. At ten, yawning, he brushed his teeth for bed and heard them still at it downstairs, still talking.

At some time in the early morning he half woke, got out of bed and opened his door. The murmur of voices continued from downstairs. Now it was Uncle Tam talking, and the only words he could make out were ". . . fair market value." They must be talking plastics, he thought.

Eight o'clock Bob galloped down the stairs, the first one down, and no wonder if they'd stayed up half the night talking about combs and bracelets. There was an empty scotch bottle in the trash. He started the coffee and went outside, ran down to the

Continuum newsstand for the papers and, on the way back, stopped at the Sweet Mountain Bakery for the strawberry-pistachio Danish they all liked. Back in the kitchen he set the table, put out the milk and sugar, took three eggs from the refrigerator, looked for the nitrate-free bacon Uncle Tam insisted on buying, heard shuffling steps behind him. It was Uncle Tam in his ratty checkered bathrobe, looking bleary and hungover.

"Oh boy, I need some of that coffee."

"How late did you guys stay up?"

"Until it got light. I just went to bed two hours ago." He looked at the table, at the three places set. He picked up one of the plates, the silverware, put them away.

"Hey, what'd you do that for? Bromo likes breakfast too."

"Not this morning. He's gone. Left at five A.M. He persuaded me to buy his share of the business out. From now on it's you and me, kid."

"But where'd he go? Why? How could you buy him out if we don't have any money?"

"He went to Iowa City where his sister lives, and from there he is going to New York. He says he wants to learn period furniture like the Keno brothers. He doesn't care about Art Plastic anymore. And you're right, I don't have any money, so I had to promise to pay him a certain amount in case I can ever unload this dump. And now, if you don't mind, let's drop the subject permanently. I've just about got brain fever from it all."

Bob had the sense to be quiet. And after a few weeks he got his first job—grocery packer at Sandman's. In addition to his wage check he got meat and vegetables, eggs and fruit past their prime. So they lived on almost-spoiled produce and high meat, with frequent bouts of diarrhea.

3

ON THE ROAD AGAIN

The morning after the celebratory steak dinner Bob was heading south down I-25 in a Global Pork Rind company car, a blue, late-model Saturn, watching out for escaped prisoners in white vans. He stopped for gas in Trinidad, got a dripping chile dog to eat while he drove, pulled over at a roadside spring below Raton Pass to clean his hands and wipe off the steering wheel.

On the passenger seat were the packages his uncle had handed him outside the restaurant.

He took twisting, climbing roads through northeast New Mexico, high dry ranchland empty of everything but cinder cones and cows and an occasional distant building surrounded by corrals. An elderly horseman herded forty cows down the middle of the road, not deigning to hurry them or turn them out of the right-of-way.

He climbed a switchback road lined with tough-looking shinnery oak. He guessed he was about an hour's drive from the Picket Wire canyonlands along the Purgatoire River, south of La Junta. When he was thirteen, he, Uncle Tam and Bromo Redpoll had rented a car and driven down to the Withers Canyon Gate, planning to hike in to the fabled dinosaur track bed.

It was a hot day, over a hundred degrees by late morning. Bob and Uncle Tam each had a canteen of water. Bromo carried a daypack of cold beers, Bob and Uncle Tam clutched plastic bottles of water. Bromo and Bob wore hiking boots, Uncle Tam his old black and stinking sneakers. The road in to the gate where the trail began was a gauntlet of washouts and boulders. At the gate a posted sign said the round-trip hike was 10.6 miles.

"Damn," said Uncle Tam, "that's almost an eleven-mile hike."

"Two hours in, two hours out," said Bromo, draining the first of his beers and tossing the can behind a rock. "Leave it alone," he said when Bob ran to pick it up. "We'll get it on the way out. You're too damn picky. Don't be such an old lady."

They set off slowly, climbing the rocky trail. The sun beat against Bob's face and within twenty minutes he knew he was burning. He'd forgotten his cap. He said, "Uncle Tam, did you bring any sunblock?" He thought they were in a terrible place, bristling with cholla, yucca and purple prickly pear. Scraggy junipers clung to frying rock. The canyon walls rose around them, shooting out heat as from ray guns.

"Shit. No. Would have been a good idea. You got any, Bromo?"

"Back in the car. Want to run back and get it, Bob? We'll wait for you."

"No." The idea of running anywhere was repulsive.

They walked on, Bromo in the lead as if he were heading up a safari. Every step raised a puff of yellow dust from the trail and their boots and Uncle Tam's sneakers, their stocking tops and lower legs were soon coated with the stuff, setting off an itchy sensation like hay chaff. At first Bob tried to make the water in his twelve-ounce bottle last but he was parched and his throat clicked painfully when he swallowed. It felt as though his throat were bleeding inside. Bromo finished his fourth beer, carefully standing the can beside the trail.

"Get it when we come out," he said as he had every time he finished one. He straightened up and a thin, arid rustle shivered the heat. Bob thought it was a cicada or a grasshopper and walked up, intending to pass Bromo, but Uncle Tam thrust out his arm with hard suddenness, hitting Bob in the face.

"Ow. What'd you do that for?"

"Shut up. That's a rattlesnake." The landscape lurched.

They couldn't see it. They stood very still. The buzzing surged until it seemed the loudest sound Bob had ever heard. Still they couldn't see it until Bromo shifted position.

"There it is," said Bromo. "Right next to the beer can. Christ, I was two inches from it."

"I want to get out of here," Bob whispered.

They backed up slowly and when they were fifteen

feet away Bromo picked up a rock and threw it at the rattler. He missed.

"Well, what do you want to do, Tam, try and find a way past? The damn snake's right on the trail."

"Hell, let's go back. I got blisters, Bob's sunburned and who knows how many snakes we'll run into? Could be hundreds in here. Not all of them rattle. People have killed so many of the ones who rattle that it's the silent guys who reproduce. One of these days they'll all be nonrattlers. Plus it's too hot. This is the kind of place you tackle in November, not June."

They left and did not come back in November or ever. But Bob had thought many times that someday he was going to make it in to the dinosaur tracks, maybe on a mountain bike, and certainly in cold weather when the rattlesnakes were hibernating. Now, remembering the aborted trip, he thought maybe he would try again on one of his trips between Denver and the panhandle. On a cool day.

North of Clayton he found a yellow-dirt road that carried him around hairpin bends, over humpback bridges and through mud ruts deep enough to scrape the bottom of the car. It was midafternoon when he came out at Teemu, not far from Black Mesa, in the Oklahoma panhandle, piñon-juniper-mesa country with cholla, hackberry, scrub oak all through the rocks. He stopped at a general store for a bottle of water and a ham sandwich, got pinned by the garrulous proprietor, a baggy man whiskered with white bristles recently arrived from California, who explained his ambitious retirement plan to make the place into another Santa Fe.

"See, my grandparents left here in the thirties. Dust bowl days. I thought I'd come back and see what they left behind. It's a beautiful place. Great potential. Got electricity too, more than you can say for California. We got craft people here, carvers and painters, we got Indians, we got people with sheds full a antiques, we got a small tourist trade that just needs working up. It's mostly a Christian tourist trade, there's the Cowboy Bible Camp that packs them in all summer. Over in Kenton they got the Easter Pageant, brings in the thousands. We even got a vineyard now, Butch Podzemny's ranch out east has went over to vines. With a little luck Oklahoma panhandle could put Napa Valley in the dumpster. Pretty good climate for vines, high, dry, plenty sun, clean air, light stony soil. The new county agent thinks we got a chance to make a real nice regional varietal. The old agent couldn't see past cows."

Bob thought the man was trying to puff the place up to himself, to smother his regret at leaving California for the bull's-eye of the dust bowl.

"I figure if we can interest *Oklahoma Today,* get them to come out and do an article on us, we'd improve business about fifty percent. But we're kind of forgotten out here. Right now I try to keep everything loose, keep a little of everything on hand so I can see what people want. I got calendars, a few groceries, lunch counter. I got the gas pump, only gas pump for thirty miles either direction. Next year is the big year. I got a friend talked into remodeling the old hotel, open a nice restaurant. Butch'll have the first wine ready to sell then. If he makes a go of it there would be a hundred others love to get out of the damn cow business and into something nice like vines. The boom is coming. Teemu will be the next Santa Fe."

It took Bob twelve seconds to drive through the bedraggled boomtown of the future, past three store-front churches, seven collapsed or empty buildings, the old school boarded up and wreathed in two-strand Wave Spread wire, past a decayed rock building with no roof and a dangling sign that read KELLY'S HOTEL— which he guessed was the home of the future "nice restaurant." Bemused by curious rock formations that resembled dinosaur excreta standing on end, he thought of the storekeeper's apparent ignorance that it had taken Santa Fe centuries to build up from its start as a trading town for Mexican hides and Indian silverwork. Several times he had gone with Uncle Tam and Bromo Redpoll to Santa Fe for the Art Plastic Society's annual convention, and while the two men slavered over cracked polymer, he'd wandered around the town with one of the free guidebooks supplied by the hotel. So, thinking of the Santa Fe Trail from Independence, Missouri, to Council Grove in Kansas, to Pawnee Rock where the route split in two, the "wet trail" going south along the Cimarron

River, the safer "dry trail" from Bent's Fort westward to Raton Pass through the Sangre de Cristo range and on to Santa Fe, and thinking how he would soon be crossing that ghostly track, he took a wrong turn.

He did not notice at first, for a road runner dashed in front of him. The road was paved, but soon it narrowed, and after fifteen miles plunged down a short hill to a bridgeless water crossing, then up and around a tight corner and onto level ground where it split away into three rutted dirt trails without signs. The mesas were out of sight, the rock formations had disappeared. He fumbled for his map but the one he had, a gas station cheapo stamped *Central and Western States,* did not show Teemu on it. He guessed that by turning right, which he took to be east, he would parallel the state line and, after a while, find a good road cutting south again.

And so he maneuvered onto a set of dusty ruts dotted with manure, a primitive road wandering through uninhabited grazing land. There were no towns, no gas stations, no houses, no corrals, no traffic. He was the only person on an endless track without turnoff nor intersection. The fine dust got into the car and choked him and he wished he had bought gallons of water from the talkative store man. It was sultry for a day in March, even in Oklahoma, and gross clouds crowded the sky. After an hour of dry swallowing he came on a weather-beaten sign, the first he had seen. It read COMANCHE NATIONAL GRASSLAND. He looked at his map. There was a green square on the map bearing the same name. He was somehow back in Colorado and heading north.

He could not bear to retrace his path to the fetal boomtown, so he drove doggedly on, believing that sooner or later there would be intersecting roads east and then south that would take him down to Oklahoma and Texas. Eight miles later he hit a right-hand turnoff without a sign but it surely headed east and gave him a view to the south of a massive wall of blue-black cloud slashed by lightning.

With an abrupt twitch the dusty road butted onto blacktop and in the distance he could see semis racing along a busy highway. He had found the road but lost the day. A northwest slot in the clouds let a narrow ray of sunlight through. There was a heaviness to it as though its rich color truly bore the weight of gold.

In another hour he was back in Oklahoma, a few miles outside Boise City, looking for a place to sleep. He found a bed-and-breakfast, the Badger Hole, where, on the front lawn, an enormous fiberglass badger stood with Christmas lights around its neck. In the tiny parking lot there was an unwashed white van with Arizona plates. A finger had written in the dust on the back door ON THE MOTHER-FUCKING ROAD AGAIN. It didn't sound like the sentiment of an escaped convict, so he took the room.

He was shown up the stairs by a heavy woman, young but fleshy, with yellow crimped hair and a beautiful face. When she spoke her mouth went up on one side as though she talked around a cigar. The room was hot and airless, the walls painted forget-me-not blue. The single bed was dainty and white, the bathroom obviously made over from a narrow closet. There was no air conditioner, but an electric fan took up most of the top of the painted chest. He pried a window open and with the cool evening air came a loose knot of mosquitoes. He turned on the fan, which roared hugely, the stream of air twitching the curtains, stirring the pages of a magazine on the bedside table—*Decorating Your Mobile Home.*

Bob Dollar opened the smallest of the packages his uncle had handed him and inside found the tie his mother had painted showing the *Titanic* going down. There was an immense gash in the ship's side and out of it tumbled people and beds and china; tiny figures struggled in the water. An iceberg shaped like a bundle of chef's knives threatened to stab the ship again. Tears came to Bob's pale eyes. He had heard his uncle say many times that the tie was his dearest possession. The other package felt like a book. Bromo always had given him books, great books, for he had an uncanny sense of what Bob would like. Inside was a slender paperback, *Expedition to the Southwest, An 1845 Reconnaissance of Colorado, New Mexico, Texas and Oklahoma* by Lieutenant James William Abert. There was a note from Bromo:

Dear Bob.
I thought the adventures of Lt. Abert might
interest you as he was the first to systematically

explore the region you are now in and at approximately your age. I hope you will take as much interest in what you see as he did. The broadly engaged mind is the source of a happy life. Good luck.

P.S. Keep away from Oklahoma.

He went down the street for supper, ate two scorched corn dogs and aged coleslaw at the Bandwagon diner and then called home collect from a pay phone.

"Hi, Uncle Tam, it's me."

"Well, I'll be damned. Haven't heard from you in twenty-four hours. How do you like it down there?"

"I'm not there yet. I got mixed up on some back roads. I'm in Oklahoma. It got too late to keep going. Anyway, I want to look over the country in daylight. Thought I'd call up and tell you I'm really happy about the tie. I know it meant a lot to you."

"Well, seemed right you should have something from your mother. I was going to give it to you when you graduated from Horace Greeley, but something told me to wait. What did Wayne send you?"

"A book by some guy named Abert. A lieutenant. I think he went through this country a hundred years ago. Looks pretty interesting. Bromo wrote I should stay out of Oklahoma but that's where I am. What's new with you?"

"Not much the time you been gone. I cut my thumb opening mail—a paper cut. Hurt like hell. And my feet are pretty bad today. I'm thinking of going to the doctor. And I entered the *Reader's Digest* Sweepstakes contest. First prize is two million dollars."

"How's the vegetarian program going?"

"Good. I got me some tofu and vegetables and fruit, about a ton of dried beans. Mrs. Mendoza down the block showed me how to cook them Mexican-style. Gave me some dried epazote. She told me where to get good chorizo but I left that out—not a vegetable. I feel a little better already—except my feet. And your old friend stopped by."

"What old friend?"

"The big jailbird. Orlando."

"Orlando's *out*?"

"Well, he must be if he came by. I don't know if he escaped or got released and I didn't care to ask. Didn't recognize him at first. You can tell he's been working out. Wanted to know how to get hold of you. Said I didn't know."

"I'll send you an address soon as I find a place to stay and get a mailbox. If Orlando comes by again get a phone number or something. I'll call you again in a couple of days."

"I hope you're not going to take up with him again. He's an ex-con now. Or worse, a prison escapee."

There was no television set in the room and he read a few pages from Lieutenant James William Abert's *Expedition,* learning, before sleep descended, that the lieutenant was the son of Colonel John James

Abert, who headed the U.S. Corps of Topographical Engineers, the agency charged with exploring and mapping the west. At West Point the son collected an astonishing number of demerits and stood near the bottom of his class in all but drawing, where he ranked first. His fellow West Pointers included Ulysses S. Grant, James Longstreet, William Tecumseh Sherman, Henry W. Halleck and others who became Civil War luminaries. Bob Dollar's heart went out to Lieutenant Abert, surrounded by military bullies, sissy drawing his only skill. The lieutenant was Bob Dollar's age when he and his friend and second-in-command, the mathematically inclined Lieutenant William Guy Peck, and a small company were ordered by the idiosyncratic and haughty John Charles Frémont to separate from the larger expedition and form the "South Expedition" to explore the territory of the Comanche, and chart the course of the Canadian River while Frémont himself pushed on to sunny California. Bob found the journal interesting, for Abert had an inquiring eye, a good nature, and he was early in the country.

The bed was heaped with puffy quilts and featherbeds, so infernally hot that he ended by kicking them all on the floor and directing the fan's stream of air at the bed. When he woke at dawn the sheets were twisted into frightful points and kinked spirals like aging telephone cords. He showered, pulled on his jeans and T-shirt. He couldn't get away from the place fast enough. The white van was gone.

4

THE EVIL FAT BOY

In every installment of life's book, Bob Dollar knew, even when he was fourteen, there was a fat boy; someone's brother or school pal, the son of a deli owner, a youth aiming his life at building a low-rider, a discontent slagged out on some sofa with a can of Yoo-Hoo in hand, the one member of the gang the police catch, the fountain of knowledge at the porno video shop, the champion pizza maker at Benny's Underground Pie Parlor. He encountered his fat boy in Walgreens while waiting in line for one of his uncle's pain prescriptions. In front of him stood a suety person of sixteen, his round head bound in a black cloth imprinted with skulls and crossbones, his chin decorated with seventy or eighty pale blond whiskers and an assortment of pimples. He was wearing overalls with enormous legs—each large enough to contain a burly man—standing sidewise in line and addressing a pregnant woman waiting on a plastic chair. His sweatshirt sleeves were so long he had torn little holes at the cuff seams and from these holes his thumbs protruded, the cuffs themselves like fingerless mitts over his warty hands. He was not like other fat boys. He was not jolly, he did not smile appeasingly, his eyes were not naïve and innocent. Bob Dollar knew instinctively that this was an evil fat boy. At once he took an ardent liking to him. He liked the fat boy because he was unlikable.

The fat boy spoke to the woman on the chair. "They had me in a wrestle hold in Kansas City. It was one of the most dangerous holds. They almost killed me. I don't know how I escaped, but I'm standing here, ain't I, waiting in line like anybody else? And that was last year. They couldn't do it now, because I'd kill *them*. I'd break their backs. And one of them was my best friend. But he is not my best friend now. He's my ex–best friend. We did some things together. One time when we were little we borrowed his mother's crème brûlée torch and melted the gumball machine, and the gumballs all came out on the floor, and they were rolling around and we picked them up and man, they were *hot*. Worse than hot, they were boiling, they stuck to our hands and burned them. See, I got gumball scars right here." He held out his palm for inspection, displaying puckered circles.

"That was my ex–best friend Mark who built a rocket launcher when he was thirteen. He was into wrecking things, me too, and that's probably why we were best friends. His aunt had all these old vinyl records, weird jazz stuff, and we threw them in the air and then bashed them with baseball bats. Mark had three baseball bats but he never played baseball, just bashed things. If I saw him now I would bash *him*. But he's safe, he's safe because he's in Kansas City and I'm here. And he plays the guitar but he's not very good. He doesn't want to be good. He wants to be loud. And he's got like these weird metal gloves that his grandfather gave him. His grandfather went to England to see the Tower of London and he brought back these metal gloves and Mark put them on and got his hand stuck in one. They had to take him to the emergency room in Kansas City and he was on television getting it taken off. The reason his grandfather gave him the gloves was to keep him from playing the guitar. That was the deal, 'I give you these English metal gloves and you not play that fucking guitar.' Excuse me, miss, that was Mark's grandfather talking, not me."

The woman on the chair stared at him with an expression of distaste but said nothing. Bob wanted to say that his uncle's roommate had been put off a plane in Kansas City but as he opened his mouth the druggist, with great heavy eyes which Bob thought sensual, came to the counter and spoke to the fat boy.

"Orlando, did Dr. Tungsten give you some samples? I can't fill your prescription. The doctor didn't sign it."

"What? No, he didn't give me samples! Just the prescription and he said, 'Get it filled right away.' He didn't sign it? What a jerk."

"Do you want me to call him?"

"Hell no, I'm going back over there," said Orlando, taking the prescription from her hand and heading briskly for the door.

When he was out of sight the clerk dialed the telephone and spoke to someone. "This is Ruby Voltaire, the pharmacist down at Young's? I had an Orlando Bunnel, claims to be a patient of Dr. Tungsten's, in here just now with a prescription for Viacomdex but it wasn't signed. So I'm not sure what the story is. Oh? Uh-huh. O.K. O.K."

The other clerk looked at Bob Dollar and said, "Your uncle's prescription is ready."

"He wants you to put it on his bill." He took the container and sprinted for the door.

In grade school he had had friends, but his freshman year in high school was one of oppression, loneliness and a sense of being an outcast, in part, he was sure, because he wore cast-off garments from Uncle Tam's shop. A month into his sophomore year he tried to explain the situation to his uncle.

"I didn't make many friends last year," he said, "but I thought it was because I was a freshman. And I thought it would be different this year. But I am still out of it. I try to be nice to everybody but nobody is nice to me. I just don't know how to make people like me. And they make fun of my clothes."

But Uncle Tam was not helpful. "Aw, what do you care? They're just punks."

After Orlando's advent Bob did not care.

• • •

He could see the fat boy at the bus stop two blocks west. He looked up the street and in the distance saw the flat face of the bus, no larger than the eraser at the end of a pencil. He began to run toward the bus stop, made it with the bus still blocks away.

"Hi," he said to the fat boy, who looked at him hard.

"You were in the drugstore," he said.

"Yeah."

They said nothing more until they were on the bus.

"Where do you go to school?" asked Bob Dollar.

"School! I don't honor them with my presence. I fucking quit school."

"Wow. Your parents let you quit?"

"Of course they let me quit. The alternative was handcuffs and forcible transport. I had a problem with the teachers. My parents don't care as long as I read a lot of books."

Bob Dollar could believe that the fat boy had problems with his teachers. He could see the potential for arousing teacher fury. "So what happened? You just didn't go in one day? You just said to your family, 'I have quit'?"

"O.K., here's what happened." Orlando spoke in a weary voice as though harried beyond bearing. "In this school I was in a class. The teacher's name was Miss Termino. We called her 'the Terminator.' And 'the Termite.' She assigned this dumb-ass paper, 'What I Plan to Do with My Life.' Everybody had to read his little masterpiece in class. It was the usual dumb shit, kids who wanted to be computer pro-grammers, software entrepreneurs, doctors and nurses, motorcycle racers, deejays."

He had touched on a subject that greatly interested Bob.

"How do they know?" he said. "How do they *know* what they want to be?"

But Orlando avoided philosophical discussion and continued his story.

"So, everybody reads their little paper except me and then the Terminator says, 'That was excellent, class.' She didn't mention that nobody said they wanted to be a scientist or a mathematician, which everybody knows is what's wrong with the country. *One* of the things wrong with the country. So I said, 'Miss Termino, I didn't read mine. You skipped me.' And she said, 'I didn't skip you, Orlando, I assumed you would not have done the assignment, as usual.' So I go, 'I did *this* one,' and I got up and walked to the front. Kind of stamping. And I read my paper. I knew it by heart. I go: 'Orlando's Ice City. I do not want to be a brain surgeon or president, I wouldn't mind being a champion wrestler or a guy who raises pit bulls or the captain of an ocean liner but first I am going to build an ice city at the South Pole and I'll get money from big corporations and hire a bunch of guys with no jobs—clean up the bums in Kansas City—to build the ice city. The buildings will all be clear ice and I'll have a big furnace to melt snow and squirt the water into molds—rectangles cubes cones and cylinders—and the bums will put them together into big ice skyscrapers and domes and I'll have all these lights inside so the ice buildings at night will shine in colors and the best and biggest buildings will be *huge* tetragons, and if people want to tour the city I'd charge fifty dollars each and that would include penguin steaks for dinner.' So then a girl goes, 'Penguin steaks! *Agk!* Gross!' and I gave her a shove because it was proof of a closed mind and penguin steaks are probably pretty good, but the girl fell on her desk and broke her teeth off just like a hockey player and the Terminator said go to the office. I said not a word but picked up my books and walked. Quit. My father—he's a jerk but so what— sided with me. Then two weeks later we moved here."

"I guess you got a good imagination or you're a big liar," said Bob Dollar.

"Well, that's for you to find out." Orlando hung from the strap so his body swayed with the bus's motion.

Bob said, "I don't get how people know what they want to be before they're old, like twenty or something."

"You don't have a clue?"

"No. Do you? I mean, after building the ice city."

"Sure. I want to be rich and rule the world. I want to be a computer geek. And I don't want to build the fucking ice city no more. That was kid stuff. Why you want to know about quitting school? You planning on doing that?"

"No. My uncle wouldn't let me."

"What does he have to do with it? What about your parents?"

"They disappeared when I was seven."

"Holy shit! What do you mean, disappeared? Ran off in the night? Abducted by aliens? Exploded? Killed by gangsters or venomous reptiles? Man, I am impressed. I wish my parents would disappear. My mother—know what she does?"

"What?"

"She cooks stuff with the labels on. Those dumb stickers they put on the tomatoes saying 'tomato' or the avocados saying 'avocado'? She forgets to take them off so you find these little labels in the salad. Or the chicken's got this metal tag on its wing and she cooks it with the tag on and there's lead and all kinds of poison comes out of the metal. So I'm half-poisoned. My father suffers the worst. He's all bent over and coughing. Poisoned by metal chicken labels."

The bus was filling up and Bob stood closer to Orlando. He could smell dirty hair and spearmint chewing gum.

"My mother and father went to Alaska to build a cabin for us to live in and I got to stay with my uncle until they came back. Except they never did. Never called up, never wrote. My uncle called the Alaska police and they put out a missing-persons report but they never found them. My uncle Xylo went to Alaska to look for them. Somehow they just disappeared. Couldn't ever find out what part of Alaska they went to. So I got to stay with my uncle forever. He runs a junk shop on Colfax and we live in the back and upstairs. At first my uncle thought something had happened to them. But later he changed his mind. I think he figured out that they dumped me."

"Man, that is weird! So are you going to go to Alaska and search for your parents when you turn eighteen?"

"I thought about it." He had never told his uncle this deep fantasy that had started a few months after they disappeared: he imagined himself flying to Fairbanks, looking in the phone book and finding Adam and Viola Dollar with an address and telephone number. Later, after he found out that Fairbanks was just another ordinary city, he had amended the scenario: now he (metamorphosed into a hirsute and muscular adult) paddled a red canoe up a raging Alaskan river, and then hiked into the wilderness as winter was coming on. Just when he was on the verge of freezing in a terrific blizzard he came upon a cabin in the wilderness. Inside was an old couple, feeble and emaciated. Their fire was out and they huddled under ragged blankets. He found the axe and the woodshed and chopped great armfuls of wood, made a fire, cooked hot dogs and mashed potatoes, fed the old couple, who sobbed with gratitude, and then he washed the dishes. There was a dog—a husky—and he fed the dog. Later he enlarged the husky to a whole pack of starving sled dogs and he fed them all and they licked his hands. The old couple exclaimed over him and when they were strong again they begged him to stay. The old man said, "We had a boy who would have been about your age but we were never able to go back to Denver and get him." And he imagined himself gently asking why and being told of a desperado—Rick Moomaw, with bushy hair and a face like a whiskered hot water bottle—on the neighboring claim, who was waiting for them to leave, even for a weekend, when he would manage to steal their entire property, even the cabin, even the deed. Finally Bob told them who he was, their long-lost son, and they fell on his neck and told him they had found gold but Rick Moomaw was after their claim. In the fantasy he laughed and flexed his arms, said he could and would break Moomaw into pieces.

Later this fantasy faded, replaced by dreams of sluttish blonds with enameled toenails, but when he met the fat boy it was still blazing. He had never told anyone about his hope to find his parents, yet within a few minutes of their meeting Orlando had guessed it.

A few months after his parents' fateful departure Bob had started thinking of his slippery self as a reindeer, and he carried his head carefully to avoid hitting his antlers against cupboards or wall projections. It became an intensely vivid fantasy. He had no idea who he was, as his parents had taken his identity with them to Alaska. The world was on casters, rolling away as he was about to step into it. He knew he had a solitary heart for he had no sense of belonging anywhere. Uncle Tam's house and shop were way stations where he waited for the meaningful connection, the event or person who would show him who he was. At some point he would metamorphose from a secret reindeer to human being, somehow reconnected with his family.

At Christmas he went with Uncle Tam, but not Bromo, who stayed behind to feed the cat and look after the shop, to Knuckle, Kansas, the family farm where his mother, Uncle Tam and the rest of the Bapp siblings had grown up. He had stayed with his grandmother many times when he was still with his parents, and saw now that even when he was very young his mother and father had not wanted him. At the holiday gatherings his aunts Lutie and Banjie made much of him and his uncles squeezed out false promises to take him fishing or hunting or to a Rockies game. At some time during the dinner his grandmother would look around the table, wipe at her eyes and say, "If Viola knew what she was missing."

"I'm sure she took it into consideration and regrets her decision, Mother," said Uncle Ket, for the extended family had theories that Viola and Adam Dollar were living somewhere in Homer or Nome, or even raising foxes in the Aleutians. Over the years the family had advanced explanations for the long silence, all built on the supposition that the runaways were not dead: leprosy, amnesia, madness, kidnapping or retreat to a very remote place could explain why they had not been in touch. Bob clung to these scenarios. Only Bromo Redpoll said they were dead, and what did he know? He was not blood kin.

On the bus Orlando suddenly said, "Hey, you want to go to the movies?"

"Yeah, but I got to get my uncle's prescription back to him. He's waiting for these pills. He said he was in agony. He hurt his back lifting a box of plastic dolls. Plus his feet really hurt."

"*Bad!* Where do you live?"

"Colfax. Way out on Colfax, out near Chambers Road. It's like almost to Kansas."

"Man, that's way, way, way out there. Can we get there on the bus? Cool. We take the pills to your uncle and then we go. The theatre is on Colfax too. The Cliff Edge, Colfax and Xerxes. It's behind a liquor store."

"I thought you had to go back to your doctor."

"Doctor? What do you mean?"

"What you told the drugstore lady. That you were going back to get your prescription signed."

"Oh, that was just bullshit. I was just trying it on. That was straight from the Book of Never Happen. I found that prescription on the sidewalk. Let me see your uncle's pills. Heh. Hydrocodone. No rush there, that's just codeine and Tylenol. But we might as well take a couple. He'll never miss them." He shook out six pills, gave two to Bob, swallowed the others.

Bob Dollar put the pills in his jacket pocket. "O.K.," he said, "what's the movie?"

"*Rat Women*. It's great. It's like this weird black-and-white flick, all grainy. It'll scare the shit out of you. It's an old horror movie from the sixties. That's all the Cliff Edge shows is horror and kinky stuff. Hey, don't we get off here? To change buses?"

Up Colfax they went, sliding past the Satire Lounge, PS Greek Pizza, past John Elway's Parts and Tammy's Nails, Air Afrik, Dragon Express and The Bomb. There was a fistfight going on in front of the Space-Age Atomic Washeteria, and Bob told Orlando that Uncle Tam's budgie had come from Jersey John's Pet Shop and that they had a charge account at the Mad Dog and Pilgrim bookstore where Bob was allowed to charge two books a month. (Bob had gone often to the branch library until Uncle Tam forbade him, for he had trouble returning the books on time and the library fines mounted up.) Orlando did not seem impressed. Finally they were past Food 99 and the Brigadier Army Surplus and there was Uncle Tam's shop, Used but Not Abused, and Bob felt a rush of embarrassment that it all looked so shabby and poor.

Uncle Tam was lying on the ratty sofa, drinking beer and watching television. He took the brown plastic container and shook out two large capsules, swallowed them with a mouthful of beer.

"So, you want to go to a movie?" he said. "Is it a good one? Maybe I'd come with you if my back wasn't killing me."

"You might not like it, sir," said Orlando. "It's an old horror film. *Rat Women*."

"Well, no, that's not my cup of tea. So I guess I'm not sorry." (He had watched Jacques Tati in *Mon Oncle* thirty-seven times for the sake of the scene in the plastic factory, the red hose emerging with swollen bladders or pinching down into a string of shining plastic sausages.) He dug a dollar bill out of his pocket.

"Here, Bob, some money for popcorn. And a paper. Bring me a *Post* when you come back."

Deducting fifty cents for the paper left fifty cents for popcorn and there was, Bob knew, no popcorn on earth for such a minuscule sum. But outside, Orlando, who had been watching, said, "I'll treat. I asked you. Anyways, I can get all the money I want. My dad drinks and when he comes home soused after he's asleep I get in his wallet and take a twenty or whatever and I got a kind of job thing." (Later Bob learned that Orlando's job thing was begging tourists for money on the Sixteenth Street Mall, a skill he had learned from a ragged man who lived comfortably in an expensive LoDo loft and who only plied the begging trade in evil weather, for it was then that pity moved passersby to dig deep. The best times were stormy afternoons before Christmas.)

• • •

The Cliff Edge was awful and the movie was awful and Bob Dollar enjoyed them both. In addition to the tickets, Orlando bought popcorn and quart containers of no-brand cola. The "theatre" was a converted storeroom behind the liquor store, the ramped floor made of bare, cheap plywood that boomed with each footstep. The wooden seats were not upholstered. The place smelled of urine and scorched vegetable oil. There were only fourteen people in the audience.

The film began with dozens of rats scurrying along a filthy waterfront street in an unidentified city. There were close-ups of rats eating garbage, rats crouching, groups of rats sleeping together in rat nests, close-ups of rats eating gristle and one lapping at a viscous substance that looked like decayed banana pudding. Then the rats scuttled around a corner and disappeared. The camera followed rather slowly. There were no rats around the corner, but eight or ten blond women leaning against a warehouse wall, voluptuous, heavily lipsticked, dressed in tight long dresses that sparkled with sequins. The women smoked and stared through dark glasses into the night. They wore shoes with sharp-pointed toes and unbelievably high heels. The camera moved closer and closer, gliding over satin haunches, shadowed cleavage, catching the wet shine of eyes and greased lips. It moved slowly down the back of the most buxom blond, her dress cut low enough to hint at the shadowy cleft of buttocks, down over the swelling rump, down the shining fabric tight over the thigh, down the full leg to the lower calf and, for a split second, there it was, hanging just below the satin hem of the dress, a muscular rat's tail that twitched suddenly like a lewd wink.

"Gross!" said Bob Dollar, but he hadn't seen anything yet. He hadn't seen the rat women on the beach in their bikinis, enticing a lifeguard under their striped umbrella where they strangled him with their tails (until then coiled in the bikinis) and devoured him, tossing the bones into the surf. He hadn't seen the nameless city's chief of police turn into a vampire and try to force the rat women to become his sex slaves. Nor had he yet seen Orlando, who had eaten the popcorn and swallowed the cola, matter-of-factly and noisily piss on the plywood floor without leaving his seat.

At the end of the film Orlando insisted they stay for the trailers of coming attractions, *Blood Feast* and *Scum of the Earth*. On the way out he pointed at a lurid poster for *The Corpse Grinders* ("In Blood-Curdling Color") and said, "That's a fucking great film," and told him about the theatre in Kansas City where he had seen it. As the audience had entered, the ticket taker had handed everyone a barf bag imprinted with THE CORPSE GRINDERS and some people had used theirs.

"I tried to, but I couldn't make anything come up. I still got the bag. It's like a collectible now. Maybe your uncle can tell me what it's worth." The Kansas

City theatre, he said, had had buzzers rigged under the seats. The buzzers went off at the moment the nurse's mad cat sprang on Dr. Glass and everyone in the audience screamed.

Bob Dollar had slept deeply that night, sated by low entertainment and drugged by the two stolen pills.

Now in Boise City, which the woman with crimped hair told him had been accidentally bombed by the U.S. Air Force during World War II, he fell asleep with the television set blabbering, awakened a little after midnight by a raucous alarm and red flashes on the television screen warning residents of May and Rosston and Slapout to seek shelter as a spotter had reported a funnel cloud moving northeast from Darouzett, just over the Texas line. The screen flashed a map and he saw the tornado was seventy miles east of him and moving away, went back to uneasy sleep, wondering if in this job he would be reaped in the whirlwind.

5

NO ROOM
IN COWBOY ROSE

The next morning was fiercely windy and as he crossed into Texas passing some purple beehives and a sign that read SEE THE WORLD'S LARGEST PRAIRIE DOG, 3 MI WEST, the wind increased, banged at the car with irregular bursts and slams. Tumbleweeds, worn small by a winter's thrashing, rolled across the road in the hundreds. Sheets of plastic, food wrappers, sacks, papers, boxes, rags flew, catching on barb-wire fences where they flapped until a fresh gust tore them loose. The landscape churned with detritus. A big tumbleweed hit the Saturn's windshield stem first and with force. A crack arched across the glass. In the distance ahead he saw a hazy brown cloud and guessed something was on fire. But the smell and an immediate choking sensation in his throat as he drove past an enormous feedlot, the cows obscured by the manure dust that loaded the wind and was clearly the source of the cloud, introduced him to the infamous brown days of the Texas panhandle, wind-borne dust he later heard called "Oklahoma rain." He passed a tannery and a meatpacking plant, saw the faces of

Chicano men in the windows of old trucks. A large metal sign, pulsing in and out as though breathing, read BULL WASH OUT. The sky was dead grey, a match for the withered grass around the railroad tracks where a chemical spill years before had killed off all the soil organisms.

He turned east, snorting and blowing his nose. At least hogs, he thought, were kept in a building (for, still innocent of direct experience with hog production, he had looked through the glossy Global Pork Rind annual report and admired the clean, low-slung hog bunkers). He passed several playa lakes crowded with thousands of ducks and geese struggling in the white-capped waves, and these bodies of water seemed incongruous under the throstling brown wind. But mostly he passed flat fields with V-8 engines pumping water, pump jacks pulling up oil, and, in the pastures, windmills lifting water into stock tanks, each tank surrounded by a circle of dirt from which radiated dozens of narrow cow paths.

By bright midmorning he was in the clear on Highway 15, looking for a town to establish his base of operations. The wind was dying down. Somewhere between Stratford and Miami he turned off Route 15 onto a narrower road, past a fence hung with dead coyotes and posted with signs that read TRESPASSERS WILL BE SHOT SURVIVORS WILL BE PERSECUTED, bumped across a set of railroad tracks and, a dozen miles on, entered Cowboy Rose, once a cattle town, then a ghost town, now slowly reviving, half-restored and idyllic, richly shaded by trees. Silver Spoon Creek ran through it, and through the center of the town, a large square of lawn edged with some drooping trees he associated with cemeteries. There were two cafés, two gas stations, and a cream-painted brick building, the front wall painted in huge red letters: TORNADO & BALL POINT PEN MUSEUM. Across the way he saw a shady park with a grand lawn edged by flower gardens. He noticed a Victorian-style bandstand. There were no grain elevators nor cylinders of anhydrous ammonia, nor giant storage tanks in sight.

He went into the Cactus Spike Café, past a hand-lettered poster that read:

18 CATTLE MISSING, MIXED HEIFERS.
WING ANCHOR BRAND.
NOTIFY SHERIFF H. DOUGH,
WOOLYBUCKET COUNTY.

He ordered the special, chicken-fried steak with milk gravy. The waiter/dishwasher, a stout man wearing rubber gloves, brought the gravy-swimming plate and Bob asked casually if he knew of anybody who rented rooms.

"Well, there's Beryl. Beryl and Harvey Schwarm. They got a room they rent out *sometimes*. But usually to a *lady*. I don't know, they *might*. They got the yellow house with the big porch on Wild Turkey Street. Worth a try, I *guess*. You a *salesman*?"

"No. Just visiting the area—a tourist, I guess. Like the looks of your town. Pretty nice."

"That'd be Beryl's sister, Joni, she's the one got the flower beds going, got them to build the bandstand. Got a band started up. They play every Friday night in the summer. Light classics, they say, but ask me it's mostly old Frank Sinatra tunes. Nobody around here knows what *classic* means. There's more and more people comes to *visit*. It *would* be handy to have a motel or a resort hotel here, but don't look like it will happen tomorrow. Best we've got is the Schwarms unless you want to drive over to Dumas or up to Perryton. There'd be motels *there*."

"I'll try the Schwarms. Thanks for the tip."

"*I'm* the one supposed to get the *tip*," said the man.

Mrs. Schwarm, wearing a blue chenille housecoat, answered the door, her nose swollen, face red and sprinkled with small yellow grains. Her hands were encased in rubber gloves and she held a wet facecloth from which water dripped.

"I'm hoping to rent a room," he said. "Someone told me you rent rooms?"

"Who? Who told you that?" She sounded extremely annoyed.

"Ah. The waiter at the café. A heavyset man . . ."

"Big Head Haley. That fool. So dumb that just tyin his shoelaces gives him the headache. I can't even have myself a facial without somebody poundin on the door and wantin a rent the room. He don't know nothin about nothin and he don't know I stopped rentin that room a year ago. If people come to Cowboy Rose they can stay with kin or bring a tent. I had trouble with a woman stayed in that room and I swore I'd never rent it out again. Come here from Minnesota and her ways was not our ways. Stay up late at night, sleep until noon and then want *orange juice*. She must a thought she was in Florida. I asked her to take her shoes off when she come in—I got white carpet on the stairs—but she never did and like to ruined the carpet."

"Mrs. Schwarm, I swear I'd take my shoes off. You would have no problem—"

"No. I'm not havin no problem because I'm not fixin to rent it out. It don't even have a bed in it now. My husband uses it for a hobby room. He makes wood ducks." And she closed the door.

He drove north to Perryton near the Oklahoma border, decorated with blowing food wrappers and old election signs. The traffic lights swung in the wind. Every vehicle was a pickup, his the only sedan, and heads turned to stare at his Colorado plates as he drove along the main street. All the motels were booked full. On the outskirts of town he found a sad, two-story building, the Hoss Barn. A large banner hung over the door reading HOSS BARN WELCOMES MARBLE FALLS BAPTISTS.

"Are you with the church group?" asked the clerk, a young man with a skewed face and scarred nose. Bob Dollar guessed him to be an ex-convict.

"No, I'm traveling on business."

"It'll cost you the full rate, then—seventeen a night."

"That's O.K." In Oklahoma he had paid thirty-seven.

The Hoss Barn sported a thin, filthy carpet on concrete stairs. Dixie cups and peanut wrappers lay in corridor corners. His room was small and shabby, with a powerful smell of perfumed disinfectant; a painted concrete floor, the television set chained to the wall, only one working lightbulb, several Bibles, including one in the roachy bathroom. Over the bed hung an enlarged photograph of Palo Duro Canyon. He could hear singing and cries of "Hallelujah!" coming from the room next door and, when he went out in the corridor on his way to find a restaurant for dinner, noticed a hand-lettered sign, PRAYER MEETING 5 P.M., stuck to the cinder-block wall with reused duct tape.

Every restaurant in town was packed full, people standing in long lines outside the doors except for the Mexicali Rose, which had only a small knot of hungry would-be diners. He waited with them and in time was shown to a tiny table next to the kitchen doors, which swung open furiously every half minute. The restaurant was crowded with Baptists and their children, who either sat passively without moving under the parents' stern eyes or raced wildly up and down dodging waitresses. He ordered enchiladas and studied the crowd. There was a booth next to his table where two very quiet children sat with their hands folded. The father and mother conversed in near-whispers, shooting narrow-eyed glances at the rowdy kids running and jumping. Bob heard the father say that if he had them in his care for five minutes he would learn them what-for, he would dust their seat covers, they would get a rump-whacking to last them a lifetime. The family's food arrived, cheeseburgers and fries for each, iced tea for the parents, enormous glasses of milk for the children.

The same waitress, wearing asbestos gloves, brought Bob a metal platter, the entire surface a lake of boiling yellow cheese. He put his fork to it and a gout of steam shot up. He expected to see the fork tines droop. Before the molten lava cooled enough for him to eat, the waitress brought the family in the booth a special dessert, ice-cream sundaes with five sauces and masses of ersatz whipped cream. Instead of a cherry there was a tiny cross atop each. The wan children could only eat a little of these concoctions.

"Give them here, then," said the mother, digging in her spoon. "We paid for them."

Very suddenly he thought of Fever, Orlando's girl-friend, of how the Baptists would shrink from her if she strode in now in her unlaced Doc Martens.

Orlando had called one day and told Bob to meet him at Arapaho and Sixteenth.

"There's like a place where everybody hangs out.

At night people in wheelchairs race there. In the day-time it's a hangout. A lot of cool kids show. Fever's going to be there."

"Who's Fever?"

"My girlfriend. Sort of my girlfriend," said Orlando, stunning Bob, for the fat boy had struck him as a loner, a singular youth who would grow up to have the classic berserk fit, shooting diners in some fast-food emporium or taking a tax collector hostage.

"How come she's called Fever. Did her parents name her that?"

"Not them! Shirley is what they picked out. But she had her tongue and lip pierced with these little bar-bells in and they got infected. Her ears, too. But they didn't get infected. She had a fever and she went around asking everybody to put their hand on her forehead and see if she had a fever so we started to call her that. Anyway, we can just hang for a while and then go to the movies," said Orlando. "There's a five-dollar special triple feature—*Deranged . . . the Confessions of a Necrophile* and *I Drink Your Blood.* The other one is some kind of atomic monster thing and if it's boring we can leave."

When he got to Arapaho he saw Orlando at once. The evil fat boy was wearing a red cowboy hat and an aircraft mechanics jumpsuit with *United Airlines* stitched on the breast. He was in a crowd of ten or twelve teens. They looked more like sci-fi movie set creatures than human beings, with spiked, shaved, dyed heads, Magic Marker tattoos, pierced lips, nostrils, eyebrows, lips and tongues, huge swaddled trouser legs and assortments of metal—neck chains of fine gold and waist chains of heavy tow-truck linkage. Bob was struck by the appearance of a rachitic youth wearing black lipstick, which went well with his ginger mustache and gilded ears.

"Orlando," he called and the fat boy spun around, waved coolly, pulled a girl from the crowd and brought her over.

"This is Fever."

He had to admit Fever suited Orlando. She was rather fat, her sleek flesh looking springy and resilient. The sides and back of her head were shaved, the top hair left long and dyed prison orange and federal yellow. Her mouth was coated with alternating vertical bands of purple and blue lipstick and a small ring hung from her lower lip. Her ears glinted with a dozen niobium rings. She wore a pair of men's white corduroy trousers. The backs of her hands were inked with skulls. Each finger showed several rings and chipped green nail polish, and her elbows were scaly gray. She wore a man's sleeveless purple satin jacket, the back embroidered *Insanity Posse*. When she turned around Bob saw a biscuit-size hole in the rear of her pants disclosing the fat swell of a peach buttock. When she sat on the concrete abutment her bare ankles showed, scabby and ringed with grimy circles.

She looked at Bob Dollar and said, "How the fuck are ya?" When she smiled he could see the barbell in her tongue.

6

SHERIFF HUGH DOUGH

Sheriff Hugh Dough was forty years old, a small man, five feet five, 130 pounds, riddled with tics and bad habits, but nonetheless a true boss-hog sheriff. He had a sharp Aztec nose, fluffy black hair and black eyes like those in a taxidermist's drawer. A line of rough pimples ran from the corner of his funnel mouth to his ear. His uniform was a leather jacket and a black string tie. He had been a bed wetter all his life and no longer cared that he couldn't stop. There was a rubber sheet on the bed and a washing machine in the adjacent bathroom. He had never married because the thought of explaining the situation was unbearable. He was an obsessive nail biter. He counted everything, courthouse steps, telephone poles, buttons on felons' shirts, the specks of pepper on his morning eggs, the number of seconds it took to empty his bladder (when awake).

Other members of the Dough family had gone into law enforcement and public safety, creating a kind of public service dynasty. Hugh Dough's half brother Doug was a paralegal, and their maternal grand-mother had been a member of the Panhandle Ladies

Fire Brigade in Amarillo at the turn of the century, with a wonderful costume of black tights, short serge dress with enormous brass buttons and a crested metal helmet modeled after those of the Roman gladiators. His father's mother's sister, Dolly Cleat, took pride of place. She had gone off to the University of Chicago early in the century where she specialized in political economy and sociology, and, after the Great War, worked her way up from superintendent of the Ohio Women's Workhouse to assistant warden at the State Home for Girls in West Virginia. His father's unmarried sister, Ponola Dough ("Iron Ponola"), was the commander of the Women's Police Auxiliary in Pine Cone, south of Waco. Before her ascension to the top position, the auxiliary had been little more than cops' wives holding bake sales to raise money for a barracks pool table or to help some trooper's family left destitute by his injury or death. Ponola changed all that and made the auxiliary a quasi-military organization with uniforms and black leather belts and boots, rigid hats in Smokey the Bear style, shirts with neckties and the like. The cookie-baking wives were forced out and in their place came Ponola's friends, muscular Baptist-Republican-antiabortion amazons who patrolled the street outside Pine Cone's only bar, looking to break up fights and twist cowboys' arms, arts in which they excelled.

But the one he was close to above all others was his younger sister, Opal, with whom he'd enjoyed a particular relationship throughout adolescence, begun on a sultry Sunday afternoon when he was fourteen and Opal twelve. They had been playing hide-and-seek with visiting cousins, big shock-headed bullies neither of them liked. They had burrowed into the hay in the barn loft. The need for silence and secrecy, the closeness of each other's body, the gloom of the loft shot through with sparkles of light from roof holes, were conducive to half-playful physical exploration which continued in many places over the next year, from the front room coat closet to the family sedan which Hugh was allowed to drive in certain circumstances. One of those circumstances was as his sister's escort to dances, for Opal was not allowed to go on dates. Instead, the Dough paterfamilias decreed, Hugh would drive his sister to and from the dance. Once there she could meet her partner for the evening while Hugh could team up with his girlfriend.

One warm September evening when Opal was thirteen and Hugh fifteen, he had driven them to the dance. He was enamored of a tall girl with long red hair, Ruhama Bustard, recently arrived in the panhandle from Click County, Missouri. He danced six times running with Ruhama, who allowed him to rub against her, then, as he begged her to come out into the parking lot, twirled away with Archie Ipworth. Aching and abandoned he sought out Opal, who was dancing with a classmate whose face was so pustulated it appeared iridescent from a distance.

"Hey, you want a go? Get the hell out a here? I'm havin a hell of a lousy time."

"O.K.," she said and turned to the boy. "See you in school Monday." He nodded and slouched away.

In the sedan he told her what the problem was, how the red-haired girl had excited him to a frenzy and left him with an ache that ran from his knees to his shoulders.

"I mean, it's terrible," he said. "She give me bad Cupid's cramps." He groaned theatrically. "Whyn't you just let me put it in? I mean, it's not much more than we already done."

"O.K.," she said and he pulled into the cemetery where they got in the backseat and began an activity that finished up nearly every dance they attended for the next five years, including the dance that followed Opal's wedding, the bridegroom an elderly rancher named Richard Head, too drunk on cheap champagne to notice his bride's absence from the festivities. At Thanksgiving and Christmas, when the Dough family gathered en masse at the old homestead, it was Hugh and Opal who volunteered to go to the store and get the ice cream or ginger ale or extension cord that was needed.

The sheriff's father, T. Scott Dough, had been a cook at the Texas State Prison in Huntsville for many years, back in the days when it was called Uncle Bud's Place, his job to prepare the final dinners for men on death row. When he died at sixty-six it was the sheriff who had to sort through the clothes in the closet, the Sunday trousers with bagged knees as though keeping a place for the dead legs. In a box of brittle papers he found four or five old German post-cards, hand-tinted, showing women leaning into or against motorcars of the 1930s, their seamed and clocked stockings wrinkled sadly at the back of the knee and ankle, their feet in T-strap shoes of dull leather. Their skirts were rucked up to disclose utilitarian garters and sweaty, bunched cotton panties. From the gaping leg openings buttocks swelled, muscular and hard. One in particular he disliked. It showed a bare-bottomed woman, left foot up on a running board, the right on the ground in a patch of grass. The woman's posture and the angle of the camera made the left buttock alarmingly huge while the right, pulled flat by the extended leg, seemed atrophied. How anyone could take pleasure in asymmetry was beyond him, yet the repellent image fixed itself in his mind and rose unbidden at awkward times.

People had always asked the sheriff's father about the condemned men, what were the nature of their crimes, what they said and did. The old man would say, "Don't know damn thing bout any of it cept what they want for their last meal. Thought when I first come in the job it was goin a be fancy stuff, but no. Country boy don't know a thing about food. The most a them ask for cheeseburger with double meat and fry. Sometime you get one steak and Worcestershire. But mostly it's your hamburger. They don't think steak. Nigger boy got better idea. They ask like fry chicken, peach cobbler and cob corn, your barbecue back rib, salmon croquette. A lot a the nigger, special your Muslin, refuse a last meal. They rather fast. Another one ask wild game—guess he thought we goin out and make a javelina hunt for him. He get cheeseburger. Had my way he would a had road kill. Lot a enchilada and taco. They ask beer and wine but they don't get it. They ask cigarette and cigar. No. They don't get no bubble gum neither. This one that kill his girlfriend want six scramble egg, fifteen piece bacon, grit and seven piece toast. He eat ever bite and lick the plate. What was comin don't affect *his* appetite. And how about two jalapeño and raw carrot for the last meal? But I tell you what—hardly a one ask for chicken-fry steak. What you make a that?"

In the bottom of the box was a chef's toque, stained and crushed. That's what his father's life had come down to, yellowed girlie pix and a flat hat. He intended to take care something of that nature did not happen to him.

For a while he collected sheriff memorabilia. He had a collar worn by one of Sheriff Andre Jackson Spradling's hounds. He had an axe that the escaped convict Jason Shrub used to bludgeon his way out of the Comanche County jail, and a photograph of the gun that a desperate prisoner snatched from Sheriff C. F. Stubblefield and then used to shoot the sheriff's tongue. He had one of Buck Lane's florid neckties and a pack of greasy cards from a Borger gambling den raid. He had a windmill weight in the shape of a star. He had a set of brass knuckles used by a deputy sheriff from Bryant, Oklahoma. There was a heavy chain used to lock prisoners to trees from the days before the Woolybucket jail was built.

Hugh Dough was reelected term after term. He did not, as some sheriffs, rely on easy banter and warmth to disarm, but had developed a mean, piercing stare and a reputation for being a trigger-happy marksman. The credulous believed in vast acreages for paradise and inferno, one aloft, the other down the devil's adit in the hot rocks, both unfenced open range. But the sheriff knew that the properties had been long ago broken up and that frayed patches of heaven and hell lay all over Texas. Most rural crimes, he believed, happened in vehicles at the Dairy Queen and at roadside rest areas, the latter having social uses that might surprise the highway landscape planners. Then there were the lowlives who stole drip gas from the pipeline, and every town had its set of wife beaters. To track the former he listened for sounds of engine knock in local cars, a side effect of drip gas use.

He was a good customer of the state crime lab and, with their help, had once solved an ugly crime in which a naked and severely bruised young ranch hand was discovered dead at the foot of a remote windmill. There were scores of circular marks on the victim's skin, and on a wild hunch Hugh Dough asked the crime lab to compare them with the decorative *conchas* on the ranch owner's handmade chaps. They matched.

There were notches on his gun handle. He had

black belts and diplomas in esoteric martial arts; in his hands a stick was a lethal weapon. In Woolybucket County he presided over certain legal rites, heard confessions, arbitrated disputes, observed the community, knew when a family was in difficulties, and he guided the errant back onto the path, sometimes forcibly.

Hugh Dough disliked politics and it galled him to run for office. For many years he had run against Tully Nelson, a six-four bully who, after his last defeat, moved thirty miles to sparsely populated Slickfork County where he was handily elected, and hence a rival sheriff. Hugh Dough also disliked teenage punks, and thought the best deterrent for a young hoodlum—the younger the better—was a night or two in the county clink. He had once locked up the state's attorney's bespectacled nine-year-old son, whom he caught throwing rocks at a dog chained to its doghouse.

"How'd you like it, then, was you chained up and some four-eyed little bastard come along and start peggin rocks at you? Believe I'll have to educate you." And he handcuffed the kid to a bicycle rack in front of the courthouse, snatched off the kid's glasses and put them on his own blinking eyes, saying, "Now let's us pretend I'm you and you're that poor dog," picked up a small stone and hurled it. It caught the kid on the upper arm and set off shrieks and blubbering that brought heads to the windows. A few more stones and the kid was hysterical.

"Guess I will have to lock you up until you quiet down," he said and dragged the bellowing child into the jail, kicked him into a cell. Of course he paid for it later, as the state's attorney was a formidable enemy.

"Ain't that the squeeze of it?" said the sheriff on the phone to his sister Opal.

"At least you got the satisfaction," she said, and in the panhandle satisfaction of grievances counted for something.

Perhaps the most irritating of his duties, aside from chasing down old ladies' reports of strangers on the highway, was keeping a balance in the ongoing feud between Advance Slauter and Francis Scott Keister, two ranchers of opposing personalities and ranch philosophies and styles. What puzzled Sheriff Hugh Dough was their lack of kin recognition, for the Slauters and the Keisters had intermingled generations back when both clans lived in Arkansas. Old Daniel Slauter had married Zubie Keister in 1833, and although she was only the first of his five wives, she bore him five of the thirty-two children he claimed to have fathered, and a marked Keister look—long ringy neck, circled eyes, spider fingers and bad teeth—had entered the Slauter genes. Later more Slauter-Keister crossings further marred the stock.

Advance Slauter and Francis Scott Keister had loathed each other since grade school (which old-timers called "cowboy college" in their sarcastic voices) when Keister, the product of an intensely religious upbringing, a 4-H leader and a Junior Texas Ranger, overheard Advance Slauter, muscular lout extraordinaire, say that he was screwing both his younger sisters and anybody who wanted a piece of the action should show up at the family ranch at six A.M. with a quarter in hand and tap on Ad's window for admittance. Hugh Dough had sniggered knowingly, later inspired to do his own homework, but Francis Scott Keister was outraged on behalf of pure girlhood. A terrific fight followed, broken up by the principal. Both boys refused to say what had started it. In fact, Ad Slauter was entirely puzzled by the attack. So the feud began and had persisted over thirty years, each man coming by turn into the sheriff's office to report the latest atrocity. Sheriff Hugh Dough would hear the complainant out and take notes, file them in the two voluminous dossiers of increasingly sophisticated criminal misdemeanor. The assaults were mostly rock-throwing and name-calling until high school when both wangled broke-down old hoopys to drive. Now buckets of paint were thrown, tires shot out, windshields broken. When Francis Scott Keister went to the Wichita Falls stock show with the 4-H group he bought a custom-designed bumper sticker that read I AM A PIECE OF SHIT and pasted it on the back of Slauter's car. Ad Slauter responded, on the family vacation trip to Padre Island, by visiting the marina store where he stole three aerosol cans of expandable flotation foam and he used them to fill the engine compartment of

Keister's vehicle. He signed Keister up for subscriptions to gay pornographic magazines ("Bill me later"). Keister released black widow spiders on Slauter's windowsill. Slauter poured sixteen gallons of used crankcase oil on Keister's front porch.

As grown men both Francis Scott Keister and Advance Slauter ran cow-calf cattle operations but there were few similarities beyond the fact that both men's cows were quadrupeds. Francis Scott Keister was a scientific rancher, methodical, correct, progressive. He had been born in Woolybucket and was belligerent and aggressive about being a "panhandle native," loathed all outsiders.

Keister lived with his wife, Tazzy, and only child, fourteen-year-old Frank, a lanky boy with wing-nut ears and broom-handle neck. He often told him to go help his mother in the kitchen as he was no help with machinery or cows. Their house was large, of the style called "rancho deluxe," the only building on the ranch not made entirely of metal. His corrals and catch pens were of enameled steel in pleasing colors. The machine shop and calving barn were heated and well-lighted, freshly painted every year. His handsome Santa Gertrudis cattle displayed rich mahogany coats and backs as level as the ground they trod. Ninety-four percent of his cows dropped a calf every spring. He kept meticulous breeding records on complicated computer charts. The heifers were artificially inseminated with semen from champion bulls, turned out on newly sprouted winter wheat in the spring, carefully moved from pasture to pasture during the summer. Keister supplemented the grass with soy meal, beet pulp, molasses, sorghum and sweet-corn stover, corn, cottonseed hulls, beet tops, cannery waste, anhydrous ammonia, poultry packer by-products (including feathers), peanut meal, meat meal, bonemeal, lint from the family clothes dryer. To this smorgasbord he added a battery of growth stimulants including antibiotics and the pharmaceuticals Bovatec and Rumensin, as well as the implants Compudose, Finaplix, Ralgro, Steer-oid and Synovex-S. At eighteen months his big steers were ready for market and he received the highest prices for them.

Ad Slauter, in contrast, lived in a dwelling constructed around an old bunkhouse dating back to the 1890s, part of a massive ranch that had belonged to a disappointed Scottish consortium. He had added slapdash additions and wings to accommodate his large family of ten girls. He was an advocate of arcane home remedies. When five-year-old Mazie, playing hide-and-seek, chose a bull nettle patch in which to hide and emerged shrieking and clutching at her calves, he urinated on the burning welts, telling her it would take the sting out, until his wife came at him with a broom. Turpentine and cold coffee was, he said, good for a fever, and drunks could be made sober if they ate sweet potatoes.

The Slauter ranch was shabby and run-down, with sagging fences and potholed roads. He ranched as his father had, letting his mixed-breed cows, mostly picked up at the cattle auctions in Beaver, Oklahoma, take care of their own sex lives. Cows preferred to nurse their calves for six or seven months, not become pregnant as rapidly as possible, and Slauter thought they knew what they were doing. They wandered where they would and were half-wild by the time of fall roundup. He bought small, young bulls every five or six years for a few hundred dollars. Only fifty-five percent of his cows produced a calf each year. Because they ate only pasture grass supplemented by baled hay in winter, they took a long time to put on enough weight for market, twenty-eight to thirty months. Curiously enough the two men's ledgers balanced out at almost the same figures, for Keister's operation was costly and his heifer mortality rate high as the champion bull semen made painfully large calves.

Hugh Dough dreaded to see either of the combatants pull up in front of the courthouse, but especially disliked Francis Scott Keister, whom he regarded as a rigid straight arrow who made too much of things that didn't concern him.

The sheriff's office had five dispatchers. They were all big, placid, middle-aged women, and not one of them understood how to separate the inconsequential from the urgent. Myrna Greiner did not hesitate to call at three A.M.

"Sheriff, I thought you ought a know we got a report that a black panther is tryin to break into Minnie Dubbs's kitchen. She can hear it a-growlin and a-scratchin at the door."

"How does she know it's a black panther? Did she see it?"

"She says she can tell by the noise it's makin. Plus she looked out that little side window in her pantry and she could see it in the moonlight standin up on its hind legs and scratchin away."

"Call her back and tell her that if it's still on the prod at daylight I'll come out there and arrest it. Tell her to put some cotton in her ears and go to sleep. Tell her to take a bath first. My granny used to say that if you don't take a bath the panthers will get you in the night."

But to the dispatchers all calls were of equal weight, for if you read the papers it was as logical to believe that a panther would slink out of New Mexico and make its way to Minnie Dubbs's house in Wooly-bucket as it was to fear that the creaking noise down below was an escaped convict bent on robbery, car theft and murder. Just such a terrifying fate had overwhelmed deaf old Mr. Gridiron, a retired rancher kidnapped from his bed in 1973, driven away in his own truck and murdered beside the road across the Oklahoma line.

The sheriff's great victory against Tully Nelson, his onetime political opponent, had occurred a few years earlier at 8:30 on a moonless June night as he was cruising the back roads. A call for backup help came from Texas Fish and Game.

"Sheriff Hugh, we got a tip-off that a gang of poachers is working the Stink Creek area tonight. Can you meet us there ten o'clock?"

He was a mile from the bridge when the call came, pulled over and doused his lights, glassed the fields with his powerful night binoculars and immediately picked up parking lights at the side of the road near the bridge. He counted four lights—two vehicles. He turned around, circled south, east, north and west on farm roads, making a four-mile loop in order to come up behind the vehicles, drove the last half mile slowly with his lights out (for he had good night vision and knew every inch of this road), stopped a quarter mile from the bridge and crept up to the parked vehicles on foot. Just off the road at the bridge stood two empty sheriff's cruisers, parking lights on. On the doors he saw a star and the words SLICKFORK COUNTY SHERIFF. The trunk of one vehicle gaped wide.

"Well, I'll be a Methodist," he murmured. It was the break he'd been waiting for. The Slickfork Sheriff's Department Annual Barbecue and Volleyball Tournament was coming up, and here, he thought, they were, fixing to get the main entrée by foul means. Out in the field he could hear grunts and panting and cursing and adjurations to keep it down, he could see the dancing flicker of a small flashlight. He used his cell phone to call the dispatcher (Janice Mango) and whispered that she should get Fish and Game out to the Stink Creek bridge immediately, call the newspapers in Amarillo, get three deputies out there with shotguns—the miscreants he was about to arrest were heavily armed. He had a newsworthy collar about to go down.

As the hunters approached the gap in the barbwire (their fence cutters had been at work) he turned on his own light, a marine searchlight that lit up what seemed to be the entire panhandle in a blast of 200,000 candlepower—Tully Nelson and his four deputies, dragging and lugging two dead deer and one Rocking Y steer, put their hands over their pained eyes.

"O.K., you're under arrest. Turn around and put your hands behind your backs. I know who you are and you're already reported so don't try no goddamn fool stuff." He saw with disgust that Tully was in uniform. He used their own handcuffs on them, collected weapons and tossed them into the open trunk.

"Come on, Hugh, let's talk about this." The speaker was Deputy Waldemar, a heavily muscled workout freak with a Hollywood profile and capped teeth.

"Nothin a say. Might as well sit down, boys. You goddamn arrogant idiots are caught red-handed fixin to pull the dumbest trick I seen in many years. I suppose this was for your goddamn barbecue?"

"Come on, Hugh. It's for the public good. Everbody comes to that barbecue," pleaded Harry Howdiboy, Sheriff Dough's idea of a garden slug reincarnated as a human. Well, he'd sprinkle salt on him.

"It was not for the public good. It was for personal

gain and advantage and it is illegal sideways, up and down and through the middle. What you done is mortally wrong and it will stay done until the trumpet blows. Advise you to set and keep still. I'm in a stinkin bad mood and the least little move or talk might make me think you are resistin arrest and tryin to escape. Time I got done with you they mightn't recognize anything except the frickin handcuffs."

In December of that year he received the Texas Peace Prize awarded annually at the Hotel Stockholm in Dallas. On the flight from Amarillo to Dallas he had had a window seat and spent the time counting the rivets in the wing. In addition to the rivets there were five small L-shapes as though someone had traced the corner of a toolbox with white paint. Then he noticed many droplets of white on the wing—clusters as though someone had struck a loaded paintbrush a smart slap. There were too many to count. During the ceremony he had counted the fringed threads on the cloth covering the award table. The large photograph of himself holding the trophy and the fifty-dollar prize check hung in his office next to the portrait of his grandmother in her Roman gladiator headgear.

7

THE RURAL COMPENDIUM

Bob stayed three days in the Hoss Barn reading the local classifieds, returning to the Mexicali Rose to eat chicken-fried steak (the never-changing special), asking waitresses and store clerks about places to rent, driving around reading bumper stickers:

MY SON IS AN HONOR INMATE AT MCALESTER

HONK IF YOU LOVE BRATWURST

WHAT A FRIEND WE HAVE IN JESUS

7-LETTER WORD FOR STINK—HOGFARM

He counted churches: the Primitive Baptist Church, the New Light Baptist Church, the Sunrise Baptist Church, the Sweet Loam Baptist Church, the First Baptist Church, the Bible Baptist Church, the Apostolic Faith Church, the Freewill Baptist Assembly, the Tabernacle Baptist Church, the Fellowship Baptist Church, the True Christian Church, the Straight Christian Church, the First Church of God, the People's

Church of the Plains, the Gospel of Grace Church, the Jehovah's Witness Kingdom Hall, the Pentecostal Holiness Church, the Bethlehem Lutheran Missouri Synod Church, the First Assembly of God Church, the First United Methodist Church, the Church of the Brethren, the Seventh-Day Adventist Church and, on the very edge of town near some run-down hovels, the Immaculate Conception Caprock Catholic Church, a tiny building hardly bigger than the smokehouse from which it was converted. There seemed to be a church for every five residents. But of apartments and houses there was nothing for rent. Everyone had a home and was in it. The manager of the Hoss Barn, Gerald Popcorn, perhaps not an ex-con after all, thought Bob Dollar, offered him a residency rate of ten dollars a night but told him he would have to move to a smaller room. A tent seemed a better choice. And outside the wind never stopped blowing.

At night he read from Lieutenant Abert's *Expedition*. There was an illustration of James William Abert at the front, but in it he seemed middle-aged. It was difficult to guess how he had looked at twenty-five: thin, a longish, straight nose, limp brown hair. Perhaps even then he was growing the mustache and beard of the sketch, even then his hair already receding. Bob imagined his friends called him "Jim," but he thought of him as Lieutenant Abert.

The account began with a description of Bent's Fort. Bob Dollar had gone to Bent's Fort himself on the eighth-grade class trip. He knew the fort was a reconstruction and the guides, blacksmiths and mountain men lounging around were only actors, but the feeling was remarkably real that he was on the border of Mexico marked by the Arkansas River in the mid-nineteenth century, the world of traders and trappers and Cheyenne Indians, of Mexicans and Texians, of buffalo hides and French voyageurs. Now, looking at Lieutenant Abert's watercolor of the fort, done from the far side of the Arkansas and showing an overly large flag flying from the fort and, in the foreground, a conical tent, perhaps a teepee, with two white men standing near, one wearing a striped shirt and, his arms folded, the other in buckskin pants and with a rifle over his left shoulder, he felt he was there again. The fort looked the same as it had on the eighth-grade trip. During the class visit Bob had been pleased to see screaming peacocks strutting along the fort's parapet and wandering through the courtyard. Now he read that in Lieutenant Abert's day there had been numerous cages at the fort containing birds of the region—the magpie, the mockingbird, the bald eagle. The parapet of the outer wall was planted to bristling cacti, which, when Abert saw them in the summer of 1845, were in waxy red-and-cream-colored bloom.

He delighted, with the lieutenant, in the groups of Cheyenne who came to the fort and did a scalp dance and posed for him while he painted their portraits. He enjoyed the lieutenant's detailed description of Cheyenne hairdressing, the men's hair long enough to trail on the ground but their eyebrows and beards

plucked out with tweezers. He thought the lieutenant's attraction to the women's center partings
and neat braids that hung to their waists a little more
than that of a disinterested observer. Clearly he fancied them and Bob wondered if he had slept with any
of them. He supposed so. And when the lieutenant
went with "Mr. Charbonard" to visit Old Bark, an
important Cheyenne (with a beautiful daughter), Bob
thrilled at the contact with the Lewis and Clark expedition of 1804, for "Mr. Charbonard" was Jean-
Baptiste Charbonneau, son of Sacajawea and
Toussaint Charbonneau, the baby whom Sacajawea
had carried on her back all the way to the Great
Water of the West. What the lieutenant had written in
1845 Bob held in his hand, feeling the long-dead
voice speaking to him.

At the end of the week, sitting in the Mexicali Rose
over a cup of weak coffee, the cook stuck his head
out of the square hole where the chicken-fried platters appeared.

"Hey, Bob Dollar, want your eggs bright-eyed or
dirty on both sides? And are you still lookin for a
place to rent?"

"Dirty. And I sure am."

"Well, I heard it there's a lady down in Woolybucket got somethin. If you don't mind stayin down
there. Pretty dead town. I got the number for you."
He thrust a torn edge of newspaper through the hole.
"And if you got smarts you'd take somethin to eat.

There's no place to eat in Woolybucket. There *was* a place about fifteen years ago, run by a old lady, well, I say old lady, but you couldn't tell if she was a woman or a man."

"Thanks. And I guess I'll get an order of fried chicken to go."

He looked on his map. Woolybucket was the next town past Cowboy Rose, down Route 444, which ran from Tyrone, Oklahoma, to Pampa, Texas. It was on the north side of the Canadian River. He called the number and a woman's thin yet rough voice told him that the place was an old log bunkhouse on the Busted Star Ranch, without electricity or running water, but sound and sturdy and only fifty dollars a month. No drinkers, no smokers, no women, no drugs. He said he would like to look at it, thinking that maybe it was the break he had been waiting for.

The wind had died down, leaving an emptied, medium-blue sky. On the outskirts of Woolybucket a sign proclaimed THIS IS THE BEST PLACE IN THE WORLD. A smaller, almost completely faded sign beyond it was illegible except for the sinister words ". . . out of town before sunset." Woolybucket was the seat of Woolybucket County. Seven gravel and caliche roads, formed in the 1890s by cattle driven from outlying ranches to the railhead, converged from every compass point. No traffic light on earth could order the complex nine-way intersection which operated first come, first served. The railroad bisected the main street. There was a white water tower on which some wag had painted the legend H_2O. Beyond it were five or six grain elevators with a dozen pickups parked in front. Bob guessed that was the major hangout place for farmers.

The center of Woolybucket featured a small tan lawn like a grass tutu around a tan brick courthouse, a tan sidewalk leading up to a portico where a sign with an arrow directed visitors to the sheriff's office. Along the street opposite the courthouse he saw the traditional lineup of small-town businesses, a card and gift shop, an empty storefront, the Old Dog Café, a law office with a sign reading F. B. WEICKS ATTY in flaking gold letters, the Lone Star pool hall, Bludgett's Pharmacy, the Speedwell Market, the Woolybucket Bank and the glass-fronted newspaper office, *The Banner*, which he soon learned the less sanguine locals called *The Bummer*. Through its plate-glass windows the Old Dog looked to be crowded with men wearing cowboy hats, and the street itself, especially in front of Clip's News & Video where young men and teenaged girls leaned against the walls of stores, against the municipal trash barrel, the posts supporting the arcade roof, draped themselves across the fenders of pickups. The town seemed vital and full of life.

The newer shops that proclaimed Woolybucket a community of modernity flanked the courthouse on the side streets. Here was an Episcopal church shaped like a wedge of cake, the Motel Caribe with a bathtub-size pool in the center of the parking lot, a Thai-Mexican restaurant, Woolybucket Cellular and a fitness center named Gym Bob's. He bought six doughnuts at Cousin Dougie's Donut Shop. A placard in the window announced YES WE HAVE LATE, which he took to be the regional spelling of "latte."

The post office was two streets back, a false-front building shaded by a small cottonwood tree. On slat-backed benches sat four elderly men, leathery, wrinkled, skinny-necked and thin, all with their right legs crossed over the left. Their pants legs rode high exposing four white shanks in oblique alignment. They all smoked cigarettes showing the same length of ash, they turned their heads in unison to watch the traffic pass. Bob Dollar was pleased to see so many oldsters and imagined them all to be proprietors of big spreads.

Another elderly man standing outside the post office, wearing chinks, cowboy hat and tooled leather cuffs, gave him directions to the Busted Star, said it was owned by LaVon Grace Fronk, told him to stay on the asphalt because they'd just bush-hogged the damn roadsides, now bristling with brush stobs sharp as punji sticks. He mounted a grey horse, saluted Bob Dollar and rode off. The horse limped.

"Come on in," yodeled the woman, beckoning him into the gloom of the house. Her voice was grainy and oleaginous at the same time, like coarse-ground peanut butter. "Will you all take a glass of water or

97

some Pepsi?" LaVon Fronk, small and thin as a fifth-grader, was a middle-aged ranch widow who resembled one of the minor Roman emperors with her intense, nervous face, small mouth barely wider than her nose, the eyes close-set under a ledgey brow, marbled hair of faded red and white.

"I'd love some water," he said, his throat parched with dust. She made a little production of getting the glass, rinsing it, putting in ice cubes, taking a pitcher of iced water from the refrigerator, slicing a lemon and perching it on the rim of the glass. The house seemed very hot to him.

"There! There's nothing like cold water, is there? I was a Harshberger from Miami"—she pronounced it "Miama"—"Miami, Texas, of course. Not the Florida place. I married Jase Fronk in 1951 and he died—well, that's enough of that."

"Woolybucket is kind of a strange name," said Bob. "Is it called after somebody?"

"Named after the woolybucket tree. I guess there used a be a lot a them grew here. Birds like a wooly-bucket. The leaves in the spring, why they are all fuzzy underneath before they roll out—that's the wooly buckets. And Cowboy Rose is named after a flar. The wine cup. That's the other name for the cowboy rose. You couldn't have a town called 'Wine Cup.' Not in teetotal Woolybucket County."

While he drank his water Bob noticed flamboyant knickknackery everywhere. LaVon said the kitchen was French provincial, though to him it seemed

Texas provincial, a clean white linoleum floor, a white Formica table with chrome legs and matching chairs, a calendar on the wall next to a portrait of Jesus constructed of macaroni and seeds, and against the walls aged and noisy white appliances. The dish-towels, stamped *Bonjour* at the bottom, showed the Eiffel Tower. On the counter stood ceramic jars labeled CAFÉ, SUCRE, FARINE. A poster reproduction of Brassaï's *Steps of Montmartre* hung over a wine rack, which contained not wine but bottles of whiskey; a good sign, thought Bob Dollar. She showed him dozens of items she had purchased through mail-order catalogs—a leather hot water bottle cover, a Moroccan oil lamp. Over the cat's basket—she had a heavy paint tomcat with a bad leg, only one ear and half a tail, the victim of an encounter with the lawn mower—a blue enamel sign declared CHAT LUNA-TIQUE. *Chat mort* would have been more accurate, for the somnolent beast lay as one dead hour after hour, rousing only when the refrigerator door opened or when the gangly neighbor boy started the lawn mower.

When he finished his water she said, "Well, let's go have a look at that bunkhouse."

"This's it," she said, driving him through a bumpy pasture, over a sullen creek toward a motte of cot-tonwood trees. There was a second fence behind the barbwire made up of old tires on end, packed three deep in overlapping rows. Under the cottonwoods stood a small log building with a porch. A rope ran around the circumference of the porch floor and LaVon explained this was to keep snakes out of the cabin. Inside were four empty bunks, on each a thin mattress folded in half, a stack of blankets, four wooden chairs at a square table. There was a tiny stove with a blackened teakettle on it and against the wall a wood box full of kindling and sticks.

"Spartan," she said. "There's no electric. Supply your own sheets and towels. You'll have to haul water. Get it down the house in the kitchen."

"I'll take it," he said without seriously considering a daily drive across a cow pasture, the labor of lugging water, no telephone, for already he was taking pleasure in the subtle beauty of the panhandle, noting the groves and thickets along watercourses, huge coils of grapevine weaving the trees into a coarse fabric. He thought the bold diagonal of caprock rim that divided the high plains from the southern plains, the red canyons of the Palo Duro striking and exotic.

He unloaded his suitcase, his new briefcase (new only to him, for it had come from Uncle Tam's shop) with its freight of Global Pork Rind flyers and papers, a pair of pinch-toe cowboy boots shining with polish, and the box of fried chicken he had brought from Perryton. It took only a few minutes to unpack. He went outside and walked around the bunkhouse, starting up a plump, chickenlike bird in the tangled vines along the creek. The sound of running water was pleasant though it made him want to piss. Against the back of the bunkhouse leaned four large logs, two of them partially shaped and carved into figures—a woman's head with flowing hair, and a roughed-out human figure that vaguely resembled Lenin. Perhaps some ranch hand had fancied himself a sculptor.

In the deepening afternoon he sat on the porch with a warm bottle of Pearl and told himself to buy a cooler and ice in Woolybucket the next day. There were several pieces of farm machinery in a large field to the west, ungrazed for some years and grown up with big bluestem and weeds. He counted five rusted wheat combines, three pickup trucks, four old tractors, various harrows and rakes, all sinking into the earth. There was a dark shape in the high grass, but what it was he could not make out—perhaps an old gas pump. In the dulling light he noticed a low rise to the south, too low to be called a hill even in this flat country, little more than a swelling as though the earth had inhaled and held the breath. But by panhandle standards it was a wave of earth that deserved the name "hill." Beyond the rise was a great indigo cloud spread open like a pair of dark wings, monstrous and smothering, shot through with ribbands of lightning, and in the distance the stuttering flash of strobe lights at the ends of the irrigation pivot water arms. The dusk sifted down like molecules of pulverized grey silk.

He left the fried chicken skin and bones on the porch floor. Sometime in the night he woke to hoarse barking cries outside the door repeated with monotonous regularity. But even as he struggled to come fully awake the barks began to recede and, peering out the window into faint starlight, all he could see was a small shadow gliding into the black weeds, whether fox or coyote he didn't know. Toward morning rain tapped the roof.

He went over to the ranch house in the morning, drew the water, then sat and had a cup of coffee with LaVon, who had the regional taste for very weak, pale brown coffee. She told him she was compiling a county history which she called *The Woolybucket Rural Compendium*, hundreds of memoirs and photographs from families of the region.

"Mr. Dollar, I have been workin at it for thirteen years."

Her mailboxes, she said, were packed full with genealogical reminiscence every noon when Doll McJunkin delivered. Elderly visitors came up the drive with their boxes of photographs and diaries, faded envelopes. The papers and photographs filled two entire rooms downstairs. As they sat at her worktable with their coffee cups LaVon gestured at the shelves of boxes.

"I suppose I'll never get it done," she said with something like pride. "I suppose I'll die and my son will throw everthing out—essentially the entire history of Woolybucket County and everbody in it."

"Couldn't you do it in several volumes?" asked Bob. "Like, get the first volume published that deals with the earliest days and then, later, you know, follow up with the later stuff?"

"No, I could not. My material is filed by family, not by year. It's alphabetical, not chronological. I sometimes think that was a mistake. But we live with our mistakes."

"Then couldn't you do like A to L? I mean, anything, just so you make room. And don't the people want their letters and pictures back?"

"They may," she said carelessly. "And they'll get them back when I'm done. There's too much new stuff that comes in that has a be added to the families at the beginning a the alphabet."

"But—"

"Do not worry about it, Mr. Dollar," said LaVon. "I'm sure you have your own work that interests you. Every pie got its own piecrust."

"Well, yeah." He did not see the trap.

"And just what *is* your work? What brings you down here in the panhandle, which has so few voluntary visitors?"

"It's kind of complicated," he said. "It's not really work at all." He noticed two semitransparent plastic sweater boxes on the table near LaVon's computer. He thought he saw something moving inside the top box.

"Oh? A vacation perhaps in sunny Woolybucket?"

"I'm looking for—"

"Yes?" She stared.

"I'm, I'm, I'm writing a profile of the panhandle for a magazine. That's why I'm interested in your *Compendium*."

"What magazine is that?"

"Ah. I haven't got one lined up yet. I thought I'd write the article first and then send it to a magazine. Maybe *Oklahoma Today*," said Bob, thinking fast.

"I *don't* think so, Mr. Dollar. Strange as it may seem, *Oklahoma Today* specializes in Oklahoma stories, and they are not even partial a panhandle Oklahoma. And that's not how you get a article in a magazine. People get assignments. You must think I'm pretty dumb. For your information I was a contributing editor to *Drip* for seventeen years." She relieved his puzzlement; "It's an ag-tech magazine devoted a irrigation."

"No. No. You're right. I'm not writing an article. Somebody else is. Was." He thought frantically. "In fact I'm looking for a—a girlfriend. My mother disappeared in Alaska when I was little, but she always told me to marry a girl from Texas."

"Oh, did she. How old were you when she gave you this advice?"

"Around seven. Or eight." He kept looking at the plastic box. There were holes punched all around the top just below the cover.

"That's a little young for someone a be guidin a child toward marriage. Unless she was Chinese?"

"No."

"Maybe she came from Texas herself? There are a lot of Asian people on the coast."

"No. She wasn't Asian. But she always admired Texas girls. And I admire them too."

"Maybe we'd better leave it at that, your admiration for Texas girls. By the way, are you employed? I'm just wondering if you'll be able a handle the rent, low as it is."

"Well, I am employed. I'm scouting the region for nice pieces of land for, for a luxury home development. Global Properties Deluxe. The company is interested in branching out into the Texas panhandle. They feel there is potential here."

"If you know how many thousands have surmised that 'potential.' But luxury home development is a new one to me. This part a the country is losin people. I'd think they would a sent you down to the hill country outside Austin with all those rich computer folks or around Dallas. Your panhandle millionaire prefers a live in a trailer house and put the money into land and horses. Anyway, how lucky you are, Bob Dollar, to have a good job in a world where so many strive hand to mouth. In that case you probably don't mind givin me a month's rent in advance? I got a be protected in case you skip."

He smiled and said he would write the check on the spot, then added, "Is there something in that plastic container? I thought I saw something move. In the top one?"

"That's Pinky." She reached for the box, set it between them and pried up the cover. Bob was horrified to see a tan tarantula with baby pink feet staring up at him. He rose so abruptly his chair tipped over. The spider reared back in alarm.

"She won't hurt you," said LaVon. "She's very quiet. I'm surprised you noticed her move. She spends most of her time in her hideout." She pointed at several pieces of heavy bark propped at the back of the sweater box. "It seems a little dry," she said, putting her hand in the box and feeling the wood chips and soil. The spider ignored her. She took up a small bottle near the phone and squirted the cage interior with a fine mist, replaced the cover.

"Long as I'm misting," she said, putting down the bottle and reached for the other box.

"You've got two," said Bob without enthusiasm.

"This one is different," she said, carefully lifting up one corner of the lid. "This is Tonya. She's a Togo starburst, an African arboreal. They're both arboreals, but Pinky comes from Latin America, from the rain forest." Bob moved closer to get a better look. "Stay back, Bob, this one can jump and she is very aggressive and bites like a flash. The bite can make you feel pretty sick." He saw the grey spider had a beautiful starburst pattern on its carapace. It was not as large as Pinky. He was relieved when LaVon put the cover back.

"I only had Tonya for a year, but Pinky almost five. She could live to be eight or nine years old. That's a short life span for a tarantula. Now your Mexican blond can live to be forty. They are long-term pets."

The sky was the color of cold tea when he went out.

On the bunkhouse porch that evening when it grew too dark to see the words he fetched his flashlight, for he was at the point in the narrative where the lieutenant was looking at drawings by Old Bark's son (who had earlier danced with "extravagant contortions"), autobiographical drawings in which the son vigorously attacked Pawnees with his lance. The lieutenant was generous, praising the execution and the "considerable feeling" for proportion and general design. Bob felt that if the lieutenant had had Old Bark's son in a drawing class he would have given him a gold star. But when the famous guide Thomas Fitzpatrick came on the scene, cautioning the lieutenant never to tie mules to bushes, for they twitched the branches, each rustle convincing them that the enemies of mules were creeping near, the flashlight began to dim and falter and after a few minutes he gave up and went early to bed. At that moment, sitting in the deep dusk, the flashlight beam weakening, the course of Bob Dollar's life shifted, all unknown to him, for he was conscious only of his annoyance at the lack of light and swore to get a camp light or candle the next day.

8

PIONEER FRONK

In 1878 in Manhattan, Kansas, Martin Merton Fronk, twenty-three years of age, the son of a German immigrant watchmaker, sat on Doctor Jick's leather examination table, coughing and wheezing.

"Well, young man," said Doc Jick, "what I think is that you are suffering from a concentration of the humid nature of our local atmosphere, which, however fragrant and delightful to the majority of nostrils, affects some few in a deleterious manner. You, I fear, are among that rare number. Your constitution is somewhat weak and renders you unable to enjoy or profit from the lowland airs. I advise you to seek a higher, drier climate where crystalline breezes sweep through the atmosphere with rapidity and frequency. I would suggest to you the high plains of Texas where other sufferers have gone before you and found themselves much improved within a year. Not a few with tuberculosis."

"Do I have tuberculosis?"

"I think not. You have a sensitivity to vapors and dampness. I have no hesitation in recommending you to the Texas high ground. There is, in fact, a very good medical man in Woolybucket—oh, these Texas town names—who has cared for and cured a number of respiratory cases far worse than yours. You can seek him out with confidence. D. F. Mugg, M.D., keenly interested in the malaises of the human body and good horse trader as well."

"I have no idea what I might do out there to make my living."

"I understand it is a fair country for farming, but even better for the raising of cattle. Many men, especially young men such as yourself, are flocking to the region seeking their fortunes through the rich grass and pure water. Once your lungs have healed in the healthful air, as I have every confidence they will do, I do not doubt that you will be yo-ho-hoing and riding at breakneck speed across the flower-spangled highlands. You might go farther north to Wyoming Territory or Montana, but those environs suffer deadly winter chill and blizzard snows. At least Texas has warmth."

Later, Fronk reflected bitterly on those words. Yet while in a state of blissful ignorance he put his affairs in order and converted most of his worldly goods into cash ($432), argued with his father, who still cherished dreams that his son would come to the watchmaker's bench. After three days of wrangling the father understood the son's departure was inevitable, and, in late April of 1878, Martin Fronk climbed onto a huffing, west-bound train accompanied by a valise and a trunk packed with such necessaries as an axe, some good hemp rope and fourteen back issues of the *Louisiana Go-Steady,* an occasional illustrated paper of incendiary political views and attractive engravings of little-known foreign regions, a class in which Martin mentally placed Texas, high ground and low. As well he had put a small sack of yams in the trunk and a paper packet of coffee beans wrapped and tied by his younger sister, Lighty.

When the train stopped for an hour in a town that seemed to consist of one large emporium and swarms of cattle, he got out to stretch his legs, entered the store and purchased three cans of oysters, one of which he opened and ate on the platform, the other two going into his valise. The train started with a terrific jerk, then settled into a monotonous and swaying side-to-side motion. In the issue of the *Go-Steady* he was perusing, a timely article on cattle raising had his rapt attention, and he barely noticed the extraordinary span of the bridge over which the train was passing, 840 feet in length, the conductor announced.

Cattle, he read, needed no care nor cosseting on the Texas plains. One turned them out and let them graze as they would, then, once or twice a year, rounded them up with the help of the children of the region (thus he interpreted "cowboys") and drove the beasts to market in exchange for money. So plentiful were ownerless cows on the Texas plains that a poor but ambitious man could make his fortune in one or two years. Coughing lightly, he turned the page and read that a cow valued in Texas at five or ten dollars would sell for thirty dollars in Kansas City. The article described the economics of driving three thousand cows from Texas to a Kansas railhead. The eleven men needed to drive them, including a cook, each cost thirty dollars per month—that was $330. Another hundred went to the trail boss, another hundred to provisions: that made $530 a month in costs. The cows could bring $90,000. Suddenly, his future seemed clear.

The article went on to explain that the most efficient and inexpensive procedure was to arrange for the services of a contract drover rather than use one's own cowboys, who were needed on the home ranch to care for the next cow crop. Or, in yet another scenario, the article presented the example of a rancher with six strong sons who managed the trail drive with animals from the ranch, sons who were paid little or nothing, for the ranch would come to them in the sweet by-and-by. But, Martin thought, one did not find six strong sons on alder bushes. He supposed it would take decades, even if he had a wife, to grow strong and cattle-minded sons. As he read on he understood that contract drovers themselves could make fortunes, and eventually purchase and stock their own cattle ranches. There was an example of one who made $50,000 in a single season driving other men's cattle north. He fell into a pleasant reverie. If his health improved rapidly he might become a drover for a few years, then set up as a rancher, he and his six strong sons. One thing he understood clearly—there were fabulous profits in cattle if you were a stem-winder.

The train tracks did not extend to Woolybucket, but ended a brisk day's ride away at a place called Twospot. There was a rough stable behind the station where he persuaded a mangy oldster to sell him a secondhand Dearborn buggy and a grey horse with ogre eyes, loaded his trunk and valise into the buggy and started west, the general direction of Wooly-bucket. On the train, the conductor, who had seemed to be as well-informed in the affairs of the MKT Railroad as a company director, had told him it was a sure thing the line was going to be extended to Woolybucket within a year, that Woolybucket was to become a major cattle-shipping point, that he, Martin Fronk, would be smart to look for land in the vicinity of this metropolis-to-be.

He twice crossed small streams, the Woolybucket and Rogers Creeks, both lined with willows and cot-tonwood, offering shade and rest to the traveler. Indeed, he saw a small party in a camp but as they looked, from a distance, like Indians, he did not care to approach. The conductor had mentioned a few peculiar habits of the Indians, especially the Comanches, who were lacking in common manners and sometimes exhibited markedly abrupt behavior.

"They got ahold of a clock salesman last year, cut open his stomach, pulled out his guts a ways, tied em to the horn of his saddle and whacked the horse. I believe they cut off different parts of him for souvenirs, too. Weren't much left but the general idea of what he'd been. Smart if you stay away from them."

A man in the seat across the aisle said, "Hell, that weren't the worst. Tell him what they done to Dave Dudley at Adobe Walls. You don't know? Well, *I'll* tell him. They got Dave Dudley who was shootin buffler at the mouth a Red Deer Creek. They carved out one a his balls, put it in his hand and tied his hand to a stake set out in front a him so he would have to look at it and think about what was happenin. Then they cut the hole in his gut and driv a stake down through into the ground, pounded it in with a axe. Used one a his own buffler pegs. And they finished up with scalpin him four ways from last Tuesday, ever hair on his head tooken. That's the kind we got here. They run out most a them now but not all."

By late afternoon the sky was a deep khaki color in the southwest though that had little significance for him. He was tired from the hot, jolting hours in the Dearborn and wanted more than anything to sink to his chin in cold water. He was thirsty, had long ago drained the canteen of water. Yet he feared going down to the river where there might be Indians. Now and then he drew a deep breath, testing to see if the high, dry air was making a difference in his breathing. It seemed to him to be easier and perhaps more comfortable. He could not really tell. The gloomy sky ahead cracked open with lightning and he cut toward a motte of trees, Indians or not, wanting some shelter.

There were no Indians in the shady grove, but a cleared area and trampled vegetation showed it had been occupied in the last twenty-four hours by someone. He made a tiny fire and laid two yams in the coals to bake while he washed the dust from his burning face. There was a small pool, somewhat murky. He cupped his hands and drank the sulfurous water. A rumble of thunder shook the ground though the air was dead still. A soft explosion from the fire reminded him that he had forgotten to pierce the potatoes and one had burst. It was a dead loss. He stabbed his knife into the other, still whole (he thought of suffering Dave Dudley and the wretched clock salesman, for the yam resembled a yellow belly), raked more coals on top of it and filled the canteen at the pool. He unharnessed the grey, rubbed it down, fed and watered it, spread his blanket on the ground under the Dearborn. When the surviving potato was done he ate it hot and without salt, opened a second can of oysters with his knife, swallowed them, drank again from the pool, rinsed the oyster can and put it aside to use as a coffee pot in the morning, crawled under the wagon ready to sleep although it was still daylight, yanking his blanket over his head to thwart the mosquitoes. A tiny fresh breeze slid along the ground, as sweet and cool as chilled water. The sky had turned purple-black, riven with lightning that showed low-scudding clouds moving at right angles to a heavier mass above.

The clouds were ragged and wild. The little breeze quickened, became a small wind, strong enough to drive off the stinging pests, lifted the corner of his blanket. It was sharply colder.

He dozed for a quarter of an hour, then woke to a terrific explosion of thunder. He thought for a moment he was back on the train, for he could hear a heavy freight not far away. How had he come to a train yard? There was a mad rattling and balls of icy hail the size of pecans bounded under the wagon. He tried to crawl out from under it but something was blocking the side, something with stiff, wet hair. It took him a few seconds to recognize the feel of his horse. The freight train was passing by just beyond the trees accompanied by a crackling of branches. The trees swayed, one fell. In the flashes of lightning he could see their writhing branches, a confetti of torn leaves, and beyond, some black and immense thing towering like a nightmare. The unseen train, running without lights, curved away into the wet night. To the west a band of colorless sky showed that the next day would be fair. Aching with fatigue and a general sense of malaise he slept again.

He woke early, before the sun was up. The vast sky freckled with small flakes of raspberry-tinted clouds. He crawled out from under the Dearborn and looked at his horse. It was dead.

In a little while he mixed a handful of cornmeal with water in his palm, laid the mass on some gathered leaves to thicken while he made a fire and heated two flat rocks in it. He baked the cornmeal cake on one of the hot rocks, roasted a few coffee beans on the other and pulverized them with the heel of the axe, boiled coffee in the oyster can. The hot can burned his hands and mouth. He strained the floating grounds through his teeth, chewed the escapees. He studied the horse again, thought it might have been struck by lightning as there was a discolored mark on its right shoulder and another near the fetlock.

He hid his trunk as well as he could beneath an overhang of dirt bank, piled torn branches in front of it, heaped rocks. He looked again at his dead horse. Finally he set off west on shank's mare, guessing that Woolybucket could not be more than two or three miles distant.

Late in the morning a new difficulty assailed him. He could feel the cornmeal cakes and coffee and oysters whirling and sloshing in his gut. His bowels writhed. He thought of Dave Dudley and the clock salesman. For the next few hours he stumbled along with frequent responses to his mad intestines. He abandoned his valise. Soon he began to vomit as well and his head ached violently. In midafternoon he quit and lay on the ground in considerable misery. After an hour, feeling fever roast him on a spit of illness, he thought he smelled smoke. He rolled to his other side and scanned the prairie. Yes, there was smoke coming out of a mound of soil—might it be a volcano? A black rectangle suddenly showed in the face of the mound of earth and a figure moved into it and hurled something that sparkled briefly. The figure turned and disappeared into the dark rectangle that he recognized as an open doorway. He began to crawl toward it and when he was only fifty feet away, two horses in a makeshift corral began to whinny and snort. The door opened a crack and Martin Merton Fronk called out "Help," in a feeble, choked bleat.

"What the blue burnin hell is *that*?" said a voice and a seven-foot gink with white hair wearing a red shirt and too-short California pants came striding out of the dugout with a Winchester in his hands. He was followed by a shorter, younger man, a bench-legged, bullet-eyed rip with a luxuriant but multi-colored beard that blew sideways in the wind.

"Who the hell are you and why the blue tarnation are you creepin up on us? You one a them fellas with a sticky rope admires other folks' horseflesh?"

"Sick. Can't walk. Meant no harm." It seemed funny that they saw evil design in him. The talking made him vomit again.

"Christ, you smell like you been shittin yourself as well as losin your okra."

"Yes. Sick. Sick." He said a few words about the cornmeal cakes and the dead horse and the sudden diarrhea.

"You get your water at Twospot? Little pond a water there?"

"Yes."

"That's squitter water. It'll make you want a die, make you think your guts is bein pulled out a your asshole with your mama's crochet hook, but you won't die and most gets better and some even drinks that squitter water again and has no ill effects. I done it. Anyways, we got the fix-up for it. Just wait here. You ain't comin into this camp smellin like shit and puke boiled with skunk cabbage for a week. You lay out here folded up like a empty purse and we'll bring it to you."

The cure, as they called it, was a tin cup of brown liquid toned up with some kind of cheap whiskey. He drank it and promptly vomited. The man with the multicolored beard fetched a second dose, which he took in tiny sips, willing it to stay down. When the cup was empty he lay in the grass and closed his eyes.

"Give her a hour or two to work," said the giant and they disappeared into the dugout.

Near sunset they reappeared with a basin of steaming water and some folded garments. They pulled his noisome shirt and pants from him and poured the basin of hot soapy water over him, threw down a flour-sack towel and advised him to get into the fresh clothes.

"My valise . . ." he said, pointing back the way he'd come.

The tall man said, "Good idee. Why have him stink up our duds with his squitter shit when he can do what he wants with his own?" He saddled one of the horses and rode in the direction of the creek camp. Martin lay naked and cold on the prairie and began to shiver but at least he was no longer racked with spasms. The multicolored beard brought him a biscuit and some clean water.

Before the sun went down the tall man was back with the valise, which he opened and went through with interest. He tossed a pair of pants to Martin and a striped cotton shirt. Martin asked for his spare underdrawers but the man laughed and closed the case.

"Sonny, no man in Texas wears them. Just slows you down whatever you got in mind. I'n use them for a dishclout."

They gave him a corner in the dugout and the tall man who said his name was Klattner, late of Arkansas, promised—as soon as he learned there were coffee beans in it—that he'd get Martin's trunk in the morning.

"We been out a coffee a month. Tried to git a little in Woolybucket but they're out too and no supply wagon due until June. So your coffee will be appreciated. What damn old Woolybucket needs is a good store. The one they got in Woolybucket now, it's not no good. There's a crazy doc half runs it when he ain't layin on a sofa dead drunk. Couldn't hit a elephant's ass with a banjo. Used a have a regular storekeeper, but he lost the emporium to the doc in a game of chance. Doc don't never order enough coffee, flour, sugar, what-have-you. All last winter no flour and no tabacca. My God, he got in a thousand pound a saleratus and not one teaspoon a flour. We horsewhipped him but it didn't do no good. Bad as ever."

"Would his name be Doctor Mugg?"

"It would. You know him?"

"No. I was told he was well-regarded at curing sick folks."

"I don't know who told you that but the informant was lyin. Doc Mugg couldn't cure a ham if you gave it to him in front of a smokehouse. What Doc Mugg needs in the cure line is the water cure—for hisself. If I was you I'd get better on my own. Fresh air and whiskey is best and plenty work."

The multicolored beard chimed in. "If I was you I wouldn't tie up to Doc Mugg for a minute. He's filled up the graveyard complete and is startin on another. Why don't you git his store away from him and run it good—run it honorable. Every man would greet you with hearty goodwill wherever you may go."

But Martin Fronk had fixed his sights on making a fortune as a cattleman, whether drover or rancher, found the idea of running a store repugnant and said so.

"I spose you want a be a cattleboy," drawled the multicolored beard whose name was Carrol Day, a curiously feminine name, thought Martin, not yet acquainted with the bearded Marions, Fannys and Abbys of Texas who, saddled by their unthinking mothers with dainty names, built savagely masculine frames of character.

"I believe I'm too old to be a boy again of any kind."

"Age don't matter. Some a the pertest cowboys is pushin seventy summers. Lookit old Whitey here," nodding at the tall man who was wrapping rawhide around the helve and head of an axe. "He's most eighty and he's more cowboy than any ten ordinaries."

"He's a *cowboy*?"

"Hell yes. Been up the trail to Montana what, twenty times?"

"Twenty-two. And that was enough. It's too cold up there. Snows all summer. You git paid there's no place to spend your money. Just turn around and come back to Texas."

"What about Miles City? What about Cheyenne? What about Denver? I understand you paid them towns a visit on your return journeys many a time."

"My money was gettin too heavy. Anyway, Martin here don't want a be no cowboy or no storekeeper. I'n see he's got bigger ideas in mind."

"I was thinking about the stock-driving business."

Both men began to scream with laughter. Carrol got down on the dirt floor and rolled, moaning, "Oh my sweet cabbage patch, 'the stock-drivin business.'"

"You idiot," said Klattner. "Make it in the stock-drivin business, you got to know cows like you know your own tweedle-dee. You got to have cowboyed, got to know the markets and men. You have to sweet-talk crazy farmers and handle Indans. We just got burned alive, me and Whitey, in the stock-drivin business. Stampedes, Indan troubles, blue-burnin Kansas farmers—"

"Indians?"

"Hell, they're no bother," said Carrol. "Just give em

one a your cows and they leave you alone. A course after fifty donations you're down fifty cows."

"They can be trouble," said the other. "There's Quanah Parker. And others. There was that clock salesman—"

He didn't want to hear about the clock salesman again.

"I could run a store," whispered Martin Fronk, giving up his plans to become a rancher or cattle drover. The waterholes were too chancy.

The next day he felt distinctly better, packed his suitcase and asked his hosts if they could spare one of their horses so he could get to Woolybucket.

"You buyin or borrowin?"

"I'm agreeable to purchase one of your steeds. Preferably one that is docile and of gentle disposition."

"That one died last year. But we can let you have that sorrel gelding for twenty dollars. He's got two names: You Son of a Bitch and Grasshopper. He don't like grass a wave in the breeze and when it does so he hops. You purchase old Grasshopper and we'll draw your wagon in next week. See if you can't git that store away from Doc Mugg and do right by the town."

The other added his advice. "And, if you do, lay in plenty coffee. And keep your supply wagon outn reach a them damn red sloughs. Look like dry riverbed places along the Canadian but you break through to the mud, stickier than boiled molasses mixed with glue, and eight hunderd foot deep. It's happened."

You Son of a Bitch disliked waving grass, birds, distant riders, prairie dogs, clouds, saddles and, as Martin Fronk came into the outskirts of Woolybucket, black-and-white dogs. One of the last named sent him into paroxysms of bucking until Martin departed the saddle. The horse stood trembling, facing the barking dog. Martin picked up a few stones and threw them accurately and hard at the dog, which ran yipping to a ragged tent. The side of the tent was painted with letters: GEN'L STOR DF MUGG MD PROP.

He went inside the tent. There was an ungodly welter of stuff, from unfurled yard goods to bullwhips.

"Got any coffee?" he asked the shambling wreck entangled in a bolt of blue daisy cotton. Was that a banjo on the cold stove?

"June. Didn't send it yet. Come back in June, sir."

He left, wondering if he'd seen the fabled Dr. Mugg, thinking he could run that store with his head in a bag and hobbles on his ankles.

9

THE BUSTED STAR

Bob Dollar thought LaVon's Busted Star Ranch, a little north of the Canadian River, a beautiful place. For the first time in his life he saw what extraordinary personal privacy a ranch family enjoyed. If he really were looking for a site to develop luxury homes this would be it. LaVon told him the ranch had been mixed-grass grazing land—bluestem, buffalo grass, gramma, wheat grass and Indian grass—when the first settlers came into the country in the late nineteenth century. Moises Harshberger, her peripatetic grandfather, arrived in the panhandle as a young man in 1879, a year after her husband's ancestor Fronk had taken over Mugg's store.

Moises Harshberger and his brother Sidney, she said, had made a journey from Tennessee to California where they bought fifteen hundred steers, then on to Montana with the steers where they sold them at profit, down to Texas where they bought more cows and drove them to Kansas City and sold at a profit. There Sidney fell ill with cholera. After a quick funeral Moises drove a small herd to Wyoming, sold them to an arrogant English lord with a face like a mustached tortilla at a wonderful profit and so again to Texas, where he bought ranch land north of the Canadian breaks. On this land he found thousands of short, sharpened stakes scattered over the prairie, used by the buffalo hunters a decade earlier to peg out hides. There were thousands of bison bones underfoot as well.

Perversely, Harshberger abhorred the shadeless plain, its grass and silvery sand sagebrush. He hired men to dig up and ship to him hundreds of sapling big-tooth maples and chinquapin oaks, five hundred young ponderosa pines, grudgingly watered by the wagon drivers on their jolting journey somewhat as Captain Bligh's breadfruit trees had been tended by sullen sailors on the *Bounty*. Nor did his attentions fail once the trees were planted around his new house. After a month of mumbling and dodging by his mutinous ranch hands, who thought of themselves as pure cowboys to whom any action that required dismounting, hefting and carrying, as buckets of water, was demeaning insult, he hired a neighbor's grown but mentally slow son, who, ignorant of the niceties of the cowboy code, daily sloshed water into the earth-reservoir built up around each young tree. Harshberger forbade the cowboys to use the saplings as horse hitches or pissing posts. But the young trees could not endure the sand-blasting wind and before he put sheltering lath fence on their windward sides, half of them perished. In time, the remaining trees, though they grew with a pronounced lean, struck

125

their roots deep and a canopy of shade dappled the house.

"He fenced ever inch a the ranch himself with but two helpers and a lot of that fence is still up today." She did not say that in fencing the land a certain balance shifted. Now Harshberger felt that the land was servant to him and it owed him a living, owed him everything he could get from it.

"Hard times come," said LaVon. "He'd somehow got hold of a few cattle from below the tick-fever line, put them into the herd and pretty soon had a lot of sick and dyin cattle. At that time the panhandle was free of ticks."

"And now it's not?"

"I didn't say that. Now the tick problem is over. We learned what a do about it."

"What?" said Bob.

"Don't you know anything about ticks?"

"I know that in Colorado the Rocky Mountain spotted ticks can kill you."

"Well, the plain old cattle tick and the southern cattle tick can kill cows. They still got them in Mexico. Southern cattle was resistant to the fever disease but northern cows—where ticks can't live—had no resistance. They were very susceptible and died in a few weeks after they came in contact with southern immune cows carrying the ticks.

"Anyway, Graindeddy's bad luck wasn't over. His calves got blackleg. Then was such a droughty hot summer that his wells quit, the grass was pretty well gone and cows died. Come the winter he lost half the remainin herd in a blizzard. In the spring it rained like crazy and heel flies drove his cattle into the bogs where a good many of them perished. On top a all that his wife went into a decline and passed on Fourth a July. He buried her wrapped in a flag. It had took him ten years to build up his life to where he got his own place and in one year he went from sittin pretty to flat broke. He was so broke he had to rustle up all them old buffalo bones and sell them to the bone fertilizer man in Mobeetie. But he wasn't a quitter. When he'd got all the bones, he swallowed his pride and took a job fencin for Griffith and Shannon. They had the contract a fence the XIT. And that sure changed everthing."

She was amazed that Bob Dollar not only knew nothing of ticks, he had never heard of the XIT. With relish she told him that this three-million-acre ranch of west panhandle range came into existence when the state of Texas deeded it to several Chicago businessmen in exchange for the construction of a new state capitol building in Austin, larger and grander than any other.

"While Graindeddy was pickin up bones and horns, he got some a his cowboys a help him and one day they hauled a wagon-full down to Mobeetie. They couldn't wait until they finished their business but proceeded a get drunk. And then they got fresh. Most a them still teenagers. They commenced a toss a few bones at hands from other ranches they seen walkin past. One a them other cowhands picked up a bone and threw it back, not your gentle toss but a hard pitch. And that's how the big Mobeetie Bone and Horn Fight got started. Cowboys was bleedin and bruised but they kept on until the wagon was near empty and the bones all over the street and the plank sidewalk. Anyway, Grainded got into fencin," she said. "The XIT was more than two hundred miles long, north to south. The fencin crews would go out with a wagon and tools. The freight wagon that carried the war all the way down from the railroad depot up near Trinidad, Colorado, was supposed a drop off four spools a war every quarter mile. That much I know."

She clawed through a file folder, pulled out a photograph of a mule team hitched to a wagon stacked with posts. A bedroll had been tied on top and on the bedroll sat Moises Harshberger. A half-grown boy wearing a wagon-wheel-size hat crouched awkwardly on the posts.

Now she was in another file and slapped a photograph of a freight team into Bob's hands. It was a long, narrow photograph showing a ten-mule team connected by a wilderness of straps and lines, the driver mounted on the left-hand mule closest to the wagon. The wagon itself was a series of wagons, two short and covered, one immensely long. He counted the wheels—sixteen—and realized he was looking at the nineteenth-century equivalent of a semitrailer truck.

"How did the driver manage that big team? How much could ten mules haul?"

"I don't know. You'd have to ask somebody like Tater Crouch. His graindeddy was a freighter before he started the Bar Owl. I imagine Tater knows how it was done."

She took a breath and resumed the story about her own grandfather. "So, after a year of it Moises got tired a fencin and quit. He took up cowboyin for the XIT, as he said, out of the fryin pan and into the fire. Every night they'd gamble. The XIT boys was a bad bunch in them days. This was before Mr. A. G. Boyce took over and cleaned the ranch up. The XIT had quite a reputation in the early days. Their hands rustled, they hair-branded, they took baby calves away from their mothers and said they was mavericks, they cut those calves' eyelid muscles so they couldn't see to get back with their mammies, they cut their tongues so they wouldn't suck and burned their feet between the toes so they wouldn't hunt out their mothers because their feet hurt so bad, they run fake tallies and counts and many a man got his personal start as a rancher with these mean practices."

"Did Mr. Harshberger do those things too?"

"He always claimed not, said what got him was the gamblin. They gambled terrible on the XIT. Monte, that was their game. The men would get right down in the road dirt and play at it. In the end he lost our ranch on the turn of a single card. He hit bottom. He said later that it is a good thing for a man a hit bottom because that's when he learns what he's made out of. The XIT lasted more than twenty-five years as a cattle ranch and never turned a dollar a profit. There was lawsuits against it for that reason. Wait a minute, I got some good pictures of my grainded."

She went into the adjacent room and he could hear her churning through papers and folders. She came back with a large soiled envelope, withdrew a handful of photographs, passed them to him. There was the usual shot of half a dozen cowboys seated cross-legged on the ground with tin plates in their laps, an arrow pointing at a small-headed youth wearing a striped, collarless shirt, chaps and a tall-crowned hat. Another showed the same young man with his left foot in the stirrup preparing to mount a muscular horse. In this picture he could see Harshberger's legs were extremely long.

"What happened with Mr. Harshberger? I mean, you've got the ranch now so he must have got it back."

She smiled enigmatically and said, "That was the *Harshberger* ranch. This here is the *Fronk* ranch. My husband's people's place. The Harshberger place is all wheat now. It passed out a the family permanent in 1947. It's over in Roberts County."

He took up the last photograph, not quite understanding what he was looking at. It seemed to be a man's back, raked and bloody, as though someone had taken the cat-o'-nine-tails to him.

"Is this Mr. Harshberger too?" He held it out.

"Yes. That's quite a picture, isn't it? He carried the scars to his grave."

"But how did he get them? Was he horsewhipped?"

She laughed. "I don't want to use up all my stories in one go," she said, sliding the photographs back into the envelope.

Bob thought there was little chance of that.

"But I will say that it was a experience made him to get married and start a family. He went back to Tennessee to find a wife and she was Fern Leake. When she was mad she told it that he had looked her and the other Tennessee girls over like horses. He didn't care about pretty—he wanted a strong woman with a wide pelvis and he just about measured them off with a axe handle."

At that moment he began to think of LaVon as a faded panhandle Scheherazade. She was the talkative type Ribeye Cluke had told him to find but his head ached with the torrent of information.

Every evening, if the wind was not too strong, Bob sat on the bunkhouse porch and, until the light failed (for he always forgot to buy a lamp), read Abert's account of riding down from Bent's Fort and then southeast to the Canadian River and across what later became the Texas panhandle.

As he read, a few hundred feet away an old windmill made a shambling rattle and, with each revolution of the bladed wheel, a stream of water arced into the tank, the liquid pulse of ranch life. The tank had been in the ground so long and so many dust storms and gritty winds had blown over it that a deep layer of silt lay at the bottom and a clump of cattails ten feet across had grown up in the center. The original corner pipes, set for a larger tower, stood a foot outside the legs, which were fastened to the corner pipes with bolts and flanges. The whole mill floated in the air on three points. The platform at the top was rotted out, a single decayed board hanging by a rusted bolt. Another board lay on the ground. Green scum covered the surface of the water except where the mill pumped in fresh, a waxing-waning stream the diameter of a quarter. The vane had been shot up, but he could still read the stenciled letters MELKEBEEK & CROUCH WIND-MILLS. At the grain elevator he'd learned that a single cow needed six to eight gallons of water a day, every day. He began to see the difficulties of the old trail drives with their hundreds, even thousands, of thirsty animals. What made a good trail, he thought, must have been access to water.

The old windmill quit pumping one dark morning before sunrise and the silence woke him. When he went for water to LaVon's kitchen he told her and by noon an elderly man and his helper were replacing the ash sucker rods, for the drop was not quite plumb and one of them had worn through and broken. In the background a dark snarl of branches showed the fuchsia blossoms of redbud.

Bob, reading on the porch that evening with the repaired windmill clanking reassuringly and pushing out its regular gush of water, discovered that the Canadian River, which he had thought named for French Canadian fur trappers, was more accurately named the Cañadian (and so noted on Abert's original map), from *cañada*, an old Mexican-Spanish word meaning "a small canyon," especially a cliff edge along a river that functioned to hold sheep on their range, a natural barrier. Government printers had dropped the tilde from the lieutenant's report and so inadvertently renamed the river. He thought it a shame. Before that, he knew, the Indians had called it the Gualpa, a name Lieutenant Abert spelled "Goo-al-pah."

Abert seemed to take particular pleasure in observing and sketching the Cheyenne, and his friendly personality and sense of humor gleamed from the fine-print pages. From time to time Bob glanced up from the book and looked west across the pasture. The odd dark shape in the grass he had noticed the first evening was still there, still unidentified, but it was too dark to walk among the rattlesnakes of the rough field. As usual the fading light left him with the book to his nose, squinting at the small type, and he stretched, went in to bed, not the least sleepy, to toss and turn for hours and wish for electricity, to swear again he would buy six lamps, a vow always forgotten in daylight.

He stopped at the ranch house nearly every day to fill a jerry can with water. The bunkhouse still showed signs of horse-oriented male occupancy—spur gouges on the porch steps, dark spots on the floor from ancient tobacco splats, and on the outhouse seat a dark brown stain. One morning, turning off her Dust Devil vacuum cleaner, LaVon said that that stain probably came from a well-known foreman of the 1940s, Rope Butt, who had suffered from a bleeding ulcer and later cured himself with coffee enemas.

"Wally Ooly, the druggist, told him a try that. Rope seen it all," she continued. "In his lifetime he seen the panhandle shift from horseback roundup days and a lonesome bed on the prairie to a pickup truck with a CD player and a cell phone."

Bob marveled that the pioneers and first settlers had strung out their panhandle towns in such a relatively straight line and at such measured distances from each other.

"I suppose that's because they were thinking the railroad would come along someday."

LaVon snorted. "Forget that pioneer and first-settler stuff," she said. "They didn't have much to do with town locations. It was *all* the rayroads. The rayroad corporations said where the towns was goin a go and that's where they went. Nothin a do with pioneers. It was all corporate goals and money and business. Then they sold lots and hoped it would all work out. The rayroads didn't care about the towns—they was after the long-term wheat and cattle freight charges. They had plans for the whole region, the whole state—the whole country—and they run things. What the rayroads done is break things up. Used a be a special kind of panhandle region here from Dodge City to Mobeetie to Old Tascosa, all tied together by the trails. I agree there was *some* towns away from the rayroad that people started, like Cowboy Rose, but most a them was out in the boondocks and they wasn't worth much. Funny, now it's those little places that people like. A course Cowboy Rose got the spur track in later but it never started out as a rayroad town. Rayroad towns was strictly about money— business street, depot, bank, couple a merchants. Not much else. It was a different place then. But everthing changes."

Although Bob was sorry to lose his idea of the pioneers bravely setting up in the wilderness, the railroad theory explained why so many towns looked like the last one and the next one. It was that way all over the west, he thought to himself, and said so to LaVon.

"Um," she said. "Who do you think settled the west? No, *not* pioneers. Business! First the traders like the Bents and St. Vrain, then the army posts a protect the traders and wagon trains, then the rayroads. It's all about business in this country. Has been from day one."

"LaVon," he said, "whereabouts would I buy a lamp? Something for camping would be good, you know, one of those propane lamps. If I want to read at night it's impossible."

"You *could* get a can of kerosene when you go downtown and I'll give you one a my kerosene lamps. Save you a few dollars. What we use when the electric goes out. I'll dig one out today and clean it up for you. You get the kerosene."

He bought the kerosene at the Drag On Crossroads Store between Woolybucket and Cowboy Rose, watched attentively while LaVon showed him how to light the lamp, trim the wick, daily wash the chimney. It was a success and he stayed up late reading on into the lieutenant's survey, the lamp casting its dim yellow light on the pages. It was slow going for the print was small and close-set and the only map was execrable—extremely small and devoid of any detail. He kept consulting his Western States road map, but, as its maker had dispensed with the smaller rivers and their tributaries, it was nearly as useless as the miniature map.

He read that the Bents had built a subsidiary fort in the Texas panhandle, "Adobe Fort," and he wondered if it were the same as the famous ruin, Adobe Walls, scene of the battle that followed the mutilation of poor Dave Dudley, a battle that marked the point where the U.S. government determined on the willful and wholesale extinction of the region's Indians. Bob promised himself his own trip of exploration. The Bents, he thought, had certainly dominated the country in their time, powerful traders. Maybe LaVon was right: business interests had wedged the west open.

And now, in his reading, Lieutenant Abert was

weeks out of Bent's Fort on his survey, down the Arkansas a few miles to where it joined the Purgatoire. At an early camp, after feasting on tender venison, they took sightings to determine their position; it was the only correct observation the expedition made, the persistent error later laid to a faulty chronometer.

He itched to see the lieutenant's sketches of the country, which were not included in this edition of the expedition. (A few years later, in the Denver Public Library, he saw an original copy of Lieutenant Abert's *Report*. And there at the back were the illustrations he had once longed to see, beautifully colored, and this, said the librarian, was probably done by Abert's own hand. Bob let his finger rest on a page that Lieutenant Abert himself had touched—a transcendental contact that never failed to thrill him.)

On Sunday afternoon, clear and breezy, the few clouds in the shapes of cowboy mustaches, Bob felt he should have a harmonica and play it sitting on the porch with his chair tilted back and his feet on the rail. He wrote instead to Mr. Cluke.

Dear Sir.
Things have been going along as well as I could wish and I have been circumspect about my interest in the region in every way. I tell people I am scouting land for a luxury home developer. Found a good place to rent, only

$50/mo., an old bunkhouse on a ranch here. It does not have running water so I have to haul some every day from Mrs. Fronk, the ranch owner. She asked for two months' rent in advance. She knows a lot about everything, very helpful but talkative in the extreme. The bunkhouse does not have a cook stove, either, so I eat out all the time. There are a few cafés, one good one. None of them have credit card machines so I have to pay cash. It is pretty much a cash society here and some swapping. So I am visiting the ATM machine a lot. There is only one ATM machine around and I have to drive quite a way to get to it. It is not in Woolybucket.

I have found out that bad droughts go with the region, this is where the big dustbowl was. On the other hand, the Ogallala aquifer is underneath everything, though they didn't have a way to pump it up to the surface until the 1960s—deep well pumps and pivot irrigators that let people get at the water and that is what made the panhandles into today's "breadbasket." If you talk to farmers here they tell you that they are saving the world from hunger by growing high-quality wheat seed, sorghum, soybeans, peanuts, cotton, etc.

I suppose you know our competitors, Texas Farms, King Karolina, Murphy Farms and Seaboard, already have a few hog setups here. There was a terrible accident at one of the

Murphy Farms places a year or two ago. A truck driver died after he backed his truck into the effluent lagoon, twenty-five feet deep. It was a tragic thing and it did not make local people feel any better about hog farms.

Water is something to worry about. Although there is still a lot of water in the Ogallala, it is shrinking very fast. One lady I met said "I'm not worried, they will find another source, icebergs flown in or something, they always do." But I don't think they will be flying in icebergs in the near future. I hear a lot down at the grain elevator and one farmer told me they've used up about half the water in the Ogallala since the 1960s and there's very little recharge. Some of the farmers take the attitude that if they don't use it somebody else will. It seems that in Texas if you own the land surface you own the water rights under the property and you can do what you want with it, so it's like a lot of people sticking straws into a big common pot of water and sucking up as much as they want (although the Ogallala is not a big underground lake, but saturated sand and gravel). Some ranchers and farmers who can't make a go of it these days are selling their water rights. They call it "water ranching." It is very controversial.

I'll just mention in closing that the entrepreneurial spirit is strong here. Most people live in small ranch houses and drive old trucks, they are conservative and frugal, and at first you think that they are still pioneers. But I am finding out there is big money in the banks and big money invested in agricultural machinery and land. The trouble is, it will all come to an end in another generation as the young people do not wish to be here. Only the Mexicans (you don't hardly see them) are poor. There are *no* black people here. Maybe you know all this.

Later Bob Dollar remembered the bunkhouse at night, the yellow glow of kerosene light, the red blanket on the swaybacked bed, the steerhide rug on the floor, stripped from some old speckled and purplish longhorn, the floor littered with the furry bodies of moths attracted to the lamp. Outside a flock of wild turkeys scratched and gobbled, flying up at sunset to sit in the cottonwood branches that hung over the bunkhouse. He had parked under the tree only once, dismayed to find the Saturn streaked with turkey excreta in the morning. A small colony of prairie dogs flourished near the cabin and he knew that where there were prairie dogs there were rattlesnakes, sometimes sharing the same burrow.

The violent sunsets came on slowly, faded to clear yellow, dimmed blue until the water lily moon floated up. And somehow, after listening to LaVon's stories, it all mixed in with Lieutenant Abert's explorations, the slangy old days of the XIT, the Frying Pan, the Matador.

Bob Dollar began to see that the two panhandles once had been part of a single region where the curtain had risen on many stages. Here the Indians had lived nomadic hunting lives; traders opened routes to Santa Fe and Taos to sell calico and took peltry from the Indians in exchange for manufactured goods; army scouts came to map the terrain and tangled with the Indians; buffalo hunters shot and skinned for the eastern trade. As the great herds disappeared, ranchers brought in cattle to run the free and open range and the sons of settlers became cowboys. Mule team freighters carried in lumber and fence posts, kettles and flour, wire fencing. The flood of people came with the railroads, small farmers who believed that drought and wind could be overcome by hard work and the plow. Finally came oilmen and flimflam tricksters, government men to tell the farmers what they were doing wrong. Now corporate agriculturists like Global Pork Rind had moved in.

The states of Texas and Oklahoma stacked like dirty pots in the sink, their handles touching. The same obelisks of sunlight fell on both sides of the state line, both shared out the same cold cuts of wind. Both lay in country of metallic light, tarnished brass clouds. LaVon told him there was much cancer in both panhandles, and multiple sclerosis, which she believed was somehow connected with owning little dogs. She mentioned the cancer centers as Perryton (benzene from the oil fields), Panhandle (nuclear weapons disassembly) and Pampa (a large chemical plant).

Slowly Bob began to think that Texas was the unnamed place lurking behind the song line "And the sky is not cloudy all day," for often the panhandle skies *were* cloudy day after day with pot-metal overcast. Occasionally the clouds drew apart a little to reveal blue wash. He could imagine that in a drought the farmers' gorge would rise at the sight of such clouds, low enough to prod with a stick but yielding no rain.

There was something, he thought, about projecting territory that worried: a pot handle can come off if the rivets fail, can bend or break under blows and weight. The Oklahoma panhandle was shaped like a finger pointing west. The Texas panhandle attached to the state like the neck of a bottle. It was the northern territory, unlike the rest of Texas, geometric, bony and high and hard-rocked, cut across by the Cañadian (in his mind he replaced Lieutenant Abert's lost tilde). It was a place defined by its position atop the caprock. As a lone tree attracts lightning, the panhandles drew end-of-the-world thunder, grass fires, blue northers, yellow dust storms and a yearly parade of dirty tornadoes. At night, the light out and limbs composed for sleep, no one could know with certainty that he or she would awaken in the morning or be carried into the sky with whirling metal and smashed wood. So there was an underlying sense of unease to panhandle life. If LaVon's stories were true, he thought, people had developed a counterpoint humor and a gift for narrative, sharpened accounts that launched ordinary life into mythic clouds of hyperbole.

It did not take long to see that there was also rivalry and mutual disparagement between the two panhandles, though Oklahoma naming a part of itself Texas County ("Saddle Bronc Capital of the World") might seem a kind of homage, along with such place names as Texhoma, and the joking reference to the Texas panhandle as "Baja Oklahoma." But Texans sneered at the poor Oklahoma roads, described their northern neighbors as obstructionist, larcenous and at the mercy of politicians on the take.

"In Oklahoma everthing was and is Standard Awl," said Froggy Dibden at the Old Dog. That narrow strip of what was once public land belonging to no state or territory, that pointing finger of No Man's Land, remained isolated, ignored by the main body of the state. Up in Guymon a waitress told Bob of a time when, after driving east through their state for a hundred miles, she and her husband came upon a sign that said WELCOME TO OKLAHOMA. Now and then an Oklahoman remarked that the Texas handle was smirched with excess pride and the show-off manners of the undeservedly wealthy. Bob Dollar gathered from the talk at the grain elevator that some ill feeling was residual from the 1880s, when Oklahoma ranchers strung barbwire along the Texas line to stop trail drives coming through with their fevered and tick-infested cattle. The Texas men cut the wire and went north and that was that. And there had been the long-running animosity over which state—Texas or Oklahoma—owned Greer County, a quarrel that still colored discourse as a few drops of ink in a jar of water imparts a blue tinge. Panhandle people had long memories.

"Even if the local kids don't want a stay here there's a galore a people retire to the panhandle from the cities," LaVon started, slicing coffee cake, "from Houston and Dallas just a get away from the lights. They can't sleep at night with those lights. They come from all over. Maybe they rather go to the hill country down around Austin but they can't afford the property prices. There's people in this town has moved in pretty recent and they are resented. Yes, you're in back porch country now, Mr. Dollar. We're like a family out here. Everbody knows everbody and has for a long time. What we got here that don't exist in the big cities is a sense a community." For LaVon, like Bob, believed in the idea of harmonious rurality, where outlying farmers and ranchers and the people of the small town were linked not only through living in a common geographical region but through kind-intentioned and neighborly interests. The way she called him "Mr. Dollar" made him uncomfortable, as though a silver-haired man stood behind him. Bob Dollar wondered aloud if the retirees were also attracted to the panhandle as a place to act out lives gilded with antique cattle-day romance.

"You could say that," said LaVon. "They appreciate the sense a history."

The more he nodded the more she told him about Woolybucket. Freda Beautyrooms, she said, was a leading light and the president of the Historical Society, though in 1994 a newcomer, Betty Sue Wilpin, who had moved from Houston to Woolybucket with her husband, Parch Wilpin, made a run to take over the society. She inaugurated an annual ice-cream social, featuring homemade ice creams of unusual flavors—mango, persimmon, pumpkin-cherry, cinnamon drop. Parch made all the frozen confections himself in the three ice-cream freezers he had bought for the occasion, for the Wilpins had money. The social was a great success and on the strength of that Betty Sue pushed for the society's presidency, promising historical programs and activities that would "wake up Woolybucket." She was overwhelmingly defeated and Freda Beautyrooms elected for the seventeenth straight year. Both Wilpins, smarting from this social slap, resigned from the society and concentrated on restoring the old stone house they had bought, once the Lazy A ranch house though the 12,000-acre spread was reduced to 150 acres, the rest long since given over to small ranches and farms.

"Parch Wilpin got so he had a have a crushed oyster shell driveway and he drove pretty near every weekend down to the Gulf to get the shell. When he got the driveway finished he started in tryin a find somebody could restore the stain-glass window in that house; it was a steer with the Lazy A brand above. A course they don't own the brand—that was sold to Bob Haywood over on the Tin Can donkey's years ago. Trouble with these retirement people comin in is they all want a change things to how it was where they come from. They want that National Public Radio. They want organic grocery stores. They want the *Houston Chronicle* delivered to their doorstep. They want likker stores. They want *restaurants*." She gave the last word a tone that equated it with "leper colonies."

She sighed mournfully. "And, a course, not everybody born here has got their act together either. The frontier character means not givin up on anything after it fails." Only repeated failures, from bankruptcy to death, put a true panhandle resident down, she said. Bob had only to look as far as the example of Jerky Baum to see this stubborn persistence.

"Jerky run cows for twenty years, same as his dad and graindad. Their ranch—the Tit Hat, after a Canadian Mountie hat—was all run down, overgrazed and dusty. The Baums never spent a penny on nothin. They made do and made do without. It got so finally there was nothin a do but declare bankruptcy and go look for some kind a job. And then, just before that happened, they found awl in his south pasture and the money begin a come in like a fire hose squirtin. Over thirteen thousand dollars a day ever day. Jerky Baum went crazy. Part of it was he hadn't never had any money at all to spend and now he was drownin in it. They built a great big stone house like a castle with tennis courts and a moat and a swimmin pool in a glass house. He bought a jet plane and hired a pilot, though he didn't have anyplace he wanted a go. Built a runway or two for the plane. Then he fell into the hands a certain men who got him a try Thoroughbred racin. He built stables and a trainin track, hired grooms and trainers, bought expensive horseflesh which never won. But now he got places a go—the racetracks—and he went: Santa Anita, Harbor Park, Keeneland, Saratoga. But his horses never won. 'Give it some time,' the horse men said. 'You're still new at the game. Give it some time.'

"Then the awl begin to slack off and the money dropped. Jerky Baum behaved like it would start up again same as before. But it didn't. Keep up all them stables and big staff all of a sudden he had a borrow money. Jerky tells his wife, 'It's like a drought. It'll break sooner or later.' But it never did and the bank took the jet and the mansion and most a the ranch land and Jerky and his family moved into one a the trainers' houses. It was pretty cramped and tight after the castle. He finally realized that the awl had run out. That's how awl is—it runs out."

"What happened to him then?" said Bob.

"Oh, he's around. Works at the grain elevator, weighs the trucks and all. You probly seen him."

Bob changed the subject. "I wondered about the radio. How come you don't have good music on the radio down here? All I can get is Dr. Laura and Rush Limbaugh and the worst kind of canned Nashville mush. And hymns."

"Well, what is it you want, Bob Dollar?"

"Uh. Some jazz? News? Classical music? *Car Talk*? Latino songs? NPR?"

LaVon Fronk snorted. "There's some tryin a raise money, get that NPR. That's not what folks here want. That liberal NPR stuff—there's only about six people in the panhandle wants a listen to that Commie stuff. And hymns suit us good."

"Then how about fiddle tunes and Texas music? Some of the best music in America came out of this part of the country. Woody Guthrie and Bob Wills and Buddy Holly and Jimmie Dale Gilmore—God, there's a hundred of them. And fiddle tunes. But I don't hear any of them on the damn radio."

"You just don't understand our ways. Here's what you got a understand about the panhandle—people here work hard, they're honest, they hold a high moral conduct and the most a them are Christians. At the same time, there's men talks hot and mean and will hurt anybody gits in their way. There's backbitin women with tongues like knives. In fact, about the only thing draws folks together these days is a funeral or a tornado. It ain't perfect, specially since the hog farms come in. I don't know if you noticed, Mr. Dollar, but we got us a condition here that might go against luxury houses. I mean them old hog farms. Anymore, you can hear fiddle tunes at the dances and clubs. You can hear that music on back porches and in livin rooms. You can hear the Panhandle Syrup Boys. You can hear the Old Mobeetie Bone Pickers. Them old fiddles squallin like bobcats. You can hear it live because it never quit here. Go over to Lipscomb some Satday night. They got a dance platform there and Frankie McWhorter and them plays. He used a be with Bob Wills. They are good. There's plenty a Texas music. It's still here. You don't need the radio to hear it neither."

"You can hear hymns in church, too, so why clutter up the airwaves with them?"

"We grew up with hymns. That's part a our lives. It's like the air we breathe!" And she began to sing in a robust voice, "I COME to the garden alooooone . . ."

"What is the Barbwire Festival?" said Bob, for barbwire sounded exceedingly nonfestive to him and he wanted to stop LaVon's singing. He wanted to get her back on track with information about panhandle denizens.

"That," she said, "is Woolybucket's day of glory. It's the biggest thing we got. End a June."

In the years 1904 to 1928, she said, the Panhandle Wire Company in Woolybucket had turned out hundreds of thousands of miles of barbwire, with the highest-grossing years linked to military sales during World War I. The factory had employed many local men and some women and when it failed the Depression came early to Woolybucket.

"So it's a way a bringin back those days when everbody had a job and business was hummin. First the parade, then the pork rib barbecue. The fire department volunteers are in charge a the barbecue and Cy Frease does the cookin. Then there's the quilt raffle, election results a the Barbwire King and Queen. And usually some kind a show for the kids. And night there's a street dance. A course there's plenty brings beer, which they are not supposed to as Woolybucket is dry, but they do and that miserable sheriff we got won't do a dang thing to stop it."

"See you later," said Bob, standing up, but LaVon kept on talking so he sat down again.

"There's other newcomers in town. There's that Frank Owsley and his so-called *roommate* Teddy Paxson moved here from Dallas in 1996 and bought the old Cowboy Rose district two schoolhouse. They fixed it up as a glassworks studio and a house. They got a truck garden out there and they talk about openin a gourmet restaurant, just what the Wilpins would love to see. Their city friends come up on the weekend and the poor things have to work out in the hot sun in the garden or pack glass in the studio all day."

"I guess I got to go," said Bob. He went out to the dusty Saturn. Even with the door closed he could hear LaVon, who had started singing again:

"Aaaaaaaaaaand, He WALKS with me . . . And He TALKS with me . . ."

In his first weeks in Woolybucket Bob Dollar discovered that if the terrain was level and flat, the characters of the people were not, for eccentricities were valued and cultivated, as long as they were not too peculiar. Crusty old ranchers who worked an embroidery hoop, or a pair of alcoholic septuagenarian twin sisters, or the man who was building a full-size locomotive in his garage, the rancher who constructed a half-size replica of Stonehenge, Mrs. Splawn who inherited her husband's Dee-Tex metal detector and could be seen on road verges seeking coins and engagement rings thrown away by spiteful and hot-headed Texas girls, were not only tolerated but admired. But dark skin color, strange accent or manifestations of homosexuality and blatant liberalism were unbearable.

Bob Dollar made the mistake of telling LaVon he was interested in everything about the place—not only the land but the people, cattle, wheat, horses, railroads, oil and gas, water, even—he laughed falsely—hogs.

"I know people don't like hog farms, but they seem to be part of this place," he said.

"There's actually plenty *want* the hog farms. Especially some politicians. They got them up near Follett. My goodness, they *requested* them, they courted the hog corporations. And, a course, you are interested in girls. Let's not forget your search for that Texas girlfriend." LaVon put a cough drop in her mouth and said the panhandle was the most complicated part of North America, the last piece of Texas to be settled. "Light soil, drought, bad wind, terrible heat, tornadoes and blue northers. And you never can tell which one is comin next. It's a weather place." She implied that the remote and level land, tempestuous blasts, tornadoes drilling down from super cells and the peculiar configuration of the territory worked with the wind to blow away the human chaff, leaving the heavy kernels. It was defeat to give up and pull out. It took sticking qualities—humor, doggedness, strength—to stay.

"Most people here *has* stayed for generations," she said, naming a dozen families, including her own, "starting with all those big ranches. It was the shiftless ones who left. Most people stick even tighter when the goin gets tough. In the dust bowl days the government told a lot of the farmers to go on to California. Or down to Arizona and pick cotton. The tough ones stayed. Look here," she said, opening a sideboard drawer and withdrawing a tiny black book.

Bob Dollar took the book in his hand. It was a miniature Bible.

"That Bible has been carried by the men a the Fronk family in seven wars. The Civil War, the Spanish-American War, the First World War, the Second World War, the Korea War, the Vietnam War and the

Gulf War. They all but one come back alive and that Bible is why." She put the Bible away. "It was lost on the Yalu River in 1950 where my husband's uncle Ditmar got killed. Some other soldier found it on the ground and it had the name Fronk and Wooly-bucket, Texas, in it—and that feller mailed it to us, just the name and the town, and it got to us.

"The cattle drives up to Montana and Wyoming went through here too. This was the original cow and cowboy country and it still is the most cow of anywhere. So people here are pretty rugged. This country was made for cows, once they got rid a the buffaloes. To live here it sure helps if you are half cow and half mesquite and all crazy." She jerked her thumb at the bookcase in the hall, packed with Texas histories and accounts of early days.

"You get in them books and you'll pretty soon learn something," she said.

He had seen for himself that right-thinking ways were supported by billows of gossip and a constant and surveillant picking at those who showed the slightest tendency to slip off the trodden path unless they fell into the category of Colorful Panhandle Characters. And work was the great leveler, work and the land, the twin assets of all rural people.

He took one of her books from the shelf, opened to pages describing a ranch leap-year party in 1884, the women dressed as men, the men dressed as women. The writer glossed over the women's attire but went into some detail for the men:

C. W. Pool, a pumpkin colored blonde, wore overskirt ecru denims, with corsage of lemon color cretonns, low neck and full sleeves. Ornaments were roller skates and plain gold. Very becoming.

Ed Miller was attired in a short walking suit of lemon-colored delaine, muscled like a grasshopper. Ornaments, cloves and lemon peel. Modest, but fascinating.

W. Strange, lovely fawn blonde. Costume, wine colored three-ply, all wool filling tartan with waist and hose to match. Ornaments, raw cotton and kiln-dried sawdust. Modest and graceful, as well as susceptible.

Bob was mildly shocked. Somehow, cross-dressing was not what he associated with old-time cattlemen.

He made a morning habit of dropping in, first at the grain elevator where there were usually four or five farmers who drank coffee and talked with Wayne Etter, the manager, about grain prices, value-added products, cursed the government and Canadian imports. Jerky Baum was the grimy little man who did most of the dirty work at the elevator and Bob tried, and failed, to imagine him as an oil magnate with a private jet and racing stables. Etter told him one day that a train had run right through a grain elevator in Marmaduke, over near Texline, and the thought was enough to send Bob to the Black Dog, a mile from a railroad track. This was the rarest café in the panhandle, if not all Texas, for it served good food, nearly as good, he thought, as must have been the fine fat doe eaten under the cottonwoods in 1845, a meal Lieutenant Abert had described with relish.

10

OLD DOG

Cy Frease had a great forward mouth, muscular and mobile, that stretched open to his back molars or, when pursed, thrust outward like a volcano cone. His face was blue with whiskers and he was built like a gin bottle with hard, square shoulders. He had cowboyed for the Quarter Moon, a big spread owned by a Chicago family who came down once a year, but in the late eighties he tired of what he called "the pukiest shit-fire-and-save-the-matches goddamn grub this side a the devil's table," said if he couldn't cook better than that he'd drown himself in his grandma's chamber pot, drew his pay, picked up his saddle and walked. He disappeared from the country for a few years, then, one day, was seen again coming down the steps of the Woolybucket County Bank, unchanged except for a new silver belly hat. When he got through shaking hands and saying hello to old acquaintances, he took a key from his pocket and held it up.

"See that? Goin a change some things." He looked around with his glass-colored eyes and would say no more, but at noon his truck (the same ratty old 1976

Chevy he'd driven away in) was parked in front of what had been Itty Bitty Petal & Posy, bankrupt and closed for two years. Now the doors and windows gaped and dust flew from them. Passersby could hear the roar of a vacuum cleaner followed by the splash of water.

"He's hosin down the walls. There's enough dirt come off to start a garden," said Big Warren, a serious wheat farmer with ornamental tufts of hair on his cheeks and chin.

Rumor ran. He was going to install a coin launderette; a suntan parlor; a saddlemaker's shop. A truck from Dumas Lumber unloaded two-by-fours, pine boards, then a carpenter from Higgins showed up one morning and began hammering and sawing but grinned and refused to answer questions. The curious put their heads in the door and saw that the space had been divided into four rooms, two very small ones at the side, one long and narrow across the back. The front room, looking onto the street, was large with a high ceiling. A truck from a Wichita Falls company, Texas Salvage, pulled up. Big Warren said Texas Salvage should rightfully be called Tornado Leftovers. Two pimpled youths unloaded stamped tin ceiling panels popular at the turn of the century, and a massive but grimy oak bar carved with figures of horsemen driving cattle. Obvious, said the gossips; the place was going to be a private club where people could bring their bottles and drink, for Woolybucket was a dry county and there were no public bars.

But a week later, the oak bar scraped down and fine-sanded golden, the club rumor died. Another truck arrived, this one from Tulsa: USED RESTAURANT EQUIPMENT—EVERYTHING FOR THE TRADE. From it came an ancient and huge gas range, a ten-foot-high stainless steel dishwasher.

"That dishwasher come out of a prison," said Charles Grapewine, who knew. "I'll say he's gettin up a café. Them little rooms at the side is the men's and the ladies'."

Cy Frease himself scrounged the panhandle for certain indispensable items: cast-iron pots, a home-made grill fashioned from two steam-cleaned fifty-five-gallon drums (found in the weeds behind the crumbling ruins of one of the LX bunkhouses). He set up the grill in the alley behind the kitchen. He went to auctions and the Salvation Army Thrift Store in Amarillo for his china and silver, covered the tables with Mexican oilcloth purchased in Cactus, fabulous designs in peacock blue and scarlet, mustard and magenta. At the back of the dining room four long tables were joined end to end. Finally he washed the windows, put up a sign, OLD DOG, with a painting of his mutt, and was in business for one meal a day, at high noon.

In the early mornings Cy did local ranch work, filling in for no-shows or making an extra hand at roundup time or in haying season, always arriving at the Old Dog around ten to fire up the grill and get the potatoes on. By 2:30 the crockery was all in the prison dishwasher and he was back at cow work. In the evenings he set his bread dough to rise, peeled the potatoes for the next day, washed lettuces and trimmed vegetables homegrown in local gardens, grabbed a few hours of sleep. Every other Saturday he drove down to Austin to shop at Whole Foods.

"Cowboys deserve to eat wholesome too," he said, opening himself to criticism (not long in coming) that he was a health food nut and probably a left-wing liberal if not a Communist.

He had a steady clientele of older men because he included on the menu eight or ten favorites from Depression days when they had been boys and their tastes set: vinegar pie, cocoa gravy over biscuits, fried salt pork and, for the old cowboys, son-of-a-bitch stew. For the earlier generation of saddle bums he occasionally made the supreme cowboy dessert, cherry Jell-O containing ginger ale and cut-up marshmallows, cut into small gleaming cubes, garnished with a whack of whipped cream and a maraschino cherry. In a place where men spent much time outdoors in heat, dust and gritty wind, Jell-O was esteemed.

He wasn't interested in *gaufrette* potatoes, but in hominy grits; he cared not for zabaglione but cherished rhubarb pie and sweet potato tart. The world contained many kinds of protein but he reduced them to grilled meat, local favorites and catfish. Once a month he did an entire spit-roasted sirloin or massive pans of barbecued ribs. Occasionally, when the mood was right, he made bierox, spicy ground beef cakes encased in dough. He kept a jar of whangy watermelon honey on hand and used it liberally.

All of the older men had memories of strange childhood meals. "Oh, we was *poor*," said Methiel Huff. "Seems like at the end a the month all we had a eat was beans and more beans. Red-letter day when we got a little salt pork to perk them up. Mother used a keep the salt pork in a crock, lid on it and a big stone on the lid, but someway Dad's old hound dog pushed the stone off and got in there and eat ever bit of it up. Ma said then the only thing we had to flavor the beans was windmill grease. That old relief truck would come around and we'd get rice, beans, prunes and powdered milk."

Bud Hank leaned back in his chair. "Them windmill beans make me think a Shut Up Now Syrup, specialty a my daddy. He was short-tempered and didn't like to hear us kids—seven boys, two girls— horsin around and he'd say, 'Shut up NOW,' and if we didn't pipe down, why he'd get out the bottle of Shut Up Now Syrup. It was his own recipe, nasty stuff, boiled up out a green persimmons and a little sugar to thicken it, but it would pucker you up so hard your mouth would ache and your stomach would clench up like a fist. God! I can taste it yet!"

Dixie Goodloe then remembered the bottom of the culinary barrel in his Depression childhood.

"We was so poor there wasn't nothin to eat pretty often, and I mean *nothin*. There was a time my daddy out a sheer desperation shot and skinned a coyote and we et coyote soup. And I guarantee you we wasn't the only ones."

"How was it?"

"At the time it was the most goddamn delicious thing I ever et."

At the Old Dog everything was set out on the long tables, with the soup at the right and the pies at the left. Customers came in, got their own silverware and plate, loaded up. Every rancher and farmer, oil rig worker, cowboy, truck driver within driving distance showed up for the big noon dinner, too many men for women to feel comfortable. It became something of a men's club, the men almost interchangeable, most past their fifties, all in grimy jeans and cowboy hats—felt in winter, straw in summer. Cy's dog slept under the tables among the manure-scented boots. Now and then Cy set him out a saucer of coffee with cream, saying, "See if that'll keep you awake."

The old lawyer from down the street, F. B. Weicks, was Cy's first customer and thereafter came in punctually at noon every day. He wore a white cowboy hat canted back, an ancient blue suit, shiny with wear. His eyes showed enormous through round plastic-lensed eyeglasses he bought at the dime store in Pampa. He had a soft, pendulous nose that resembled a penis, and every day Cy handed a special plate to him containing a large potato stuffed with creamed tuna fish. He never spoke to anyone, sat in the corner eating his potato and drinking two lime Dr Peppers. He always left a quarter tip and saluted Cy from the front door before he stepped back into his lawyer's life.

Within a week of the Old Dog's opening, graffiti began to show up on the men's room walls. The first read: *Okies, the rock candy in the urinals is not for you*. But over the months more appeared:

JESUS IS COMING!
(and in a different hand) *We'll git him agin.*
Toilet paper compliments of Texas sand and gravel.

The Old Dog became Bob Dollar's hangout, and here he learned from men sprawled and akimbo, like abandoned machinery, that a center-pivot irrigation system could cost as much as $100,000 per quarter section; that the region was too cold for cotton, but grew staggering amounts of wheat, milo, sorghum, alfalfa, corn and soybeans for domestic and overseas markets and to feed the hundreds of thousands of feedlot cattle and bunkered hogs that gave the panhandle its distinctive odor. "The stink of money," said Harvey Dimple, an independent hog farmer inexorably shoved to the wall by the big factory farms. Bob, who had introduced himself as a land scout for luxury house development sites, was quiet, taking it all in, but keeping his ears tuned for indications that someone wanted to sell out. The talkers were glad for a fresh and attentive audience.

"Yes sir, them farmers learned how to make the panhandle say 'money' stead a 'grass,' and that's when they started a call it the Golden Spread. That drew the big boys, you bet. They smelled money all the way from New York and Japan."

"That's right," said Mark Farwell, hollow-faced and narrow-shouldered, greasy hair flopping over his eyes, who made a good living supplying the estrogen market with urine from his pregnant mares. "Right here is the richest farmland on earth, long as we got the water."

There were two elderly local men, both named Bill Williams, which people got around by calling them by their mane colors—Buckskin Bill for his cream-gold hair and dark beard, and Sorrel Bill for his red-dish brown head, armpit and crotch. Now Buckskin spoke.

"Hell, we ain't like California where they got central irrigation and water co-ops. Your Texas farmer is an independent son of bee and does everthing on his own—wells, pumps, ditches, pipes, labor. The Ogallala? It can't win over this drought and the heavy drawdown. Sonny, when it's gone, it's gone."

A lanky, grey-haired man, all elbows and shanks, came in, got a cup of tea and sat at the end of the table, nodded at Grapewine.

"Bob, this here is Ace Crouch—keeps the windmills runnin. Ace, Bob here is lookin to buy land for developin fancy retirement estates."

163

The windmiller gave Bob a searching look as though he saw through that. Bob blushed and kept his head down.

"You're the feller stayin at LaVon's place? The one got an appetite for all her windies?" He picked up his cup and swallowed almost all the tea in it.

"Yes sir. She tells some good stories." Everyone in the Old Dog, he thought, ate and drank as though ravenous and thirst-scorched.

"She ought a with all them diaries and letters she's got out a folks. God save Woolybucket if that house catches afire. You stay out there very long, you won't be able a wear no earmuffs."

"What do you mean?"

"Why, she'll talk the ears right off a your head. The most can't take it."

But Bob thought that Ace himself was a strong contender for the talk championship.

All around him, in the broad variety of regional talk, he heard snatches of conversation about panhandle life and arcane jobs, worries about foot-and-mouth disease leaping the Atlantic and destroying Texas beef. He shuddered when the talk turned to farm and ranch accidents—fractures, lacerations, concussions, deathly falls, maimings and fatalities. Every man, young and old, who ate at the Old Dog had scars to show.

Rope Butt, an ancient cowboy in for a fast cup of coffee, turned to the tables and snapped, "Jesus jumpin jackstraws, don't none a you got any work to do? Just set around gassin all the time. If you don't, I do," and he hitched up his jeans and left. Bob felt a twinge of guilt. Was all of this listening getting him closer to men who wanted to sell out?

Fragmented conversations again blew by like trash in the wind. Again the talk turned back to drought and, inevitably, to the Great Depression when the sandstorms raked the panhandle. Ace Crouch looked at Bob. The old man emanated a kind of authority.

"Irrigation with Ogallala water saved everthing, proved that if you toughed it out you'd get your just reward. What nobody seen at first was how it would backfire, open the door to this agribusiness and corporate farmin."

"They say we live in a global economy," said Bob, echoing Ribeye Cluke.

"Yes, they say that. But some a the big corporate boys was homegrown like the Hitches up in Guymon. They got giant hog farms a go with their cattle feedlots. They got right into the money like ducks into water. So, some say"—and he drilled Bob with his pale old eyes—"that the Ogallala and technology— pumps, telephones, good roads, radios, computers and telvision, all that stuff—made the panhandle a Garden a Eden. But that same technology has kept us from *adjustin* to the bedrock true nature a this place and that's somethin will catch up to us one a these days. The water is playin out. The people built their lives on awl money expected it would last forever too. The awl is pretty much gone. And they told us the Ogallala would last forever. Now the Ogallala is finishin up."

"One thing's sure," said Charles Grapewine. "The people descended from those tough old settlers are sellin out and goin off to Dallas."

"Things change," said Bob. "Isn't it like a law of nature that nothing stays the same? And what about the Indians? They were here before those settlers."

Ace snorted. "They were, but they didn't *live* here. They were nomadic. They'd come into the panhandle, hunt for a few days. Mostly they used hereabouts as a buffer zone between tribes. No, the first people tried a *live* here was those old farmers and ranchers. The pioneers. Now one man with the right machines can do it all—except pay for the machinery. Machines do everthing but suck eggs."

A man Bob heard called Jim Skin beelined for the food table, helped himself to two ham steaks, piled on the pineapple rings. His face resembled the face of a snake, sleek and smooth, round-chinned and thrust forward in searching extension, the wide mouth seemingly closed on a smile. Small ears tight to his head seemed no ears, and his short, fine hair was mashed flat by a cap emblazoned *Murphy Family Farms*.

"Goddamn, I *like* pineapple," he said to the man across the table who was staring with disbelief at the yellow circles. "Good. Hey, I was watchin the tee-vee last night, they had a special on astronomy, the things they can see with that Hobble telescope. *Wagh. Wagh. Wagh.*"

"You believe that stuff? That's all made up on a computer. It ain't real."

"You hear the Fronk kid got kicked out a Texas A and M?"

"I thought I seen him last week pumpin around on that dumb bike. How come?"

"It's one a your more bizarre things. And I don't know no details. I heard they caught him down in the bull barn there at the university. They got those champion breeders there? Well, he was shovin a piece a pipe up a bull's ass. And that's all I know about it. *Wagh!*" He cut a pineapple ring into small trapezoids, ate the pieces rapidly. The snake jaws opened and the pineapple disappeared.

"Jesus gosh amighty!"

"Yeah. Ask me, they should a put him in a pasture with the bull. *Wagh!* Take care a the problem." He ran his finger along the side of his tongue. "Goddamn. Now I got canker sores from that pineapple. Does it ever time to me."

"Well, I tell you what caused it. She put that kid out in the day care from day one. Jase was runnin the ranch alone and she was workin for that irrigation magazine, havin herself a career, and the kid was dumped in day care."

"I wouldn't blame it on that. The kid was always a little wild. And he got in with that bad Christian crowd, that born-again bunch used a come inta town and stand up in back a the pickup and preach and holler. Real excitable people. *Wagh!* They did drugs."

167

"Well, *he* sure did. Drugs and the rest of it."

"You ever see them tattoos he got? *Wagh! Wagh!*"

"Why the heck don't you get you some cough syrup? And quit eatin pineapple if it makes your tongue swell up."

"This your panhandle hog farm cough. I been workin over at Murphy Farms haulin waste. It's occupational. But I got laid off last week so it's gettin better." Jim Skin got up and headed back toward the food, bypassing the pineapple rings and helping himself to soothing macaroni and cheese.

Ace Crouch turned his bitter old eyes on Bob.

"A bad cough goes with a corporate hog farm, Mr. Dollar. And those waste ponds that Jim Skin has been dumpin into pollute the water table and are surely leakin into the Ogallala."

Bob, thinking of the Global Pork Rind brochures, said, "I read that the lagoons are lined with nonporous plastic and that they are emptied out and the manure is spread on the fields to improve the fertility of the soil."

The old man laughed without amusement. "Sonny, there is no liner known a mankind that will not leak. And the manure on the fields, why there is so much of it I'm frightened. A little bit a manure is one thing, but when it's a foot deep year after year the excess nitrogen has to go somewhere. And if you think the lagoons and exhaust fans make a stink, wait until you get a whiff of a field fresh spread with hog poop. The ammonia will burn your eyes out a your head.

Your hair will fall out. They could make the stink better by coverin over the waste ponds or aeratin, but that costs money. Cheaper to just let it sit there. And the state don't care."

"But hog farms make jobs for local people. I mean, this is a region where there aren't many jobs, so that's something. Helping the economy and all? Mr. Skin there had a job from them."

"Why Bob, you are innocent a the facts a life. One hog farm site makes a very few jobs at minimum wage. They run three shifts but everthing's automated and computer controlled. The corporations don't buy locally. They buy bulk supplies in the world market, truck it in. Good business. The hog farms come in, they look like they're bringin money into the region so some a the locals just lap it up. Give them tax breaks. Then, where there was eight thousand pigs all of a sudden there is fifty thousand. They polluted Tulsa's water supply. They poisoned the rivers in North Carolina. They run wild in Oklahoma until very recent when Oklahoma begin to lay out some rules. That's when they commenced a come down here into the Texas panhandle. What a you think hog farms do to a rural panhandle community?"

"I don't know," said Bob, thinking the old windmiller must have been brooding over these hog farm arguments for years. Privately he resolved to visit a hog farm and see for himself what was so awful.

Jim Skin was back at the table with his plate of macaroni. He had been unable to resist the pineapple and a ring of the fruit crowned his pasta. "Uh-oh. Ace's off and runnin again," he said to Bob. "He's on the hog farms."

And it was true. Ace's eyes were gleaming as those of a wolf closing in on its prey. His voice rose. "Hog farms create uninhabitable zones just as sure as if land mines was planted there. Does a corporation have any kind a right come into the panhandle and wreck it for the people rooted there?"

"Ace, they're here and you can't get rid a them. People got a right a run businesses." Jim Skin cut a wedge from the pineapple and winked at Bob.

"Up to a point. It is a matter a what Brother Mesquite calls 'moral geography.' In the old days you had no hog factory farms. Maybe fifty, sixty farmers and ranchers raisin a few pigs the traditional way. Each one a them families bought local. The kids went to school local. People got together for dances and dinners, they banked local and the money enriched the region."

"Don't hogs on small farms stink?" asked Bob, feeling he was scoring a point.

The old man cut him down with a hard look. "Sure, but they are spread out and they are in the open air. The smell is nothin compared a closin in a massive number of animals. You drive past a herd a cattle grazin in a pasture. There's no smell. You drive past a feedlot—it stinks. With the hog farms, we are talkin a large number a confined animals. There's the health factor. My brother Tater lives downwind from a hog farm and he gets sick from it. The Shattles live real close and Shattle's in the hospital. Look at Jim Skin coughin his lungs out."

"Amen. *Wagh! Wagh!*" said Jim Skin.

"Headaches, sore throat, dizziness. Them hogs are pumped full a antibiotics and growth hormones. Eat that pork and it gets in *you*. Bacteria and viruses adapt to the antibiotics so the day is comin when if we get sick the antibiotics can't help."

"Hell, Ace," said Jim Skin, "don't think a the hogs as animals—they are 'pork units' like corn or wood. That's what they told us when I worked there." The remainder of the pineapple ring lay untouched at the side of his plate.

"Jim Skin, I despise that idea. What do your own eyes show you? Pigs are livin creatures, not corn or wood. Frankly, it turns my stomach the inhuman way corporate hogs are raised."

"They're just pigs, aren't they? I mean, they *are* animals?" Bob ventured in a tone as though he were making a joke, ready to laugh.

Ace ignored the joke but homed in on the question. "Pigs *are* animals, yes, but they are also intelligent and they like fresh air and the scenery, they make nests and frolic and take good care a their babies. But these—just cooped up to breed and breed, no nice dirt or weeds, no friends. Pigs are gregarious animals but not in them damn hog bunkers. Makes me sick." And the old man got up and went into the bathroom.

•   •   •

There were days when there was a big rush on and Cy was swearing his way through platters that emptied as fast as he could fill them. Bob, who had always helped Uncle Tam with household chores, couldn't stand watching the man whirl and scrape, got up and cleared the tables, loaded the prison dishwasher.

In a quiet moment Cy got him aside. He looked at Bob. "Preciate the help. You give me a hand, you eat free."

So Bob hustled dishes and turned the steaks on the grill, always rushing back to his chair to hear more about farm and ranch troubles, hoping for leads on landowners ready to sell out. Things got lively when Ace Crouch was on hand to rail against corporate agribusiness and hog farms, and Bob listened to his rants with guilty excitement (what if he were found out?). Charles Grapewine complained against the fates and mistakes of the ancestors and Bob hated to miss any of his impassioned remarks.

"People first come into this country after the big outfits bust up," said Grapewine, who farmed 15,000 acres of wheat and sorghum, "and they believed that old sayin, 'Rain follas the plow.' Feller made that up broke a damn many hearts and backs. Rain don't folla no plow."

"That's right," said Buckskin Bill, sucking at his coffee mug.

Grapewine went on. "Work? My God, you wouldn't believe how hard them old grandaddies worked. And most a them buckled at the knee. Think about what they had a do just a git a crop started. Had a bresh out the fields, catclaw, mesquite and the most a this was handwork, week after week. After the bresh they had a root plow and rake. Hitch up the horses to a plow that had a deep-cuttin blade would slice through them bresh roots."

Buckskin Bill, who had done his childhood time on the farm added, "Keep sharpenin that plow blade, too."

"That's right, Buckskin. After you got *that* done you hitch the horses up to a heavy rake that would yank the roots out. Then you'd git out there with the kids and the old woman and pile the roots and bresh into big heaps, let it dry. The best part was firin the bresh pile. Then you got a level off the field with a heavy blade, smooth out the lumps and hollows. Finally you're ready to plow and harrow. And you'd use a real heavy breakin plow that turned it over at least a foot and as big a harrow as the horses could pull."

"Don't forget, if you was goin a irrigate you had a make the ditches."

"Yes. And after that, if you wasn't dead, it was easy—plantin, irrigatin where you could, weed-pullin, cultivatin, worryin about grasshoppers, hail, drought, flood, prairie fire. People today can't work like that. Those old boys, their whole lives was crisis. There's never been nothin else here but ranch or plow."

Buckskin Bill reminded them of oil, the boom-and-bust days when a ranch kid could hire on as a weevil or roustabout, work his way up to tool dresser and eventually driller, could see the world, or at least the part of it that lay over the Permian Basin, moving along from rag town to rag town with the drifters and cardsharps and whores.

Charles Grapewine preferred to skip past oil. "Today we are *still* in crisis. There's counties in the panhandle where they've had a go back to dry farmin. We got maybe twenty-five more years on these farms and then it's gone. Last year my alfalfa made four inches. That's all. I'm tellin you, it's over."

Bob's attentive posture attracted some notice.

"By mercy God, Grapewine, you'll shoot your mouth off to anybody, won't you?" asked a lean scrag Bob had only heard addressed as Francis.

"Hell, I wasn't sayin nothin that ain't common enough to read in the paper."

"Well, let him *read* it in the paper then." And the man picked up a copy of the *Amarillo Daily* and tossed it on the table in front of Bob, jostling his cup so the coffee slopped out. He stood ready for a response, grimy, limber, with long hard muscles. "You don't know who he is. You don't know if you're blabbin to some government man or one of them hog scouts, do you? Or somebody holdin paper on a man in this room?"

Cy Frease had been watching from under his now-greasy hat, the pearl-grey darkened by sweat and sauce to an organic brown, the panhandle equivalent to a chef's starched toque.

"Francis," he said. "You want a job warshin dishes and clearin tables?"

"Rather eat hot cow shit." The rancher glared.

"Then leave Bob alone. He's workin part-time for me and I told him he ought a get to know folks eat here. I lose him from you talkin ugly and you will take his place."

"I hope you don't regret hirin him," said the rancher, tilting his hat back. He walked to the food tables where Cy stood with a pan of hot biscuits, took one, jammed it into the whipped cream and swallowed it whole.

"You cook so good it's a wonder lightnin don't shoot out a your ass." Outside he got into a fenderless truck hauling a saddled horse in an open trailer and drove off.

"One a these days," said Jim Skin, belching pineapple fumes, "*Wagh!* Somebody is goin a whack him a good one right between the horns."

"Who is he?" asked Bob.

"Hah!" said Grapewine hotly. "Francis Scott Keister, a bullheaded rancher who got all the answers. Born in Woolybucket and never left home but knows about everthing. You don't want a get on his bad side. I got a be goin." He scraped his chair legs across the floor and left.

"There's many a farmer and rancher," Ace said softly to Bob, "who will tell you how much they love the land, but then they sell out to the hog farms, or you go look at their sweetheart place and what you see is overgrazed and overcropped, live water dried up, weedy and poor. You'd pass out did you know what kind a government subsidies them birds was pullin down."

Buckskin Bill nodded. He took a breath and said to Bob, "Our ranch got pretty run-down. What was left of it passed to me back a few years."

Jim Skin nudged Bob and said, "He's headin up to it, boy—goin a tell you how come they call him 'Buffalo Bill.'" He sniggered.

Buckskin Bill lowered his voice. "I let that ranch set there. I don't know what I was expectin, but the damn place stayed the same, full a weeds, maybe the grass grew a little taller. When my great-grain-daddy come here from Alabama he wrote to the folks back home what a rich grass place he'd found. Bluestem to his belt buckle, grama and buffalo grass. What made the land so good? I didn't know, so I talked a Walt Sunbale, he was a real good aggie agent we had here, told me he wasn't sure but he thought it was the buffs—buffalo. He says people think they was the same as cows, but there was a lot different about them. Their whole style was different and they evolved with the grasslands, so they must a been doin something that matched up pretty good. Just their whole style was different."

Bob waited to hear more but a BMW convertible pulled up outside the Old Dog and the driver, a good-looking dark-haired woman, honked and pointed up at the sky when she saw old Bill.

"There's my waf," said Buckskin Bill, getting up. "Fixin a rain. I expect I'll see you again around here?"

"Right," said Bob, trying not to goggle at the sultry and beautiful brunette in the convertible, about fifty years younger than her aged husband. The sky was a deep and dirty yellow. A peal of thunder shook the Old Dog. The convertible top slowly began to rise.

The minute Old William was out the door Jim Skin sidled over and sat in his chair. "What'd you think a her? Some peach, right?"

"Right," said Bob. "A little bit younger than he is?"

"Just a little bit! I notice he didn't tell you how they tapped into the natural gas on his old ranch about six year ago. He's one a the well-offest men in Woolybucket County, now, him that used a work at the carbon-black plant. That's how come he got a lovely young waf and that car. That's how come he can run buffaloes on that ranch, because he don't have to worry about the bottom line. He's like Ted Turner that way. He ain't pore like me. All's I got is a little bit a dried-up land in Oklahoma."

"You ever think about selling it?" asked Bob.

"That's the only thing I *do* think about. That and gittin laid."

A rattle of hail spattered the front window.

11

TATER CROUCH

For the first few weeks every morning Bob Dollar ran for forty-five minutes along the ranch road and out to Farm Highway C, a long caliche road that rose up a hill with a single tree near the crest, then past the oldest cemetery in the county. On the caliche roads he sometimes felt he was running in tinted face powder, boxes of silky dust in blush, dawn and moonglow, in peachy sunset light, at midday chalk white pulver coating the grasses at road margins, and on rainy days the color an earlier century called ashes of roses.

Many times he noticed twists of flattened baling wire on the road, crushed into curious whorls and loops. What, he thought, if the whirlwind came in the night and this was his last memory, twisted baling wire?

He enjoyed mornings at the log bunkhouse almost as much as the slow evenings. The long porch faced east and there he brought his cup of coffee, made on the small camp stove he had bought, watched the Busted Star horses, the tired colts spread out in the grass like throw rugs. The legs of the running horses twinkled like spinning coins. Even the dust they raised sparkled so that he thought of them as ever moving in clouds and splinters of reflected light. A few of them were known for dodging through half-open gates and drifting toward parts unknown, sometimes seven miles west to the small spread of Rope Butt, now in his nineties yet agile. LaVon told him he ought to go over and talk with Rope.

"These days he's raisin fightin cocks. He runs fights in a old airplane hangar over the Oklahoma line. It's legal there, what you'd call 'a custom of the country.'"

In fact Bob had seen and heard Rope Butt at the Old Dog snapping out the merits of sweater grays and bluefaces, of green leg hatches, Kelsos and battle crosses, of gaffs and knives and the depredations of great horned owls in his cranky old voice. He had seen the cuts on the old man's hands and, driving the back roads, came across his strange garden of upturned plastic barrels arranged in long rows, each with its tethered fighting cock. From a distance these chicken huts in orderly rows resembled a cemetery.

Sometime in that week he decided he would go to a cockfight if the opportunity came along, but only after he had explored a hog farm for himself and found someone who wanted to sell out. On his mental list he kept the names of Sorrel Bill and Jim Skin. He wrote to Ribeye Cluke.

Dear Sir.
    I realize I have not come up with any solid prospects yet, but have been feeling my way. I

have been spending quite a lot of time in the local café trying to get a line on which ranchers are having difficulties and might be ready to sell. Most of them are having difficulties, pecuniary and matrimonial (a deteriorating relationship seems just as much a reason to sell out as anything else), but they are stubborn about holding on to the land. I have a few in mind who might be amenable to parting with their acreage. My landlady, Mrs. Fronk, has been very helpful filling in the backgrounds of local people. She is garrulous to a fault but a mine of information. She told me about one fellow who was very rich a few years ago with oil income but subsequently lost his place through excessive spending and now works at the local grain elevator. But the bank seized his ranch. Do you think I should talk to local banks about foreclosed properties?

It has been difficult to catch the rhythm of the place. At first I could not tell if it was the shift of the seasons driving the agricultural community, or the market fluctuations of beef and pork, or what. Every ranch and every town has acres of exhausted machinery. I think that saving this junk is linked to the frugal German habit of holding on to things that might come in handy someday. The derelict machines strike me as private museums of past agricultural work. There are many kinds of vehicles here—

gravity boxes, folding drills, feedyard scrapers, livestock haulers, grain trucks, hot oil units, lined frac trucks, acid trucks, rig workover trucks, and everyone drives silver pickups or white vans. It wouldn't surprise me if the diverse work character of the trucks reflects the regional inclination to multiple jobs. Many people hold down two or three jobs. Specialization does not seem to be the panhandle norm.

I have become aware that it would deepen my understanding of the pork-raising industry if I could tour one of Global Pork Rind's hog farms. There is so much talk against them here that I feel I should be able to refute their arguments but as I have never been inside one I have no basis of fact. Can you arrange such a tour for me?

In the *Rural Compendium* LaVon devoted many pages to what she called "customs of the country"; tipping over outhouses while someone was inside, killing snakes, saying "rabbit, rabbit, rabbit" before bed on the last night of the month, spying on neighbors. Bob Dollar, who was frequently reported to Sheriff Hugh Dough as a suspicious stranger, learned the hard way that many people watched the highway through their front room curtains and were not slow to call the law and tell what they suspected. There were activities in the panhandles that needed reporting: jogging, odd clothing, unusual vehicles, out-of-state license plates, dark skin, children unattended or quarreling, loose dogs, large house cats (invariably reported as "panthers"), people with flat tires or engine trouble who might be escaped convict decoys. Yet dead cows lay sometimes for weeks in the ditches waiting for the rendering truck.

LaVon did not share Bob's enthusiasm for Cowboy Rose. She told him that in the 1890s Cowboy Rose and Woolybucket had tussled over which would be the county seat. Cowboy Rose won the vote, then cancelled its legitimacy by stealing the courthouse papers from Woolybucket in the dead of night before the official proclamation. The vote was cooked as well. An aged ferryman, French John Bullyer, had voted forty-one times, once in his own name, forty times more masquerading as sons of himself, a parade of Bills and Toms and Bucks and, when his powers of invention failed, whatever his eye fell on as it roved around his cabin, a catalog of never-ending amusement to the region. An anonymous jokester ordered a tombstone with the forty names cut on it, stolen decades later by a touring professor of American history from Dartmouth College in New Hampshire:

Here lieth the Great Clan of Bullyer,
All were keenly interested in local politics.
Abraham, Abner, Barney, Bill, Shiloh, Ormy, Wake
Up, Rabbit Eyes, Acme, Plate, Matches, Spurleg,
Buck, Dishpan, Dutch Oven, Teacup, Whisky,

TATER CROUCH

Chauncey, Caleb, Digger, Fantod, Garry Owen,
Hercules, Ichabod, King James, Keg, Dram,
Money, Stump, Nine, Prince, Quill, Robert, Bob,
Buck, Tom, Calendar, Candle, Fido, Zeke, Buck
and Dutch Oven, Jr.
April 4, 1887–April 7, 1887.

One morning, the sky filled with fresh blue and not a breath yet drawn from it, Bob Dollar put his head in the door and called to LaVon but she did not answer.

"Getting some water, LaVon," he said to the silence and entered the kitchen, letting the screen door bang a little. When the container was half-full LaVon's truck pulled up and she came in carrying a large carton, headed to the dining room, which she had turned into an office. She dropped the carton, which sounded like it was packed with concrete blocks, reentered the kitchen, laid a small photograph on the table, went for the coffee pot.

"*My* lucky day," she said.

"How's that?"

"Got my hands on Tater Crouch's scrapbooks. Tater is old now, and it is a miracle he ever give these things up to me. But only for a week. I got to work through them and get them back to him next Friday. Guess he figured he was safe to live that much longer. He's a cranky old feller. You look at him now, crippled up, limpin around, face like a dried mushroom and all them sad lines, then look at this photograph here his sister snapped in 1931 when he took over the ranch, twenty years old and a real good worker, a wonderful hand with stock." She looked at the picture, a small black-and-white square with wide white margins and toothed edges.

"Just a big, fresh-faced boy, and he sure looked good. Broad shoulders, good muscle on him, kind a lean and rangy. See how his mouth's hangin open a little like he was gettin ready to say somethin or laugh? Ever picture a him I seen it's the same. Even his kid pictures showed that. His mouth still hangs open but there hasn't been a tooth a his own in there since he was thirty and now he don't wear the dentures. But see how neat he parted his hair on the left, straight as a stick and slung over his forehead white above the hat line. Big ears but flat from his mother taping them down when he was a baby. They used a do that, tape baby's ears flat so they wouldn't stick out. Done it with my own boy. He looks good in his white shirt and fresh-ironed jeans and his best boots greased up, don't he? Too bad them jeans was high-waters and tight. Twenty years old and I believe he was still growin. Tight enough so's you can see everthing he had over on the left. They say a man will generally keep his goods on the side he parts his hair, balance out his handedness, I guess. Tater is right-handed but I bet you could wrap him in see-through plastic now and not see a thing. It shrivels up pretty good when they get old. He's the one you want to ask about the freight team."

"What freight team?"

"That photograph I showed you. You wanted a know how the feller managed a drive it."

"Oh yeah. LaVon, on the way over this morning there was a grey horse on the ranch road. I couldn't see the brand. Suppose it's one of yours, but I don't think I saw it before. Maybe you bought some new horses and this is one?"

"Grey? Certain not one a ours. My graindad, like most a the old cowboys, said that light-colored horses attract lightning, wouldn't have one on the place. Kind of a tradition. I half believe it myself. There was a family down at the crossroads about six years ago, come up from Houston, he was in awl in some way, three kids, bought each kid a horse and one of them horses was a real light grey, one a sorrel and the other a bay. Wouldn't you know it, a storm rolled in, lightnin like flies on sugar, and sure enough, one of them horses was hit and it was the grey one. So I don't know, maybe there's somethin to the old sayin. I wonder if birds is ever hit by lightnin. There's some will fly around in a storm like they don't care. That horse could be from Sanderson's place down the road. I'll call them up and see. Anyway, I bet you know Tater's graindaughter, Donna Crouch—she works in the office at the grain elevator."

"Big tall lady with a blond ponytail?"

"No, that one's Lou Ann Bemis. Her and her husband run the Java Jive Café in Waka on weekends. Donna is real short, red hair parted in the middle, wears big round glasses, never says a word."

"I'll see you tomorrow, LaVon."

"Have a good day now, Bob."

The next morning began with gritty, stinking wind that increased in velocity and abrasiveness. Bob came into the kitchen banging his water jug against his leg. LaVon was rummaging through the photographs.

"Pour us out some coffee, Bob, will you? Thanks." She held up a studio portrait of a young curly-headed blond boy who could not have been more than fifteen. He was togged out in cowboy rig that fit too comfortably to have been studio props.

"No idea who this boy is. Looks a little bit like you, curly hair, big baby blues. Tater said he'd writ down who everbody was on the backs of the pictures, but I find he missed quite a few. And I can't hardly read his writin. Done my best to work through these but some a them are complete mysteries. So. I'm goin over there to the Bar Owl tomorrow and set down with him and talk him through the ones I don't know. If I can get him loose of the telvision. You can come along, you want. He was the real thing, you know, a good solid rancher who knew cows and men. And still does. He's got stories and stories if we can get him goin." She held up another photograph showing a group of men and horses standing around a fresh grave mound. White ink letters spelled out "A Cowboy Funral." She looked at the back.

"Not a *clue* who was gettin buried. Oh! Here's one

you'll like. It's the main street a Cowboy Rose around 1911."

She handed Bob a brown photograph showing a few false-front mercantile buildings, a blacksmith shop under a shady tree with the smith bent over a horse's hoof, a grassy track that was the main street extending east into the distant plain. He recognized two of the buildings; they still stood, the blacksmith's shop and the tiny bank.

He spent the evening with Lieutenant Abert, using his Texas road map to puzzle out the locations of the Bents' panhandle trading posts, for the notes told him the trader brothers had built something called "the Adobe Fort" on the Canadian around 1840, and, in the spring of 1844 put up another trading post a few miles distant. Even with the big gazetteer, *The Roads of Texas,* he could not locate the marker streams, Bosque Grande Creek and Red Deer Creek. He supposed the map was not detailed enough or that the streams had been renamed. Later, from LaVon, he learned what he suspected, that this "adobe fort," after the Bents abandoned it, was the famous Adobe Walls, the scene of a battle in 1874 between a war party of several hundred Comanches, Kiowas and Cheyennes (including the young Quanah Parker), led by the Comanche warrior Coyote Droppings (who claimed his medicine made him and those with him immune to bullets), and twenty-eight sharpshooter buffalo-hide hunters. The Medicine Lodge Treaty of 1867 forbade white men the right to hunt south of the Arkansas River, but white men did as they pleased. The same treaty forbade the Indians from raiding panhandle settlements, but the Indians continued to swoop down on homesteads. On this fine spring morning the Indians made a classic dawn attack. But the buffalo hunters had been awakened at two in the morning by the snap of the breaking ridgepole. They had repaired the pole and, sparked with coffee, decided to stay up and get an early start on the day. When the cry of "Indians!" came, they were awake and alert. They held off the Indians for three days. After a number of the attacking men fell, the main Indian body retreated to the ridges above Adobe Walls where they rode back and forth out of rifle range. On the third day the plainsman Billy Dixon snapped off a shot at one of the distant riders with his .50 Sharps rifle. The Indian fell dead from his horse and soon after the demoralized attackers, who had believed their strong medicine protected them from bullets, left. It was the beginning of the end, and a year later the panhandle had been ethnically cleansed of its native people. Billy Dixon's long shot became a pillar of western myth.

They drove to the Bar Owl over miles of pale caliche road, LaVon's scarred Chevy pickup raising milky dust that hung in the air, a translucent scrim that dimmed the road behind. It was a blinko day, clouds skipping across the sky. A windmill in the distance flashed a new blade with every revolution. When Bob remarked on it she said owls broke the blades by flying into them, and that the panhandle was thick with owls, and that Pee-Wee Fischer, who raised falcons, shot them whenever he could. Bob saw again what beautiful country it was when he looked past the clutter of tanks and pumps, colored by yellow light so thin and clear it slipped off the sky in huge slabs and in narrow straw-colored pipes glancing off flying birds, windshields and plate glass, throwing winks from cars and trucks. And it was crazy country too, some of the flattest terrain on earth, tractor-chewed and rectangled, rugged breaks and plunging canyons, sinister clouds too big to see in one look, rusty rivers, bone white roads and red grass—the oddly named bluestem. The wind had died down and LaVon gestured at an unmoving windmill in a heavily grazed pasture. Against the sky it looked like a combination of tripod and meat grinder. Half a dozen small birds sat slant-legged on the edges of the blades, and as a little breeze came up again the blades began to turn, the birds slid a few inches down the blade edges and flew.

"In the days when the big ranches started sellin off land," she said, "it was dry, dry country. The XIT had hundreds a windmills and full-time hands to tend to them. And when the nesters come in, without windmills they couldn't of made it. Not a one. Of course they didn't make it anyway. They didn't have a blessed clue to what was under them. I mean the Ogallala. All that water they didn't even know was there. In those days if you wanted a be a rancher you had a have live runnin water or a hand-dug well, somehow pump it out a the ground. If you had stock and kids you *had* a have hundreds a gallons a day. It was all shallow wells and windmills until pretty much in the 1960s. Well do I remember. I grew up in the windmill days. They was the only thing made the west possible to live in."

Bob said, "What did your husband do? Was he a rancher?"

"Not at first. He got into land sales. He was panhandle born and raised and heard the stories how Mr. Borger done the job back in the 1920s—soon as they found awl Mr. Borger bought up a couple hundred acres a land and laid it out in lots, fifteen hundred dollars a piece, called it a town site. Named the streets. When Mr. Fronk got in the land sales I did quite a bit a that. That's a job I liked. No Main Street or them First, Second and Thirds for me—I'd go for colorful names like Red Hot Poker and Bramble Lane and Messican Hat. In one day Mr. Borger took in over a hundred thousand dollars. So Mr. Fronk was inspired and he got into that kind a thing. Course there's nothin new in that. It's how all these towns was laid out—somebody, usually the railroad headquarters, decided where they was goin a have a town and then they sent in their surveyors to plat the lots or they used a land agent and then they sold them. There was good money in it. Mr. Fronk wasn't a railroad man but he was friends with many an awl man and when somebody brought in a well he was right there, buyin land. He platted it himself. There's a few towns in the panhandle he started—Auger, Gusherton, Rich and Seaview."

"Seaview?" asked Bob.

"He thought it sounded good, and if somebody said somethin, he'd turn it on them and say it was a sea of grass or enough oil underground to make a sea. To make it sweeter he sold lumber, too. Two years after we was married there was plenty to buy this ranch. In a way, Bob, you remind me of Mr. Fronk."

"How so?" asked Bob.

"Because you both believe in what you are doin. Mr. Fronk would get real excited about the new towns. He wanted them to do good. It's like you and these luxury home sites."

Bob held the box of photographs on his lap and looked at them again on the way over. The photograph of Tater Crouch as a young man seemed familiar and somehow comic, though he did not know why. Then it came to him that Tater's too-small jeans, ending well above the ankles, were the same highwater length as those worn by Jacques Tati in the Mr. Hulot films, Uncle Tam's favorites.

The entrance to the Bar Owl was a loose plank bridge over Two Year Creek. LaVon pointed out the old bunkhouse, a small, pitched-roof, board-and-batten building with a lean-to on the east side. The doors were gone, the shingle roof holed, chimney attenuated, window glass shot out. The gaping doorway showed bales of hay, darkened by weather and mold, stacked to the ceiling. A tilted cross, all that remained of a clothesline support, stood in the mesquite. On the ground in front of the building in a little patch of grass, the head and blades of a windmill lay facedown. In the brown distance another stood, but the blades did not turn and the stock tank at its foot sparkled with bullet holes. The land rose and fell, not flat enough for irrigated agriculture, the thin grass heavily punctuated with mesquite, showing lenses of bare sandy ground like rents in cat-clawed fabric.

A hawk sat on an electric pole and LaVon told him that one had started a grass fire when its wings touched two wires and it fell dead and blazing into the dry grass below.

"Tater tried to sue the electric company but he didn't get very far."

They passed a tractor dragging a bush hog through the mesquite, a spray of twigs and dust flaring behind it. The driver raised one hand as they drew abreast. In another mile LaVon pointed out the original ranch headquarters, a matched pair of narrow sandstone houses facing one another and joined by a high stone wall that enclosed a kind of patio with two or three shade trees. LaVon said that a hundred years ago old man Crouch, Tater's grandfather, had taken the plan from the design stamped on the bags of Arbuckle coffee beans. The twin houses had been abandoned in 1974, the Crouches shifting into a characterless pre-fab ranchburger with contemporary plumbing and heat, an attached three-car garage.

As they pulled up in the yard LaVon said, "Now don't say a word about Mrs. Crouch. She passed last year in terrible pain. She needed to go on but Tater could hardly bear it. And before that he lost his only boy. He was a bull rider and a big Braymer named Grannyknot got him down and mashed him."

A heavily made-up woman of late middle age opened the door.

"Hello, Louise," said LaVon, and from the way the woman answered, "Come on in, Miz Fronk," Bob guessed she was the housekeeper. The interior of this house, which might have been lifted from any sunbelt suburb, was as dull as its exterior, seven-foot ceilings coated with an off-scale rough finish embedded with sparkling plastic chips, in the hall a brown carpet with a pressed-down track to the kitchen. The living room walls were ranged around with tables, each stacked with tottering cliffs of account books, tally books, ledgers and maps, newspapers, for, LaVon had said on the ride over, Tater Crouch was roughing out a history of the Bar Owl which some grandniece, enrolled in a creative writing course at Southwest Texas U, would smooth into prose during the summer.

He thought it was the ugliest room he had ever seen. The walls were papered with a design of giant red hummingbirds. Against the wallpaper hung small sets of antlers, hardly more than spikehorns. The curtains clashed with the print upholstery, the plaid table runner, the patterned rug, as though every surface had had a digitized pattern applied to it. There were two benches upholstered in white plastic. Enormous lamps with frilled orange shades stood on side tables.

Tater Crouch sat in a wheelchair near the south window where he could watch the driveway.

"Tater! Here's LaVon! LaVon's here! Tater!" the housekeeper shouted.

"Well, *I* know it. I seen her drive in, didn't I?"

The old man turned his deflated-football face toward them, the nose almost flat, the white hair cropped, the short white face whiskers like the fur of a laboratory rat. The eyes were standard, red-rimmed Texas blue. He began to cough and spit into a handkerchief.

Bob was shocked. He had carried the image of the twenty-year-old man in his too-small jeans to this house and was now confronted with sixty years of change. He could see nothing of the young, clear-eyed man in this old wreck. He would not let old age happen to him.

"Well, Tater," said LaVon. "I hope you don't got the flu. You sound bad."

"Hell, it ain't the flu. It's that damn pig farm over on Coppedge Road. They turn them fans on, sucks out the ammonia and sulfide and if the wind is right, like it was this mornin, we almost die of it. It just plays smash with us. They say it gives you pneumonia and artharitis. They say it'll turn your eyes yeller."

The housekeeper, nodding agreement, wheeled his chair to one of the tables, moved the papers on it and cleared a space for LaVon to spread out the photographs.

"Tater, those hog farms are a crime. But I don't know what we can do about them. Anyway, I've brought Bob Dollar with me. He's visitin Woolybucket and stayin in the Star bunkhouse. Thought he'd like to meet you. And, like I said on the telephone, I got these mystery photographs. Appears you missed puttin the names on one or two. Do you recollect who is this boy?" LaVon held out the studio portrait of the young blond boy in the black hat. "There is not a name on the back."

"Why, that's young Fanny. 'Muddy Fan' we called him after he got bucked off and landed in a waller and come up mud hat to boot heel. He was the best-liked boy there ever was on our place. Five hard men, dirty and rough, at the funeral and ever one of them made tears for that boy. We won't see his likes again, not theirs neither. It was a sad thing."

"Is this it?" said LaVon, pulling out the cowboy funeral photograph.

"Yes, it is. Oh, how we hated to bury that boy. That's me over there on the left. I had my head down so's the photographer wouldn't catch me bawlin like a calf. I weren't much older'n Fanny. Could a been me dead." He gave a crackling laugh like a dead bush in a drag, twigs snapping. "Cowboyin was hard in them days. The young guys today don't know nothin about it. Take your brandin crew, twenty, twenty-five men— the wagon boss, cook, couple a ropers, wrangler, eight or ten flankers a throw them down and hold, couple men to work the irons, a knife man, a vaccinator, a dehorner, a guy to paint the stumps and cuts, and your guys holdin the herd. You'd get at it before light and keep at it until dark and then sleep on the ground until you started again. It would be dark when you got up and the wrangler had to lay down on the ground and skylight the horses. We'd always brand after Fourth a July. Forty-five dollars a month for that."

"And who was this Fanny that everbody thought so high of?"

"He was just a kid, drifted in from somewhere, I don't recollect where, but he was a pure-dee wonder with horses, just the finest kind a rider. Fanny the Wrangler. Wasn't nobody better. Limber as a piece a raw bacon. Good enough he could a been a contest hand. Cheerful, good-natured, give you the shirt off his back. And smart. He thought hisself out from a problem, didn't just bull through. Worked for my deddy two year before the Reaper cut him down."

"So he wasn't kin to folks hereabouts?"

"Naw. Missouri or Montana or someplace with the letter M on the front, could a been Maine or Minnesota. I think it *was* Minnesota, him bein so white-headed and pale-complexioned. He'd be a old man now like me if he'd lived, but I remember him like I seen him ten minute ago. I can see him noddin his head to one side and twistin his tongue around his teeth like he did. He had bad teeth and we had to pull a few for him."

"Was that what did him in, bad teeth? I know there *was* boys died from bad teeth."

"There was, but he wasn't one. He died for love of a little bitty pigtail girl, seven year old. Red Poarch was one died from bad teeth, head swole up like a watermelon. Now, there's a death I wouldn't wish even on the worst pig farm man."

The old man stirred the photographs, held one of a severe woman for a moment, dropped it dismissively and took up the portrait of Fanny again.

"There was a dance. We *had* dances in them days, went from supper to breakfast. This one was in the schoolhouse at Cowboy Rose, when it *was* a school-house, not like now, all fixed up into a house for two funny boys and the kids sent on a bus to a far-off school, and it was a box supper. After World War Two the box suppers stopped. They got in the movie show in Woolybucket and the diner and that's what people wanted a do, step out and get entertained. It was the women wanted it. Anyway, that dance. Didn't get much work out a none a us that day, we was so busy scrubbin and smoothin and brushin our hats and puttin grease on our boots. Quite a rough road a Cow-boy Rose and everbody a-horseback set off after noon dinner a get there in time to bid on the supper boxes. Some drove in a automobile, though there wasn't so many of them around here and most of us stuck to the horse. One or two rode a tractor over. You know how that box supper game goes—the girls make a fancy dish and put it in a fancy box and the men bid on the box and whoever wins a box with a high bid gets to set with the lady that made it. Somehow or other ever cowboy always knew what his favorite gal's wrap-up was to be—flary paper with a flar in the knot, wood crate with strawr packed around some pots a keep somethin hot, pink paper and jingle bells and all manner of foofaraw getups. Some reason, Fanny come in late after all the others, and they'd already started the bids. He's climbin up the steps when this little shirttail girl hardly reaches his belt buckle comes out carryin a bowl and the tears runnin down her freckles like rain.

"'What's wrong, little girl?' says Fanny, or so I hear.

"'I didn't know I was supposed a wrap it up,' she says and commences blubberin. She was the youngest kid a Jake Ahrns, ranched north a White Deer, the Double Circle near the Franklyn spread. 'I don't got nothin a wrap it up in.'

"'Well, what is it?' says Fan.

"'Strawrberries and cream,' says the girl. Now, you don't know how hard it was to git cream in them days, but the Ahrns kept a milk cow and the girl had hustled around for the berries in the season. They was preserved, I imagine, as the dance was near wintertime. Nobody had a freezer in them days.

"'Well,' says our Fan, 'I got just the thing,' and he

whips his new red bandanna he's wearin in that photograph off his neck and ties up the girl's bowl. 'Guess I'll have to bid on it to git my rag back,' he said and give her a smile. When that boy give you a smile it was like the sun come out.

"So, in they goes and the girl puts her red bandanna bowl up with the fancy boxes and the biddin recommences. Mr. Kresskatty was the auctioneer and he was good at it, the same old patter he used when he sold cows and it was funny hearin him extol the merits a the fancy wrap-ups and the savory smells comin out a the boxes. After about five minutes he holds up the little girl's bowl wrapped in Fanny's bandanna and says 'What am I bid for this fine wild rag and content, not too heavy, not too light and comes with two spoons, probly a mess a sugar grits.' He hardly got the words out when Fan was on his feet biddin two dollars. Now, your usual sum for a box supper was a dollar or a little more. Nobody said nothin except Mr. Kresskatty, who said right fast, 'Goin, goin, gone! Sold to the cattleboy without no rag on his suspicious neck,' and everbody bust out laughin and Fanny set with the little gal and they eat strawrberries and cream. Fanny told it later she reminded him of his little sister back in Missouri or Minnesota. But the next Sunday he rode all the way over to the Double Circle to visit with that little girl. She couldn't been more than seven year old. Sally or Susy. He talked with her, he took her for rides, he played dominoes with her and her brothers and sister for he was only a half-growed boy hisself and I think circumstances might a pushed him to man's estate a little early. He got about like one of the kids a that family. Then one day we heard the fever was in amongst the Ahrn kids and that little gal was sick and askin for Fanny. Wasn't he fit to be tied? Nothin would hold him. Away he went without leave and we didn't see him for a week. Deddy said he was fired. The news got back to us. That little Ahrn girl was dead and Fanny'd held her hands all through the last hour and the child's fatal last words was, 'Fanny, won't you come see me next week?'"

The old man's voice speeded up and he fairly rattled off the rest of the tale. "And so he did. A week to the very day, we buried young Muddy Fan, dead of the same ailment that killed the girl. There was a song made up about it and everbody on the range knew it and knew who it was about." And he began to sing a wavering line through his nose, though what the words were, beyond "*. . . as ever I did see,*" Bob Dollar could not tell.

"Sir, Mr. Crouch," said Bob, taking LaVon's photograph of the freight team from the manila envelope he carried. "LaVon showed me this picture and I was wondering how the driver managed that big of a team."

The old man looked at Bob for the first time, brought the photograph close to his eyes and studied it.

"I think the driver is Hefran Wardrip. Freighter. Freightin was big business before the railroads come in, specially when the big outfits started fencin. When I was a boy freightin was all done. But my granddeddy done it and my deddy would tell how when he was a boy he used a see one a them trains goin north, another one headin south or east. The rivers run west to east but the most a the freight trails and later the cattle trails run north and south. There was freight kings in the old days like they had cattle kings later."

"I thought the Santa Fe Trail was the only trail," said Bob.

Tater Crouch snorted. "That was earlier and different. The main one in the panhandle region was the Jones and Plummer Trail, started from a military road and grew, run from Dodge City to Mobeetie and over to Tascosa. They dreaded two things—crossin the Cimarron River and crossin the Canadian. Both a them was treacherous with quicksand and could come up fast. Both them rivers is soft-bottomed."

He looked at the picture again, tapped it with his fingernail. "Harnessin up and drivin a big team like this one was a skill and it took years to learn if you didn't grow up to it. There was a many men could do it then. There's hardly nobody alive now knows how except you see some old fool at the rodeo once in a while show off his skills backin a freight wagon into a imaginary dock. Them drivers knew the country like the back a their hand. The mail wagon drivers—P. G. Reynolds had the mail contract—used horse

teams, Morgans, they say, and those boys had a perilous existence. There's one feller in the blizzard a
1886 froze to death settin on the box and the passengers never even knew it until they got to Fort Supply
and the driver didn't get down and open the door.
Couldn't. He was froze dead. But I can tell you that
on the freight wagons where they used mules the
driver always set on the left-wheel mule and he drove
them with a single jerk line. That jerk line run
through the bridle bit ring of each team and fastened
to the left lead mule's bit. I still got that harness
somewheres, attic or barn loft or I don't know
where."

"LaVon's been telling me about the XIT and the
barbwire," said Bob.

"Oh, the XIT? What the XIT done with the barbwar
was show the ranchers that it could be profitable.
There was a lot a opposition to barbwar early on. It
cut the common range up like a pie where the big
boys thought it should be all for all, and the early war
they had was vicious—and they called it 'vicious
war'—hurt the cattle bad and then the screwworms
would get at them. The XIT used a different kind a
war, a ribbon war, wide and flat and the prongs was
clamped on. It would prick the cattle but not cut
them up like the Glidden stuff. But the XIT was not
the first in the panhandle to use barbwar. That was the
Fryin Pan, the ranch that Mr. Glidden himself backed
though it was his salesman, Henry Sanborn, that persuaded him to put up some a the money for the ranch.

They called it 'the Panhandle' and they had a brand of a pan with a long handle, but some old cowboy took a look at it and said, 'Panhandle, hell, that's a fryin pan,' and the name stuck. Mr. Glidden was old then and he didn't want a have nothin a do with the ranch life, rather stay up in De Kalb, Illinois. But he backed Sanborn with barbwar money. He made a fortune with the barbwar. But Sanborn liked it here and he settled in. Bossy fella, local folks didn't much like him. He was a great one for public works and it didn't make no difference. He started Amarilla. There's a piece a that war from the XIT over on the wall. I got it myself. Found a roll of it in a draw."

The old man suddenly dozed a little and the photograph fell from his hand. Bob picked it up and after waiting a few minutes LaVon said, "That's it. Let's go."

But as they went out the door the old man raised his head and croaked, "She ever tell you how her granddeddy got them lash marks all over his back?"

"Not yet," said Bob.

"Come on, come on," said LaVon, pushing him in the small of his back.

"Wait a minute. Show you somethin," said the old man struggling out of his chair. He came to the door where they stood, plucked at Bob's sleeve and pointed out a small roundlet fastened to the wall with a single screw. Outside the wind shrieked. Tater Crouch pushed the roundlet to one side with his finger.

"See that hole?"

"Yes. Yes sir."

"It's a crowbar hole. The wind gets blowin, you stick your crowbar out and let it set a minute, then pull it in. If it's bent, it's dangerous a venture forth." He laughed an old man's dry wheeze.

"Come on," said LaVon.

On the way down the drive Bob remarked to LaVon that Fanny's was a sad and touching story. She snorted.

"That was the biggest load a horse poop I heard in years. So happens Sal Ahrn was a hale and hearty woman when I was a girl, she married Darwin Lawson. I never heard a word a that story about that Fanny and his bandanna. I'll look into it."

"I wish you'd look into telling me about that photograph of Mr. Harshberger's back."

"All in good time," said LaVon.

As they passed by the old bunkhouse Bob rolled his window down to get a better look and within seconds regretted it, for the wind had shifted and carried a full load of hog farm flavor, a huge fetid stink like ten thousand rotten socks, like decaying flesh, like stale urine and swamp gas, like sour vomit and liquid manure, a ghastly palpable stench that made him retch.

"Don't you dare throw up in my truck, Bob Dollar," said LaVon, stepping on the brake.

"Go!" croaked Bob. "Let's get out of here."

• • •

A few days later when Bob came for water LaVon said, "Well, I have checked out that Muddy Fan story. I went to the Babtist graveyard and found the stone of Sarah Ahrn Lawson who died in 1962 at age forty-nine. She was born in 1913. Up in the Bar Owl buryin ground I found a stone for Fanny Wallace Meers, 1904 to 1920. I went over to the Prairie Home and talked to old men and women, and some a them remembered Sal Ahrn. Some of the men, especially Gardaman Purt, Vivian's brother, Gardie we called him, remembered Muddy Fan, said he had a gift to ride. Then I went up to the library in Cowboy Rose and looked in the back issues of the *Cowboy Rose Yippee* and there wasn't a thing about fever, but I did find a small item that said a Bar Owl cowboy had died in a 'mishap.' It gave his name as Fane Wallace Moors. A 'mishap' could mean anything from a fit a chokin to a bullet. And he was dead ten years before Tater's famous box supper."

There was a long silence. The phone rang.

"Oh, hello, Tater. We was just talkin about you. Yes? Yes, I found that much out."

He could hear the old man's voice squawking over the line.

"You don't say. Well, Tater, I appreciate your call. It's good a get these things straight as we can." She hung up, frowning.

"I wish he'd remembered all that before I wasted two days runnin around. That was Tater and he said he was goin through his deddy's letters and found one from Fanny's folks thankin his deddy for his letter of condolence and it all come back to him. It was somebody else died for love of a little girl. It seems young Fanny had a worse end." But she did not tell Tater's revised version. Nor, Bob thought, had she explained the photograph of her grandfather's scarred back. He wondered if LaVon's *Compendium* accounts of local families stopped short and left the reader wondering.

Before he fell asleep an idea hit Bob like a bite from a fire ant: Tater Crouch's Bar Owl Ranch would make a prime hog farm location. The smell was already there.

12

ROPE BUTT

A cruelly battered pickup and horse trailer came on, straddling the center line. The driver, Rope Butt, spat out the window, spoke aloud the great and dark poetic line that had come to him at sunrise, *They say an old cowboy just ain't no good.* He did not force the search for the next line; it would reveal itself. In a region once made up of the great ranches all but the tattered remnants of a few had fallen away, cotton growing up against the foundations of the houses, verandas buried in the dirt, the costly imported stained glass windows slivered by bullets. Rope Butt believed himself to be the only living cowhand of proficiency still alive in the panhandle for all that he was in his nineties. Despite his age he could still do a hard day's work and had a slightly worn reputation as a good hand, for what he lacked in strength he made up for with experience and cow sense. He had been a real nut-cutter in his day but now he was an old, old scorpion, solitary, bitter, and knew it.

He was irascible and quick to take offense, could not abide correction or gainsaying. He preferred working to staying home in his tiny three-room

house. When he was younger anything could cause him to quit and move on to another outfit. So often did he fire up that the sight of his truck with the horse trailer attached inspired wits to remark that they guessed Rope Butt was "full a quit again." But it had been twenty years since he had ridden full-time for a brand, for not many ranchers in these days of health plans and litigation liked the idea of hiring an antique cowboy. He stuck with his horses and raised a few fighting cocks to make ends meet. He regretted that most ranches had reduced the number of their horses in favor of trucks and ATVs. He remembered when the Cutaway Ranch ran three hundred horses. Now the ranch belonged to a Minneapolis insurance company and there were thirty horses on the place, half of them rarely used. The calls for Rope to fill in when some hand fell ill or had to go to court came only once in a blue moon, and his melancholy thoughts turned to cowboy poetry.

As the truck swayed down the highway, three more lines came to him. First he repeated the good first line: *They say an old cowboy just ain't no good.*

Then, *His campfire has went out,*
Though he done all he could.

But the only rhyme he could summon for "out" was "sauerkraut," which lacked poetic glory. He let it go. The right line would come in time. That was the thing about poetry. It crept up through the draws and coulees of the brain.

He had known the best men and the worst men.

The panhandle attracted some strange people, from Harvard graduates to crims on the lam. He didn't much care for the two nancy boys who had lately come up from Dallas, but he was willing to live and let live, for certain bunkhouse friendships were not unknown, though little talked about. It was Francis Scott Keister who hated the two—Frank Owsley and Teddy Paxson—with incendiary intensity, who talked about tar and feathers and worse. "Woolybucket County don't need no damn fags," he said. "I rather see the old schoolhouse where many a Cowboy Rose kid learned his ABC turned over to a hog farm than to them homaseashells." But Rope had bought a red bowl from their glassworks studio and ate his mush from it every morning, finding it cheered him considerably to have such a bright blaze on the table. He imagined Francis ate out of the cook pot.

Because of what had happened in later years he especially remembered the crazy Dutchman, Habakuk van Melkebeek, who showed up on the Cutaway one spring day in the 1930s looking for work. He claimed he came from the town of Kampen in the Netherlands and that he had been working in Oklahoma as a hired man on a wheat ranch. The Cutaway foreman at the time was Hermann Slike, a crusty old German-Texan with nostrils like the entrances to twin caves. He'd grown up in an overpopulated soddy and escaped before he sprouted whiskers.

"You know anything about windmills?" he asked the Dutchman, sizing up the spindle legs, the spider arms. The fellow had too much face—pillowy lips, a big curved nose with a bulb of flesh on the end, eyelids thick as piecrust and brows like weeds. There wasn't a cowboy in the outfit who'd voluntarily work on the mills, and when one or two were forced to get up on the towers with their grease cans they cursed Slike from breakfast to bunkhouse and, after one man was blasted by a lightning bolt, a Cutaway cowboy had only to hear the word "windmill" and he would quit. There were tall weeds around windmills, good places for rattlesnakes, and a tool dropped in the weeds was there forever. It was said that the Cutaway ran three crews of ranch hands—one coming, one going, one working. So Slike himself had spent many lonely hours on greasy ladders skinning his knuckles on recalcitrant metal and worn gears.

"*Ja.* I know pretty good."

Slike gave Rope Butt a quick, conspiratorial glance like a conducting wire.

"Well, we'll try you out. I need a good windmill man. Hell, I'd take a bad windmill man. Most important man on a ranch if you ever seen cows dead from thirst. Cows got a drink. We got forty-one mills in twenty-eight pastures on this spread. Rope here will show you where they are. You'll be responsible for mill maintenance, keepin the tanks in good repair. The cattle business is a business and water is the name a the cattle business."

"*Ja,*" said Habakuk. "I need pencil, paper. I write them mills down, where, pasture, number, how bad, write some records. Mills make money. *Daar moet de molen van malen*—that's what the mill has to grind, no?" Although Habakuk came from Kampen, which had a reputation for breeding dunces, he considered himself shrewd and was wary of others whom he suspected of trying to get around him. He was clever, but it was the sharpness of a fairy-tale Hans to whom good things happen by luck, not through smart figuring.

"I guess so," said Slike, wondering what the man had said. "Rope, show Milkbeak where he can put his things and give him a couple a real tall horses. Git him some pencils and one a them brown tally books on the shelf in the office. That ought a fill the bill. Take him out there after dinner and start showin him the mills. Keep it up until he sees ever fuckin one. Make sure he gets a full tour. Maybe we'll get lucky." And he walked away, his face twisted with a complicated expression, partly sour as if he'd raised a tumbler he suspected was filled with vinegar, partly pleased as if he'd swallowed champagne. A few yards away he turned and said, "Show him the toolshed and the repair shop. Show him the windmill wagon. Goddammit, show him everthing. Maybe we'll get lucky."

Over the next weeks Slike's humor improved. Habakuk van Melkebeek was an inspired windmill man, brilliant and efficient if somewhat quirky. Although he was tall he was catty and as flexible as spring steel. There had been a few practical jokes in the bunkhouse, remarks about his comical accent, suppositions that "Dutchman" meant German, resentment that he was getting paid almost twice a cowhand's wage, but the jokesters' sense of humor dimmed when the big man responded with a joke of his own, squirting windmill grease into their boots while they slept, and, in his mild voice saying, "If I go another place, *you* fix the windmills. Be nice, I stay, fix them good." It didn't take long to see that the crane-shanked Dutchman was a little crazy but indispensable and that he earned his seventy-five a month. In the distance riders would often see his lanky figure balanced atop a rickety mill, or his cranky wagon dusting across a pasture, and they would thank God they were horseback cowboys and not windmill monkeys.

After Rope Butt's guided tour, Habakuk was on his own and often, because the press of work was great and traveling time a waste, he slept out on the prairie instead of coming in to the bunkhouse. Traditionally the mill locations had been named by direction and incident—The Terrible Swede in the canyon pasture, Red Mill (for a swatch of nearby dirt), Short Fingers where a well driller had maimed his hand, Hard Luck where a hapless cowboy had fallen off the tower. But Habakuk painted a number on a mill's vane and its tank, dedicating to each several pages in his tally book.

Every possible ailment afflicted the Cutaway windmills: leaky tanks, worn leathers, broken sucker rods (in many the copper rivets had been replaced with bent nails), broken furl winch wires, missing sails, helmets ventilated with bullet holes, motor cases in desperate need of oiling, channels plugged with sludge, tailbone pivot bolts worn, washers, rings and bearings worn, bearing bars broken, tail chains broken and wedged in the mast pipe, crows' nests on several nonworking mills, stopped because the wheel's vibration had shaken some of the birds' treasures—marbles, bolts, pieces of bone, shiny pebbles—loose from the nest to lodge in the water column and ruin the cylinder. Around a few of the mills Chinese elms, cottonwoods or willows had grown, and damn the shade, he said, these had to go, for the roots would sniff out the well bore, converge on it and choke it. And not a few of the mills were the old wooden tower Eclipse models with soft metal babbit bearings that needed weekly lubrication, for years the special dread of every cowboy on the ranch. These, Habakuk told Slike, should be replaced with steel-tower, back-geared rigs, which, with their working parts enclosed in a metal helmet, only needed fresh oil once in a blue moon. But Slike said they would have to make the Eclipses last and only when one wore out "tee-total-tot" would they think about replacing it.

At the end of his survey Habakuk told Slike there was enough work on the ranch to last ten windmillers fifty years and that he couldn't do all the work alone, especially if he had to replace the babbit bearings in the old Eclipses. He'd have to remove the big eigh-teen-foot wheel and two-hundred-pound head from each one, a two-man operation, melt the old babbit out of the head and pour in new. He had to have a helper or even two. Slike nodded and said he'd get him one—somebody. He had Rope Butt in mind but Rope, who was twenty-eight at the time and saw himself as a deep-dyed Texas cowhand, balked.

"I like Habakuk," he had said, "but not enough to be a mill jockey. I won't do it. I'd sooner quit than do it. Whyn't you pick that kid come in the gate last night?"

There had been a gangly kid looking for work, and Slike's impulse had been to send him home to his mama, and he had done so, telling him brusquely, in his hot, nasal voice, to hit the grit, but on second thought he might do for windmill work. Barely enough muscle on him to help Habakuk, but he'd develop. He was skinny but probably strong like most ranch kids.

"How old you think he is? He still around?"

"I'd say fifteen, sixteen. No, he ain't still around after you told him a pick up his hat. But I can guess where he's at, probly. Spose he went home again. He's at the Crouch place out past Coppedge's Twenty Mile. Kind of a solitary place. Big old stone house and a lot a weeds. There's him and some brothers and sisters."

"Well. Ride over there in the mornin and see can

you git him back on my side a the pen. What's his handle?"

Rope Butt said, "Name's Ace. Ace Crouch. He's a likeable kid."

"If he can fix windmills with Milkbeak he'll be plenty likeable to me."

It was around that time that Rope Butt had written his first cowboy poem, twelve lines that took four hours to compose. It was burned into his memory.

> Ridin' ol' buddy down the draw
> I seen a cow jaw
> but it had a flaw
> it was broke in two
> could fix it with a screw
> and some glue.
>
> That cow jaw made me think
> of my uncle Leon Sink
> he wore out four saddle in his life
> and four wife
> once he give me a pocket knife
> it cut like stink.

The next morning he rode down to the Crouch place. The kid, Ace, had been pleased and excited at the thought of going to work, and he did not seem disappointed that the job was windmill repair assistant under a man who twisted the language into Dutch pretzels. Rope could understand why. The Crouch place was run-down and lonesome, the grass over-grazed, the fences mended and mended again into knots and bobtail ends, the cows scrawny and yellow-backed with maggoty infection. There was a windmill near the house, an aged wooden tower that he bet had seen plenty of emergency repair. Though it worked, it screeched horribly from lack of grease and a dozen other ailments. Rope thought that an instructional course in windmill repair for a member of the family would be a boon to the Crouch ranch.

But while Ace was getting his things together, old Mr. Crouch, who had a face like a gizzard and showed in his every gesture and word that he came down hard on his sons, bargained over young Ace's labor, insisting that three-quarters of the boy's pay had to come home.

"I'm givin up the work he could be doin here. We need all the help we can git." He waved his hand vaguely. "Anyways, what does *he* need money for if he's got board and lodge? Just spoil him, y'know?"

Rope smothered the impulse to say that the kid might want a new shirt or a pair of pants that wasn't holed and patched, that he might appreciate boots that fit or even that he might want to put some money aside for a new saddle or a horse or a down payment on a house should he get married in a few years, and remarked instead that he guessed Mr. Crouch would have to ride over and speak to Slike about the kid's pay. The way it worked usually was that a hand drew his money and it was his, for he had done the work that earned it. Just then the kid came charging out onto the porch with his change of raggedy clothes and an ancient kack that looked as though it might have been used by the Spanish conquistadors when they passed through.

"Your dad needs a talk with Mr. Slike about the money arrangements, first," said Rope Butt, feeling sorry for the kid, who was clearly crazy to get gone from home that minute.

It was deep-sleep night, the bunkhouse rattled with snores and stinking of cowboy bean farts when Rope was awakened by the sound of the door sighing on its hinges, a few stumbling steps, something eased down to the floor—the squeak of leather indicated a saddle—and a tired sigh. Somebody had come in and was going to sleep on the floor. He couldn't think who it was—Habakuk van Melkebeek, the only one missing, was out in some pasture with his bedroll and chain tongs. Then a new thought came to him; the windmiller might have taken a fall and dragged himself in for medical attention.

"Habakuk?" Rope said softly, "that you?"

"It's me, Ace. Ace Crouch."

"God sake," said Rope, sitting up and fumbling for the light string.

The kid was a wreck, his nose swollen to twice its earlier size, his lip split, both eyes black and a gash in his forehead that would leave a white scar.

"Your dad do that?" said Rope.

The kid nodded. "He did, but I got the best of it. I got out a there and he ain't goin a bother me no more. Any money I earn, it's mine."

"Good," said Rope Butt. "You didn't kill him, did you?"

"I wanted to but don't think I did. I hit him on the head with the shovel and it made a sound like hittin a kettle and he fell down. He was cussin and half up again when I took off."

"Glad a hear that," said Rope Butt. "They come down hard on kids that send their daddies to the happy huntin grounds. I'll take you out to Habakuk in the mornin. He's out with one a them damn old windmills. You got a bedroll?"

"No," said the kid.

"You lousy? You got lice?"

"*No.* We was poor but we wasn't dirty."

"Well, now you're in a place where you will be poor *and* dirty. Long as you ain't lousy, you are welcome a take my old bedroll. I got a new one couple months ago. Never throw anything out. Old one's kind a thin but it's comin on good weather so you won't freeze. Payday, you'n go into Woolybucket and get you a new one and a tarp."

"Thanks," said the kid. And that was that.

In the morning Rope took him on out to the canyon pasture and they found van Melkebeek, attired as usual in clean striped overalls and ironed white shirt, wrestling with a stuck cylinder valve. How he managed to iron his shirts out on the prairie no one could figure, and there had been long bunkhouse discussions on the possibilities, ranging from helpful nearby widow women to an ironing board and sadiron among the windmill gear in the truck. Habakuk was glad to see young Ace, and said, as though the boy had been working with him for years, "Hallo, Ace. *Ik ben Habakuk van Melkebeek.* We do some work. I think you are *een goede werker, ja*? Lot of work in a windmill job, lot of digging. Big deep holes she don't fall over. Anyway, this well right here, she was never cased and now she got *een* hole in her water column. And so we pull it. Good you come."

"How the hell you keep so neat, Habakuk?" said Rope, looking at the white shirt. By God, he thought, it *does* look ironed. He looked around the camp, not trashy with discarded sardine tins and bottles like most, but rigorously tidy, not a scrap of junk in sight. A spare windmill vane, weighted down with stones, was laid out on two packing boxes to serve as a table. Habakuk's bedroll was stowed in the truck cab and he had dug a fire pit and lined it with stones. A bubbling coffee pot sat over the hot coals.

"Water. Always around water, so put soap and water in bucket, put dirty clothes in bucket, drive around, like a washing machine, get all clean. Easy. Dutch people like clean. *Waar of niet waar?*"

"You got a sadiron out here too?"

"*Ja,* sure. Shoe polish, razor. O.K., now, Mr. Ace,

we got work to do. I got a checklist for every mill, says what's wrong. We are fixing mills one by one." He looked at the kid. "Payday you buy a new skirt."

"Skirt?"

"*Ja,* skirt." And he plucked at his shirtsleeve.

"Shirt," said Ace. "Mr. Melkebeek, that's a *shirt.* Girls wear skirts." And he sketched an imaginary skirt around his knees and twirled. Rope Butt got the sudden good feeling that the kid had a disposition to make everybody his friend. It must have gone against the grain to whack his old daddy with a shovel.

Habakuk laughed. "Anyway, *een overhemd.* Shirt, skirt. You get what you like."

Habakuk's checklist was formidable, drawn from his early weeks of inspection, which included checking a tower's girts and braces, its bolts; examining the wheel from rivets to hub; noting helmet bullet holes; inspecting every part of the furling device, the vane and tailbone; cautiously testing the strength of the wood platform and looking underneath for wasp and bee nests. The oil collector, the gears, the pitmen arms, plugs and cotter pins called for close scrutiny. He was thorough.

He started young Ace out lashing blades in place with green rawhide strips.

"When they are dry *zo hard als staal.* Need a hacksaw to cut."

Young Ace learned neatness from Habakuk along with windmill repair. He was a quiet, solid kid who worked like an ant and as time went along his shoulders broadened and his muscle thickened with all the digging, climbing, hauling and lifting and Habakuk's savory cooking, for in addition to the clean white shirts and finicky insistence on windmill record keeping, Habakuk van Melkebeek had a taste for Indonesian curries and *sambals,* whose esoteric ingredients came to him in a large box each month. And always, at the end of every meal, he looked sternly at Ace and said, *"Wij zullen afwassen,"* and handed him a clean dishtowel.

While they did the dishes Habakuk lectured on windmills.

"Mr. Rancher does not like a high tower—he is afraid he has to climb up on it. But the higher the better. Turbulence near the ground, breaks up the windmill. If a mill is near a building it got to be high. Make it high. Never put a mill in a canyon. Bad downdrafts."

Two years after Ace Crouch started at the Cutaway Mr. Slike took on his younger brother, Tater, as a horse wrangler. At first Tater tried windmilling with Ace and Habakuk, but he was not impressed with the slender stream of water that issued from the pipe of a well they had sweated on for days.

"Hell, I can piss fastern that thing can throw out."

"But you can't do it for so long," said Habakuk and knew that Ace's brother would not make a windmill man. He sent him to Slike.

Ace and Tater didn't see much of each other except on weekends when it fell right that they went into town together. Ace had taken Tater to Murphy's Dance & Saloon Hall where, at age fourteen, Tater experienced for himself what he'd only seen bulls and cows perform. Habakuk van Melkebeek never went to town, preferring to wash and mend and iron his clothes, read his Dutch newspapers and add up long columns of figures.

Once, back at the bunkhouse, where he rarely slept, "How come you git so spruced up, Hab?" asked Ercel Dullet, shuffling cards like a dog scratching an itch. "You plannin on gettin married? I ain't seen you with no lady, so sure it must be a whore you got in mind, right?"

"Hell," said Hawk Cream, "he don't never go to the whorehouse, so how could he even meet one? Hab, what a you do to git relief? You just put a little wind-mill grease on it and jerk off?"

They laughed, but Habakuk laughed too, and said mildly, "I don't want no wife. I seen all I want about wifes."

It was not much fun to tease someone who laughed and stayed mild.

"Ace, we got to put a good concrete apron around the tanks," said Habakuk one day. "Cow hoofs can't wear down in this sandy dirt and they get too long. Mr. Slike is worried. They come for water, walk on

222

rough concrete, does their hoof good." So they spent months pouring concrete.

There had been a second helper for a few months, Glen Corngay, but he couldn't stand the intensity of work, he did not like curries, and he thought he knew a great deal about the world, windmills included. The end came in a freak accident.

The wind had been blowing for days, a sand-laden wind that hissed against the big steel windmills and dulled the paint on the truck, ground the glass of the windshield. There was sand in their bedrolls, sand in the food that crunched between the teeth and at the bottom of their coffee cups tiny lunettes of sand. They pulled up to a large steel mill Habakuk and Ace had put in the year before. The flow had been weak from the beginning and Habakuk wanted to see how much it was pumping. Corngay was the first out of the truck and he walked toward the mill.

"Corngay," said Habakuk softly, "do not touch the mill, wind blows too much sand on it. No good. Static electricity."

But Corngay, shooting him a scornful look as if to say he wasn't cowed by wind, sand or any metal tower, reached for the handle of the winch that worked the pull-out wire. His fingers never touched it. The electric charge built up in the mill by days of sand friction leaped the space and hurled him into the cactus.

Habakuk laughed immoderately. *"Hij heeft een*

klap van de moelen gehad. He's had a *klap* from the mill." To him each windmill had a distinct personality and it was clear that this one was ill-disposed toward the disrespectful.

But then they were one down, for when he could stand up again, Corngay quit, staggering across the landscape toward the dusty ranch road where he might catch a ride.

Although Habakuk never made a wrong move, Ace made quite a few and had his own accidents. He learned that the worst place to recover from a hangover is atop a windmill in blazing heat. But nothing happened as awful as the dismal end of a rancher miller on the ZZ Ranch up in Wireline on the Oklahoma border.

The rancher, Archie Frass, took shortcuts when he could. He had found some used pipe and jury-rigged a tower by sticking sections into wet concrete and welding cross-members for a base, spot-welding minimal points to hold the forty-foot tower together, not bothering to construct a proper base section, nor putting up guy wires nor checking to see if the tower was level. The pipe sections were hollow and Archie did not think to cap them. Rainwater gradually got in and, because of the concrete pad, the pipe legs could not drain. In the winter, hard freezes weakened and even burst some pipe sections. The tower developed a slight list to the southeast. After several years the windmill head wore out and had to be replaced. Frass and his unwilling son tried to haul up the new wind generator using a gin pole and pulley system, but neglected to run the gin cable to a pulley at the base of the tower, fastening it instead to Frass's truck with the son as driver, Frass on the tower as top man. As the cable came off the gin pole the son drove the truck forward and Frass, expecting the generator to rise up to him, shouted "Whoa!" in horrified amazement when the tower buckled, the rusted and weakened pipe legs folding. Frass, the windmill, the gin pole, the truck, the wind generator and the son all came together in a tangle of flesh and steel pipe red with blood.

"He done everything wrong," said Habakuk van Melkebeek with the satisfaction of a man who does everything right. "Comes to anchor your legs in concrete I'll show you a little trick. You got to be sure the tower is level before you fasten it down."

He went to the truck and got his coyote-shooting rifle. Ace, wondering, watched Habakuk rest the rifle on the truck hood and take aim at the tower, squinting through the scope.

"Your cross-strut got to line up with the horizontal crosshair, and the pump rod got to line up with the vertical. It's a quick way you can tell if the tower is level."

In 1938, after five years of working the Cutaway windmills, Habakuk made Ace Crouch a business proposition. They both sat on upturned fruit boxes drinking cocoa, Ace's specialty, for he made it with

double-condensed milk and white sugar and topped
each cup with a marshmallow. When the marshmallows became stale and stiff, Ace threw them into the
bunkhouse stove or the campfire, where they charred
into a graphite-colored mass like coal clinkers.

"Goed," said Habakuk, sucking the sweet froth off
the top. "Ace, I had ideas since I started working for
the Cutaway. Mr. Slike is a good man and I get along
with him O.K., but since I come on this ranch I want
my own business, not work for nobody. I thought
first I come to this country and I go back again, but I
change my mind. I like the panhandle. I like Texas
where it's flat. I like flat. Another thing, the water
table she sinks beneath us. I come here the wells
was twenty, thirty feet deep. Now we got to set pipe
deeper and some wells down to eighty, a hundred
feet. Windmill can't lift water that deep so we got to
put in a pump. Water table is dropping. Remember
that number forty-three in the north pasture? One
hundred twenty-two feet. I bet you we'll go deeper.
And it's all over the panhandle—now everybody has
to go way down for the water. My idea is get off the
Cutaway and make a business that does well-drilling,
puts up the mills and does repairs. Work for myself.
I save my money a long time now and I got enough
for a good drill rig."

It was true that Habakuk spent much time adding
columns on the backs of envelopes, figuring, scratching out the numbers, writing new ones down. Though
he had left school, he said, when he was eight years

old, he was a dab hand at adding and subtracting. Of decimals and fractions he knew little and did not care, for who needed them? Accumulation and loss were the great math processes.

"I like you be my partner. We be van Melkebeek and Crouch. We make a lot more money that way. Pretty soon I have my own ranch. Or maybe you want to stay here and Mr. Slike will give you my job, seventy-five a month. What you think? Stay with Slike or come with me? You come with me, you won't be sorry."

Ace Crouch said yes to Habakuk because he couldn't imagine himself staying on the Cutaway alone, wrestling with the windmills by himself or with some reluctant cowboy for a helper. The idea of an economic adventure pulled at him. How about that, in just a few years he had come from drinking root coffee out of a tin can and dodging the old man's fists to being a young businessman with a partner; he was advancing.

At the same time cowboy Rope Butt felt he was in retreat. Nothing went well. The range was chopped up into barbwire rectangles and farmers were taking over ranch land, plowing pasture. He disliked the food they served him at one ranch or the other, he hated the bad horses that came his way, he took no joy in frolic. Only drink, betting on horses and fighting cocks, and his poetry interested him. He had two ex-wives in different counties, several children by each. All he could do was quit and move to another outfit, work a while, quit again and move on.

And now, a lifetime later, driving along the highway and looking back through the deep channel of time past, he was amazed all over again by his own bad luck and Habakuk van Melkebeek's good fortune. What or who decided where gold would shower and where cactus thorns would pierce? Sixty years later he still could not understand why the Dutchman had fallen into the land of plenty while he, Rope Butt, had nothing but a few roosters and arthritis.

Then, as he had known it would, a closing line for his poem came to him: *"Time that he went up the spout."*

13

HABAKUK'S LUCK

Habakuk and Ace had more work than they could handle and eventually hired and trained two field crews. They were all over the Texas and Oklahoma panhandles and into New Mexico. More and more Habakuk handled the paperwork at the office in Woolybucket while Ace worked with both crews in every sandy, cactus-studded pasture for a hundred miles around, sleeping on the ground or the front seat of the truck, stirring up rattlers, half-frozen in the icy northers that roared down, packing up when lightning threatened, for millers died on steel towers. Habakuk resisted putting up wooden towers even when ranchers claimed wood was their dearest wish, for a wooden tower was slow, heavy work and they rotted out and threw off splinters like a sapwood fire throws sparks.

Two events shifted local opinion toward steel towers. An itinerant windmiller, Daisy Boy Pocock, tried to increase his business by setting wooden towers afire. Then a plague of grasshoppers in whirring, rustling flight settled on two old wood mills on the Seven Range and ate them to beanpoles.

Increasingly the work was with deep wells and gasoline pumps. Still, money came in and by 1939 Habakuk, who was of a saving disposition, had salted enough away to buy land for his dream ranch. He knew the panhandle intimately, knew every ranch pinched by hard times and drought. One morning, when Ace was in town to pick up pipe, he stuck his head into the warehouse and called to him, *"Kom binnen."*

Ace came into the office where every paper was neatly aligned, the windowsills sandless and gleaming. Habakuk was fussing with a coffee pot on the hotplate. *"Wil je koffie of iets sterkers?* I've got some gin. If you like."

"Coffee for me. I can't drink in the mornin. You know it's no good go up on a mill half-lit."

But Habakuk could and he chased his black coffee with a small tumbler of neat gin, said *"Ahh!"* with a sound like a steam engine.

"So, the Wilcox job O.K.? We had trouble with him last year. The gate."

"Yeah. The gates was locked, all five a them. I went up the house and he weren't around, nobody around but the missus. She said, 'Do what you have to do, them cows need water.' So we cut the locks."

"Ja, cut the locks, but when you finish the job weld the gates shut. That one, Wilcox, never paid us for the work last year."

"Jesus," said Ace, picturing the Wilcox place with its shambles of low buildings and rutted approach, the broiling sun that heated truck fenders like frying pans. "That's a little harsh, weld a man's gates. Could be he don't have no money. I hear their place is for sale. Anyway, when I was out there it was hot enough to loosen the bristles on a wild hog and Mrs. Wilcox give me a glass a cold buttermilk. Best thing I ever drank. So I don't want a give them trouble."

"He gets a good lesson," said Habakuk complacently. "And he asks too much for that place. I been looking at land. For my ranch. Good time to buy land. Plenty of land for sale. I will get Roughbug land cheap enough, I think," he remarked to Ace. "I ask down the land record office and they say whole town belongs to one family, only one left of a broke syndicate in Ohio. They had the land since 1885, failed in the cattle business after a hard winter. I wrote the people a letter saying 'how much?' Waiting to hear. So, you go back to Wilcox, fix his cows with water. Fix his gates with welding."

But when Ace went out he decided to make a last try for the key and pulled up at the Wilcox shack. Before he could climb the porch steps he heard a yoo-hoo from above and there, on the platform of the mill that pumped the house water, sat Mrs. Wilcox, knitting something blue. He couldn't imagine how she had climbed up the bent re-rod angles that served the mill instead of a ladder. It was a sorry mill, the ash sucker rod lashed onto what looked like an old bed rail.

"What are you doin up there, Mrs. Wilcox?"

"Why, I heard a terrible growlin a while back, some

wild animal, I don't know what, black panther or worse, sounded like it was in the house, so I come up here where it couldn't git me. Wait until Mr. Wilcox gits home and he can shoot it."

"You want me to look in the house?"

"Thank you kindly, Ace. I would sure appreciate it. And take your gun. It might be in the back room. The door is open because I was airin it out."

He expected to find nothing, but there was a large and irritable badger with a mousetrap on one toe backed into a corner and ripping at the wallpaper. He prodded it outside and shot it, brought it to the windmill for her to see.

She started down with her knitting bag slung around her neck, breathless and sunburned. He stood below, looking up her dress, seeing her pale legs, her pink rayon panties descend.

"You deserve a reward," said Mrs. Wilcox. "Would you rather have a glass a buttermilk or go in the bedroom?"

"Both," said Ace, who took his rewards where he found them.

A letter came to Habakuk from a lawyer in Chillicothe representing the interests of Mrs. Gladys Armenonville. Mrs. Armenonville, he wrote, would let Habakuk van Melkebeek have the 17,000 acres that made up her Roughbug holdings at fifty cents an acre, cash in hand only. Habakuk caught the train to Ohio the next morning and clinched the deal.

He named the ranch Kampen after his old home-town, and, in a play on words, registered a triangular tent shape for the brand.

"See?" he said. "'Kampen' out in the tent." He dragged two abandoned houses from the outskirts of Woolybucket to his land and, after renovation and many coats of paint (renewed twice a year, as the wind scoured paint away nearly as fast as it went on), referred to one as headquarters and the other as a *slaapverblijs*. He hired five luckless cowboys who, though glad to have the paycheck, disliked being called *boerenknechten* and made to stand clean-shirt inspection every morning. He put them to work con-structing stock tanks at each tower site. There were no cows, for water came first. The cowboys learned that they would help drill wells, and, with the field crew, put up windmills over the next months, ten of them, all steel, all the best mills. When they protested that they were not mill monkeys Habakuk glared at them and said, "You will do this or you are unemployed." Only one man walked, but Habakuk no longer trusted those who stayed, for they were afraid of heights, their claims to be tough hands hollow when it came to high platforms and slippery steel ladders. He replaced the deserter with a good fencing man, for there was barbwire to be strung, miles of it.

But worse was to come in his labor relations with ranch hands. Habakuk's cousin, Martin Eeckhout, and his wife, Margriet, came from Java for a visit, bringing boxes and hampers of viands and schnapps, curry powder, mango chutney, Bombay duck, coconuts and bananas, almonds and rice and a hundred other necessaries to make a twenty-boy *rijstafel*. Margriet would do the cooking, but what of the serving, the line of boys in sarongs with fragrant platters on their heads?

"The *boerenknechten*," said Habakuk.

And so the feast was served by furious cowboys defiantly dressed in chaps and spurred boots, cowboys who stuck their grimy thumbs into the prairie chicken curry, who scowled and made retching sounds as they shoved the serving dishes (washbasins purchased hastily from Steddy's store in Woolybucket) in front of the diners. Ace Crouch, who had eaten Habakuk's fare now for several years, tucked in with relish, heaping his plate with rice and then adorning it with curry and spoonfuls of side dishes. One of the cowboys said audibly that he would as lief eat skunk turds.

"Possible a certain *boerenknecht* will be looking for the new job tomorrow," said Habakuk darkly. There were muttered threats and insults when the servers learned that their own supper was to consist of the leftovers. And yet all the food was eaten, the chutney jar interiors wiped clean by cowboy fingers, and no one quit. The feast passed into local legend as "damn good Dutch pepper-belly grub." A few days later Margriet Eeckhout made ranch culinary history with a *sambal* so cruel it swelled the diners' lips. The regular cook sidled up to her and, in a low voice, asked for the recipe, which she wrote out in a spidery European hand, promising to send him certain fiery chiles. Within a few months tins of curry powder and jars of mango chutney appeared on the shelf behind the counter at Steddy's store and several ranch cooks made it their business to use both liberally, the beginnings of the famed Woolybucket curry chile, always served at the Barbwire Festival, the recipe jealously guarded.

Windmill work on Habakuk's ranch began on a calm but cloudy morning following a sunrise like molten slag. Ace and one of the field teams arrived with the drill rig, a powerful old Model A Ford truck that could and did go anywhere and a rotary drill that gnawed its way downward. Van Melkebeek and Crouch had a second drill which they used in sandy soils, a jet type with weights that slammed down repeatedly on a T atop the pipe, driving the pipe into the ground. Inside this pipe was a smaller-diameter pipe and down it they forced water under pressure, pushing out the detritus sand and gravel which floated up to ground level. But while some of Habakuk's ranch lay on sandy soil, many of the proposed wells were aimed at water beneath limestone and shale. As he finished each well Ace topped the pipe with a large rock that served both as a marker and a cover, moved on to the next site. They would put up the towers after the wells were drilled. Three of the more shallow well locations would take thirty-foot towers and relatively small-diameter windmills, but there were deep wells and big towers in the more remote pastures.

The work went smoothly enough until the seventh well. The site was dry, level ground. It was to be an unusually deep pump well, perhaps two or even three hundred feet. On the fourth day of drilling a twenty-minute rush of gas, followed by stuttering gouts of oil, erupted. Ace watched the oil come out for an hour and a half and, when there was no decrease—indeed, an increase—in the amount of flow, jumped in the truck and raced for the house where Habakuk was nailing on shingles.

"Habakuk. Your number seven's spoutin awl. You better get a awlman out here. It looks interestin. And I don't think cows can drink it."

Habakuk van Melkebeek drove out to number seven and looked at it. He was more than a little annoyed, for he wanted to start his new life as a rancher.

"We let it run tonight. I look in the morning and see. We don't need oilmen here. She runs in the morning we drill somewhere else."

"But Habakuk, awl is worth money."

"We'll see."

Before daylight Habakuk awoke to a curious sound, the roar of many truck and car engines laboring down his sandy road. He got up and peered out the window. A string of headlights jounced and winked as the

vehicles came along the rough road. Some, headlights pitching wildly, showed that their drivers had
forsaken the road and were coming across the open
prairie. He counted seventeen sets of headlights.
Habakuk got into his pants and shoes, went downstairs, rustled the stove into life and put on coffee.
Then he went out on the porch to drink his coffee and
smoke his morning cigar and wait for the first vehicle
to come up. The eastern sky paled.

The car stopped at the bottom step of the porch and
a medium-size man got out. He saw the glow of
Habakuk's cigar and spoke.

"Howdy do, sir. H. H. Potts, lease man for Condor
Awl out a Oklahoma City. I hear you got a water
well that's spittin awl."

"That was last afternoon. Maybe it stopped now."

"Why I'm here, take a look at the situation, let the
geologists and formation testers see what they think."
He waved his hand at the headlights now filling up the
yard. "Soon's we git a little light from old Sol we'll
have us a look. Funny, comin out here. So dark. Most
a the panhandle's lit up pretty good with gas flares.
But it's dark out here. We'll fix that, maybe, eh?"

Habakuk disliked this man, saw he had his sleeves
full of tricks. The fellow was on the porch now, rocking on his heels.

"Wouldn't have another cup a that coffee, would
you?" said H. H. Potts. "I left Oklahoma City in the
middle of the night, only had a hamburger and a bottle a pop."

"No," said Habakuk flatly.

In the silence that followed something shifted subtly, but in a beat or two, as the yard filled with yawning and stretching men and the sky turned the color of watermelon juice, H. H. Potts said in a flat voice, "Well, then, let's just go take a look. If there's awl we can make you a lease offer."

Habakuk insisted on leading the caravan out to the site himself. He did not want to ride with H. H. Potts. And someone had to show the way. The well was nearly two miles from the porch, almost in the dead center of his property. The jolting headlights in his rearview mirror irked him. He had a suspicion that the peace and contemplative quiet of Kampen Ranch was being profoundly disturbed. How had this man away up in Oklahoma City found out about the oil? Why did they need all those geologists? If there was oil, there was oil. No need to guess and estimate something visible. As he went through the last gate, which Ace had left open for there were yet no livestock on the range, he could see the black silhouette of the drill rig against the pink sky and closer, the satin sheen of a lake of oil on the ground reflecting the dawn. He stopped at the edge of the oil and got out. Behind him H. H. Potts pulled up. They could both hear the escaping gas hissing through the oil.

"My God, it stinks," said Habakuk.

"That's a money stink," said the lease man. "It's a flowin well, all right. By God, it's pretty far east a be part a the Amarilla Arch, but what else could it be? You sure enough got you a shallow discovery well. How deep did you drill?"

"I don't know. It was my partner. We figured maybe two, three hundred feet, so maybe around there. I don't know. He didn't tell me. Four, five days' work?"

"That's awful shallow. Your panhandle wells is usually around three thousand feet. Cable tool drill takes sixty to ninety days to git it. This could be just some little maverick shallow pocket. I reckon we ought a talk business. Who knows what's down there?"

"What do I need you for?" said Habakuk. "I do everything myself my whole life. I got an oil well here already been drilled. I don't need you."

The geologists were twittering like birds behind them.

"Mr. Milkbeak," said H. H. Potts. "You got you a little shallow awl well but no field tanks to keep the awl in, no way to git the awl from the well to the tanks you don't got, no gatherin lines to connect to the trunk pipeline, you got nobody a buy your awl, you got no casin in that well and for all you know, it could be cavy and slump in. And what will you do when she goes into the decline curve when she'll have to go on the pump? You don't know the awl-gas ratio neither, and you don't know the formation pressure. It takes thousands and hunderds a thousands a dollars to set up a awl field. You got no idea the size a this awl field. There's surely more to it than one little pissy well. The Texas Railroad Commission has to

239

come out here and take their data so it can be pro-rated. You can't have a well just spittin out awl on the ground like you got here. Awl is a complicated and expensive business, sir, and a cooperative one."

Habakuk slumped. Potts was right, he knew noth-ing. He was no oilman. He would have to go along with this fellow whom he disliked. But he would not be fleeced.

"How much?" he said.

"Well, sir, the lease could be for five or ten years and as for long thereafter as awl or gas in commercial quantities is produced. You, as the landowner, git a royalty. Condor Awl bears the full expense a drillin and settin up the wells, they build the tanks, put in the pumps, lay the pipe and—"

"How much?"

"The standard royalty in the awl business is one-eighth."

"But the land is mine. All the oil under the land is mine too!"

"But the company bears the considerable expense a construction and maintenance. Awl under the land is not the same as awl in a pipeline."

"I don't care. One-eighth is not enough. I want a tenth!" Ha, he thought, at the look of stupefaction on H. H. Potts's face, he can't get around *me*. He took the strange play of expressions across the man's fea-tures as his realization that he had been bested, and, when Potts said, "Mr. Milkbeak, I guess I'll have to give in to you. We'd better go up to the house and work through the contract before you change your mind and ask for one-twentieth." Habakuk smiled broadly.

Two hours later the man departed, still without coffee, after scratching out all references to "one-eighth (1/8)" and substituting "one-tenth (1/10)" and having Habakuk initial each change in the margin on the six-page printed lease form. Habakuk's signature was on the dotted line.

By noon a team of men were fitting pipe over the head and installing a pump to move the oil. A crew of pipeline men were laying pipe. A begrimed man with a mule team and a fresno were shaping an earthen tank.

Around noon Ace pulled up at the house.

"Hear you had a lot a traffic out here this mornin. How'd you make out?"

"My God, it was something. Seventeen cars. The geologists are still out there. It is an oil well. There was this fellow from Condor Oil, said he come from Oklahoma City. I didn't like him but a man not in the oil business can't do it alone. I signed the oil and gas lease for ten years, but I got the best of the bargain."

"Did you?"

"Oh yes! He was only going to give me one-eighth royalties but I said I wanted one-tenth and after a while he gave in."

"Habakuk, he offered you one-eighth royalties and you held out for one-tenth?"

"That's right."

Habakuk was disconcerted to see the same curious expression on Ace's face that he had seen on Potts's. "Why? What's wrong with that?"

"Habakuk, important you come to town with me *right now*. I mean it. Save you a lot a grief in comin years."

And so they went into Woolybucket, Ace driving. He pulled up in front of the Good Time bakery, went in and came out a few minutes later with two boxes. They drove out of town, pulled off at a roadside picnic table, Ace saying not a word, ignoring Habakuk's querulous demands for an explanation, for he had begun to suspect that something was wrong, though he could not pin down what it was.

At the picnic table Ace opened the boxes disclosing two pies, one apple, one cherry. He put the cherry pie in front of Habakuk, the apple on his side of the table, and took out his horn-handled jackknife.

"Watch," he said. He cut the apple pie into eighths and handed his knife to Habakuk. "Now, you cut that there cherry pie into tenths and we'll see who got the biggest pieces."

As he cut Habakuk learned the vital difference between fractions and percentages. His rage at having outwitted himself was awesome and he stamped and swore terrible Dutch oaths while Ace looked on, shook his head and ate pie, one slice after another, favoring the eighths.

"Just the same, I fool myself this time but never

another. I am through with the cattle business. Now I am a oilman. You wait. I beat them at their own game."

"Better get up pretty early in the mornin then. Awl people is smart."

But Habakuk put his mind to it, discovered that beneath the flat panhandle lay a buried granite mountain range, the Amarillo Mountains, staggeringly rich in oil, natural gas and helium, the site of a great strike in 1916. He devoured books on oil, buttonholed oilmen, followed crews and dogged lease men and invested the money from his one-tenth Condor share in a dozen oil ventures. By the end of World War II Kampen Oil was a small but powerful corporate entity.

Five years later Habakuk visited his cousin in Java and, his eye sharpened for oil, he bought promising land, a few years later leased it to Shell–Royal Dutch, which pumped more than two million barrels a year from the field. He was in Kuwait and Qatar, he had interests in Venezuela. In 1961 Kampen Oil seized Condor in a hostile takeover. By then H. H. Potts was long underground, but Habakuk van Melkebeek went to the Oklahoma City Freewill Baptist Cemetery and found the gravestone.

"You are fired," he said to the basket of faded wax lilies.

14

THE YOUNG COUPLE

The Cutaway missed Habakuk van Melkebeek and Ace Crouch badly. Instead of assigning a pair of cowboys to the job Slike contracted out to the new partners for mill maintenance.

"Hell, they know the Cutaway mills inside out. In the long run it's cheaper," he explained to the owner. For Habbakuk and Ace it was steady income during the hard years.

Ace was twenty-two, strong and quick, not unattractive in a rough way, though his eyes were too close together and his limp brown hair hung over his eyes. But he was tall and strong, the bony shoulders wide, his chest deep with muscle, and he was quick to smile. He started going to the Saturday night dances in Cowboy Rose, but rarely drank, the memory of his terrible hangover day on the windmill still strong in memory. He stopped at a single beer and, while other young men hung around the trucks drinking and guffawing, fighting like beetles with clumsy swipes at each other, rearing and pawing, falling onto their backs and kicking up again, he danced. He danced rags, polkas, swing, breakdowns and two-steps until

244

he knew every girl, every dance call, every fiddler for miles around. It was the height of Texas swing and on Saturday nights he'd drive to barns, dance halls and honky-tonks a hundred miles distant to hear Billy Briggs and his XIT Boys, Rip Ramsey and the Texas Wanderers, the Lone Star Playboys, Dub Adams and the K-Bar Ranch Hands. There were great bands in those years, Shorty Bates and his Texas Saddle Pals. He often slept in the car, ears ringing with the thump of "Rattle Snake Daddy" and "Motel Blues."

One night he met Valentine Eckenstein—Vollie— the full-breasted middle daughter of a German wheat farmer in Twospot. She worked at the government relief office food distribution center, packing boxes with staple goods for families on relief, but her pleasure, as his, was the weekly dances. She was a pushover for the musicians on the stage of the dance hall, standing at the edge and gazing raptly at them, singing, "Old Tascosa and CanAYdiun, dah-da-dah-da-dah."

She was not pretty, but there was a freshness to her strong-boned face with its shapely mouth, and hazel eyes accentuated by straight thin brows. Beyond this her features were symmetrical, perfectly balanced, which gave her a kind of lasting beauty. That physical symmetry was enough for Ace, indoctrinated by a windmiller's predisposition for balance. Vollie's hair was thick and curly, and the color of butterscotch; she mashed its wildness under a beret. She was strong, with a good-natured laugh. She had a sense of humor and saw the jokes of life. After two months of "Banjo Boogie" and "Holes in My Soles," Ace went out to the farm to meet her parents.

Old man Eckenstein was not, as he had feared, the truculent and aggressive German father who believed his every sentence was meant for a stone tablet; he was one of those men who could throw peanuts into the air and catch them in his mouth. Here was the source of Vollie's dazzling smile. The old man greeted Ace with a kind of jovial relief. Vollie's mother, an example of the faded brightness of middle-aged farmwives, wore wire-rimmed glasses whose lenses often fell out, causing a huge uproar until the missing glass was found and replaced, gave Ace questioning looks. He wanted to ask her what was wrong, but some instinct held him back.

The family liked ice cream and on Sunday afternoons they sliced fruit, or took a jar of strawberries from the root cellar, mixing the sweet preserves into the cream and sugar, packing in the salt and taking turns cranking the ice-cream maker. Ace gained four pounds courting Vollie.

Ace got on well with the other daughters: Maxine, the oldest, dressed always in georgette frocks and high-heeled pumps to fit her position as second assistant town clerk; Honey, rather fat and with silken braids, who was a champion breadmaker; and Hilda, the youngest, homely with blond eyelashes and pinched mouth, who wanted badly to be an aviatrix and badgered old Eckenstein to let her learn to fly with Rupert Bayliss Rigg, a Charlie-at-the-wheel crop duster. There was a toddler in the family as well, Little Emily, with straight black hair and a peevish elf's face. Bob gathered vaguely that Mrs. Eckenstein was taking care of the child for someone. It was only after he and Vollie were married in the tiny stone Lutheran church in Twospot in 1936 that she told him her sister Maxine was the baby's mother, the baby an unplanned accident.

In September of 1939 war broke out in Europe. Ace thought it inevitable that the United States would get into it. Habakuk said that steel windmill parts would be hard to get if that happened and they began stockpiling gears, trusses, heads, blades in the big warehouse. Roosevelt changed the date for Thanksgiving to the fourth Thursday in the month, persuaded that more shopping days for Christmas would improve the economy. In stores one could see the new flickering light tubes filled with neon gas, said to be more efficient and cheaper to run than lightbulbs. King-size cigarettes and cup sizes for brassieres made news. The world was rushing along. There was more work for van Melkebeek and Crouch, deep wells and big pumps as the panhandle began to expand into something called the "Golden Spread." The talk was all of irrigation and increased crop production and sometimes a single field would have eight or ten windmills pumping water into tanks that fed irrigation ditches, and still it wasn't enough.

"They say there's big water down below, deep down. Deeper than any little old windmill can pump," Ace said to Habakuk.

"Well, that's where it's going to stay until they get better pumps than we got now."

Ace and Vollie lived in the old bunkhouse on the Eckenstein place, and it was a red-letter day when Ace ran a telephone wire from the main house to the bunkhouse.

Ace called her one day. "I'm out at the Wrink place," he said. "Ah, I need you to go to Amarilla, to our supply shop and pick up a rod-type O'Bannon cylinder. Habakuk's not there but José will have it waitin for you. I just talked a him. He'll put it in the back a the car. I need you to bring it on out. There's nobody at the shop can do it. José don't drive and nothin to drive if he did. The rest a them's all out in the field. So bring out the damn thing out to me," he said. "County Road J and turn north on Wrink Road. Watch the tracks, the wheel tracks. You go through Wrink Crik. Shouldn't have a bit a trouble, just gun it and keep going, good hard gravel bottom. The water's only about fourteen inches deep. Turn off at the sign for Wrink Ranch. There's a cattleguard and just past it a kind a wet place, big clump a willers and just past the willers a dead cow in the goddamn ditch and you head out left. About half a mile and there's a gate. It's kind a hard to open so I'll git somebody a keep a watch for you and open the gate. Now I don't

248

want you to drive dangerous, but we need that damn cylinder soon as you can git it here."

The trip into Amarillo and then the drive to the Wrink place took two hours, but Vollie was glad to get out of the cramped little bunkhouse and away from the washing machine with its churning scum of windmill grease.

She pulled up at the gate. It was made of barbwire strands stapled to a post that was firmly held by fixed wire loops at bottom and top. It was the tightest, most difficult gate in the county, and the maker clearly had taken great pride in making a gate that only one man in a hundred could open with anything approaching ease. She could not budge the wire and even prying up on the top loop with a heavy screwdriver from the tool jam on the passenger floor did not move it. There was no one in sight to help get the damn thing loose. She heaved on the post and it gave a thousandth of an inch. She got a crowbar from the truck and began to pry at the wire loop. It was so taut it made a fine singing hum every time the crowbar moved.

Then she saw the rider coming toward her through the grass. Disheveled and panting, her fingers red and grooved by the wire, she waited for him.

As he came near she could see the sweat patches on his blue shirt, the wet fabric almost black. He stopped at the gate, dismounted, letting the reins trail. He seized the post, pulled it toward the main gate upright, jamming the loop up over the post with the heel of his hand, though it took three or four punches. The gate, tension released, collapsed into limp strands. He smiled at her.

She looked at him and there was light on the water. The sky flared up in black leaps and she stepped an involuntary step toward him. He was the most beautiful human she had ever seen, the right one for her. Heavy shoulders and arms inside the plaid shirt, the square masculine face, four-day growth of reddish bristles catching the light, narrow eyes, squinted enough not to disclose the color, hidden by dark lashes. His thick, dark red hair stuck out carelessly from under a cap. He was dirty and pouring sweat, the shirt showing a few dry patches at the shoulders, the rare face red and sweat runnels down the cheeks and jaw and into the wet hollow of his throat. He gave her that easy quick smile, drew back the gate so she could drive through, his sleeves rolled up and showing heavily muscled forearms, hairy.

"It's a tight one," he said.

She wanted badly to touch the wet throat hollow, wanted badly to say, "Wait, it's all been a mistake, I didn't know you were coming, please touch me, please look at me." Her blood was filled with slivers of fine steel all forcing against the inside of her skin, aligned to his pull. She stepped helplessly toward him as though to help with the gate, but he was dragging it back, turning from her and she saw his perfect body, balanced, a tall man, the dirty jeans full of the

fine legs and buttocks. He held the gate back and
there was nothing for her to do but get in the car and
drive through. She came abreast of him. Now he was
working a fence tool into the back of the top wire
loop, reworking it into a wider loop. The sweaty hollow of his throat showed a line of dirt at the bottom
curve, as fine as a hair.

"I thank you—" Her eyes were stinging, smoke
burning, nothing to do with the gate.

"Bet you can git it open now," he said.

"You must have built this gate," she said. He did not
answer and she drove across the dirt-colored grass
toward the windmill rig, barely steering, watching
him in the rearview mirror jerking at something on
the gate, one elbow moving back and forth, then saw
him go to the horse, remount, take off his hat and
draw his hand over his face.

In the evening, sitting with Ace on the top step of the
trailer house, sharing a bottle of beer, she said, "That
guy opened the gate for me, who is he?"

"Oh, Ruby? Ruby Loving. He sings at the Spearman dances sometimes. He works for the ranch, just
a hand, but the situation changed some recently. He
got married two weeks ago. Married the rancher's
daughter."

The pain of that disclosure made her gasp, and she
disguised the gasp with a swig of beer. A venomous
hate for the unknown rancher's daughter poured
through her.

"Hasn't made no difference so far because he's still buildin fence, but I imagine it will. I imagine he'll get his hands on the ranch one day. Why, he wasn't sulled up or nothin about openin the gate, was he?"

"No. No. He was nice. He was *nice*. But he never said his name, so I wondered."

"Ruby. Ruby Loving."

Well, that was the perfect name. She couldn't think of anyone better made for loving.

"What is the rancher's daughter's name?"

"Honey, *I* don't know. Her last name has to be Lilian. Her father's name is John Lilian. He owns the Wrink place. But I don't know what her first name is."

She found out in a day or two. Of course it was Lillian—Lillian Lilian—and of course they called her Little Lilly. She was a barefoot five feet tall and with kinky orange hair and flat-chested. Thank God.

She did not see him again until late in the month. Ace was almost done with the Wrink windmills. The May day was sultry and packed with dirt blown by a fitful hot wind. She heard a truck in the yard and went onto the porch. The interior of the truck was shadowy and at first she couldn't make out his face, didn't recognize the truck. He got out and the moment she saw him come around the front of the truck her stomach turned over. Light on the water, the black current catching her. She went down the steps, stood facing him on the shady side of the truck.

"Hey. Mrs. Ace," he said. "Ace wants me a tell you that he had a go in to Amarilla and that he will be late gettin back, you are not to worry."

"Well, what on earth for? Go to Amarilla?"

"Two more wells. Boss wants a see two more wells long as he's got Ace on the ground." He leaned against the truck, crossed his heavy arms across his chest, crossed his right ankle over the left. He was wearing a baseball cap and was not as sweaty as the last time, though the hollow of that fine throat, red throat, almost turkey-skinned, was glistening and there were half-moons of wet under his arms. He was chewing gum. She could smell its sweet winter-green flavor, see the flash of pink between his large white teeth. The blue work shirt was half-unbuttoned. There was a streak of dried blood on the back of one hand. He was talking about something, the weather, she guessed, but he pulled her attention so hard she couldn't focus on anything like talk, staring was all she wanted, all she could handle, from the scuffed toes of his cowboy boots up the dirty line of packed jeans to the narrow waist and heavy studded belt, the triangle of waist to shoulder, the hot bare skin and dark hair, the stubbled jaws moving, chewing with wet and juicy speed while he talked, pointed at the clouds in the southwest with his chin, looking at the pure white masses swelling upward and saying something about keeping an eye on them.

She did it without thinking. An animal urgency seized her in its jaws for a few minutes, shook her wits loose. She stepped forward and lightly pressed the palm of her hot hand into his inner thigh, against the long shape of his sex. He stopped talking but did not move except to turn his eyes from the cloud to her eyes. His face was expressionless. He continued to chew the gum but very slowly, his eyes steady on hers. They were fixed in a tableau, he leaning against the truck, arms folded, legs crossed, the mound of his sex prominent, she, facing him, looking at him, with her hand in his groin. She could feel him hardening and lengthening under her hand. Whatever she expected it was not what followed.

"Hot," he said in a conversational tone. "Sweaty."

But sweat was what she liked about him, and the smell, strong, stinky, salty, tobacco, horse, dirty hair. Ace often came home hot and dirty but he put out a more acrid body odor, smells of chain and metal, grease and brackish water. Ruby Loving was different.

Then he winked, stepped back, got in his truck and drove off.

Three months later she saw him again. She was in Borger with Ace, shopping, and there he was, wearing a new black felt hat with a braided leather band, coming out of a bar with another cowboy. Instantly her body flushed with electric shock, heat followed by slow somnolence. She watched the man with him turn into a barbershop. Ruby stepped along until he came to the pharmacy. A few minutes later he was back on the street holding a blue sack, the kind the druggist used for prescriptions. She wondered what he had bought—if he was sick or had a headache, or if the bag contained something intimate like rubbers. He walked down the street toward her. She looked hard at him, opened her mouth to say something when their eyes met, but he did not notice her and walked quickly past.

She was sitting in the car when Ace came out of the hardware store.

"What a you say, let's eat at Greune's roadhouse, have some a that chile."

"All right."

And there he was again, hat pushed back like Casey Tibbs, sitting at the counter drinking ice water and waiting for his food, a plate of chicken-fried steak with white gravy.

"Hey Ruby," said Ace. "How's it goin?"

"Ace! Goin good. Pretty much."

"Member my wife, Vollie? Opened the gate for her when we was puttin in the mills at your father-in-law's place?"

"How do," he said, raising his hand and index finger as though they had never met, a denial of her bold hand that hot day months earlier.

"Come on over and eat with us," said Ace, shifting his chair. "You still singin?"

"Yeah. There's a new group started up, the Texas Coffee Cowboys. Some a the old Line Rider boys from Dalhart."

He brought his plate, the ice water, a cup of coffee, spilling the coffee and slopping gravy. He was there. She thought she would faint sitting across from him, unable to eat, watching his red hands, warts on the fingers, dent the white bread, mop it through the gravy. He hardly looked at her, talking to Ace about water and mills. At the end Ace said, "Hear you guys are startin a family, that right?"

"Well, looks like it. Bound a happen, I spose."

It was years before she pulled out of the feeling, scared, maybe love, or whatever it was for him. If she took a plum from a tree after fog or rain, beaded with droplets moisture, she thought of him, thought of that hot sweaty Texas time.

In 1942 Ace and Vollie's only child, Phyllis, was born, a handful from the start, a wild, headstrong girl with a heart-shaped face and a tiny, squeaky voice. By the time she was six she could sing all the words to four songs—"You Are My Sunshine," "Barbecue Bob," "The Panhandle Shuffle," "Smoke! Smoke! Smoke! (That Cigarette)." Every Saturday night after supper Vollie made a big bowl of popcorn and they listened to *The Hit Parade* in the dark, in summer out on the porch, in winter in the parents' bedroom, lying on their big bed, Ace warning Phyllis to watch out for stray popcorn, complaining that he was tired of getting up in the morning with hull dents all over his body. On the porch Ace and Vollie, drawn back in memory to the weekend dance halls, would sometimes get up and dance a little on the creaking boards, sun-dried and warped, while Phyllis would hang on to their legs and dance with them, singing the lyrics she knew.

"I guess you are goin a be a singer when you grow up," said Ace.

"Yep. And you can come with me and lift me up on the stage," said Phyllis.

"Why, I'd be proud a do that," said Ace, but when she was seventeen Phyllis ran off to Tulsa, hoping to get a job singing with some band or other.

Phyllis, nineteen years old and sitting on the edge of a thin mattress, face white as lard, trembling hands, suffering from a near-fatal hangover. The man hauled his jeans up, fastened an ornate buckle, having a little trouble with it as the catch was bent.

"You seein me at my worst," she said.

"Doubt it." He had some experience of women at their worst. He reached under the sheet, felt for something.

"Listen. I got a ask you something. Did you—"

"Naw. You was too drunk. Be like fuckin a corpse." He was pulling his boots on over bare feet. He took a comb from his shirt pocket, ran it through his tangled hair, took his hat off the lampshade, put it gently on his head, tilted it over his eyes.

"You did. It's wet down there."

"Naw." He limped to the door, took up the guitar

case that leaned against the dead heater. "See you."

The door closed softly and she heard him going down the wooden stairs. She got up, head banging with old drink, looked down into the dirt parking strip. He emerged below, foreshortened. She supposed he would hitch back into town. The motel was on the west end of everything, a place of last resort. He was walking fast and she saw the wink of metal in his hand. He went straight to the dented-fender Mercury, got in. A torrent of blue smoke came from the muffler. She struggled with the window.

"That's my car! You bastard, that's my car!"

He was on the highway, heading north toward Oklahoma, and she still hadn't got the window open.

She sat on the edge of the bed again, wondering if she should call the police. In the end she called Ace.

"Dad. I got all kinds a problems. Now don't ask me questions about any of it, but I am in the Oak Leaf Motel in Lubbock. I guess it's time I come home if you and Ma will have me. I done some stupid stuff. I'm flat broke, too. Looks like I was robbed. And my car is gone. What? It's stole."

There would be more phone calls over the years and Ace always came to bring her back home to Vollie and the child, Dawn. He thought to himself, remembering Vollie's sister Maxine, that getting in the family way ran in the Eckenstein blood. Though Vollie had never produced another kid.

15

ABEL AND CAIN

The late April morning panted in record-breaking heat. Bob stepped out of the bunkhouse into a glowing haze like a sauna fitted with an amber bulb. The paint tomcat, banished from the ranch house by LaVon after he knocked the tarantula boxes off the table, allowing the evil Tonya—still at large—to escape, lay on his side panting. Bob opened the Saturn's door. Already the steering wheel was too hot to hold. He should have put the windshield screen in place the night before. Gripping the wheel with the feed cap he'd gotten at the grain elevator, he drove first to town to pick up the mail, then to LaVon's house to help with her furniture moving.

A letter from Ribeye Cluke lay on the seat beside him. He thought he would wait until the end of the day to read it.

On Tuesday afternoons the Round Robin Baptist Bible Quilt Circle gathered at the house of one of the quilters. It was LaVon's turn after many months, and all day Monday she cooked and baked treats and made ice cubes, had enlisted Bob's help in moving boxes of papers and photographs intended for the

Rural Compendium out of the living room, followed by all the furniture.

"Are you all from the same church?" asked Bob.

"Almost everbody, but not a hunderd percent. The most is members a the Sweet Loam Babtist, but there's some from different ones. Rella Nooncaster's Gospel a Grace, and Mrs. Stinchcomb is a pillar a the Freewill Babtists, and Freda Beautyrooms is a Methodist, though she don't hardly go except to Babtist gatherins."

In the emptied room they set up an enormous worktable made from two painted sheets of exterior plywood on sawhorses. He carried folding chairs down from the attic, four at a time, thinking to himself that what comes down must go back up. The roof timbers creaked and snapped as the heat built and he believed that LaVon could bake a cake up there. In the kitchen he got a glass of water from the refrigerator, sweet, cold Ogallala water pumped by the windmill. It was so cold it made his temples ache, a beautiful chilliness as the heat swelled up outside. The day's heat pounded like blood pulsing through veins, struck down from sky tinted like a windshield, darker at the top, and embedded in it the malevolent grilling sun.

The refreshments would be served on the shady porch, said LaVon, for it was forecast to cool off in late afternoon, and, if Bob truly wanted to hear about Woolybucket folks, he could stick around, help set out the food and iced tea. (LaVon was, she said, fixing to serve limeade sherbet floats, canned oysters and cold rice salad, recipes from her 1955 *Esquire Party Book*.)

"You'll hear more about the old days and what made the town work than if you lived in Woolybucket for fifty years. We started the quilt circle in 1978 with five women. There's twenty now. We meet for three hours each week. That's sixty hours a week times fifty weeks—we don't meet Christmas or Easter weeks—equals more than three thousand work hours in each quilt. You can't put a value on them. The first one was the Garden of Eden and you wouldn't believe how beautiful that quilt was. It only stayed in Woolybucket for a little while. It was raffled off—they are all raffled off—to raise money for a new roof for the church and by the strangest stroke Father Christopher, the priest at the Harmonica Catholic Church up in Popeye, Oklahoma, won it. Then he gave it to some folks I won't name who didn't hardly have any blankets and it deep winter. Well, wouldn't you know, they turned right around and sold it for fifty dollars, I heard they bought cigarettes and beer with the money. The quilt ended up in Dallas at some art gallery and there was a picture of it on the cover of a fancy art magazine. I had a copy somewhere, but I couldn't find it now if you jabbed me with a cattle prod."

"I wouldn't dream of that," murmured Bob.

"At first they were raffled off at the New Year's time, right on New Year's Eve. That used a be the *big* holiday in Woolybucket County. The German people always made a big thing a New Year's. But now it's just when we get it finished. This one we're workin on has to be done by June. They're rafflin it at the Barbwire Festival. If I do say so myself, the quilts are beautiful. We're lucky to have women in this community that sew with the evenest, tiniest stitches you can imagine, almost invisible, and silk thread which comes finer. That reminds me, I better get the silk thread box out a the back room. Well, here's that magazine I didn't think I'd find, *Art in America,* funny name for a magazine. I'll be back in a minute." She disappeared into the small rooms at the back of the house.

He looked at the quilt pictured on the magazine cover. Even he could see it was a fabulous work of stitchery, embroidery and appliqué. In the center of the Garden stood a magnificent apple tree loaded with shining satin apples, and twined in its branches was an oversize diamondback rattler with a tongue of tiny black beads that seemed to flicker. In the cocoa-colored soil grew Mexican hat, Tahoka daisy and rabbitbrush, with purple groundcherry creeping around two knobby boulders. Adam was naked except for cowboy boots and a hat, which he held in front of his crotch. He was stitched all over with black curly hair. Eve, chatting gaily with the snake, her back to the viewer, showed long pink buttocks. She was wearing a charm bracelet, each charm sharply detailed, and Bob could make out a dangling state of Texas. An apple core lay on the ground.

"Adam seems pretty hairy," Bob called to LaVon, who was in the next room.

"Yes, he was modeled on Cy Frease, runs the Old Dog now but back then he was just a local cowboy. I don't know who brought it up to make Adam hairy, but it seemed a be the right thing to do. And Cy, why he's the hairiest man in the county. Why I won't eat there. You don't want a find one a them hairs in your gravy."

LaVon returned, shaking a wooden box. "Then the *second* quilt Doll McJunkin won, he's the one delivers mail, and he sold it for a thousand dollars to the Texas Christian Museum in Wichita Falls. I believe it was Jonah and the Whale. I remember the whale's little bitty eye like a watermelon seed. It was some old jet button Freda Beautyrooms found in her sewing box. They used a make really beautiful buttons in the old days. I can see why people collect them. The whale was divin and it filled up the whole quilt. All you could see a Jonah was his legs stickin out of the leviathan's mouth. And there was his empty boat at the top a the water. There's been other church groups, especially the Missionary Babtists, started up tryin a make quilts like these, but they haven't got the know-how. They haven't got the feel. You wouldn't *walk* on one a their quilts compared a ours."

"What subject are you all working on this year?" asked Bob.

"This year it's Cain killin Abel. Wait'll you see it."

At one o'clock sharp the first truck, an elderly grey

Ford from the late 1940s, arrived. Two white-haired women headed for the front door, carrying cross-stitched sewing bags with wooden handles. The driver took a long time to descend from the truck and helped herself along with a cane. They all wore flowery, shin-length dresses, and when the wind swept the skirts forward they seemed Botticelli's *Three Graces* (panhandle-style) grown old.

They had just finished exclaiming over LaVon's new cobalt blue fleur-de-lys trivet when two more trucks pulled in, each disgorging several women. The male drivers moved the trucks near a corral and got out to stand together and lean on the rails. One lighted a cigarette. Within fifteen minutes the house was full of women, almost all of them elderly or middle-aged, though there was one beautiful girl with black hair who looked to be barely twenty. She was heavily pregnant, so swollen and clumsy Bob feared an obstetric emergency. LaVon introduced her as Dawn Crouch, the granddaughter of Ace Crouch, the windmill man, and said that she had made her grandparents Ace and Vollie a fine quilt in the wind-mill blades pattern.

"Yeah, and I put a lightning-streak border in it," said the girl. Bob noticed she was not wearing a wedding ring. As fast as the older women were introduced he forgot their names, except for Freda Beautyrooms, a short woman with heavy bowlegs whom Bob guessed to be seventy until the old lady crowed she was "ninety-three years young." She gripped a black leather case the size of a box for child's shoes.

"Well, I see Archbell isn't here again," she said in a savage voice, lowering herself onto a chair.

"That's right," said LaVon. "She's been havin a lot a difficulty the last few months. She forgets, she's unsteady, and her temper's none too good."

"She's old and she's crotchety. She was never the brightest bulb in the socket anyway. Remember the year her son and daughter-in-law gave her that nice pink electric blanket and she sat there workin away for hours, until she pulled out all the wires? Didn't have a clue." She opened her case revealing hundreds of needles in graduated sizes, thimbles, scissors like cranes' bills.

"She never snapped back from those burns. When her gas stove blowed up? Just melted the nylons right onto her poor legs."

"Why *I'd* never wear them pantyhose." She handed her chosen needle to LaVon for threading, saying her eyes were too old to find the needle's eye.

The women arranged the sections of the Cain and Abel quilt on the table. The ground was a great tawny pasture dotted with mesquite and Spanish bayonet. In the distance there was a corral and a figure bending over a branding fire. In the foreground, a burly farmer, his face contorted with rage, stood over a recumbent shepherd, preparing to smash his face (which resembled that of James Dean) with a huge rock. Three blue-eyed sheep looked on. Blows had already been struck and copious blood stained the ground. The killer's blue overalls were spattered with red satin gore.

LaVon explained to Bob. "We had quite a discussion about whether a put Cain and Abel in those stripy robes and sandals you always see in Bible pictures, but in the end we voted a go with the way people around here dress. To make it more real-like."

"Drive the message home," said Rella Nooncaster, a sallow woman as thin as a chopstick, her white hair in a spiky butch cut. She spoke in a whiny slur without moving her upper lip. The bottom lip twisted and curled prodigiously.

Another woman, middle-aged, with crimped brown hair like auto upholstery stuffing, came in.

"Here is Mrs. Lengthy Boles. Mrs. Boles is our artist, Bob," said LaVon. "She draws out the quilt designs. She went to art school. And she makes gorgeous whitework quilts and art. That picture a Jesus in the kitchen made out a corn and seeds? That's one a hers."

"Yes," said Mrs. Boles to Bob. "Crop art. It's called crop art. Mostly religious pictures or family scenes or local landmarks—I done the bank, the school with the schoolbuses all corn, but instead a paint I use seeds, all kind a seeds, the bounty a God's hand. I got over three hunderd kinds a seeds that I use. Some are wild. I like the plum pits for belt buckles." She unrolled a quilt section that showed a half-finished cactus in bloom, quickly threaded a needle she plucked from her dress collar and, after a fuss to find the right color silk, began working on the fleshy leaves.

On the main panel the fallen sheep man, Abel, wore jeans and a plaid shirt with pearl buttons. His dented cowboy hat lay on the stained ground near several broken teeth. Nearby a Border collie snarled at Cain.

"Abel looks something like James Dean," said Bob.

"Didn't you see *East of Eden*?" said Dawn Crouch. "I embroidered that face and I *wanted* it to look like James Dean. *East of Eden* was based on the Abel and Cain story. We studied it in English class. When I was in school." She smiled at Bob in a way that made him uneasy, then turned back to working up a sheep, the effect of curly wool achieved through French knots.

"I didn't see it," said Bob, thinking suddenly of *Rat Women* and the films he had seen with Orlando—*Mudhoney*, *It's Alive!*, *Psych-Out*, *The Tingler* and *Sin in the Suburbs*.

The women worked at separate pieces to be added to the scene.

"These mesquite leaves are the worst things to sew," said the sallow woman. "Would have been easier to embroider them."

"Oh Rella, remember the deer antlers when we did Noah's Ark? Now *those* were terrible." Mrs. Stinchcomb, grey and self-effacing, spoke as though pleading.

"Yes, they were. I'll say it, they were worse than mesquite leaves. But there's so many a these I might go blind before I get done."

"Well, I wonder if it's goin a storm, it's so hot out there," said Jane Ratt, a hefty woman with yellow hair scooped by side combs into a froth atop her head. "Rella, let me borrow your little scissors. I left mine at Hattie's last week." She cut a trailing thread.

"I think it might. It's got that feeling. I can feel that old ache in my pelvis."

"Tornado weather."

"Knock on wood."

Jane Ratt glanced out the window, saw her grandson Billy tear open a package of potato chips and pour them into his mouth. It was his twenty-second birthday and she was still smarting from his rejection of her little gift.

She had asked around to discover where to get one of the metal fish she saw fastened to so many fishermen's cars; that would make a nice present. At the garage they told her the only place that carried them was over in Woodward at the Christian Superstore. It seemed an odd place for fishing supplies, but she had driven over, found the store, found the fish, purchased it and had it gift wrapped. The store wrapping paper was printed with tiny crosses. She had given it to him that morning.

"What's this, then?" he said, feeling the hard metal through the paper.

"Open it. Go on."

He tore the paper away and the chrome fish lay flat in his hand. He looked at her.

"What's this for, then? What the hell is *this* for?"

"It's because you like fishin, honey. It's so you can put it on your truck and the other fishermen will know you like fishin. A friendly kind a thing. It means, 'Hey, I rather be fishin than drivin this hot old truck around.'"

"Grandma, that ain't what it means. Where'd you git it?"

"Over in Woodard."

"*Where* over in Woodward*?*"

"Oh, I don't know. Some store. I seen it and I thought you'd like it."

"I *would* like it if it meant what you think it means."

"All right, you're so clever, what do *you* think it means?"

"I know what it means." And he would say no more.

Outside the men continued to lean against the corral rail, although there were no animals in it. Many of them were young, and Bob guessed them to be the sons or grandsons of the sewing circle women. Now they had paper cups and an older man was pouring something from a thermos. Bob doubted it was coffee.

Freda Beautyrooms looked directly at Bob Dollar.

"Young man, we're not used to having a visitor of the opposite sex when we sew, and I hope you don't get the wrong impression of us. Don't expect us to talk about poetry and philosophy and politics, though there's plenty could. We are just good friends and Christian women who enjoy making quilts for a good cause."

"LaVon explained that to me," he said, feeling his face go crimson with embarrassment at being noticed. Then he caught his breath, for pinned to the old woman's navy polka-dot dress was the most striking brooch he'd ever seen. And it was some kind of plastic. Uncle Tam would kill for that brooch.

"Don't get him flustered, Freda. He'll leave us and go out with those fool men to smoke and chew and act the fool. I see him lookin out there," said LaVon.

"Young man, I'm ninety-three years of age and I have seen more than you can imagine. I was born in Roughbug in 1907. And I have no interest in learning the computer. I had seven years of piano lessons as a girl and that was enough."

"Actually, I don't have much interest in computers, either," said Bob, shifting his chair to get a better look at her brooch.

LaVon said, "Roughbug is no more, Bob. It used a be quite a place. It was about sixteen or eighteen miles from Woolybucket, once upon a time full a cattle people and cowboys, then fell on hard days when the rayroad passed it by and was a ghost town. Then this big old Dutchman, used a work for the Cutaway as a windmiller, bought the town up for a ranch and he was drillin for water and struck awl. In the old days there was cowhands, then come farmers, and when the Dutchman made his lucky strike here come the awl workers, gamblers and bank robbers and murderers and bootleggers, all mixed together, a regular Sin City. Worse than Wink or Borger. I remember how greasy everything was. You'd pick up a plate—greasy; doorknobs—greasy; the car windshield—greasy. And that smell a sulfur and awl and garbage and likker just everwhere. It was all shinnery and sand, jammed with cars and horses and men afoot in ankle-deep mud when it rained, dust when it was dry. Just turned into a rag town. There was women a the night there too. Prostitutes, bold as brass. They'd go to the beauty parlor, get their hair done, and after, when a good Christian woman come in, the beautician would have to fold a newspaper and lay it on the chair where the other one had sat or the Christian woman would not stay. Woody Guthrie lived there for a while—where they say he wrote that song 'Throwed the Old Man's Shoes in the Broomcorn.' One day a tornado just pulverized the place. The mornin after it hit you couldn't tell there'd ever been a town there. Gone. People said it was the wrath of God."

"That Woody Guthrie was a Communist," someone muttered.

Freda Beautyrooms looked at LaVon. "Wiped Roughbug out. By then the Dutchman had got most of the awl and wasn't *he* livin high on the hog. Had a big ranch over by Amarilla and a house in Dallas. Yes, Roughbug was one of the livelier places in its time. The cowboys from the old Box Three used to come in Saturday afternoons and how the dust would fly! Wally Snow was the foreman."

"Was not he the one who used a shave with an axe? My mother remembered that." Babe Vanderslice looked around for someone who recalled. She, too, was working on cactus, delicate single-thread spines.

"Bob," said LaVon. "Babe here is *The Banner*'s crack reporter. She keeps an eye on everthing."

"He was. Vain as a peacock. Wrote poetry too. Horse poetry and stuff about sunsets. Made your skin crawl to listen to him recite. He had a voice like a woman. They say a horse kicked him in the Adam's apple when he was a boy. Some say the kick was lower down."

"Wasn't it the Box Three cowboys all decided a get married in a bunch? They ordered brides from one a them matrimonial magazines they had in them days and got a cut-rate delivery charge from P. G. Reynolds, ran the stage line. My mother used a tell about it. Fourteen or fifteen women come in on three stages, *and* a Methodist minister to do the marryin and some a them was pretty awful, no better than they should be. But those cowboys, all except one, kept their courage up and went through with it. I won't mention names because some a the women turned out a be a strength to the community," said Freda Beautyrooms, looking around the room, no doubt tallying the offspring of those mail-order marriages between rachitic cowboys and poxy whores.

"One time they had them a so-called dance over there at big fat Pa Murphy's dance hall, and the girls was goin a wear fig leaves and nothin else. But the panhandle is not fig leaf country. Some dumb bunny went down by the river and picked a basket a poison oak leaves and that's what some a those poor girls put on."

Bob Dollar stared at Freda Beautyrooms' brooch. It was a large Art Deco rectangle of pearlized celluloid with a black border. Two rhinestone chevrons were flanked by varicolored pennant shapes, handpainted and incised with fine black lines.

"The tornado that wrecked Roughbug was not as bad as the one that come through in 1947, the one started in White Deer and went all the way to Woodward. Wiped out Glazier, almost wiped out Higgins and Woodward. There was another bad one in Amarilla in 1949. People get them mixed up. And then years later some Texas airline made the offer that if anybody could prove they was in that forty-nine tornado they could buy a one-way ticket to Las Vegas for forty-nine cents. Wally Ooly, used to have the drugstore, he'd gone to Amarilla for the day when it happened, took them up on it, flew to Las Vegas and never come back until a year ago. He can't seem to adjust back to the panhandle and he's talkin about leavin again. Good riddance to him, I say."

"I thought it was 1947 that tornado came through."

"It was."

"And that one that hit Pampa a few years ago, the one with the pickup trucks flyin around in the air like mosquitoes. The worst one though, they say, was in Wichita Falls in the seventies. Killed fifty people."

"If we was to write down ever terrible thing that happened in Roughbug we'd be writin for days," said Phyllis Crouch, mother of the pregnant girl.

"Isn't that the truth. *And* Woolybucket. *And* Cowboy Rose. You girls are too young to remember this, but back in the twenties Joy Spide opened a beauty parlor to give permanents in Woolybucket. Everbody went, ever female had a have her hair marcelled. It was a rage. And in those days Joy was usin celluloid curlers. What happened was when this lady customer, her husband owned a big spread over in Roberts County, was under the heat lamp—that's how they made the hair set, chemicals and heat lamp—one a the curlers touched the heat element and it caught on fire. Well, those a you who remember celluloid know how fast it could burn. Just a terrible flash. And this poor woman, her whole head was afire. It was her first permanent wave, and her last. I believe she suffered brain damage afterwards. Certainly had a wear a wig. It was just tragic. She became a recluse. Her husband came into town and he wrecked Joy's beauty parlor. To this day there's never been another one in Woolybucket. Why we have to drive a hunderd miles, get our hair done," said Rella Nooncaster.

Bob noticed that she, too, was wearing a handsome piece of early plastic, a necklace of cream and lime-green pendants.

"Well, I'd say the best thing about Roughbug was Steddy's store," said Jane Ratt.

There was a murmur of agreement from the older women.

"Mugg's Emporium in Woolybucket was right good too," murmured Mrs. Pecan Flagg, a plump woman with dyed coal-black hair and rouge circles the size of biscuits on her cheeks.

"Bob," said LaVon, jumping between the poles of conversation like an arcing electric current, "my husband's graindaddy bought Mugg's store from the old doctor started it. Though they never used the name Fronk on it. It always stayed Mugg's. And Mrs. Flagg is very interested in the prairie chicken. Part a their ranch is a prairie chicken refuge. They got a award over it last year."

The woman looked at Bob. "They respond very well to good grass cover, and we enjoy seeing them do their funny mating dances in the spring."

"Mugg's Emporium was orderly. Jed Steddy's store was messy but how we all loved it." A rod of sunlight struck through the window and the needles glinted.

"I remember them metal cowhide stretchers hangin down from the rafters and my dad swapped him a used saddle for six a them. And a big box a that greasy yellow soap." The sunlight dimmed as clouds moved in, the needles dulled.

"Yes, that's right. And they say he never got the

worst of a bargain. What all didn't he have in that place. I remember shell cases that Mr. Steddy said was from the Indian wars, some old picket pins stamped U.S. Cavalry and a great big cone a twine. We'd get one or two of those when my deddy was raisin broomcorn. Remember that big old dusty dinosaur tooth they found on the Double Z? There was a glass case on the counter with all sorts a things for cowboys. My brother Ivon would get his bottle a Glacier Rub Scalp Stimulant and work that stuff into his hair before he went to a dance. It sort a smelled like almonds. He loved that store, all the cowboys loved it. Steddy called them 'cattleboys.' Never called them 'cowboys.' It had everything for them, tobacco, used saddles and riggin, varmint traps and slickers, liniment and vetnary cures, feedbags and saddlebags."

"One thing about those old days that's gone and good riddance is fire. There was always smoke and fire, grass fires. The smell of smoke would just scare the thunder out of you." As though the word had conjured the event a rumble shook the air. Out in the yard all the men looked up.

"I'll say another thing about those fires. There was nothin on earth so beautiful as the Texas prairie the season after a burn."

"Amen."

"But it wasn't all good times and going to the store. There was heartbreak and meanness. Remember that poor girl died of the infected leg? She got a goathead sticker in her foot and it got bad infected? And those fires, you know, had some good in them. They burned out the weeds and helped the grass. Nobody ever burned up in one. It wasn't that hard a get away. You just stepped over into the part that was already burned. It was the houses and buildins that suffered."

"I think that was Helen Leeton had the bad leg. Her father raised broomcorn and they were awful poor. I remember she had a brother, Nutsy Leeton. Swear terrible like a mule skinner or awl driller, smoked cigarettes from the time he was seven or eight, drank. Old Mr. Leeton threw him out when he was around thirteen and he lived in a grove a trees by the river. Helen always said he wasn't her real brother, that they found him in the bushes, but he was the spit and image of the Snises—the mother was a Snise— skinny and tall and with coal black hair and Indian eyes. Looked like Lyndon Johnson."

"The grass come back real good after a fire but Steddy's store burned out years before the boom days and that was that." There were ticks of rain like insect wings against a lampshade.

"My father always said Jed Steddy set the fire for the insurance."

"Doubt he had any insurance. Few did in them days. Maybe money troubles is what caused him to end up in the asylum. The Insanity Board declared him unfit. It seems so strange now that they had such things as Insanity Boards."

"I believe they did just as good a job as all these expensive shrinks that people go to."

"What I think turned his mind was that awful accident with his boy Duffy and the baby."

"Oh Lord. Just tragic."

Janine Huske, who had only lived in Woolybucket County for sixteen years and was still regarded as a newcomer, said, "What happened?"

"Oh, well," said Freda Beautyrooms, and with a glance at Bob she lowered her voice to a whisper. He could not hear what she said until her voice rose again. "And later poor Duffy went bad when he got up in size. He got to be a bank robber in the nineteen and thirties and robbed banks in the panhandle and up in Oklahoma. Him and his gang went into the Antelope Hills and took to the willers."

"Chirdren did used a die bad in those old days," said Rella Nooncaster.

"Indeed they did. I lost my little Mina to the catarrhal fever, she just coughed herself into the angels' arms."

"You know, even with all these ballet classes and music lessons kids nowadays get to take, I think parents loved their chirdren more in the old days. We was more involved in the work of the family. A boy or girl knew they had value."

"That's true. Chirdren today are not valued. Contraceptions, abortions, shows you how much value they put on young ones."

The pregnant girl's head was bent low over her French knots. Bob guessed she found the conversation uncomfortable. Had she considered an abortion?

"But in them days, even if it was nothin a do but throw rocks at something, chirdren knew how to make their own fun. My daddy told me that when *he* was a boy they had a terrible winter, so cold that hunderds a antelope froze to death. And the kids, why they dug out those froze antelopes and dragged them to a good place and stood them up in the snow. My daddy had twenty all in a line in front a the dugout. He'd talk about his big antelope bunch as if they was registered cows. 'My antelope herd,' he'd say. Come spring they commenced a rot and draw a crowd a vultures. His sisters said, 'Your vulture flock.'"

"These abortion parlors, they take the poor little babies and"—she lowered her voice conspiratorially—"*cut them up!* They sell the body parts to godless scientists. Evolutionists."

"I heard something even more horrible."

"What *could* be?" Needles paused, all hands still.

"I heard that in Warshinton, D.C., the abortionist doctors cut up the babies, cut off the identifiable parts and *sell the rest to Chinese restaurants.*"

Exclamations of disgust and outrage followed. Bob Dollar was disturbed to see how easily they believed this grisly statement. But Freda Beautyrooms glared at Parmenia Boyce.

"How can a woman a your age believe such claptrap?"

"I accept it on faith. I heard it from a friend whose cousin lives in D.C. and her daughter is a waitress there. It's common knowledge."

"It's common foolishness."

"We should trust to the Lord to guide us and pray for our enemies and that the killer abortionists will accept Jesus and give up their foul trade."

And from around the room came soft amens. And they all agreed that hailstones were bigger in the olden days, men and the wind stronger, and the sweetness of life rarer but more intense.

Bob Dollar, who had been vaccinated against religion by Bromo Redpoll's atheistic cynicism and Uncle Tam's neutrality, thought to himself that maybe the Lord had a mean streak, or maybe what happened to people was all chance and circumstance. "It beats me," Bromo had said, "how anybody can support a religion that takes a scene of capital punishment for its central image."

"My fingers is stiff as a fork," said Freda Beautyrooms, getting up and going into the kitchen where she ran hot water over her cramped hands.

"My father's brother died of tuberculosis," said Jane Ratt. "Years he had it. But you know, that long sickness gave Grandmother time to adjust to the end. She could see it comin and almost welcomed it for it ended the poor boy's sufferin. She said later she heard the angel wings beatin in the air ever time she went in his sickroom." She shook loose threads from her quilt section and glanced out into the yard. The men were all in the trucks, out of the rain, which fell gently, a fine thready rain like silk stitches.

"It's a wonder as many lived as did. Just a little

scratch could get infected but somehow healed up. We didn't have no Band-Aids but my mother would get some awl weed and break it and the sap would drip on the cut and make a nice a coverin as you ever seen."

Freda Beautyrooms came back in, flexing her fingers. "The sickroom. Now *there's* a room folks don't have these days. But there was always somebody in the sickroom on our ranch. If not one of us chirdren, then some hurt cowboy. It's a wonder those fellows lived as long as they did, foolhardy, messin with guns and around half-broke horses."

Mrs. Vera Twombley, a small, wizened woman who had said nothing, now spoke up. She looked older than Freda Beautyrooms but was, in fact, four years younger. "Do you all remember DesJarnett's melons?" She said it with such longing that Bob was moved, and he glanced around the table, imagining all the old women as young girls, slender and lithe, cutting open the sweet melons and never dreaming they could be old women, ever.

Freda Beautyrooms said, "And then the Depression. Hard years everwhere. Those awful sandstorms. Everbody had a drag a chain behind their car to cut the static electricity or the engine would just quit. And it would build up in the grass from the wind until sometimes it busted into flames. Especially that dry buffalo grass. And people went crazy with the dust, some a them."

She put her needle back in the case, clearly finished for the day, and went on. "There was plenty a tragedies, but it's strange the ones you remember as the biggest of all. I'm thinkin of a time after the World War One. I remember I was in grade school and it must a been around Memorial Day, always a big holiday, because I had a new dress and it was ruined. I had a little dog, Big Boy, we named him that because he was so small and spirited. I don't know what breed you'd call it. Just a little black-and-white feist dog. He used a walk with me to school and then he'd run back home. In the afternoon he'd come set by the school door and wait for me. Like I said, it was just around Memorial Day and folks had put little American flags on all the graves of the boys who died in the war. You know how the wind blows here in the panhandle. Well, you'd walk past the cemetery and those little flags would be a-snappin and a-crackin in the wind. Big Boy just went crazy. He couldn't stand that noise so we'd run past to get beyond them quick. But you know, you can't watch a spirited little dog ever minute. One day he come to school with me and went back home as usual. When school was over I went out and he wasn't there. I started home and when I come up to the cemetery I could see something layin on the grass. It was him, dead, he'd been shot. Well, I carried his little body home just a-bawlin and cryin, and my dress got ruined with the blood. We had a burial for him out under the woolybucket tree. Somebody told us later that a man in town had shot him. Big Boy'd run into the cemetery and started tearin up them little flags, just ripped them to shreds.

They said he'd got about seven of them before somebody seen him and said it was 'Dishonor to the Flag
and a Insult to the Nation.' So that man shot him. I
never liked those little flags myself, afterwards, and I
never put one on a grave, even when I had call a do
so."

"That shows the Depression wasn't the only bad
time," said Mrs. Herwig, "though bad enough."

"You know what was the worst thing about the awl
days? Warshin clothes. The old Maytag would just be
a-throbbin for hours ever day."

Phyllis Crouch, the mother of the pregnant Dawn,
had been silent but now she spoke with mock exasperation. "With all due respect the early settlers and
the folks had to live through the Depression *did* have
a hard time of it, I know, but my granny and my ma
never quit harpin on their old troubles. Ma had seven
or eight thousand Depression stories about babies
blowed off into the sky and people's teeth all wearin
down because they ate so much sand, and Dad could
tell you about windmills so choked up with sand they
couldn't run. But why in the world *we* have to rake it
all up again I don't know. It all happened long ago.
We'd be better off talkin about today's goins-on."

There was a general laugh and someone freshened
up a piece of scandalous gossip.

Bob Dollar counted the oldest women around the
table—seven. He had gathered that they were all
widows, all owners of substantial properties, some of
which might be the acme of perfection for hog farm

sites. He resolved to call on each one of them under the guise of learning more about the past, and check out the real estate, any possible heirs. And Tater Crouch as well.

LaVon went into the kitchen to take the refreshments out of the refrigerator. The rain had slacked off, leaving a satiny gloss on the world. Bob carried the plates and chilled food to the porch. A delicious cool breeze slid over the ladies as they sipped their limeade sherbet floats. The men were out of the trucks, calling to their mothers and grandmothers not to drink too deeply.

Bob sidled up to Freda Beautyrooms.

"Mrs. Beautyrooms, I was fascinated by what you had to say. About the old days here in the panhandle. I wonder if I could visit you sometime and hear more?"

She looked at him and smiled.

"Mr. Dime, or Dollar, or whatever your name is. I learned long ago that when a young man is interested in pursuing my acquaintance it is not because he is interested in me or the old days, but because he is determined to persuade me to invest in some foolish venture, or make an attempt a buy my property for a song. I have discovered that young men's blandishments are simply *too much pie.* So I will decline your request."

The word "rebuffed" leapt to his mind. He had been rebuffed.

• • •

On the way home Billy Ratt explained to his grand-mother about the metal fish.

"It's a sign some Christians put on their cars, sort a like that bumper sticker, 'Honk if You Love Jesus.' But a little more sophisticated. Has to do with Jesus turnin them five loaves and two fishes into enough to feed all them people. The fish is better than the loaves. Think how hard it would be for them to make a sign a bread shape—one a them Middle East round dudes? Or a slice a white like you get in the Piggly Wiggly? Or one a them long French ones looks like a bear turd? No, they had a make the fish."

"Well, then, what's wrong with that? Seems to me you would be proud a let people know you was a Christian."

"Grandma—" he said and stopped, knowing he was on the wrong end of the argument, that when they got home he would be affixing the metal fish to his truck. He was already thinking of a way to attach a heavy wire that would resemble a fish line. He could set the fish on an angle to show it was caught, and spot weld a flashy lure in its mouth. If it wasn't sacrilegious.

16

CURIOSITY KILLED
THE CAT

As the last quilt lady rolled down the driveway Bob said, in a comradely voice, "All right, LaVon, what's the story on that girl?" as though she had been keeping back a secret. They were in the kitchen loading the dishwasher.

"What girl is that?" asked LaVon innocently, measuring coffee into the percolator. "That cold stuff is all right but I need a good hot cup a coffee."

"There was only one girl there. The girl who's going to have a baby. Dawn."

"Dawn. Yes. Well, it's the old story. Dawn wasn't any better than she had to be. I'm glad Coolbroth never got mixed up with her. Do you want coffee?"

"Yes."

"She got in trouble. The same thing happened to her mother, Phyllis, that was there today. That's how come they both carry the name Crouch. Never married. Phyllis, she left home real young, went off to be a movie star or actress or whatever. You know, girl's dreams. And got herself in trouble. Ace had to go rescue her in Houston or Tulsa, I forget which. So he

286

brought her back and few months later *he* showed up, the feller got her that way. Ace took one look and ordered him off the property. Said he'd see him in hell before he'd let her go off with *him,* or let him stay with her. That's how it went." The coffee's heavy fragrance filled the kitchen and Bob got the two last clean cups from the cupboard, pawed through the refrigerator looking for milk.

"Use that cream I whipped for the floats," said LaVon, pointing at the bowl. The coffee cups had a gala look with puffs of whipped cream riding high.

"And Dawn—that was her baby—was the smartest, sweetest little girl. Ace just spoiled her rotten, got her anything she wanted—a pony, stuffed animals, a telescope. She graduated from high school top of her class. She was goin a go to college. And then! Just like her mother." It was quiet in the kitchen.

"It's nice of the quilt ladies to be so kind to her," said Bob, not sure that it was. "I mean, an unmarried mother and all—"

"I told you, Bob, it's a Christian ladies' group and we try to extend a helpin hand to the unfortunate. Some wasn't so nice to Phyllis years ago. That's why she made that sarcastic remark. Besides, Dawn's a good little quilter and a cheerful girl. At least she had the moral fiber to carry her child and not go to some filthy abortionist."

"She's very pretty," said Bob after a while.

"Ah," said LaVon in the sour voice of one who had never been pretty. "You see where it's got her."

And although Bob had more questions LaVon did not want to answer them. A frost settled over her. "Curiosity killed the cat," she said, and they finished the dishes in silence.

In the bunkhouse Bob read Ribeye Cluke's letter.

Bob Dollar.
I have your note in hand. Please know that Global Pork Rind's company policy prohibits site scouts from entering operational units. You do not need to know anything about the operations side of the industry to do your job. Nor are we paying you for a sociological analysis of the panhandle. Bob Dollar, if you want to be in Global's Big Shot League you will have to get out there and hustle. This procrastination is going to have to be stopped. It is useful when casing a region to get in with the oldsters of the community who know the goods, but the time has come to ACT. I expect to hear some GOOD NEWS from you very soon. Let us have your cooperation.

17

THE DEVIL'S HATBAND

LaVon washed the cups and saucers, Bob carried the chairs back to the attic and disassembled the work-table. LaVon vacuumed up the scraps of cloth and threads and Bob hauled the ordinary furniture back in, her boxes and books and papers. While they sorted out the piles of paper LaVon talked about Jed Steddy, the storekeeper so many of the older women had remembered.

"My graindaddy had dozens of stories about Jake Steddy, but the one we liked best was the contest between the barbwar salesman and Ab Skieret, a big rancher around here in the early days. Bob, I think I want a bring down a bookcase from the attic. There should be a green one up there. Would you mind?"

When the bookcase was in place and thoroughly vacuumed, to get any brown recluse spiders hiding in the joinery, she continued.

"You have to remember that it was all open range here until the barbwar was invented. Texas is the first place they tried out that barbwar for ranchin. Ab Skieret, owned the Woolybucket Cattle Company, and him and his foreman, Blowy Cluck, they was important men in Woolybucket, and both looked it. Skieret had a black handlebar mustache that hung down on his chest and Blowy Cluck was one of them bossy, picky men that could never let anything alone, big round head, round ears like bear's ears, real brown teeth from chewin molasses plug.

"So, one day these two ride up and wrap reins around the hitch in front a the store. Both a them pretty dusty and old Skieret, who had a rough way a talkin, says, 'Let's have a blankety-blank cutter here.' Course he used strong language which I won't repeat. Part a Steddy's counter was a kind a bar for privileged customers. Both men took the whiskey down in one gulp. Then Blowy Cluck turns and looks over the store stock, and he notices the reels a barbwar. He was one for practical jokes and such. He knew Will Rogers when Rogers cowboyed over to Higgins.

"So Blowy says, 'If you was to wrop up in that and roll down a hill, wouldn't be much left a you at the bottom. I wouldn't leave any cows git near such a cruel and unfriendly stuff,' he says. 'There'd be plenty a-wounded and drawin screwflies.'

"Old Skieret puts in his two cents' worth after another dustcutter. He looks Steddy in the eye and says, 'Don't your physiognomy tingle with shame for sellin such a devil's hatband stuff?' When my grandfather told the story, the way he made Skieret say 'physiognomy'—all puffed up and show-off—made us roll on the floor laughin. It was a big word for a rancher.

"Steddy says, 'Why no, Mr. Skieret. Reckon you ought a git acquainted with it some—there's about a hunderd miles a barbwar right around here. There's a rumor after while there won't *be* no open range. Dividin it up. Fencin it in. All be gone in ten more years.'

"Skieret didn't care to hear this. He says, 'Them nesters, them dumb farmers. I'm just a goldarn full a them buggers. I give em a brisk time, cut their barb fence and wrop it around their necks. Oh, there'll be open range long as *I'm* kickin.'

"There was stories about Skieret: that he once pulled a loaded cart half a mile with a rope in his teeth. And an awful tale about him blowin up a Finn farmer.

"Mr. Steddy quiets him down, says to him, 'Don't git carried away. There's the barbwar salesman comin along now,' and he is peerin out the window where a fella in a striped suit is takin down a green drummer's satchel from his wagon seat. 'That's him. Billy Gates. Travels for the Barb Fence Company out a De Kalb, Illinois.'

"'Hell, he is just a kid,' says Skieret, 'he ought a be at home bringin sticks for his mam's woodbox stead a horsin around pretendin a be a growed drummer.'

"The drummer, Billy Gates, comes in, nods, asks for a bottle a sarsaparilla.

"'Ho, little boy, still like soda water, do you?' says Skiert to him, squintin up his hot old eyes.

"'Yes I do, on a hot dry day such as this.' He nods at Mr. Steddy. 'And how are you, Mr. Steddy?'

" 'I was just tellin Mr. Skieret here that he ought a become more acquainted with your barbwar. He is a free-range man and vows not to become accustomed to it.'

" 'Devil's hatband,' roars Skieret. 'Look at the blankety-blank skinny stuff—you expect me believe that'll hold a thousand stampedin longhorns? Don't care if it's got stickers on it the size a knittin needles, you git them beasts on a run and they'll bust it like a spiderweb. You got yourself into a trick Yankee business here and it is bound a fail, for there are too many good Texas men who are loyal to the Great Cause and free grass, and we ain't takin on no Yankee barbwar.' That's how they talked back then.

"The drummer answers him back. 'Mr. Skieret, I appreciate your sentiments, but the days of free grass are in jeopardy. Many American farmers wish to work this rich Texas land, but they fear the ravages of uncontained cattle who trample crops as they will. This fencing, the most excellent in the world, all steel and miles of it, is the answer for them. It protects their labors from stray cows, sir, and increasingly cattle roaming unchecked on the plains are regarded as nuisance animals. This remarkable wire fence can contain the most unruly critters. This barb fence is making Texas a farmer's paradise.'

" 'I don't like to call a man a liar, but I doubt this hatband war can hold two sheep, sure enough not crazy longhorns. And never in aitch can't make Texas a paradise.'

"The salesman drinks the rest a his sarsaparilla.

"'Willin to put it to the test, sir? If you will supply the longhorns and make an interestin wager, we'll see by demonstration how well the war holds.'

"Jake Steddy tries to warn Skieret. 'Don't take that wager,' he says. 'He'll win, he'll win over you good and hard.'

"But Skieret can't be told nothin and he takes the bet. They arrange to set up the barbwar corral out on Skieret's place and then drive some cattle in.

"Says the salesman, 'If they break through, it's my fifty to you and I'll take my war elsewhere, to where men are reasonable. If they don't break through, you pay me fifty and buy a boxcar of war. I'll learn your men how to set the posts and string the war tighter than a fiddle string. But it'll take me two days a build a barbwar corral for this test.'

"Even with help it took three days set the posts and string eight strands of war, stretchin it tight with a wagon wheel. The two hands Skieret supplied were dirty old codgers; neither one see fifty again. They worked at it, spittin tobacco and gruntin, makin remarks about the war which cut their hands pretty bad. One a the reels slid off the back of the wagon and ripped the old feller's boot from top to heel.

"'You'll sing its praises one day,' says the salesman. 'It's the cowhand's friend.'"

LaVon stopped talking and began to straighten up the alignment of the sideboard.

After a minute Bob asked, "Did the barbwire salesman win the bet?" for it seemed to him that once again LaVon was going to leave the story high and dry.

"Um-hm," she said, arranging the boxes on her worktable. He thought nothing more was coming but after another long silence she continued.

"Where they had the test was empty ground except a braked windmill and a empty stock tank. See, that was Skieret's trick.

"On the day people ride out from town, gather a safe distance away from that war corral, which looked mighty flimsy to them. The old cowboys ride off, and come back a hour later hard-drivin a big bunch a nasty-tempered longhorns. Mr. Skieret is with them. He wasn't takin chances, had kept those old cows away from water for two days until they got ugly. After the cows is in the war corral, Skieret goes over to the windmill, real casual-like, and releases the brake. The water begin a pump out into the tank, and a course them cows smelled it.

"Them thirsty critters can't see much of anything between them and the rest a Texas, so they charge the war, jump back from the sharp barbs, rush again until the blood run down. After about fifteen minutes they mill and stand there with their sides heavin, and they don't move, even when the salesman hurrahs and slaps his hat, prods them with a long stick. Skieret shouts and screams but in the end he has to pay up."

Bob, enchanted by LaVon's windy, said, "I don't suppose you'll tell me about your grandfather's scarred back, now, would you?"

"Someday," said LaVon enigmatically. "And thanks for your help."

Bob got in the Saturn and drove to the pay phone outside the Woolybucket post office. A telephone company truck was parked beside it, a middle-aged telephone employee turning the inside bolts on the floor.

"Are you fixing the phone?" asked Bob Dollar.

"Fixin? We are removin it. Phone company's pullin out all the pay phones in the panhandle. Maintenance costs too much. Use your cell phone."

"I don't have a cell phone."

"Better get one. These babies are gone. There's one we ain't pulled out yet over at the café, if you got a make a call."

"You can't take that one out. Must be fifty people a day call on that phone."

"Hey, don't blame me. I don't give the orders." He deftly blew his nose on the ground near Bob Dollar's foot, turned back to his work.

At the Old Dog he put in his call.

"Hey, Uncle Tam. They're pulling out the pay phones down here. I got to get one of those lousy cell phones."

"They're talking about taking them out here, too. Call it 'progress.' Glad to hear your voice. It sure is lonesome here by myself. Anyway, what's cooking down in Texas?"

"Chicken-fried steak. Not too much else. I sat through this old lady quilting bee. But Uncle Tam, you should have *seen* the Art Plastic pins and necklaces these old ladies were wearing. Fantastic stuff." He described Freda Beautyrooms' brooch and heard his uncle's breath quicken.

"Old ladies? Can you make them an offer and buy these things? You know, say five bucks? Old ladies always need a little money for pills and slippers and stuff."

"I don't know. I can try, but don't hold your breath. These are real sharp old gals. Most of them are well off. These are panhandle ladies. They live to be a hundred fifty years old and smarter and richer every year."

"Well, make them an offer. Go as high as twenty. If you have to. Try, anyway. Maybe I should come down there myself?"

"No. It's complicated enough. These are real suspicious people. I been reported to the sheriff five or six times for running on the road. It's like nobody does that down here. It's like if they didn't do it in the old days they don't do it now. I'm in a time warp zone."

"Bob, do you remember how to tell whether something is Bakelite? There's a lot of celluloid and acrylic that looks like it."

"It's the smell, isn't it?"

"Yes, Bob. Good for you. But you have to be quick. Rub the piece very hard and fast with your finger and then, real quick, smell it. Bakelite's got that funny musty smell. That's the phenol. Another way is to hold it under hot running water for about thirty seconds and then smell it. Or dip it into boiling water. And it makes a certain sound, too, if you tap it against another piece, a kind of miniature dull thud, but recognizing that only comes with practice. The other plastics and celluloid make a higher clacking. It takes practice."

"Uh, listen, Uncle Tam, are you still in touch with Bromo?"

"Yeah. We talk pretty often." His tone was guarded.

"Next time please ask him if he knows of any more books like the ones he sent me. That Abert report is pretty interesting but I'm halfway through with it now. I don't know, all that stuff, Bent's Fort and the old Santa Fe Trail gets me going."

"Well, sure, I'll ask him. When are you coming up for a weekend?"

"Pretty soon, actually. I got to pick up some different clothes. It's hot down here and getting hotter. And I'd like to see you and catch up on the news. Orlando still around?"

"There's not that much news. And I haven't seen your big friend since he showed up here right after you left. I suppose he's around somewhere. But not so I can see him. It would be good if you came up for the weekend pretty soon. I can show you about the Bakelite."

18

JUST A FEW QUESTIONS

On a windy April morning Sheriff Hugh Dough was not pleased to look out the window and see Francis Scott Keister's truck and horse trailer pull up. He wondered if the horse's tail had grown back in after the military cut Slauter had inflicted on the animal. He listened to Keister's cowboy boots on the stairs; taking them two at a time, an indication he was smarting over something.

"Good day, Mr. Keister." Keister's watch had many dials and hands and the sheriff tried to count them.

"Yeah. Listen, what do you know about that guy's stayin at LaVon Fronk's place? He's around everwhere but it ain't too clear what he is doin here." His voice dripped with contempt. "He's from Colorado. City boy from Denver. He hangs out at the grain elevator and he helps Cy Frease a little at the café when it gets busy. Cy claims he's workin for him. Parttime. But the guy says he's workin for a luxury home developer, lookin for land with a nice view and some water. You ever hear such crap?"

"Well, maybe he is."

"Yeah, and maybe he's a government man too,

lookin into anything—land prices, lifestyles, water use study. Who the hell knows? Not me, but I'd like to. Can you find out who he is and what he is doin down here? Name is Bob Dollar. He's drivin a late-model Saturn. I wrote down the license plate number. Goddamn, I'm a Texas native, I was born right here in the panhandle, right in Woolybucket. Us native panhandle Texans don't whine and bitch about wind and dust and hard times—we just get through it. We work hard. We're good neighbors. We raise our kids in clean air. We got a healthy appreciation for the out-doors. We pray and strive to remain here forever. We are Christians. We are bound to the panhandle like in a marriage. It's like for sicker or poorer, richer or healthier, better or best. Livin here makes us tough, hard and strong. The women are tough too, the ones can stick it out, anyway. This is horse and cow coun-try and ever dollar you squeeze out a the place, by God you've earned it. This jerk came in here and starts snoopin around. Let him haul his sorry ass back to Denver. Let him pack up and git on the road."

"I'll make a few inquiries." Five dials and seven hands.

"O.K., see what you can find out and maybe I'll vote for you next election. You don't find out, won't *nobody* vote for you."

Bob Dollar was driving north and south, east and west, exploring back roads with a stack of maps on the seat beside him, looking for rundown properties, which he would check on at the county land records office. When he found a promising site he sought out the owner and brought the conversation around to selling and buying acreage without ever saying the words "hog farm" or "Global Pork Rind."

One late afternoon he was under the brow of the caprock hiking along a trail of orange dust so fine it seemed a kind of defiant liquid, climbing a slight incline through shrubs and violet-colored cacti like spiny cow tongues. In the undergrowth cardinals turned leaves and scratched up fallen twigs. Above him rose a landscape of red baguettes headed by the grey crust of stone, the great caprock layer, a section of the limestone escarpment that wavers diagonally across the Texas panhandle, intersecting with the Canadian River to make a huge crooked X. To the north and west were the dry high plains, the treeless Llano Estacado, and to the south and southeast the moister southern plains of ordinary Texas. He squinted his eyes at the landscape, trying to imagine a sea of hog farms.

The trail crossed a sinuous stream again and again, water a few inches deep braiding thinly over gravel the color of tangerine peel. The cliffs were streaked with chalky raptor excrement. On a projecting knob flattened and heeled like a human foot, wild rock doves clustered. A cloud came, unloaded hail and rain; the river rose, the steep, eroded trail ran with red water and in the encroaching twilight the butt end of a mule deer looked fleetingly like the face and muzzle of a wolf. As Bob Dollar left and headed back to Woolybucket a ringneck pheasant burst out of the grass and flew low across the road.

He was on the edge of Woolybucket by sunset and running east on a caliche road colored by low sun to the blond of raw sugar with deep blue undertones in the shadows. He knew this property belonged to a cantankerous woman in Lubbock who, when he drove down and talked to her, behaved as though he had made an assault on her honor. He was startled when a siren went off behind him and the sheriff's lights flashed. He couldn't think why he was being pulled over and kept on driving for another half mile. But there was no one else on the road and in the rearview mirror he could see the sheriff gesturing and pointing to the side of the road. Fearing sagebrush stobs he pulled over gingerly.

"Let me see your registration," said the sheriff, silently counting Bob's fingers, then his own by twitching each one. "No, not your license. The registration."

As he handed the paper over it dawned on Bob Dollar that the registration was undoubtedly in the name of Global Pork Rind. He had been found out.

The sheriff was silent for a long minute, then he said, "You'd better come down to the office and see me sometime tomorrow. We need a have a little talk." He counted the seconds—five—before Bob said, "All right."

•   •   •

Bob Dollar stopped at the Busted Star for water.

"You know," said LaVon, who heard the door slam and came out of the dining room to shovel extra sugar in her coffee, "I been meanin a tell you. The *real* interestin one of the Crouches is not Tater, but his brother, Ace. Ace Crouch is a windmill man, sold em, put em up, fixed em. That was in the old days before they got the deep pumps and the irrigation. Now he mostly fixes the old ones. Ace lives in Cowboy Rose. He quarreled with old man Crouch and walked off the ranch at an early age, and that's how come Tater got in the saddle. By rights the place should a gone to Ace, but his daddy left him a deck a cards and a pile a sucker rod. He tried a git the will broke but it didn't do no good. Their daddy was real destructive to boys and if he taken against you, you'd never please him. He was a old man when Ace and Tater was born and he never did understand boys. He had went to work on the Panama Canal way, way back. He was a dynamite man, handled the dynamite. He told it that there was so many accidents human flesh flew through the air like birds. You go on the cemetery road north of Cowboy Rose and there's a little old stone buildin there? That was Ace's windmill shop when he was partners with the Dutchman. Before they had their big place in Amarilla. Ace lives up in Cowboy Rose to this day. His mean old daddy is in the cemetery here in Woolybucket. My husband worked for him when he was a boy. Ace, I mean, not the daddy. Ace and the Dutchman. Ace's wife would like to sell off their place. She would like to move to California. She'll probly have to wait until Ace passes before that comes to happen. Their grand-daughter was at the quiltin day last week back. You might remember her. She was the pregnant one. Dawn. Her mother, Phyllis, was there too, and I have to say she was as bad as Dawn when she was young. Ace and Vollie has had a cross to bear. Ace was a important person around here. His daddy was big in the Klan back in the twenties. They say he was the Exalted Cyclops." She saw the expression of distaste on Bob's face.

"Now Bob, you come down here from Denver and you do not understand this place. Probly you never will, seein you wasn't brought up here. In them days the Klan was not a bunch of crazy supremacists but decent men who was strong Christians, very patriotic and chivalrous. They more or less watched over com-munities and promoted Christian morals. It's true they didn't care for Nigroes, but no more than they didn't care for Catholics and Jews. And that wasn't the point, anyway. They wanted to see people behave decent. The women a the Ku Klux Klan was strong on community morals. And they had to be!

"But the KKK set out to improve. They'd get the men to build onto them two-room shacks so they could separate out the boys and girls. They talked a the mothers. The girls that was in trouble, why they carried them over to Amarilla to the Unwed Mothers' Home. They kept their eyes open and they could tell if a girl was *that way* before she knew it herself. At Christmas they packed up baskets a food for poor families, called it a present from 'Santa Klaus.' No, you won't hear me say nothin bad about the Klan. It was a community organization dedicated to decent Christian behavior. I tell you, everbody wanted a join. I personally think the panhandle is a better place because a them."

There was the sound of footsteps on the porch and a tall youth, thick blond hair in a ponytail, came in. He was wearing magenta tights and a black jersey, worn cycling shoes. A gold chain glinted at his neck. His face was thin and narrow, tanned, and where not stubbled, gleaming with the oily exudate of sweat. There were raw scrapes down his right leg and arm, beaded with tiny drops of blood. He looked intensely angry.

"Well, look what the cat dragged in," said LaVon.

"Look," he said, opening the refrigerator and tearing the leg off a cold chicken, "I am tired, I'm dirty, I'm hot, I'm hungry, and I hurt because some son of a bitch run me off the road, so I'm in no mood for sarcastic little gibes. Got any beer?" he said, turning around and spotting Bob. "Who the hell is he?"

"No beer. Coolbroth, this here is Bob Dollar; Bob, this is my son Coolbroth. He skolps. It was him carved them figures out by the bunkhouse. He turns up ever now and then. Cool, Bob is rentin the bunkhouse. You will have to sleep in graindaddy's room."

Coolbroth Fronk turned and looked at Bob Dollar. There passed between them a cold and immediate animosity.

19

THE SHERIFF'S OFFICE

Dutifully Bob went to the sheriff's office in Wooly-bucket the next morning. There was no receptionist, only Dispatcher Christine Logevall putting green polish on her toenails with painful effort, as her spare tire and arthritis kept her from bending close to her feet. She did not look up when Bob came in, and after hesitating he knocked on the frosted glass door labeled SHERIFF.

"Yep," said a noncommittal voice and Bob pushed the door open.

He had never been in a sheriff's office before but quickly grasped that it was an uncomfortable place unless you were the lawful inhabitant or his deputy. The walls were the dull pistachio green beloved of small municipalities. An aged dog collar held down a stack of papers whose corners were riffled by the sheriff's electric fan. Despite the fan the room was stuffy and stale. There were bars on the only window. An axe hung on the wall and a flowery necktie dangled from the coatrack. On the wall behind the desk Bob saw a photograph of the sheriff embracing a trophy the size of a teenager and, below it, in a shadowbox, a pair of oversized handcuffs with explanatory lettering saying that these had been custom-made for Jack "Big Wrist" Derrida. Two hulking computers from the 1980s, black with grime, buzzed on the sheriff's desk, and in the corner a table bore a printer, a dinosaur fax machine and an electric coffee pot from Sears. The telephone also was a relic from the past, the plain black 1949 Bell 500, a rotary dial instrument with the loud drill of a movie telephone where the heroine lets it ring four times before answering.

The sheriff looked up.

"Do for you?"

"Yesterday. You told me to come in. Bob Dollar."

"Right, right. Sit down."

Bob sat in the only chair, an orange, soiled plastic Eames knockoff. All the furniture looked like fifty-year-old castaways and everything was shiny with the patina of old hand grease.

"What's your business in Woolybucket County, Bob?" asked the sheriff mildly, but his eye was so penetrating and cold that Bob began to tell his history: how his parents had left him on Uncle Tam's doorstep, their disappearance into Alaska, his life of poverty with Uncle Tam (he left Bromo out of the account as an unnecessary complication), his first job. But when he came to describe hiring on with Global Pork Rind, he veered violently around the truth. Yes, he said, he *apparently* was employed by Global Pork Rind and looking for hog farm sites, but in *actuality* he was acting for Global Deluxe Properties, a subsidiary of GPR interested in rural acreage for luxury home communities. At last he fell silent.

The sheriff said nothing for some time. His gaze had not softened.

"I spose you got a reason for sayin what you say," said the sheriff, "but you might have boxed yourself into a corner. You got a couple tough locals interested in you and what you are doin here. You might want a know I checked with GPR. You're scoutin pig farm sites, pure and simple. Nothin a do with no Global Deluxe Property, which don't exist. Now, there's no law against searchin out property for swine production, but it could be unhealthy to tell folks you're a real estate developer front man when it ain't true. My guess is that the price differential between agricultural land and property folks think is goin a be developed is enough so's you won't make many hog site buys. You may think because most a these old boys didn't git too far in school they will be suckers for the easy deal. I'll tell you what. These illiterate old coots can figure you right out a your socks. I don't know why you are lyin about it. There's two others workin the panhandle and ever one a you is pretendin a be in some other business. I'm goin a be keepin an eye on you."

"Who?" said Bob. "Who are the others?"

"You're so smart, you find out," said the sheriff. "Anyways, I was you, I wouldn't give no time to that chickenshit hog farm work. How much they pay you?"

"Twenty-four," said Bob, sure that the sheriff of this panhandle town made far less than that judging by the antiquated equipment in the office.

"If you was as smart as you think you are, you'd be down in Austin with the computer Dellionaires," said the sheriff.

"No," said Bob. "The bottom fell out of all that. It's over."

"Then you ought a think about prisons."

For a moment Bob thought the sheriff was threatening him with jail time, but the man went on calmly.

"There's good money in prisons. They are ideal for rural towns on hard times like Woolybucket. Look at this place. Just a bunch a old farmers livin on government crop-support handouts and ranchers usin the last a their oil money to support cows. A prison is a good, stable source a income for the town and the county. Hires locals, pays taxes, pays for water and other utilities and services, pays sales tax. And attracts other businesses. Prisoners' visitors need motels, restaurants, gas stations, bus depots and Wal-Marts. I'd purely love to see a great big Wal-Mart in Woolybucket. It would make this place hum. They got them a *good* prison over to Pampa."

"So how do I fit into that?"

"Why, you ought a be scoutin for a prison-builder corporation stead a hog farms. There's one up in Nashville. They pay good money, I bet, to fellers finds them a sorry little town at the back a everthing that's perfect for a good prison. Your best prisons are in the rural places. You get in touch with that Nashville outfit and tell them you know some good places in the panhandle perfect for prisoner incarceration. Put them inmates next to a hog farm, see how fast they reform." Suddenly he got up and put on his hat. "In the meantime, I'll be watchin you. Now git."

As he drove out of town he noticed a new restaurant sign down the street from the Old Dog.

HEALTHY CHRISTIAN CAFÉ it read, and in the window a small sign announced

Afternoon Tea 3–5 P.M.
Assorted Pastries

The windows, in contrast to those of the Old Dog, were sparkling and a lace edging frilled the sides; potted geraniums enticed. A brisk stream of elderly women, many wearing flower-sprigged dresses and white gloves, were going in and he slowed to better see the crowded interior, glinting water goblets, a waitress in a muslin apron pushing a trolley of creamy pastries, an elderly lady raising a demitasse cup to her withered lips. A large billboard beside the window with moveable red plastic letters spelled out

THE SHERIFF'S OFFICE

WELCOME TO WOOLYBUCKET.
HAPPY BIRTHDAY TAMMY
Congratulation
Today Carrot Cake

So, he thought, the Old Dog had competition. Of a sort. And because he liked carrot cake very much he parked and went in, nodded to many of the women whom he remembered from the quilting session. There were no men in the shop. He glanced at the short menu, which featured chicken salad and egg salad sandwiches, a cream soup du jour, a blue plate special and assorted pastries to accompany coffee or tea or hot chocolate. It was obvious every customer was there for the desserts.

"Is there any carrot cake left?" he asked the waitress, who also looked familiar, her shining black hair parted in the center, her pink uniform snug.

"Your lucky day. It's usually all gone by now but we made extra and there's a good piece for you. There's plenty a rice puddin. And cream horns."

When she brought the confection he recognized her as Dawn Crouch, Ace Crouch's pregnant granddaughter who had embroidered James Dean's face onto Abel.

"You had your baby," he said. "Was it a boy or a girl?"

"Twins. One a each. I named them James and Jeanette. My grandmama takes care a them while I work. How you doin?"

"Pretty well," said Bob. "Out of curiosity, what is the blue plate special today?"

"Today it was tuna melt, but it is all gone now. Real good. We still got cheese sandwiches."

"No thanks. So, who owns this restaurant?"

She laughed. "We all do. It's a cooperative multi-denominational church venture." She lowered her voice conspiratorially. "But the First Primitive Babtists are the real ones. Same as the quilt. We pretty much do the work and did the setup. It's nice."

"Yes," said Bob truthfully, "it is nice. Very nice. Did you all ever finish the quilt?"

"Looks like it will be finished in a couple weeks. There's the big rodeo at the Barbwire Festival on the third weekend in June, and that's when it will get raffled off. Five a'clock. You be sure you buy a bunch a tickets. And the Babtist ladies will serve a good supper. It's usually the same thing—bierox, french fries, coleslaw, baked beans and a kind a tutti-frutti Jell-O or sugar snakes. Course, Cy runs the barbecue."

Bob could not imagine what sugar snakes might be and he was going to ask but a bell tinkled somewhere in the back and she went to fetch a plate of sandwiches to a table near the back and was soon talking with the group of women exclaiming over the sandwiches embellished with radish roses, black olives and parsley bouquets. Bob could see that the cheese peeping from the bread was the supermarket utility grade colored federal yellow.

20

EVERYTHING'S O.K.
SO FAR

The way to the Beautyrooms' Axe-Head Ranch began with a letter from Houston on thick grey paper.

TEXOLA PETROLEX

Dear Mr. Dollar.

A mutual acquaintance mentioned your name to me, saying that you are looking for attractive panhandle property to be tastefully developed as luxury home sites. My siblings and I believe that the family ranch left to our mother, Freda Beautyrooms, at our father's death in 1955, would admirably suit your needs. It is a beautiful ranch of 8,000 acres with rolling terrain through which Big Lobo Creek flows, feeding a small lake of the same name (on the property). At this time most of the pasture land is leased to local cattlemen. I would like to speak with you about the possible sale of the ranch should my siblings and I persuade our mother (93 years young) that such an event would be beneficial to all.

Given Woolybucket's high level of interest in others' affairs, it would be best if you could come down to Houston and discuss the possibilities with me and my sisters. We would be pleased to give you a real Texas dinner.

Please let me know if this is possible. I hope to meet you soon for a mutually gratifying talk.
Sincerely yours,
Waldo Beautyrooms

He called the Houston number and got Waldo Beautyrooms' secretary. The man came on the line, sounding like a camel in distress, apologizing for his guttural voice with the explanation that he was just recovering from a throat operation.

"I'm eager to meet you, Mr. Dollar," he grated. "I think we have *nearly* persuaded Mother to come down here and live in a very pleasant retirement home. We worry a good deal about her. If she should chance to fall or have a dizzy spell . . . well, she's an elderly woman with an active mind and will not admit that she cannot ride or work in her garden as she once did. If you think you can come to Houston for a day we could discuss the possible sale of the ranch."

"Yes, I think I can," said Bob Dollar who, despite the sheriff's warning, was losing sight of hog farms and now more than ever believed in the luxury homes. Perhaps Waldo Beautyrooms would turn out to be a man of sense, who understood that hogs, too, needed a place on the planet. Or perhaps Global Pork Rind would diversify into luxury homes. He reminded himself to write to Ribeye Cluke and suggest this. They might give him a raise for being so attentive to ways of expanding the company's business. "How about Thursday next week? I'd like to drive down, see more of Texas. I guess it might take a day and a half to drive to Houston?"

"You could easily take two days driving from Woolybucket to Houston. Do you know Houston? No? I'll send you directions on how to find the Texola offices. We'll look for you next Thursday around noon."

On the drive he banished boredom by counting dead skunks on the margin of the highways. (Sheriff Hugh Dough had mapped most of the state in average numbers of dead skunks between towns, depending on the season. He contributed to the number as often as he could, for he believed that running over a skunk fostered a wealth of common sense in the driver.) He passed oddly named side roads—Greasy Corner Junction, Wrinkle Road, Diving Board Road. Shortly before noon on the Thursday Bob turned onto the 610 loop road. He had counted seventy-three dead skunks between Woolybucket and Houston, slightly above the sheriff's average sixty-eight.

Texola Petrolex was near the Saudi Arabian consulate on Post Oak. He got out of the Saturn into a wet heat that had him sweating in seconds. By the time he reached the enormous glass doors he was drenched. Inside the doors a blast of arctic air coated him with light frost. On the seventeenth floor a sneezing receptionist buzzed Beautyrooms' office.

"Blease take a seat, sir," she said. "Mr. Beautyroobs will be with you in a bobent."

He sat and leafed through slippery copies of *Texas Monthly* and an awkwardly large book titled *Texola Petrolex, Building a Bigger Texas*. After leafing through the bright photographs of folksy, grinning roustabouts on offshore rigs, he closed the book and his eyes.

"Mr. Dollar?" It was the same hoarse voice he had heard over the telephone. Waldo Beautyrooms stepped up, presenting a curved, silver face surmounted by a tremendous pile of white hair like Hokusai's *Great Wave*. There was a snowy bandage around his neck. He held out a thin hand.

"I thought we might hit the Trail Dust for lunch," he rasped. "They have great Texas steaks." They rode the elevator down in silence. Outside the enormous glass doors the wet heat fell on them like a barber's towel. They drove to the restaurant in Waldo Beautyrooms' Cadillac. "A lot of executives like the Lexus," he said, "and they say this is old-fashioned, but I'll stick with the Caddy. My sisters will be joining us," said the man hoarsely. "We thought it best that we all meet you. I must confess I guessed you would be an older man. Your voice on the telephone sounded older."

EVERYTHING'S O.K. SO FAR

At the restaurant they headed for a corner table where two thin and remarkably similar women sat drinking blue cocktails. "Bob, let me introduce you to my sisters, Eileen Moon and Marilyn Tyrell." The women looked at him and smiled. The thinner one, arms like pool cues, asked if the drive had been boring. He nearly told her about counting the skunks but thought better of it.

A few feet away three men sat at a table for six, their briefcases on the empty chairs, papers weighted by salad plates, a map draped over the fattest briefcase. A cadaverous man with slick grey hair the color of a wet mouse talked to the other men, showed them photographs, pointed to a crude circle on the map. Bob heard the words "weed killer," "carrying capacity," "erosion," "riparian recovery" and "back from the dead."

Waldo rubbed his palms and cracked open the menu. "It's all Texas meat, Bob. Are you hungry?" The silvery face bent toward him.

"Starving. I could eat a horse."

"Then I recommend the Bronc Buster's Special."

When his plate came he thought for one terrible moment that it actually contained the larger part of a horse. An enormous, four-pound slab of meat covered the sixteen-inch plate. The waitress, a blond girl in the restaurant's uniform of cowboy boots, miniskirt and tight T-shirt emblazoned *Trail Dust Saloon,* unloaded an array of side dishes—grits, mashed potato, gravy boat, pickled beets, cornbread, fried onions, stuffed mushrooms, sliced beefsteak tomato, a pot of freshly grated horseradish, stewed okra and a bowl of tiny, lethal chiles.

Waldo had ordered cream soup for himself and both women dabbed at lobster salads.

One of the women, the one whose lips were edged in cracks, spoke—he had already lost their names. "About the ranch," she said, winking her eyes rapidly. "Have you been over it?"

"No, ma'am," he answered through a mouthful of bloody meat. "Your mother wasn't receptive to that idea."

"You have a treat coming, then. It's truly beautiful, and we think it would be wonderful if the other luxury homes were modeled after the original place. The house was built in 1891 of local limestone. It overlooks the lake. The living room and kitchen have hand-hewn beams. There is a separate guest cottage once used for *very* distinguished visitors, for our parents knew everyone in Texas and entertained lavishly, but now, alas, it's rarely in use except when one of us visits. The outbuildings include corrals, chutes, a barn, machine shop, three line camps. There are many rare plants and a diversity of wildlife on the ranch. We've always been guardians of the land. The selling point, of course, would be that the ranch would continue to give enjoyment to people as a site for fine homes."

Waldo Beautyrooms mock-frowned at his sister. "Now, Eileen, don't rush ahead," he said. "We haven't even told Mr. Dollar—Bob—the possibilities. Or the good news. How's your steak, Bob?"

"Delicious," he said, swallowing a great painful lump and swilling his glass of beer.

"The good news is that our mother has tentatively agreed to the sale. She says she'll move down here to Oak Shadows Village. I've talked with several real estate men about what we might expect for the property, which is *exceptional* as it has live water and a twenty-eight-acre lake, as well as the house, which is on the Historic Register, and the ranch outbuildings, and eight thousand acres of prime grazing land and the natural attributes my sister mentioned. They tell us a fair price, if it's going to be subdivided and developed, would be nine million dollars."

Bob Dollar had been sampling a chile when Mr. Beautyrooms floated the figure. His quick intake of breath carried the chile with it and in a second he was strangling and retching. A nearby waiter, trained in the Heimlich maneuver, rushed over, wrapped his muscular arms around Bob's lower chest and jerked. The chile shot across the table and, wet with saliva, stuck to Waldo Beautyrooms' silk necktie. Although the chile had been dislodged, its fire had not and Bob continued to choke and weep. He seized his water glass and emptied it. He went for the beer glass and swallowed the contents. Desperate for relief, he ignored the expressions on the Beautyrooms' faces and took up the gravy boat, drank deeply of the soothing mixture. He excused himself, went to the men's room where he vomited, drank water out of the faucet, washed his face, drank more water, heaved again, and finally returned to the dining room. Only Waldo Beautyrooms remained. Bob was grateful to see the remains of the steak had been taken away.

"Bob, are you all right?"

"Oh, better now," he croaked. "It was a pretty hot chile."

"My sisters had hairdresser appointments so they've gone on. But here is what we would suggest you do. Go back up to Woolybucket. Visit the ranch—I'll tell my mother you are coming. Steve Escarbada can show you around—he's a kind of ranch manager, even though we don't run our own cows anymore. He grew up on the place and knows everything about it. Take all the photographs you like. Send them on to your corporate principals. Invite them down to see for themselves. We're confident that there isn't a more beautiful or historic property in the panhandle."

"Why don't you live there yourself, Mr. Beauty-rooms?"

"What! Live in the *panhandle*!?" For the first time the man lost his aplomb. It was as though Bob had suggested he move to the near east and become a camel drover. "No, Mr. Dollar, I think not."

"All right, I'll look at it. It sounds like a beautiful place."

"It is. And this, I think, may be the break we've been waiting for. Otherwise we might have to sell the water rights to T. Boone Pickens and let the place go to desert."

"But he'd never pay you nine million dollars for water rights," said Bob Dollar hoarsely.

"Oh, wouldn't he?" asked Waldo Beautyrooms, smiling, turning his silvery moon face toward the waitress and making scribbling motions for the check. "I've known T. Boone since he was a kid in Oklahoma and I think I know better than you what he might do. Just so you get the drift of it, in 1997 the Bass brothers sold forty-five thousand acres of water rights for two hundred and fifty million dollars to a southern California water utility. Up in the panhandle the only dependable Ogallala water left is what's under Roberts County. And T. Boone has got control of the water under a hundred and fifty thousand acres of Roberts County. In quite a few panhandle areas they've had to give up irrigation and go back to dry farming. So the water's an asset. A very big asset."

They said goodbye and shook hands before leaving. Bob headed back to the men's room, his gut rumbling. When he came out of the cubicle the cadaverous man from the next table was washing his bony hands. He looked at Bob in the mirror.

"You look like a decent kid," he said. "What are you doing in the dirty subdivision game?"

"Sir?" said Bob.

"I was listening to you fumble the deal with those assholes. You got any idea what you're doing to the country when you chop up one of those ranches? You're bringing in powerlines, roads, increased water consumption for Kentucky bluegrass lawns, giant trophy homes. You're bringing in people who don't know and don't care about the region, so long as they get theirs. All so some greedy little pipsqueak developer like you can make a buck." He glared at Bob.

"I'm not a developer," said Bob.

"I overheard you talking about the 'luxury homes' that are going on the property."

"Maybe," said Bob, "if you didn't eavesdrop you wouldn't get wrong ideas."

The man stood there scowling at Bob, who walked briskly to the door, then turned and said loudly, "For your information, mister, I'm in HOG FARMS," relishing the man's incredulous and horrified expression. At the exit he realized he had come to the restaurant with Waldo Beautyrooms, and now had to call for a taxi to take him to the Texola parking lot on the other side of Houston, using his last cash to pay for it.

There were several entrances to the Axe-Head Ranch, all but one behind electronic gates set between upright posts bridged by a hand-forged arch that carried the brand, an axe head in a triangle. He could see corrals inside each of these gates. The main gate was open and Bob drove down the graveled road and through a short tunnel of trees near the bridge. As he emerged from the trees the pale rock house appeared in the distance, long and low. It did not look particularly imposing or large but as he came nearer he could see wings and ells. In front of the house there was a hitching post and a horse trough, both obviously still in use judging by the piles of manure.

A large black bell hung beside the door, a twisted piece of rawhide attached to the clapper. He jerked it sideways and the bell made a sonorous clang. No one came to the door and he rang again. Minutes passed. He opened the door a few inches and called, "Hello? Mrs. Beautyrooms? Anybody home? It's Bob Dollar."

A young woman in an apron came suddenly into the hallway.

"Come in, come in," she said. "She'll want you to wait in there," pointing to an open archway on his right. Before he could say anything she was gone again.

He entered the room and looked around. On the floor was a sand-colored carpet with deep indigo borders in oriental design. The furniture was old-fashioned, leather club chairs, a big square piano (beneath it a fossil mastodon leg bone), a high-backed sofa upholstered in tufted black leather. On a side table rested a brass tray holding a bottle of seltzer water and amber-colored tumblers. Paintings of western scenes crowded the wall. Velvet drapes the color of dried mushrooms hung at the windows. A clock ticked. In front of a window stood an ancient windup phono-

graph with a thick black record on the turntable. He
went over to it to see what it might be: Wyclef Peeler
singing "Ate Some Burnt Hoss Flesh." In a corner was
a curio cabinet filled with rocks and fossils. A small
bookcase showed faded buckram spines with such
titles as *Bella Donna, Broncho Charlie, Tiger
Smoke*—the sort of books found in secondhand book-
shops. There was a silver cigarette lighter in the shape
of a howling coyote on a table and he flicked it to see
if it worked, startled when flame leapt from the coyote's open jaws. An entire glass-fronted cupboard
was given over to objects carved from Oklahoma
alabaster: many squirrels, and a bust of Sam Houston.

The room connected to a smaller room and from
the arched opening to it issued Freda Beautyrooms'
voice. He could see her, her face turned toward the far
corner out of his sight. She glanced at him and waved
her hand but kept talking.

". . . lean but broad-pelvised from his mother's
side. All the women in that family had babies real
easy. My two daughters inherited that. O.K.'s mother
was old-timey. She believed all that folderol about
babies—rub the baby's knees with greasy dishwater
and he'll walk early. Read poetry and think kind
thoughts and the baby will be a good person. He had
big feet nothin could fit, couldn't find store-bought so
he had his boots made. Over in Amarilla, at Oliver
Brothers. Expensive. He held up a long time. Big
hands, big feet, big strong bones. You'd never know
when he was born his head was the size of a teacup, or

so his mother said." She glanced at Bob Dollar again and called to him.

"I let you come in, Mr. Dime, just a keep Waldo quiet. He thinks I'm goin like a lamb to the slaughter and you're the man with the axe. So we'll just have us a little visit. In a minute. You just set and wait." She resumed her conversation with the corner of the room. "The reason they called him O.K. was on his first job, cowboyin, the other hands called him O.K. because a his way a sayin, 'Everything's O.K. so far,' tryin a look on the bright side, you know. It stuck. His given name was Satrap, but I was the only one called him that, and I usually said 'O.K.' Unless I was mad at him. O.K. was what he answered to, and that's what we put on his headstone. He had a trick a pretendin not to know much and that got him out a a lot of things, being hazed by the other men, work, responsibility. He didn't like to be the one up front. When push came he could do anything but he never let you hear about it and he'd hang back until there wasn't any other way, then step in and do it, whatever it was, just as cool and smooth and right. He got to be well-known for that."

She sighed and went on. "He did some dumb things too, had a taste for mean pranks, about as much manners as a goat, liked a drink a whiskey pretty well. But don't write that down. Let the dead sleep comfortable. There was a long list a things he wouldn't do, that got him insulted if you asked him, like cut lawn grass. He was your stiff-neck proud cowboy type. But he was a pretty good man, not special or outstandin except when it come to handlin horses and stock. There was very few animals didn't act right under his hand and you knew where you was with him. Look on the table in there and you'll see when he was twenty-two, that face gettin ready to smile at you, and see how strong and willin he was, walkin straight, *he* thought, into the happy days. Don't seem like his faults earned him the whippin he got from his life. That's Waldo he's holdin, eight months old and just a-wigglin so he's all blurred. He was our first baby, born September 4, 1939, our only boy. Named Waldo after a kind of bakin powder I liked. 'Waldo's Cream Powder.' The other two was girls. I rather have boys to raise than girls. A girl will sass and flout you and lie until you don't know the day of the week."

A voice came from the room beyond. "That is probably enough for today, Mrs. Beautyrooms. I've got to make some phone calls before three so I'll have to run. What about tomorrow? Maybe we can talk about your son, Waldo. He's quite an important man in the oil business."

Freda Beautyrooms snorted. "That's what *he* likes to think. But I guess it's all right." She paused and added, "My husband's mother used a say he was too smart to live. If a child was too smart he'd die young. A course Waldo didn't die so I guess he wasn't all that smart."

A very short blond girl appeared in the archway.

She held a small tape recorder and a sheaf of loose paper, each page filled with sloped writing.

"Oh, hello," she said to Bob. "I'm Evelyn Chine. I'm writing my M.A. sociology thesis on Woolybucket. Mrs. Beautyrooms is one of the oldest citizens and remembers the town before the streets were paved." She seemed nervous, looked over his shoulder rather than directly at him, one of those who avoided direct eye contact.

Bob shook her hand and mumbled. He was wild with envy. Why had he not thought to say *he* was a grad student working on a paper about, say, land values and usage? What a great cover, a million times better than the luxury home dodge.

Evelyn Chine left, a wire trailing from her recorder.

"Get on inside," said Freda Beautyrooms, pointing at the inner room. "That was my husband, O.K., I was talkin about to her. I just got a the point where I was goin a tell about how O.K. come to die when she jumped up and run off. It was because a Waldo. Waldo was crazy about swimmin and he got into these school meets where they race each other in swimmin pools? I thought it was a lot of foolishness myself but O.K. got pretty excited when Waldo won a ribbon or a trophy of a half-nekkid feller. When Waldo was fifteen there was this big swimmin contest with other panhandle schools and Oklahoma, too. Maybe New Mexico. A long time ago. It was held up at the college in Goodwell. Waldo won the first part.

Poor O.K. got so excited and jumpin around and screamin 'Waldo! Waldo!' that he lost his footin on a wet place and fell into the deep end. He didn't know how to swim a stroke and went straight to the bottom like a stone. He was drowned before they could get him. And it was Waldo who had to pull him out, too. He didn't race the second part so he never knew if he could a won or not. I don't believe he went in swimmin again in his life."

"That must have been quite a burden of guilt for Waldo to carry through life," said Bob.

"'Burden a guilt'? I don't think so. I don't think Waldo ever felt a twinge a guilt about a thing. Now he sends you along to twist my arm about buyin the ranch, and I'll play along with you for a while, but I just want you to know that you are not goin a buy it. Not even if you was to offer a million dollars."

"Waldo is asking almost ten times that amount of money for the property," said Bob.

"What! Why, that little snake. I suppose Eileen and Marilyn's in on it?"

"They were both there when I met with your son."

"Them snakes! I just got a mind a do it and keep all the money myself. Did he tell you to look around or what?"

"He said somebody named Steve would show me the place."

"Oh, Steve? Estefan Escarbada, you mean. Haven't seen him for years. I thought he moved a San Antonio. You better go look around on your own." She seemed anxious to get him out the door. Her hands were shaking and the lined face was beaded with sweat. Suddenly Bob was afraid she might be having a stroke.

"May I help you to a chair?" he asked.

"Bed," she gasped, waving at a green portiere on the far side of the oak table. He helped her toward it, pushed aside the curtain and revealed an immense bedroom carpeted in pale pink. A king-size poster bed, as ornate as a wedding cake, stood unmade in the middle of the room. He noticed the film of dust on everything and wondered if she did not have a maid or cleaning lady. He guided her to the bed and almost as soon as she touched down on it her eyes closed. As he left the room he looked around a little furtively, noticing the big windows with the view of the lake, the leather-topped table strewn with rings and necklaces, a basket of papers and unopened mail and magazines. The plastic brooch he remembered lay in a drift of powder. Once past the green curtain he kept on going, got in the Saturn and decided to drive around the ranch by himself.

Outside he could see a track that circled the lake and headed west toward a motte of trees. Because it had turned into such a rare scented day, cool and blue, millions of wildflowers coloring the fields as pastures of heaven, he lowered the car windows and, with the delicious air streaming in, mashed the accelerator and headed for the lake track.

He was a quarter of the way around the lake, the

track gaining altitude as it rose and ran along a white bluff a hundred feet above the lake, when a yellowjacket flew into the car and could not seem to fly out. It flew angrily around his head, weaving figure eights. He could feel the air stirring under its wings. He flapped his left hand trying to drive it out, but it suddenly came at him and stung him just below his right eye. Instinctively he put his right hand up to his burning eye, which felt as though washed with acid and the car swerved off the track. He tramped the brake but the front half of the car was already projecting over the bluff, the rear tires still on land, the entire vehicle teetering when he moved. His eye had swelled nearly shut. The yellowjacket was still with him but there was no question now of shooing it away. Even if it stung him a hundred times he was afraid to move. His heart pounded in his throat. He would sit quietly. It was only a matter of time before someone saw him. Freda Beautyrooms. But how long would she sleep? Would she look out of the window at the lake? Surely he must be in sight of those big windows in her bedroom. He wanted something to wave to catch her eye. He gingerly picked up his grain elevator cap and slowly moved it up and down before the windshield. The yellowjacket came at his hand and stung him on the thumb. The car gave a sickening shudder. The edge of the bluff was gradually breaking off and pulling the car forward toward the lake.

There was nothing else for it, he had to get out

somehow. He had to get in the back of the car. There was a space between the two bucket seats and very slowly, very carefully he raised his buttocks and shifted over into the gap, sliding gently backward as he went. The car hardly trembled. Cautiously he moved toward the backseat, but as he pulled his legs up, more of the cliff broke away and the car nose tilted downward a terrible inch. He pissed his pants, hardly noticing. But now he was in the backseat, his hand reaching for the door handle, opening it as slowly as possible, and then rolling out onto the blessed ground. He crawled away from the edge, hearing the patter of clay falling into the water below. But from the outside the car looked more awkward than perilous, canted over the bluff as though peering at the water before a dive and refreshing swim. In fact, he thought, if he could get a tow truck out here there was a good chance they could pull it back to the track. He headed for the road and only then realized his pants were sopping wet and, as he walked, chafing his thighs. His right eye was swollen shut. He guessed it was eight miles to town. In this wind his pants would dry long before he got there, or someone might come along and give him a ride. Not if his pants were still wet. He had a choice, of course. He could go back to Freda Beautyrooms' house and ask to use the phone, call a tow truck. What could he say when she remarked on his wet pants? Or he could walk to town. He wondered briefly if the yellowjacket was still in the Saturn and decided to walk to town.

Out on the main road he walked along, turning around and walking backward, thumbing a ride, every time he heard or saw a vehicle in the heat-quivering distance. A rattletrap truck packed with three cowboys passed him, then two Mexicans in a well-maintenance truck. The third vehicle stopped and Sheriff Hugh Dough opened the passenger door, glancing at Bob's wet pants, and said, "Car break down?" then, seeing his swollen eye, "Have a accident?"

"'Down' is part of the problem," said Bob. "I was driving around the lake to look at the ranch when a bee got in and stung me and I lost control. The car is kind of at the edge. I almost went into the lake. So now I got to call a tow truck."

"Happen I got tow straps," said the sheriff, glancing again at Bob's damp crotch. "Get in."

When they got to the Saturn the cliff had given way several more inches and the car had the posture of a diver leaning forward before the plunge.

"I don't know," said the sheriff, "that weak old yeller dirt could come down any minute. I'd say you need a tow truck."

"That's what I said."

"You need a tow truck and a prayer. So tell me, Mrs. Beautyrooms ain't thinkin a sellin you the Axe-Head, is she?"

"Not exactly. It's complicated. Real complicated."

"You can spin me your yarn while we wait for

Albert." And he called the dispatcher and told her to get Albert Dent out to the Beautyrooms' place.

"We got a car half off the bluff over the lake. He needs a get some speed on it."

21

TRIPLE CROSS

It was another grey morning, the low-hanging clouds bulging with hundreds of grey udders that threatened hail and worse.

He spent the morning writing to Uncle Tam and Mr. Ribeye Cluke, drove into Woolybucket on a road the color of grapefruit pith and mailed the letters. The weather was closing in, sticky, damp and dark. In his mailbox was a plain brown envelope postmarked Denver. He tore it open. It was the Global Pork Rind newsletter, *Ribs*.

A sudden burst of wind threw hailstones against the post office window. Lightning flickered as he ran for his car. On the way back to the bunkhouse the wind shoved and hustled the Saturn. Hail and rain mixed, the hail increasing in size, smacking the car, the road, and rebounding with dull purple flashes. The lightning shot around him in blinding streamers. He pulled off near Saddle Blanket bridge and parked under a black willow for some shelter. The wind was terrific and frightening. The sky flickered, its sickening strobe light revealing torn clouds, leaves flashing white. Rain and hail and twigs and plastic bags scraped over the windshield. He could just make out hailstones the size of walnuts lashing the stream into froth. It was less frightening to watch the brown ripped water than to look at the jittery horizon. A brown wave swept down the Saddle Blanket, no longer pencil-size, but a snarling river. He watched in horrified amazement as the water swelled out of its banks and began spreading over the road behind him, then, with thin, watery fingers, crept over the bridge roadway. He saw he could be cut off and swept away in the flood.

Quickly he started the car and left the shelter of the black willow, back into the full force of the hail and wind. The wind, gusting and veering, pushed the Saturn toward a deep ditch that ran alongside the road filled now with rising water nearly up to the asphalt. Slewing and skidding he fought his way through the wet detritus on the road. The lightning flashed, the brassy light revealing carbuncled underclouds. A dozen cows, pelted by the hail, ran in front of him, their hooves splashing, the young calves blatting in fear and pain. A piece of metal roofing hurled past and tumbled end over end across the prairie. The hailstones were bigger now, and it seemed a dozen roofers with nail guns were attacking the Saturn. All at once the windshield cracked and crazed in a dozen places. He could not see through it and had to put down the window and drive peering out the side. A large dark hump in the road turned into a dead cow and somehow he steered around it. No wonder, he thought, that panhandle people were a godly lot, for they lived in a sudden, violent atmospheres. Weather kept them humble.

By the time he reached the Busted Star gate, the hail was slacking off. He knew the Saturn was ruined, pocked with ice pellet dings. It was not possible to drive across the stream to the bunkhouse and he took refuge in LaVon's kitchen, his rain-wet mail stuffed under his jacket. He was sorry not to get across the creek, for Lieutenant Abert's *Expedition* was there, facedown on his pillow.

"Oh Bob," said LaVon, "there's a tornado in Hutchinson County, just about twenty miles away. I was worried about you." The kitchen radio was on, emitting a blatting horn sound, the signal to take shelter. The television was flashing red warning signals. A hollow voice finished the tornado announcement and said ". . . Service has issued a severe thunderstorm warning for Woolybucket County until three-thirty P.M. This line of thunderstorms can produce golf ball/baseball–size hail, torrential rains with flooding and high winds. Take shelter in a sturdy place."

"My God," said Bob, "are you sure the tornado isn't right here? It's terrible."

"This is just the edge of it," said LaVon. "If it was right into the tornado, why, you'd be whirlin around the sky. It's on the telvision. You'n see it, that red patch there? Good thing not many people lives in Hutchinson County. Anyway, you better stay here tonight because you can't get across to the bunkhouse until that water goes down and that probly won't be until tomorrow. There could be more storms. They're sayin there could be a bunch a them touch down. I'll make up the couch for you." Outside the lightning trembled and shivered.

Bob plotted to steer LaVon toward the story of her grandfather's scarred back. To soften her up he helped her rearrange her kitchen pots and pans. Through the window she pointed out the storm cellar door in the backyard.

"If a real one *was* to come, that's the place to be. If I'm not here you just get in there and stay put, anytime, day or night. It's fixed up pretty good down there. There's a old tee-vee and some canned goods and candles and such. Couple cots and a chair or two."

"How often do you have to use it?"

"Never have used it but once," said LaVon. "Tornadoes don't hit here very often. We get the fringes. They'll follow the rayroad tracks, though. Why I wouldn't want a house next to the tracks. I believe it's lettin up now." And, in fact, the lightning had shifted to the northeast and the southwest showed clear.

Bob sat at the kitchen table drinking coffee, remembered his mail and took up the Global Pork Rind newsletter. Much of the content was devoted to pie charts and financial prognostications, but the two back pages were intended for the location crews who were, Bob saw, scattered all over the globe. He learned for the first time, for Ribeye Cluke had not told him, of the Global prize-winning system.

TIME'S AWASTIN, SCOUTS, BUT THERE IS STILL TIME TO MAKE SURE YOU GET *YOUR* HANDHELD DEVICE WITH LEATHER CASE STAMPED WITH THE GPR LOGO! Why be sorry when the end of the month rolls around and you are not one of the fortunate boys and girls sporting a sleek new PALM DEVICE?

At the bottom of the same page, in a pink box bordered by magenta, was a list of the previous month's outstanding site scouts, the ones who had secured the most acreage for Global.

SALES WIZARD	HOW MUCH	WHERE
CN Barker	900 acres	La Junta, CO
Evelyn Chine	6,000 acres	Guymon, OK
Mrs. Freda Bigley	1,600 acres	Johnson, KS
Clay Leak	120 acres	Blue Hill NE

These fine representatives now all enjoy last month's prize, an attractive overnight bag by Calvin Cline. Lack of space prevents listing all of our outstanding site scouts. If your name does not appear this month, make sure it does next month. Evelyn Chine and Mrs. Fred Bigley, for breaking the magic thousand-acre barrier, also received Global Explorer Portable Receivers, an advanced short-wave radio that pulls in Moscow, Paris and London *in English* with crystal clarity. Evelyn Chine also received a Megapixel Digital Camera with Carrying Case and Compact Memory card for her terrific accomplishment! Atta girl, Evelyn, show the guys how to do it!

LaVon was not in a storytelling mood, balancing her checkbook and muttering. In the afternoon, restless in the French provincial kitchen, Bob decided to drive into town and arrange to get the windshield replaced, see what kind of damage the storm had done to Woolybucket. Outside he saw that the Saturn was not too bad, maybe a dozen dents. The worst was the windshield.

He was surprised to find the sun shining and the roads dry and pale as powdered milk just a few miles from the Busted Star. In Woolybucket he parked at the Old Dog, went in and helped Cy load the serving platters, pineapple-glazed ham steaks, twice-baked potatoes with sour cream, asparagus with butter and lemon juice, raisin pie.

"It didn't even rain here, did it?"

"Nope. We could see the storm, though, and the wind kicked up some. It's that way sometimes, bad weather a town over and nothin here or vice versa. And it was real muggy earlier, hot enough to cook a bear. Anyway, you get used a rapid weather change.

It's part a the character a the place. Stick around, you'll hear some weather stories."

But Bob was thinking about LaVon's tale of rancher Skieret and his foreman, Blowy Cluck.

"Cy, did you ever hear about an old-time rancher named Skieret?"

"Hell yes, everbody knows the stories about him. He was supposed to blowed up some Finn farmer. Back when they was havin war over fencin the range. They found the Finn a mile from Skieret's ranch blowed up by dynamite. The cowboy found him said it looked like somebody had rammed a stick of dyna-mite up the Finn's popcorn popper and lit the fuse—the head and neck and shoulders was intact and unmarked, as was the legs from the knee down, but everything between the knees and the clavichords had nourished the prairie in shreds smaller than a toothpick. Skieret was one of them hard-ass old boys who did what he wanted and devil take the leavins."

Bob said, "LaVon told me about the barbwire con-test he lost."

"There's a hunderd stories about that outfit. They was real colorful. Skieret's still got kin here, still on the old ranch. Janice Sue Palace, champion golfer, is his great-granddaughter, still runs Skieret's place. She's a good rancher, too, could she quit draggin home husbands. And you mentioned Blowy Cluck? He's got descendants here all over. I'm a little bit kin a him myself."

An unusual truck pulled up across the street. Bob

craned his neck to get a better look at it. It had so many dents he could not tell if any of them were fresh. The magnetic sign on the driver's door read ACE WINDMILL. Ace, looking more than ever as though he had spent his formative years in a trouser press, got out, pulled his wallet from his back pocket and examined the contents. Bob thought he might be checking to see if he could afford the Old Dog's lunch. Apparently he could, for he headed to the door.

Inside, Ace looked around slowly, nodded to Bob and several men but chose a table near the window, away from the rest of the room. He came up to the food tables but only poured a cup of coffee.

"Waitin for Brother Mesquite," he said to Cy, who nodded and kept turning ham steaks in the giant fry-pan. "Bad weather in Hutchinson County. They had them a little tornado."

"So I hear," said Cy.

The place filled up quickly and Bob was busy hauling foil-wrapped potatoes out of the oven, but not too busy to notice the whispered excitement in the room. Something was going on. He caught the name "Flores" several times and guessed there was a cockfight on the calendar, but could learn nothing more. When the crowd thinned out he noticed that Ace was still nursing his cup of coffee and looking at the food tables with a hungry face. Once he got up, went to the door, opened it and looked up and down the street. He got another cup of coffee and resumed his wait.

"Looks like he's tied up somewheres, Ace," said

Cy. "Or else he got caught in the storm. You might as well get your dinner while there's still some left."

"I'll wait a little longer," Ace said, then added, "anyway, here he is now."

A second truck had pulled up behind the windmill truck. The driver, something of an apparition, thought Bob, ran across the street through the glittering sunlight and opened the Old Dog's door. Here was a sight; a bearded monk in a grubby cassock hitched up at the waist high enough to show a pair of jeans from the knees down, cowboy boots, a battered Resistol on his head.

"Ace! Real sorry I'm late. Storm caused a truck to roll over and they had them a chemical spill on the highway. Had the traffic blocked off. I turned around and come the long way on the farm roads and it was some mess, high water, trash all over. Man, I'm starved. Let's get somethin a eat. Sure smells good, Cy."

The two men filled their plates and went back to the table. The monk-cowboy bowed his head and mumbled, Ace said "Amen," and their knives fell on the ham steaks. From what Bob overheard Ace was talking about replacing a windmill head on the Triple Cross range. The monk-cowboy listened attentively, asking a few questions. When his plate was clean he got up and went back to the food tables, took more salad and a spoonful of grits.

"Pretty good, Cy. Especially the salad dressin. Don't suppose you'd part with the recipe? Or come over and spend a day in our kitchen teachin us a few things?"

Cy, who received few face-to-face compliments on his food, blushed and said he'd write down the salad dressing ingredients, "Nothin to it, just fresh-made mayonnaise. I only put in a hair a garlic. The boys'd shoot me they known they was eatin garlic."

"I'm serious about a teachin day."

"Well, you know, between runnin this place and the ranch work, I hardly got time to take a—to relieve myself. I don't know when I could do something like that."

"Maybe we could send down a apprentice. He'd help out and sort of watch how you did things."

"Well, sure, that might work out. Bob here's been helpin me when he can, but it would be fine to have an extra set of hands. I do most of my prep work real early, four or five in the A.M. That's the crazy time I need somebody."

"Howdy, Bob," said the monk-cowboy turning to him. "Brother Mesquite from the Triple Cross. You're doin a good job here." And to Cy he said, "I'll ask who wants a get a early start on the day. Brother Sammy's up before light and he'd enjoy to ride his bike more than he does. And he's good in the kitchen. Makes a mean pizza."

He carried his plate back to Ace Crouch and they began to talk again. Bob got a cup of coffee, sat at the next table and listened.

Jim Skin came in, plastered with grease. "Hey there,

Ace, Brother Mesquite. Cy, what's good today?"

"Ham steaks with gravy, mashed taters, new green peas, rhubarb fool."

"Nothin with pineapple?"

"Matter of fact there is. Pineapple on the ham steaks, and pineapple-tapioca puddin. Only made a little bit. Right there on the end. Most people prefers rhubarb."

"It's O.K. But pineapple is so goddamn good it ought a be against the law. For everbody but me."

He brought his plate to Bob's table.

"How you doin?" he said. "I'm Jim Bob Bill Skin. Just call me Jim." He had a bad neck, long, as though stretched, and thick, with an Adam's apple as large as his knee. Dark hairs grew unevenly on it in whorls and clusters, disappearing into a chest mat like moldy black hay.

"Bob Dollar. Doing good. How about yourself?"

"Good as a pig in a waller. You try this pineapple puddin? It is *good*." He was eating the pudding first as though it might get away.

"I'm not crazy about pineapple. Rather have the rhubarb stuff."

"Rhubarb fool. *Wagh!* My mother used a make it. If us kids managed a steal a couple stalks from some old biddy's garden. I know who you are. You're stayin out a LaVon's, right?"

"Yeah. In the old bunkhouse."

"Well, you can answer me something. I heard she keeps tarantulas and scorpeens for pets. That right?"

"Tarantulas, yes. But she's only got one now. The cat knocked the other one's cage over and it got away. No scorpions far as I know."

"Holy Jeez. So it's loose somewheres? The tarantula? *Wagh!*"

"Seems like it. Somewhere in the house. I walk real slow whenever I go in and keep my eyes open. It's the bad one got loose. Big grey bugger with a design on its back."

"What she ought a do is get in one a them termite guys and gas it to death," said Jim Skin, coughing, *"Wagh! Wagh!"*

"She doesn't want to kill it. She wants to find it. She says it's a very valuable animal."

"Come on! Who'd pay good—*Wagh!*—money for a fuckin spider?"

"LaVon, I guess. Now I got a question for you."

"What?"

"Somebody told me to ask you about your daddy—said he was quite a local character."

"He was. And not exactly local. *Wagh!* See, I don't come from here, and neither did my deddy. I was born up in Guymon, Guymon Oklahoma. My deddy was from Struggle. That's Oklahoma too, west a Guymon. Actually he was born in Arizona. His folks went down there pickin cotton in the dirty thirties. In Oklahoma they was tenement farmers growin cotton in Custer County, not in the panhandle, but the whole system collapsed and they went to pickin cotton in Arizona. *Wagh!* Thirty-seven out a forty families pulled out a the Oklahoma panhandle them days. It was worse there than down here in Texas. But he *is* known all over, Texas and Oklahoma, parts a Colorado, New Mexico. *Wagh! Wagh!*"

"Why was he so famous?"

"Partly it's because he got married so much. Fourteen times. And all fourteen a them slipped away from him. He couldn't hold a woman. He could get em but he couldn't hold em."

"I guess that's true for a lot of people," said Bob.

"He had a little word or two for each one a them, like a little song. Here's what he'd say: 'Harriet was a deep-water storm, blowed out all my—*Wagh!*—sails; Calvina was a Texas mule trade; Josie was jinglebobs and blue honey; red-headed gal was paradise lost; that old horseface Brigitte belonged in a corral, but she didn't like mine; Jean was all cob and catalog; Lucy reminded me of a—*Wagh!*—camel's ass; and old Susie, she was moonlight and a whiskey bottle on a white rock.' He'd just reel that off. That was my—*Wagh!*—mama, old Susie. And she did like to drink before she got religion and spent all her time in prior. But from all these women only three squallin kids made it into the world, me and my half-sister; we used to call her Little Girl with Her Hair All Hangin Down, just 'Little' for short. And my brother Hoit. He died when he was around nine or ten. Was supposed a bring a pitchfork to deddy down in the hayfield, but he sort a got to runnin, pushin the pitchfork along on the path in front a him, and it cotched a tine in a bunch a grass roots and as he was movin pretty fast the handle jammed into his gut real hard. Ruptured his gut. He bleeded a death inside before they could get help. Doctor said that even if he'd been right there with all his instruments laid out there wasn't nothin he could a done. Oh my God, we was dirt-poor. Here I am, forty-six years old and have yet to own my first bicycle. My sister's in the entertainment binness in Vegas. When my deddy died they buried him in—*Wagh!*—Struggle. He is buried in the lightbulb cemetery—*Wagh!*—up there where a man's worth is spelled out by the watts a the lightbulbs set in the ground around the grave. Know what old Susie picked for him? Three burned-out refrigerator bulbs. She said he didn't deserve no more. *Wagh! Wagh! Wagh!* I always felt bad about that. I always told myself I'd go up there and put in bigger bulbs for him. Hoit's buried up there too."

"What was the other thing your father was famous for?"

"*Wagh!* His dick. That's how he got all the women. He had a dick like a stallion. That's how come he's so good known. Some guy thought he was heavy built would come up and say, 'I hear you got a big one. Ten bucks says I'n beat you.' And then they'd lay the money out, and other guys would bet and then they'd unzip. My deddy always won. *Wagh!* It was never even close. By rights I should a inherited some a that, but it didn't work that way. All I got was the average. *Wagh!* Don't seem fair."

"I'd like to see that graveyard," said Bob.

"Well, I'll tell you the truth, it's known a some as a nigger graveyard. My deddy wasn't no nigger but he had Indan blood and Indan kin in that—*Wagh!*— boneyard and that's where he wanted a be laid. There is whites in there too. But nowadays it got to be known as the nigger lightbulb cemetery. But if you'd like—*Wagh!*—to see it, I would admire to drive you up there. Get me some fresh lightbulbs for his— *Wagh!*—grave."

"O.K. When you want to do it?"

"Sattaday? I could—*Wagh!*—do it then."

"Well, I guess I could too. What time you want to meet?"

"Say nine A.M. right here."

They shook on it.

"Wagh!"

"By the way," said Bob casually, "when's the cock-fight?"

"Tonight, ain't it?" said Jim Skin. "At Flores's barn in Wasp, just over the Oklahoma line. It's behind the old Esso gas station. Why, you goin?"

"I might."

He drove slowly through the back streets of Wooly-bucket, many of them unpaved, the traffic kicking up enough dust to keep vacuum cleaners humming. There were many vacant lots in town, some of them places to store old machinery and vehicles, others garden plots where residents worked on their tomatoes and string beans in the cool of the evenings. A few people still kept horses and it was not unusual to see them riding slowly around town, to the post office (where the old hitching rail was still handy) or the feed store. A bald man everyone called Red was the local expert on animal diseases and the complaints of large stock, and many of the riders stopped by his front yard for advice.

The asparagus days were upon them. LaVon had been busy pickling slender stalks and freezing the stouter ones. Everyone had special asparagus recipes—stir-fried beef with asparagus, cream of asparagus soup, asparagus strudel, asparagus and noodles. LaVon had insisted he try her Salade de Saint-Jacques, a knot of defrosted scallops heaped in the center of a plate and radiating from this hub fourteen asparagus spears, atop each a thread-thin raw enoki mushroom. The sauce, composed of equal parts of horseradish, gin, tomato paste and whipped cream, took his breath away.

"It's unique, LaVon," he said, and she nodded, pleased.

After the dishes were in the washer Bob drove over on the floury back roads to Cowboy Rose. There was a tiny bakery there and on Wednesday—cookie day—they had vanilla-pecan wafers, for which Bob had developed a strong affection. The bakery was strategically located across the street from the elementary school and if he didn't get there before three o'clock there would be no cookies left.

Cowboy Rose looked as though a certain amount of wind had swept through it, for trash was scattered and there were twigs and branches in the road near the highway picnic pull-off. The sky was shaved clean except for a stubble of pale clouds on the horizon.

He came out of the bakery with his warm sack of cookies and drove to the tiny park with its shade trees, where he planned to enjoy the first half dozen. He found an empty bench near the playground, swept the fallen leaves and twigs from it and, while he ate cookies, watched two or three preschoolers play, their mothers sitting on the concrete curbing around the sandpit. An older girl, certainly old enough to be in school, perhaps the fifth grade, was twirling around a maypole affair, clutching a leather strap attached to a nylon cord. Each time she swung herself off the ground for a spin she cried, "Wheee!" in a high, put-on voice. He was instantly, with the speed of a slammed door, transported to some swing in his childhood, a tire swing tied to the branch of a shady tree and himself swinging and saying "Wheee!" in exactly the same way, saying it, not out of glee, but because it was what you said when you swung around, and remembered himself alone and marked for solitude, beneath his feet the oval of hard dirt where the grass was worn away, feeling sick from the motion of the swing but still saying "Wheee!" as though he were having fun, although there was no one to see nor hear him. He could smell the tree and the tire with its little slosh of water from the last time it had rained, and a very bad feeling of desolation, of aching loneliness, flooded through him and into the taste of the cookies, which he knew he would never like again.

Instead of going back to the Busted Star he went along to Wasp, looking for the cockfight. On the way he found a barbecued-rib counter at the back of a grocery store and brought the smoky red meat with him to Wasp, a hamlet so small there was nothing there but the ancient Esso station in a state of collapse. In a muddy field half a mile beyond stood a galvanized metal building surrounded by broken machinery and parked pickup trucks. Some of the trucks he had often seen parked near the Old Dog.

An enormously fat woman in a magenta pantsuit sat in a director's chair at the door. She took ten dollars from him and stamped his hand with a purple circle that enclosed the word "member." The light was dim inside. The underside of the galvanized roof had been sprayed with some lumpy plastic insulation and thousands of feathers stuck to it. The seats were tiered bleachers and there were only about fifty people in them, many of them very large men in overalls but also twenty or so short, slender Mexican and Vietnamese men in T-shirts and jeans. They had wide jaws and soft throats, round eyes like black spots and small mustaches barely larger than the wings of a moth. Everyone was smoking. The smell of smoke, feathers, hot birds and sweating humans was palpable. The atmosphere was hot and odorous. He sat next to a four-hundred-pound farmer in a plaid shirt limp from many washings.

Below lay a rectangular pit with two smaller fenced areas at each end. A sign on the wall announced that this was a PRIVATE CLUB. Another sign read NO GAMBLING, but Bob saw fistfuls of money changing hands.

"Where do all these folks come from?" asked Bob, looking around, for Wasp lay in a singularly unpopulated region.

"Hell," said the fat man beside him, "from all over. And I mean *all over*! Dodge City, Garden City, Amarilla, Texhoma, they even come from Denver and Lubbock, from Wichita and Oklahoma City." As they spoke more people came in and Bob could hear roosters crowing. The fat man introduced himself as Byrd Surby, said he was an insurance agent from Fort Supply and had just started raising fighting cocks himself. "It's poplar all over the country, not just Oklahoma where it's legal, but places where it ain't legal. California is a tough state for cockfightin. Will Rogers introduced the sport to Hollywood. But things got tough when William Randolph Hearst, who tried somethin funny, was barred from competition. And out a spite he went to the legislators and pushed through the toughest laws in the country.

"That's Stick Flores," he continued, pointing out a tall man with close-cropped hair and a long, creased beeswax face, his lips the color of genitals, broad yellow hands with curved nails, climbing into the announcer's cage. A teenage boy entered the pit and began marking opposing lines in the dirt with a plastic ketchup bottle of flour.

The action began. A referee and two handlers, each holding an extraordinarily beautiful bird with a short knife bound to one leg, entered the pit. One handler was young, slouchy and fat, a farmer's cap on backward à la mode; the other severely wrinkled, his face a stretch of gravity-ruined muscles and slipped wattles, in extreme contrast with the brilliant blueface he held. This rooster was an oriental carpet of a bird with a hard red head, tail of iridescent green, a golden cape and a back draped in chestnut red like a fringed piano shawl. The fat young man's rooster was a brown hennie, which Bob thought less attractive than the blueface. The men shook hands and then, still holding their birds, allowed the birds to peck at each other.

"That's to git their blood up," said Bob's neighbor. "See, they're usin spurs, not knives. They match up by weight."

Then the bird owners separated, stepped behind the flour lines, bent and released their birds on the mark. The roosters rushed at each other. Everything went too quickly for Bob to follow. The brown hennie bird leaped on the blueface, stabbing. The blueface struck the hennie's leg with its wing and Bob heard a dull pop. The brown hennie, listing to one side, sprang forward, the spur on its good leg a jet of light. A shout went up from the audience. Someone screamed, "Kill im, Pee-Wee!" and Bob felt he was surrounded by ruffians. The beautiful blueface sagged, its beak touching the dirt. It coughed and Bob could see dark spots on the dirt. The handlers rushed forward, picked up their birds and blew into their mouths, then set them on the line again. The hennie rolled back and tried for a shot with his good leg, but was stunned by another wing blow and lay twitching. The blueface struggled up and stretched, then a gout of blood came from its beak and it fell. It was a dead winner. The old man picked up his bird by one foot and threw it toward the dark recesses of the back of the barn. Immediately another pair of men, one of them Rope Butt, stepped up with their birds, the teenage boy drew fresh flour lines and a new contest began.

Bob stayed for nearly two hours watching match after match until he began sneezing from the chickeny dust and feather effluvium mixed with smoke. There was something mesmerizing and terrible about the birds, the rank and sweaty crowd. Gradually he had understood that the cocks represented their owners, that the grossest lout, the skinniest Asian, mingled his psychological identification with that of the sleek, beautiful and dangerous birds. He said goodbye to the fat man and eased out. In the parking lot a heavy farmer was pissing on a tire. He glanced up at Bob.

"Lost me nine hunderd bucks in there," he said.

"Sorry to hear it."

"Not half so sorry as I am. I believe my waf will kill me."

Bob drove back to the Busted Star feeling he had been present at some dark blood sacrifice older than civilization, a combat with sexual overtones rooted in the deepest trench of the panhandle psyche.

22

RIBEYE WRITES

Bob had been in the panhandle for nearly three months. He had written six letters to Mr. Cluke describing the ladies' sewing circle, the interesting talk at the grain elevator and the Old Dog, had written a long explanation of how the unsettled weather had kept him from pressing the owners of land to sell. He had discussed the possibilities of the properties he had in mind—Tater Crouch's place, Freda Beauty-rooms' ranch and several others he thought might fall into his hands. He wrote nothing about luxury house sites. In return he had the GPR newsletter. But on the hot, cloudy Saturday morning he was to go to Oklahoma with Jim Skin to place high-watted light-bulbs on his father's grave he found two letters from Mr. Cluke in his mailbox, both short, sarcastic and biting in tone.

Dear Bob Dollar.
   Don't try to line up any properties. Just put in your time letting people see what a swell guy you are. You never can tell—they might just decide to sell all on their own. Of course, if they

do, it'll probably be to Texas Farms who have a very smart operator in the field. Sure, send the office a list of names you *think* might go for it. Boy, we really sit up and take notice when we see how many prospects you have lined up. Global Pork Rind is glad to have a popular fellow like you, Bob Dollar, to represent them! Be sure to tell the office if a miracle happens and one of these people decides to sell. Just keep on telling us how hard you're working, how bad the weather is out your way. Comment on everything you can think of, and tell us what you intend to do next week. Hot dog, you'll really give us fits of joy then!

The second letter was shorter.

Bob Dollar.
    More business and less letter-writing. I thought we got rid of the writing bug with the last fellow. Magazines will pay you for writing. GPR is paying you to find sites for hog farms. How about you pin those wrestlers to the mat and let us know when we can send the Money Offer Person down?

After these blasts Bob thought he had better not go to see Jim Skin's father's grave, but that decision called for a cup of coffee and a doughnut and the only place to get them was the Old Dog, where he found

Jim Skin at a table with a box of floodlights in front of him. He couldn't back out, so bought a sack of raised doughnuts and two take-out coffees.

"Let's us take your car," said Jim Skin. "My old truck is runnin with the help a Jesus the tires is so bad. And it's got that gas ping real bad. *Wagh!*"

They drove north, Jim Skin regaling Bob with the story of his life and his father's adventures—". . . one time he used a umbrella cover for a condom. Bob, you know why I like you?"

"No." He couldn't imagine why anyone would like him.

"Because you're—you're—I like you because you're laid-back. You just drift with whatever. At first I figured, that boy's on drugs."

"No," said Bob, wondering if Jim Skin was on something himself. He seemed hyper and a little crazy.

"The old man was pretty good with a lasso, too, let me tell you. There was one time back in the fifties when these three guys held up the bank. My deddy still rode his horse into town, hadn't never owned a vehicle up to that point—car or truck like. So he's comin down the street, not a thought in his head, when these guys run out a the bank with sacks a money in their arms. My deddy—didn't even think about it—started after them, got his old rope a-whirlin and cotch two a them in one loop. The other one got away. Before the sheriff come—not the sheriff we got now, but his main old deddy used a cook at Huntsville for the death row—my deddy heped hisself to one of them bags, hid it under his shirt and told the sheriff the other robber done run off with it. First thing he done was get hisself a nice automobile, big white Studebaker. A course it was a car like no cowboy would never have the dough saved up to buy and the sheriff figured that one out pretty quick. My deddy had that car about two weeks and then the sheriff convocated it. He just taken it with a big small on his face, caused a star to be painted on the side and deddy went back to his horse. He used the rest a the money to buy his ranch. It was in Oklahoma and he settled there and that damn main old sheriff couldn't touch him. Got me a red dirt dog, too. Old Woody. Named him after Woody Guthrie. He's dead now. Got killed by a bicycle feller carryin a gun. Shot him."

As they drove north Bob said that it was remarkable how different the contiguous panhandles seemed.

"Why not? Different people, different laws. Oklahoma is more southern in a way, and Texas is more your western state. Texas got the smart ones, smart guys watchin for the chance. It's been said Oklahomans is main-spirited and can't take no criticism, but you ask me your average Oklahoma person is pretty straightforward except he feels like Oklahoma always gets the shitty end a the stick. *Wagh!* When that McVeigh blowed up the federal buildin in Oklahoma City we just nodded and said, 'That's right, that's how it goes. Pore old Oklahoma.' And a course people didn't like that musical neither, until they made a movie out a it. *Oklahoma.* Then they liked it."

"What do you do for a living, Jim?"

"This and that but mostly I'm a musician. I play the guitar, write songs. If country music was to be tooken away tomorrow I'd kill myself. Specialize in Oklahoma material. We got us a group, the Okie Dokies. Play here and there. Down in Amarilla quite a bit. Guymon, Boise City, Beaver. You hear a lot a bad stuff about Oklahoma and I'm tryin a set it right."

After several hours of driving, Bob listening, they entered a particularly desolate stretch of wind-scoured sand and sparse grass. Jim Skin jerked his thumb to the right.

"That there is my deddy's ranch," he said. *"Wagh!"*

Bob slowed and looked at it. It was perhaps the poorest land he'd ever seen, eroded, dry and sorely used. The wind had blown Kentucky Fried Chicken boxes into the bluestem. A lifeless windmill leaned east, apparently ready to fall. But with great effort he could imagine it grassed, buffalo moving across it.

"He worked it some years. In the early days it wasn't too bad. They run cattle. That there pasture is where he calved for years and I mean thousands and thousands a years. Then come the big droughts and the wheels fell off the wagon."

"Who owns it now?" said Bob, expecting to hear it was part of the National Grassland system, that government effort to rescue the worst of the eroded dust bowl lands from their improvident owners.

"Well, I do," said Jim Skin. "I'd sell it, but there's nobody wants a buy. It's pretty poor and I guess I'm stuck with it. No good for farmin or ranchin. No sir, there ain't no corn on *that* cob. But it was a ranch once, long ago. Part a the drift fence they run across the Oklahoma panhandle a keep cows from strayin down into Texas was here. But that was open range days. Don't know who owned it then. Probly the 101."

A thought came to Bob's mind. "It would be O.K. for a hog farm," he said, keeping his tone neutral.

"Well, it would, but you know, not one a them guys ever come near me. I'd do it—it's a burden to me. But hell, for all you hear about them, them hog farm people are shy, they don't eat their dinner in Woolybucket and I wouldn't know where or how to find a one a them."

Bob opened his mouth, then closed it again, reopened it.

"You own it free and clear?"

Jim Skin shot him a sharp glance and paused a minute. "Well, half shares with Ace down in Cowboy Rose. He's the one fixes windmills. He's sort a my uncle. I got kin on both sides a the line. But Ace, he's pretty much got the say about this old ranch. Seein he pays the taxes." He waved his hand at the land again.

Jim Skin went on. "He ain't blood kin. He married one a my deddy's sister's friends—Vollie Eckenstein. He's brother to Tater Crouch, owns the Bar Owl. By rights Ace should a owned half the Bar Owl, but his old man left it all to Tater. I think it was part comprehension for that miscarriage a justice that my deddy left half a his place to Ace. They was always pretty good friends."

Bob felt the world getting smaller. While they had talked he watched a slowly twisting groin of cloud, a muscular mass that seemed to draw all other clouds into its huge torso. It reminded him of Timmy Potelle, the school exhibitionist, striking poses in the shower after gym, showing off his well-shaped body while several weedy hangdogs watched out of the corners of their eyes.

"This's her," said Jim Skin, jerking his thumb to the left. They drove under a wooden arch with the words STRUGGLE CEMETERY worked in twigs, and up a slight hill toward a plot fenced with barbwire.

"Here we are," said Jim Skin, "the cemetery. His grave's up in that corner, I think. We better get out and hoof it." As he walked, he coughed.

"The ghosts come up out a this place ever night like a flock a bats," he said.

At the front of the cemetery tidy rows of graves faced east, each set in stone curbing and covered with white pea gravel. Farther back the grave rows straggled and many were scraped earth, decorated with plastic ferns and flowers, slabs of rock, a broken accordion, a flashlight.

Near the path Bob noticed the grave of Mrs. Venus Hogg, whose headstone was carved with the image of a Princess telephone and the somewhat sinister inscription, "Jesus called. . . ."

They passed an open-sided tabernacle in bad repair, the benches along the sides splintery with weathered wood. In the near distance rain shafts shaped like the roots of wisdom teeth moved toward them. As the Law of Circumstance ruled, by the time they found Jim Skin's father's grave, drops pattered down and the Texas gloom fell on them. The grave was near the barbwire fence at the back. A cluster of the plants known as antelope horns for their odd leaves grew at the base of the stone.

Jim Skin kicked the refrigerator bulbs away and rammed the floodlights into the wet earth and they sprinted for the Saturn. But again Bob's eye had been caught by a name and he turned back to read the stone:

Here lieth Fanny Walter Morris,
a Young Cowboy
Born Rockhard, Main, 1904.
Died Woolybucket, TX Nov 17, 1920

It seemed Muddy Fan had more graves than he needed. They drove away as the thunderstorm closed with bulging clouds like portly buttocks in white underwear.

"Deddy had the Hunter's Special for his coffin," said Jim Skin. "Camouflage shell and the liner was camo too. And he wore his camo jacket and hat. It was a nice send-off except them little bitty bulbs."

23

RICH ORLANDO

It took several days for the creek to drop enough to allow crossing. Bob felt as though he were coming home after a long journey. He sat on the porch with his bottle of Pearl and read of Lieutenant Abert's encounter with a remarkably similar storm, which coated the ground with an inch and a half of hail that, lodged against the bluestem, formed small dams until the prairie was ankle deep in water. The lieutenant made a sketch of the remarkable sight. But, he wrote huffily, "It would have been a laughable scene to a disinterested looker-on, if I may judge from the effect a rude sketch produced on an untutored Indian."

As the days passed the pressure to make a deal increased. Finally, Bob Dollar tossed and turned at night, unable to concentrate on Lieutenant Abert's observations of rugged cliffs and prairie dogs, a sentence drumming in his head, "Get a property, get a property." He wanted to nail down Tater Crouch because there already was hog stink in the air. The Beautyrooms ranch was too fine for a hog farm; it really would be an extraordinary site for upscale houses. He thought briefly of contacting a Denver developer but then he imagined himself explaining that the property was in the Texas panhandle and that the owner wanted nine million dollars for it. Still, if he went up to Denver the next weekend, he might talk to a real estate outfit about the Beautyrooms ranch. But for the hog farm, Tater Crouch was the real target. And after Tater, Jim Skin and his so-called uncle, Ace Crouch. How would old Ribeye like it when he brought in two properties at once?

The pay phone in the Old Dog still hung on the wall and from it Bob telephoned Tater Crouch and asked if he could come out and talk to him the next morning.

"Yes, you can come out but I don't know as I can tell you much more about the freighters. We might have some of that mule harness in the top of the barn. You are welcome to look."

"I'd like to see it, but actually I want to talk to you about something else."

"What?"

"Well, I'll come out tomorrow and explain it all."

"I see." The old man sounded suddenly crafty.

Bob Dollar ate two bowls of Cy's corn and chile soup, dunking slabs of buttered bread into it. He drove back to the Busted Star and stopped at the ranch house for water. LaVon was sitting at the kitchen table, gnawing on a plate of defrosted and reheated chicken wings.

"I should have brought you some of Cy's soup," he said.

"What kind was it—noodles out of a can with big hunks of celery whacked in?" she sneered.

"No. He doesn't make that kind of stuff. Corn and chile with onions and cilantro and cream and plenty of homemade bread. It was really good. He's a great cook."

"Well, it sounds good. I don't know if I'd care to go in there, though. They say the sweat drops off his nose into whatever he's cookin. That I can live without." She threw the wizened chicken wing down on her plate. "Too sultry a night to eat. That reminds me, a fella come lookin for you. I told him you'd probly be back before dark. He said he'd come back, if not tonight then tomorrow. Drivin a fancy car. One a them Porches."

"Who was it?" He couldn't think who would come looking for him aside from the sheriff, and certainly not in a Porsche, but surely LaVon knew Sheriff Dough.

"He didn't say his name."

"What did he look like?" Maybe it was Orlando. His sense of expectation flared.

"Great big muscled-up fella covered with rings and tattoos. Yellow hair. Kind a main-lookin."

"Muscled-up" did not sound like Orlando. "Fat? Was he fat?"

"Not a ounce a fat on him. Looked like Charles Atlas."

"Who's Charles Atlas?"

"Oh, forget it. This guy looked like a tee-vee wrestler and said he'd come back tonight or tomorrow mornin."

"That's too bad. I'm going out tomorrow morning. Going over to see Mr. Crouch."

LaVon half rose from her chair. "Don't tell me Tater's goin a let go a the Bar Owl!"

"We're just talking. If that guy comes back, tell him to leave me a note."

The stranger did not come back that night and the next morning Bob Dollar headed out for Tater Crouch's Bar Owl.

A bronze Polaroid light tinted the pasture as though a massive lens were clenched in the sun's eye socket. Bulky clouds flared red. It was stifling hot, not a breath of moving air. As he drove over the ranch bridge, the planks rattling, he caught the smell of the hog farm on Coppedge Road, a mile distant, but strong enough to bring tears to his eyes. In a way it made him feel better; the Bar Owl was already ruined; another fifty thousand hogs couldn't hurt. Tater Crouch would be better off in town, close to the amenities of the livestock auction, the Dixie feed store, and, of course, the Old Dog, where he could visit with his cronies.

So he knocked on the door with the pleasant feeling that not only did he have a done deal, but that he was doing a good deed; he would tell Tater that the stink of the neighboring hog operation left him no choice and follow up by pointing out the pleasures of Woolybucket, such as they were.

The housekeeper answered the door, snatching it open with such force that Bob's shirtfront was sucked inward. She glared at him with malevolence and he stepped back, catching his heel on a nail protruding from a board.

"He's in there," she snarled, pointing with her elbow at the ugly living room. As soon as he stumbled through the door she slammed it and rushed off toward the kitchen.

Tater Crouch turned his wheelchair slowly around and smiled at Bob. There was a dusty mass of leather lines and buckles spread over chairs and tables, across the floor and into the hall beyond. The aged leather was stiff and unwieldy and twined like Laocoön's snake.

"Well, Mr. Nickel, you'll be pleased. I got Louise a go up in the barn loft and look for that ten-mule harness a my granddeddy's. It wasn't there but then I thought it might be in the crawl space over the tack room and sure enough, it was. So we been tryin a spread it out here the way it would a been used. You got a imagine there is a team a ten mules here."

No wonder, Bob thought, the housekeeper had glared if she had spent the hot morning on hands and knees in an oven of a crawl space, dragging out stiff and dirty hundred-year-old mule harness. He pretended interest in the rig but kept well back when a nimble spider emerged from under a buckle and ran across the brown carpet, disappearing under shelves that held figurines of horses. He tried in vain to change the subject from mule teams and mule harness to ranch properties, hog farms, and the pleasures of Woolybucket, but Tater Crouch was among the days of yesteryear and not to be deterred. The best Bob could do was herd him away from mules and toward horses and from horses toward Mr. Skieret, who hated barbwire.

"A course that was way before *my* time," said Tater Crouch, "but we all knew the stories. Plenty a them. Abner Skieret and Blowy Cluck. What a pair. You ever hear about Blowy's horse and the train whistle?"

"No," said Bob in despair, wondering how to turn the direction of conversation.

"It's a well-known story. Blowy had hisself a horse, Old Razorback, didn't like trains in any shape or measure. He got fractious and nervy when he had to be around em. In fact he hated em. Well, horses back then did not have an affection for trains, but the most did not lose their minds and bust in half when one heaved up over the horizon. Old Razorback did. So one time Blowy was out on the prairie ridin, a long, long way out yonder. He was all by his lonesome and you know, Mr. Nickel, how far Texas stretches here, so there ain't nothin *but* yonder. Well, Blowy, he was kind a tired a bein out there, nothin but grass and sky and his horse's ears, so he thinks he'll pert things up a little. He goes ahead and makes a sound like a locomotive whistle far away, *whoooo-ooooooo!* That old

369

horse stiffens up. Probly would a been O.K. if that was all, but no, Blowy has to do it again, a little louder, like the train is comin closer at forty miles a hour. Well, sir, that did the trick. Old Razorback jumped fifteen feet into the sky and turned hisself inside out, dumpin the locomotive on the ground and he don't stick around neither to see how much steam it's got up. Horse come into the ranch all lathered up and they thought sure Blowy was out there dead or worse. Bunch of em rode out to find the corpus and there was the locomotive puffin along on two blistered wheels and swearin swears never heard before in Texas.

"Hell, I didn't mean to get sidetracked like that," he said. "About them freight wagons. I knew you was interested so I called up my old pal, Almond Yuta, works over to the Panhandle Plains Museum in Canyon. He knows a lot about wagons. He collects the damn things. Funny, he told me there's not a single entire freight wagon from the old days been preserved anywhere. I told him there was a big old Studebaker freight wagon up in Guymon, but he snaps back that it's just pieces and some a the runnin gear and a wheel or two throwed together, but the entire, original wagons are gone. Not a one saved and they used a be in the thousands, just thousands crossed over this country. Them wagons made the United States. The big outfitters was Russell, Majors and Waddell—sixteen thousand yoke a ox, fifteen hunderd employees—bull whackers and mule skinners, and they had terminals in St. Louis, Nebraska City and I don't know where-all. That was big business then. Then they started the Pony Express, a good idea but the end for them. It busted them flat. Only lasted a year and a half and then the telegraph got operatin and nobody needed a send a letter by rider at five dollars a stamp. Yes, them freight wagons made this country side to side."

"Before the railroads came in," said Bob, thinking of LaVon's lecture.

"Yes. Before the railroads. Different museums got a Conestoga or two, they got buggies and Dearborns and Rockaways and Jersey wagons, but no freight wagons like we seen in that picture you showed me. Maybe one up in Utah, but in real bad condition. Mostly it's just pieces and parts is all that's left.

"He says them extra wagons hitched on the back end was trailers. That's what they called them, trailers. Like we'd say 'trailer truck.' He said that if one turned up somewhere in some farmer's barn or ranch house let him know. But it was the railroads killed them. Railroad in, mule team and freight wagon out. Folks just left them out on the prairie to weather away. Started fires with them. Not a single person looked out the window at the old freight wagon and said, 'By God, that'll fetch a good price to my great-grand-chirdren,' and put it up safe. So Almond said if *ever* you come across one—I told him you was interested in mule teams and wagons—call him up because it would bring a very sweet price. Unless the owner wanted a donate it as a part a Texas's past history."

And now Bob saw himself slipping away from the hog business and the luxury house business and becoming a freight wagon searcher, a finder of rural vehicles and implements. Who knew what would be valuable half a century on, a hundred years later? Was this how his uncle and Bromo operated, making silent bets on future values? Who could guess? The drivers of mule teams and homely but utilitarian freight wagons would have guffawed.

"Well, at least we've got photographs," said Bob.

"Not so many. Who in their right mind would take pictures a freight wagons?"

"The driver, proud of his mule team?"

"Right. Them drivers had all the money in the world a take pictures a their mules. Probly carried it next a their heart."

"How much could those wagons carry, anyway?" said Bob diverting the old man from sarcasm, hoping to get him talked out of the wagon subject and onto the idea of selling out.

"From what he said, your Santa Fe wagon could carry around sixty-five hunderd pound. You could get a secondhand wagon and a six-mule team for around eight hunderd dollars. Imagine what that would cost today. They called them Santa Fe wagons because they was always puttin out from Kansas City and Westport bound for Santa Fe. There was grand trade there. Almond tells me the most a them wagons was made in Philadelphia. Back in the east they had the hardwood they needed for them—locust and elum and oak, ash and poplar and I don't know what else. And all the special machinery. Lathes and planers."

The old man looked at the clock and nodded. "It's time I hit the hay for my mornin nap. Thank you for comin over, Mr. Nickel, and I hope I answered your questions about mule teams. I'll be goin a lay down now." And he shuffled out into the hall briskly, leaving Bob sitting on the white plastic chair.

The housekeeper came in, stood wordlessly, waiting for him to follow her to the door. There was nothing to do but leave.

"I'm sorry," he said to the housekeeper. "I'm sorry you had to—" but she slammed the door and he was alone in the odorous morning.

As he neared the highway he had to move far to the right to accommodate a big green SUV pulling into the Bar Owl gate. It whipped past him, spattering the Saturn with dust and gravel. He had only a glimpse of the driver, a scowling blond woman wearing large dark glasses, so short she could barely peer over the steering wheel, her lips moving with what he took to be invective. He thought her scowl uncalled for, looked in the rearview mirror and saw a sign he could not read in reverse. He braked, put the window down and craned his head out the window at it: ENTRANCE ONLY. Now he remembered that he and LaVon had come out a different way.

Nearing the Busted Star Bob saw a silver Porsche with Colorado plates parked in front of LaVon's. As soon as she heard the Saturn she was out the door and onto the porch, gesturing to Bob to put down his window.

"That man come again. He's down at the bunkhouse." Bob waved and drove on.

He could see a hulking form on the bunkhouse porch, a huge man with shoulders too wide to fit through the door except sideways. Bob parked, got out and looked at the colossus on the porch. There was something familiar.

"Bob!" The basso voice came up through the plinth of neck. The creature held out a monstrous hand. He bulged with muscle. He wore a black rayon short-sleeved shirt handpainted to show a barroom interior with a pneumatic blond on a green bar stool drinking a martini. The shirtsleeves could hardly contain the great biceps.

"Orlando? Orlando! I would never have recognized you—" They were slapping each other on the shoulder and laughing.

"Lifted weights. Prison's ideal for working out, exercising, bulking up, carb loading. Goddamn place looks like Mr. America–land. And since I got out I got into steroids. Hey, I'm on my way down to Austin. Got a partner there, but I wanted a see you. Got your address from your uncle. He looks pretty old."

"That Porsche—that's yours?"

"You bet, Bob. I got another one just like it only red. You are looking at one wealthy son of a bitch."

"But how? When did you get out? I mean—am I missing something here?"

"In the clink I played the stock market through my dad. Tech stocks and we sold when everything was high dollar, just before the crash. Lucky. Then, in there, a bunch of us used to do silly things and we made this weird CD that we sold through my dad on the Internet. It's done good. Every fraternity has to have one of these."

"What, singing fraternity songs?"

The colossus brayed. "No. It's called *Live Fart Rock Hits from Prison* and that's what it is. In prison you discover some surprising things about your body, and some of us noticed a variance in fart pitch. And we had one guy was a real star. Nothing he couldn't do—basso profundo to coloratura, whistles and quavers, tremolo. The Louis Armstrong of the asshole. It was simple after that. I just recorded samples—I had this little Casio digital sampler that looks like a wrist-watch—and when I got out I spliced them together. People love it. We got 'Jailhouse Rock' and 'Freebird' on there, but 'Stairway to Heaven' plays for eight minutes and it is dynamite. A lot of studio work, but worth it. It wasn't like we all got together in the Tabernacle Fart Choir—technology made it happen. And I had a couple hits after that, not farting, but in the same mode."

Bob did not want to know the nature of the subsequent successes. He could imagine a series of grunts and slobbers and wet smackings rendered as tunes and the delight such renditions would cause in fraternal circles.

"What about the computer scene? I thought that was what you wanted to do."

"Ah hell, I don't got the savvy for it. All the good times was back in the seventies with Cap'n Crunch and the Phone Phreaks. It's all different now. It's no good since the crash. Now I'm focused on CDs."

"I suppose there'd be a market for these with the Elks and the VFW too?" said Bob. "Firemen and oil rig workers and National Guard guys? How about the military?"

"Man! What a great idea. I hadn't even thought about those guys. Bob, tell you what, how about you sign on with me—be our sales manager. I got a partner down in Austin—my old cellmate, Smoko—but there's room for you. You got good ideas. We want a get into Dolby five-point-one mixes of fart stuff that can be played on DVD home systems—with video. We can really clean up. But getting the cash together for the console—hell, it's real expensive." He looked critically at the mud-stained, dusty Saturn. "You could buy yourself a Lexus or whatever. What do you say?"

Bob did not want to refuse his old friend within ten minutes of their reunion but the thought of selling fart records to old veterans and Elks was repellent. He thought Orlando's difficulties in getting the money together for his console were negligible compared with the problems of making a watchable video based on fart music.

"I'll have to think about it," he said. "I've got a pretty good job."

"What? What is your 'pretty good job,' Bob, that you're living in this hole in the Texas panhandle? Come on, Bob, it looks like something out of *The Texas Chainsaw Massacre*. Remember that girl in the hot pants? And the meat hook?" His dismissive glance took in the bunkhouse, the Saturn, the landscape, the Busted Star horses, the weeds in the ditch, the turkeys scratching in the leaves, the cloudy sky. "Look, Bob. I been in prison and I made a success. You been out in the world and what have you got to show for it?"

Bob said nothing. He doubted he could make Orlando understand about Global Pork Rind and following through on something he'd said he would do no matter how much he hated it.

"Well hell, let's you and me go on out and get some barbecue and get drunk."

"We'll have to go up to Guymon in Oklahoma, or over to Woodward, or to Amarillo. Woolybucket County is dry and there's no barbecue joints."

Orlando's expression was incredulous.

24

VIOLET'S NIGHT
ON THE TOWN

They ended up in Amarillo after a long and fruitless trip to Woodward. In the vicinity of Fort Supply the headlights illuminated a sign: HITCHHIKERS MAY BE ESCAPING INMATES. They turned west, roaring across the Oklahoma panhandle to Boise City and down through Stratford and Cactus, where they became entangled in a slow, slow parade of low-riders. Orlando played Jim White's "A Perfect Day to Chase Tornadoes" over and over. It was after eleven when they reached Amarillo and engraved in Bob's mind was the line ". . . *sometimes I feel so goddamned trapped by everything that I know.*"

The whole trip Orlando had storied along, telling about the zine collection of his cellmate, Smoko.

"He had maybe fifty, sixty. See, he was in for hacking too. But he got just a bushel a zines—not *2600*, they wouldn't let him have that one, but *Dishwasher, Whackamole, Mouthnut, Tripwire* and *Bill of Kansas.* That was the best one, *Bill of Kansas.* It's like a comic book showing this religious farm youth's struggle to combat science. Smoko always read it first and he'd kind of spoil it by saying what happened. He'd say, 'Poor Bill's up against it this time. He's trapped in a cave by a gang of geologists who are tryin to get his dad's farm. The dad's pretty far gone too. He don't even go to Wednesday night prayer meeting no more.' 'Come on, Bill,' he'd say. And I had to give him cigarettes to let me read it. The drawing was good too. Bill was this geeky guy with an incipient bald spot. And he wore overalls. Old Smoko. He got out a month before me. He had like his little tricks, you know? Everybody's got some physical talent, like the farting thing, usually something you discover when you're a kid, like wiggling your ears or whistling through your teeth or bending into a hoop shape. Smoko could work up a little spit into a foaming lather, made him look like a fox with rabies. And he used to do that if somebody hit on him. He would make this foam and it saved him from getting porked. The guy would see the foam and say, 'What's wrong with you?' and Smoko would sort of bubble through the foam and say, 'Just a disease thing, like,' and the guy would get real nervous and say, 'Git way off away from *me*, dude.'

"Route Forty cuts right through the top of Texas," said Orlando portentously. "And where there's trucks there'll be clubs," as they eased into Amarillo. He had changed to a tight black T-shirt stamped with the words "If I Gave a Shit You'd Be the First One I'd Give It To."

"There's one," he said suddenly, pointing at a low-slouched cinder-block building with a red door. "I knew it. We should a headed to Amarillo first."

A neon sign threw its red light on a man standing in the doorway, coloring his cigarette smoke a devilish crimson. *TEX'S JOINT*, read the blinking sign. *COME ON IN*. Bob pulled into the parking lot among a dozen pickups in various stages of dissolution. They made their way to the red door, jumping puddles in the cinder parking lot.

"Must have rained here," said Bob.

"You could paddle a canoe across this one," said Orlando, skirting an enormous brown puddle edged with glistening mud.

Before they reached the door they could hear the music, loud and punchy, a stentorian male voice bellowing. The drumbeat was slow and physical. They opened the door and went inside.

"Jesus!" shouted Orlando above the music. "This's like *Violet's Night on the Town*. Remember that movie? Remember Violet, this big-butt blond, gets a box from the florist and she opens it and it's a bunch a goldenrod? And she reads the card and it's from a guy she doesn't know? But he gives his address as some club? And says if she wants to come down she can have free drinks all night? And she goes? And this guy with a diamond belt brings her a drink? And tells her he is the one sent the flowers? And he gets her in the back room and gives her an injection? And she goes crazy? You gotta remember that one! There's the shot where they stick a baby crocodile nose-first up her skirt? You loved it. This place is just like it. Same layout. And look at the bartender! He could double."

Bob did not remember the movie nor the actor who played the bartender in it, but he glanced at the man behind the bar, extremely thin and very old, his carefully combed white hair hanging to his buttocks. He was wearing a grimy rhinestone-studded shirt and looked like Gravel Gertie.

"Get you," the bartender said to Orlando.

"Two Maker's Marks," said Orlando, ignoring Bob's head shaking. "And a couple Fat Tire chasers."

"We don't stock that stuff. Four Roses and Bud work for you?"

"I guess," said Orlando unhappily. "I guess it's that kind a place."

"Oh yeah. It's that kind a place," agreed the bartender, looking at Orlando's tattoos. "But I'll tell you what. Ten years ago you couldn't get in the door it was so packed."

He slid the drinks to them and they carried them to a table in the corner.

"I don't see how you remember those old movies," Bob said.

"Remember? How could I forget them? We did that in the clink, told each other the plots of old movies. There was one guy, Reg Curl, specialized in westerns. He'd seen hundreds of westerns and he remembered them all pretty good—the stars, the set, the characters' names, but actually I had the best ones. All those great horror and weirdo flicks.

Remember *Locked in a Bank Vault with Three Nymphos*? Remember *Re-Animator*? They must a used a hunderd gallons a fake blood makin that. I only seen one movie since I got out—*Cyberspace Duchess*. This Jap woman dressed in Mylar with live ants glued on wins the title 'Cyberspace Duchess' because she's so fast at web surfing. But see, because of her speed she makes a mistake e-shopping and instead of sending her boyfriend a birthday card she gets involved with some hard-core criminals."

"That's great. Telling the plots." Bob laughed, shook his head and looked around. There were fifteen or twenty people in the place, most of them old, oddly shaped women: a bony, braless woman of about fifty with dyed black hair gazed worshipfully at the singer, a pudgy woman with white spiked hair danced alone. All the women seemed to stare with various degrees of longing at the singer bellowing into a mike, an octogenarian with a red toupee. A sparkled sign on the edge of the stage read RUBY LOVING. A heavy blond with a beer gut, leaning against the sleazy faux-tweed shoulder of her date (perhaps a retired coal stoker who feared ablution, judging by the ingrained black lines in his face), kept crying to the singer, "Oh Ruby, oh Ruby, you beautiful man."

"More like *Night of the Living Dead*," said Bob.

Ruby Loving's huge, pendulous ears were so wrinkled and knotted they resembled strings of dried mushrooms. He was toothless, but his shirt was unbuttoned to the waist and beads of sweat sparkled in a lawn of white chest hair as he shouted *"Don't let the stars get in your eyes . . ."*

"Orlando," said Bob. "You got us into a senior citizens' club. There's not a person here under sixty-five. And the bartender's got to be eighty. He's an octogenarian."

"Yeah," said Orlando. "But I dig it. And there's liquor. What the hell, you want a drive around some more?" And he called out to the beer-gut blond, asking if her name was Violet.

"Nah. Della," she answered, looking at Orlando with interest. "You been here before?"

"No way. I been in prison. Me and my buddy"—he gestured at Bob—"just got out."

"Orlando," Bob mumbled. But there was no stopping the muscle man. He invited the woman, whom he insisted on calling Violet, to sit with them. Her black-seamed date came too, rather eagerly, no doubt figuring, thought Bob, that he was in for a night of free drinks. Well, let Orlando pay for them. He claimed to be rich.

"I'm Della and this is Bob," said the woman, patting the shoulder of her dark-lined companion.

"Oh now," said Orlando. "We can't have that. Already got one Bob. You're Violet and your friend is—Bram." Bob guessed that the name Bram Stoker had come to Orlando. "Violet and Bram." He waved for drinks and paid, tipping the old bartender, who shuffled over with a slanting tray.

But the elder Bob didn't take to Bram for a name.

"My name is Robert Bodfish," he said loudly and belligerently, glaring at Orlando. "And you call me Robert, or Bob, or Mr. Bodfish. Got that?" He thrust his hand into his jacket pocket.

Orlando's face fixed in a sneer as he opened his mouth but he saw, at the same time Bob did, the glint of metal rising from the man's pocket.

"Sure, Bob," he said smoothly. "Whatever you like. And you," he said to Bob Dollar, "I'll call *you* Bram. Want a dance?" he said to Violet, who nodded and jumped up. As they moved toward the floor Bob heard Orlando say, "Honey, I'd like to get you over to my side a the seat," and in a few minutes they were gyrating to "Itsy Bitsy Teenie Weenie Yellow Polka Dot Bikini." The two Bobs sat silent, their eyes down. Finally, as the singer segued into "Moon River," Bob Dollar said, "Uh, Mr. Bodfish, what's your line of work?"

"Hogs." The dark-seamed man lit another cigarette and shot out a stream of smoke that would have done credit to a cigar.

"I beg your pardon?"

"I said 'HOGS'! Pigs. Swine. *Oink oink.*"

"Do you raise them or sell them or butcher them or what?" He knew there was a meatpacking plant up in Cactus, but had thought it was beef as it was near a feedlot.

"Manager. Hog farm manager. Day shift." He said the last two words with some pride.

"Is that right?" said Bob. "What's the name of the

outfit? I mean, who do you work for? I mean, are you an independent? Are you with Texas Farms?" The other Bob's eyes were fastened on Orlando and the blond. Orlando was saying something to her and she glanced over at the table where the two Bobs sat, and frowned. There was something about her expression. Bob tried to connect it with *Violet's Night on the Town,* but in place of the film a memory of himself leaving Tater Crouch's place and a dusty SUV in a cloud of gravel appeared with its frowning blond driver, followed by the lightning recollection of the back page of the Global Pork Rind newsletter and the woman with the tape recorder interviewing Freda Beautyrooms.

"My God," said Bob Dollar, as the images clicked into place, "Evelyn Chine!"

"Nah. Global Pork Rind. Big outfit in Tokyo. Japs own it. I manage one a the farms. Used a be a pipe tester for Texola but this pays better. And it's not so much stress. Your pipe inspector's got a lot a responsibility. Especially on the gas lines. Take down in Garland where the drought was so bad the soil is cracked and the gas line leaked. The gas, travelin through the cracks, got into some houses and they blowed up, killed three people. At least hogs don't kill you so sudden. I got a second job too. At the carbon-black plant in Pampa."

That, thought Bob, explained the dark creases in the man's skin. He was ready to ask a hundred questions about hogs, thought that at last he'd found a way to get into a restricted plant, but Orlando was steering back to the table. The beer-gut blond was making her way to the sign that read GIRLS.

"Hey," said Bodfish to Bob, "you ever check out that Alley Bates flint quarry? Over by Lake Meredith?"

"No," said Bob. "I been meaning to go have a look at it. What's there?" He had been pronouncing the word "Alibates" as Ali-BAH-tees.

"Flint. It's a flint quarry. The Indans used a knock out these flint blanks and make arrow points and knifes and such. It's real pretty, too, different colors. Indans that lived there on the Canadian was rich, compared to other tribes. They had this flint everbody wanted. I got started at flint knapping couple years ago. Hobby. It's a lot harder than you think. But I got so I'm pretty good at it now. Course you can't get the Alley Bates stuff, they got it all closed off to the public. You got a go with a guide, watches you. But there's other places along the Canadian got it too, and I get that. What I do, see, is make up a bunch a arrowheads, bury them a year or two so they look old, keep them in my glove compartment. I go someplace like, say, Michigan or Kentucky, if there's Indan ruins or places they was known I drop a few a them arrowheads. Them archeologists get all excited, think they found some big trade route."

Before Bob could respond to this evil confession Orlando threw himself into his chair.

"Man, she's a good dancer," he said. "But this

music sucks. Lot a times in prison I'd whistle and dance by myself in my cell. Keep the muscles toned up. But you don't learn the new dances that way. So I missed a lot. But this old stuff, hell, anybody can dance to it."

"They used a be good music around. The old days they had good dance music. Bob Wills used a play that Texas swing before he went to Tulsa. Before my time but I got a collection a CD music from the fifties when the swing started a come back. Merle Haggard got Asleep at the Wheel goin," said Robert Bodfish.

"How about Jim Skin? You ever hear of him?" asked Bob.

"That Okie fathead? Give me a break."

"Orlando, I got to go," said Bob. "I got some major business tomorrow."

"Go? Hell, we just got here."

"Yeah. I was thinkin maybe Mr. Bodfish here could give me a ride. I got stuff I want to talk to him about anyway."

"Whereabouts to?" said Robert Bodfish. He did not seem eager to abandon his date to Orlando.

"Woolybucket," said Bob.

"Woolybucket!? That's half the hell over the other side a the panhandle. That's damn near in Oklahoma. And it's over roads no more'n turkey track trails."

"Yeah, but don't you work over there?"

"Hell no, I work just north a Amarilla, bout eight miles from where we are sittin, close to life and bright lights. Except when I'm at the Pampa plant. They close up Woolybucket at six P.M."

"Just about," said Bob.

The blond woman came back to their table, lips glistening with a fresh coat of metallic purple.

"You sit here," said Orlando, patting the chair beside him.

"Della!" said Robert Bodfish. "This guy wants me to drive him way across the panhandle. What a you think a that for brass balls?"

"You go ahead," she said to Bob Dollar, "and drive *yourself*. I'll give Orlando here a ride back to wherever he's stayin. I want a finish tellin him about that killin where the kid run over the other one, the punk with the purple hair." She looked at Bob and said, "The one done the runnin-over got off with probation. They don't like purple hair in Amarilla."

"No intention a *doin* it," said Robert Bodfish to Bob Dollar. "These two got a plot goin. *That* one"— he pointed at Orlando—"he's thinkin a couple feet deeper than he shows, and I know about what, too."

"Mount down off your high horse," said Orlando. "Tonight I'm stayin in Amarillo. I got no purple hair and a strong feelin this is where I'm meant to be," and he moved close to the blond. He looked at Bob Dollar. "I'll skip your damn bunkhouse crap."

"Hell with this," said Bob Bodfish, turning to Bob. "O.K., I'll give you a ride a Oklahoma City, you want."

"O.K.," said Bob, getting up. "If Orlando intends to

stay in Amarillo—" He would be happy to get away from Orlando, who was no longer a fat, evil boy full of outrageous stories and movie plots but a loud-mouthed, conniving, ex-con muscle man. "But I'd like to get together with *you* sometime," he said to the other Bob. "I would like to talk about the hog business. I'm in the business too. I work for Global Pork too. I'm a scite sout. I mean site scout." He wanted to persuade Robert Bodfish to give him a tour of his hog farm.

"Anyhow, tell you the truth," said Robert Bodfish, "I just as soon not talk business in the evenin when I'm out drinkin. They don't like us a talk about what we do. You're welcome a stop in sometime, seein you're with the company. We're up in Parch, County Road M. You better call up first though, so's they'll let you past the gate. Bring your I.D. tag. We run a tight ship."

In the parking lot Bob, bemused by boilermakers and music, sloshed into one of the giant rain puddles. He got in the Saturn with soaking feet, turned on the heater to dry out. He opened the window to equalize the temperature disparities in the car and saw the moon bleached and small as a dime. He decided to go north and take the back roads.

25

TOP SALES

He had a twinge of conscience about leaving
Orlando behind as he drove across the dark panhandle, but told himself that if anyone could take care of
himself it was Orlando and he would certainly be
along the next day to pick up his Porsche and go on
to his career in Austin. What played more vigorously
on his mind was the discovery that Evelyn Chine, top
saleswoman for Global Pork Rind, was in the territory and she was going after Tater Crouch, whom
Bob thought of as his own find. And after Freda
Beautyrooms, too—Bob was not fooled by the thesis
ruse. But was it her territory? Hadn't her big sales
been up in Oklahoma, near Guymon? What was she
doing in Bob's area—poaching? Yes, decided Bob,
she was poaching. She recognized Bob Dollar as a
neophyte and saw a chance to muscle in and steal his
sales. He would have to cinch Tater Crouch in the
morning. He would have to get Tater to go for it.
Unless Evelyn Chine, the driver of the green SUV in
Tater's drive yesterday morning, had already bam-
boozled the old man into signing on her dotted line.
Bob didn't doubt that she used feminine wiles on the

old boys as well, giving a glimpse of flesh, making suggestive innuendos. As Freda Beautyrooms might say, the woman was a snake. And then there was Ace Crouch and Jim Skin. Jim would sell, he knew, but what about Ace?

He found himself on Coppedge Road just outside Woolybucket. A single lighted sign and a small glass-windowed booth inside the gate broke the panhandle darkness. KING KAROLINA FARMS INC. He was past it before it registered. He stepped on the brake, backed up and stared. No mistake, it was a hog farm and the gate was open, the guard booth empty. His chance! He turned in and parked beside a silver pickup with a bumper sticker that read TEXAS FARMERS FEED THE WORLD.

Bob walked as slowly and quietly as he could over the crushed gravel toward the door. There were no windows in the building. Suddenly, with a sound like a dynamo, the great ventilation fans at the back of the building started up, the rising pitch drowning his footsteps. He was only ten feet from the door when two brilliant spotlights activated by motion caught him. Inside he could hear an alarm bell. He turned and ran back to the Saturn, started it and backed out in time to see the automatic chain-link gate swing shut. Red lights atop it began to flash. He was trapped, for there was no other exit.

No one came out of the building and after five minutes he blew the horn. Still no one appeared. He got out and went to the building's door, tugged at the knob. The door was locked. He looked up and saw a surveillance camera. So they knew he was there. He knocked on the door and called. Nothing. He pounded. Nothing. At last he went back to the Saturn and sat waiting. They'd have to let him out when the day shift came on.

But after fifteen minutes or so he saw, far down the road, twinkling cherry lights. He knew before the vehicle pulled up who it would be.

As the sheriff's car drew up to the gate the electronic lock relinquished its grip and the gate slid open. The sheriff was out of his cruiser and in Bob's face in seconds.

"Well, well, well, look who I got tryin a break into the hog house. What's the idea, Dollar? You goin a steal a few pigs for yourself?"

"Look, this is going to sound stupid, but all I wanted was to see what goes on inside."

"That's what the Defenders a Wildlife say, that's what PETA says when they try to break in. Who are you workin for, Dollar, and don't give me that shit about Global Pork Rind. I got your number. You're a front man for a animal activist group. Plus you been drinkin. Drunk drivin on top a everthing else."

"I'm NOT!" screamed Bob, snapping like a dry stick.

The sheriff spoke into a cell phone. "Yeah, I know the guy. I'll take him in."

He got Bob out of the Saturn, put handcuffs on him and made him sit in the backseat of the cruiser while he drove the Saturn to the side of the road and parked it. Then he drove Bob to the jail.

"What is the thing about you and hogs, anyway?"

"It's a job. It's just my job. I thought I could do better if I saw the inside of one of the hog farms, but my boss, the one you talked to, says it's company policy not to let site scouts into them. I thought I'd just try to do it anyhow."

"Must be, if he really *is* your boss and you're not a reporter or a bloodthirsty activist, must be he got a reason to keep you out, don't you think?"

In the morning Bob was groggy and his head ached. It took nearly until noon before he was released after the sheriff had had a long talk with Ribeye Cluke. The sheriff drove him back to the Saturn and handed him the keys.

"Your boss is kind a upset at you."

"Yeah," said Bob.

"I told you once before you ought a git another job. You ain't cut out for this one. Now stay out a trouble."

It had rained in the night and everything was wet, the low clouds like a grey lid overhead, the silvery drops giving the landscape a lustral glow. Bob went straight to the bunkhouse and made coffee. It was hot and good and gradually his head cleared and he felt better. He thought about the sheriff. He thought about the oldsters' nightclub in Amarillo. He thought about his imminent meeting with Tater Crouch and what he would say.

He got into a clean shirt, combed his hair and sallied forth, bringing Lieutenant Abert with him, as after the meeting he planned to eat a sandwich under a shady tree along the Canadian where Abert himself might have stopped a century and a half before. On the way he noticed waxy yellow blooms on the cactus and the yucca stalks just unfolding their creamy towers of blossom.

"What, you again?" The old man was not pleased to see him.

"Well, I have something to discuss," said Bob. He took a breath and went straight at it. "A business proposition. I want to buy your property. For a hog farm. I represent Global Pork Rind."

"That's pretty blunt," said Tater Crouch. "What makes you think I would sell it for such a vile purpose?"

"Because, sir, the hog farm smell is already here and it isn't going away. It annoys you. You can't sell the property to anyone but a hog farm because of the stink. And just think, if you lived in town you could stop by the Old Dog every day, eat Cy's special and see your friends. You could do research at the library." The Woolybucket Library was a wonderful place and Bob imagined that anyone writing a ranch history would enjoy happy hours in it. From the expression on Tater Crouch's face he could see that for once he had said the right thing.

The library was in the old Frontier Bank building, high-ceilinged, sunny, paneled and fitted with walnut shelves shipped up into the panhandle after they were taken from a Galveston mansion wrecked by the great hurricane that brought the city to its knees in 1900. Over the years the library board had somehow resisted selling off the good books and replacing them with romances, westerns and mystery fodder. There were hundreds of scarce Texas books on its shelves, but the treasure, Bob thought, was in the storage room, boxes and boxes of papers and account books from regional ranches, rolls of maps, scrapbooks of photographs, huge bound volumes of old newspapers from Texas and Oklahoma panhandles and from Kansas and New Mexico, including the *Crookly's Border Star, The Weekly Western Argus,* the *Woolybucket Expositor, Roughbug Bee, Council Grove Process* and the like.

"You could really work on your ranch history then," said Bob, and he mentioned his own affection for Lieutenant Abert and said that if their situations were reversed he would hightail it to Woolybucket and work on a book about Lieutenant Abert.

Tater gazed at him, his expression warming. "You know, a couple years after that Lieutenant Abert come through the panhandle, the Topographical Corps sent out another fella, Lieutenant James H. Simpson. He was supposed a find a good southerly route to the California gold fields. In 1848. He's the one *I* like. He was a smart one. He thought the panhandle population was too scarce for any railroad a come through then but said there should be forts and military roads first, and then they ought a make a start on towns and wagon roads—which is what happened. It was freight wagons and stages opened up the panhandle region, not the hide hunters and not the cattlemen and sure not the railroad. The wagon routes established a line of supply—goods, mail, communication. The railroads didn't come until the late 1880s. The Fort Worth and Denver City come first in 1887 and then the Rock Island across Kansas a little later and the rest a them. Anyway, where would I live was I to move to Woolybucket?"

"I suppose," said Bob, thinking on his feet, "that you could have this house moved onto a town lot if you didn't like any of the houses in town." This was easy, thought Bob.

"Of course I *would* like a house in town. Decent runnin water, not have to worry about the well goin dry ever summer or the electric blinkin on and off. I could get that satellite tee-vee, too. My sister lives in town, Ivy Nomore, and I'd like to see her once in a while. Closer to Ace's place, too. Not gettin any younger. I know I'm supposed a get all upset and miserable about leavin the ranch, but I been plannin a do it anyway for a long time. Only thing is, Ace. I'd do it, you see, but I got a talk to my brother. Ace owns half a this place. I can't do a thing unless he agrees."

"I hear he owns half of Jim Skin's place too, up over the Oklahoma line."

"Ace does? First I heard of it. Ace don't have a pot to piss in. He's a good man but he wasted his life fixin windmills. That's how come I put him down as half owner on this place. Our deddy should a split it fair and square and left it to us both but he didn't. I fixed it up after my wife died so's half of the ranch belongs to Ace and if I die first, it all goes to him."

"Do you want me to talk to him or would you rather do it yourself?"

"Oh, I'll do it, I'll do it. Ace is contrary, you know. I git along good with him but not everbody does. Never asked a soul for help in any way. He fell off one a them damn windmills once, caught a strut and there he hung until somebody come along a hour later. Helped him down and he never said a word a thanks. He takes care a hisself and hates a be beholdin. I'll talk to him. See, Ace is the older one but I can talk to him. What kind a price are you offerin?"

There it was. They were down to dollars and cents and he had no idea.

"I don't actually make the offer," said Bob. "Someone comes down from the Denver office."

"So, you're not lookin for luxury estate property at all."

"No sir, that was the lie I told."

The old man slapped his knee. "I knew it, I knew it was a lie. You had that look on your face of a liar. That little bitty girl that come around here yesterday, she was a liar, too."

"What girl?" said Bob, knowing it was Evelyn Chine.

"Comes up to your elbow. Said she was workin on a thesis about panhandle folks. Looked me right in the eye. How I knew she was lyin. That's the sign, when they look you right in the eye. Then she starts with questions—I been asked before—that all lead to disposin a the ranch property. Wouldn't I like to see Dallas, was I thinkin about the old folks' home some-day, oh not *now,* a course, did I have any chirdren, was I married, all a that. I knew she was movin toward the property but I couldn't make out why or what for or how much. Finally I tells her, 'You just run along, miss, I'm not goin a sell my property to you.' Got red as a tomata but she went."

Bob was embarrassed by Evelyn Chine. Her approach did not sound subtle. How had she man-aged to rope in that six-thousand-acre property up in Oklahoma and win the attractive overnight bag, the Global Explorer Portable Receiver and the Megapixel Digital Camera?

"You know," said Tater, looking out the window at the ranch horizon, "this whole region was held together in ever way by those old north-south roads. That's how the panhandle was set up. That's how it was here. But the railroads had east and west in mind. That's how *they* thought. People believed they'd do the sensible thing and lay the tracks beside the old freight trails but they didn't. The old important towns—Mobeetie, Appleton, Tascosa, Wilburn—was killed. The new towns was Miami, Woolybucket, Canadian, Panhandle City, all on the railroad line.

Once the whole place was linked with Dodge but that come to a end. That's when the people stopped knowin each other over the big sweep a land. That's when the people started to talk about the 'good old days.'"

Tater Crouch promised to call Bob by the end of the week, after he had talked with Ace.

"Now don't you go rufflin him up about that business with Jim Skin. That don't amount to nothin anyway, for Ace don't own it no matter what Jim Skin says. You don't believe me, go look it up in the county courthouse. Teach you not a believe everthing you hear. And you get me an offerin price. I'll talk to Ace."

Bob Dollar took Tater's advice and discovered that the only name on the deed for the Oklahoma property was James Robert Alamo William Skin, no mention of Ace Crouch nor anyone else. He went first to the post office where another letter from Ribeye Cluke lay smoldering in the box, then on to the Old Dog looking for Jim Skin but Cy, basting a rib roast, said Jim had been in, ate two pineapple brownies and skedaddled out the back door when he saw Bob coming.

"You must a done somethin a get on his wrong side. Jim Skin would talk the hind leg off a statue. He's almost as bad as LaVon. I thought you was gettin along good."

"So did I," said Bob. "But I guess I frightened him off asking about that property he's got up in Oklahoma."

"Oh, the old Skin place? I hear a gas company is talkin to him about that property too. They're supposed a make some kind a offer. Even if it's five dollars an acre he ought a take it. You can't be wantin it for no high-class development. That place is like Mars."

"Yeah," said Bob, as it slowly dawned on him that Jim Skin had invented an authoritative role for "Uncle" Ace while negotiating with the gas company. "It is. I thought it would work pretty good for a hog farm."

Cy looked at him but said nothing.

When he drove up to the Busted Star in the late afternoon, tired, sweaty, looking forward to a cold beer on the porch with Lieutenant Abert, Orlando's Porsche was still parked in front of the hitching post. LaVon came out onto her porch waving a dishtowel.

"Bob. Bob, I wonder if you would do me a favor?"

"Sure. What is it?"

"It's Coolbroth. He's got some kind of problem with the sheriff. The sheriff's got him down there at the—" She couldn't say it.

"Jail?" prompted Bob. The sheriff, he thought, was a busy man.

LaVon nodded her head. "He's an impulsive kid," she said, "and sometimes he does things that are not quite ordinary. I'd appreciate it, Bob, if you picked him up and brought him home. He needs a ride because the sheriff has confiscated his bicycle, or at least that's how it sounds to me. Coolbroth was so upset on the telephone he could hardly make himself clear. The sheriff is anything but obliging. In fact, he's a miserable, main-hearted, lyin no-good. His people was no good and he's no good."

"Just let me change my shirt, LaVon, and I'll go."

But as he started the Saturn, thinking he would bring back a pizza from Woolybucket and enjoy it in solitude after he dropped off Coolbroth, an oversize Silverado pickup with double wheels, roll bar and more lights than an ocean liner pulled up behind him and Orlando got out, making kiss faces at the driver. Behind the wheel was not the pot-bellied blond of last night, but a tall brunette wearing a red cowboy hat and red blouse.

"See you later, honey," called Orlando and the woman gave him a dazzling grin and revved her engine. Orlando called to Bob. "Hey, wait up. Give me a ride over the creek to your place. I need to get my stuff at your cabin." He jumped in beside Bob.

"What stuff?" said Bob.

"I left my bag there. On your porch. I'm goin a shave and clean up and meet that little honey back in Amarillo."

"What did you do with the blond?"

"The blond? Oh, her. Della. She went off with that greasy guy—'Bob'—after I got talkin with Veronique—that's the honey in the truck that brang me here. She just burns my house down."

"At that old folks' bar?"

"Nah, we went down the road to another place that the greasy guy knew. It was O.K. You ought a get out and explore Amarillo some time. Lot a baaaad action if you know where to look."

At the bunkhouse Bob glanced longingly at the cooler where he kept his beer.

"Damn!" said Orlando. "You got no shower? And no place I can plug in my shaver?"

"No electricity," said Bob. "That's why. Want me to heat you some water? I got a regular razor you can borrow."

"Why, Bob, you sure are up-to-date. Is it one a them old straight razors and a great big leather strop? No thanks, I'll get a motel room in Amarillo and clean up. Probably goin a head down to Austin tomorrow or the next day anyway. Slacker City. Plenty a cute college girls and rich dumb Texas kids. And Smoko is there. Get our business cookin. Hey, you think about that sales manager position. You could make some real money with me. Are you goin out again?" he asked, seeing Bob change his shirt and comb his hair.

"Yeah. I got to go get LaVon's son from the sheriff. Some kind of problem."

"Well, give me a ride back over your damn creek so I don't have to wade," said Orlando. "It's been good seein you, Bob, and I want you to think the job offer over. You could do good with us."

"Thanks, Orlando. I'll think about it. But I might go back to school. Or something. But we'll stay in touch, right?"

"That's a good thing too. Get some more smarts. Damn right we'll stay in touch."

As they started to ford the stream Orlando opened his bag to rummage in it. "I think I got a extra CD here, just want you to—*AAAAAAHHH!*"

Bob slammed on the brakes midstream and looked at Orlando, who was straining back against the seat so hard Bob heard the metal frame crack. A grey object emerged from the interior of Orlando's bag, leaped on his chest and ran up his neck and onto his shoulder, across his back and down the other arm and into the dark crevice between the seat and the door. Tonya had been found.

Bob drove across the stream nervously, glancing down between his feet to see if Tonya was crouched there.

"Are you bit?" he asked Orlando.

"Christ, I don't know! I need to get out a here. What the hell was that thing, a tarantula?"

"Yes," said Bob. "It's one of LaVon's pets. Missing for a couple a weeks. Check yourself over, make sure you didn't get bit."

"I'm afraid to move."

But Bob was pulling up in front of the hitching post and both of them leaped from the car and rolled in the dirt like stunt men, leaving the doors wide open. LaVon came out on the porch and stared curiously at them.

"Check yourself over," said Bob to Orlando, who was gingerly plucking at his shirt and looking at his bare arms. "It's Tonya," he called to LaVon. "Somehow she was hiding in Orlando's overnight bag. Don't know how she got on that side of the creek."

"She's arboreal," said LaVon. "Where is she now?"

Bob started to say that the animal was in the Saturn under the seat but they all saw Tonya climb up onto the passenger seat (recently vacated by Orlando), as though waiting for her chauffeur.

"I'll get her box," said LaVon, disappearing inside. Immediately Orlando picked up a rock and threw it at the spider on the seat. It missed, but dented the Saturn's door frame.

"Don't hurt it, Orlando. She's going to get it in a minute. It's quite a valuable spider."

"Nothin I hate more," said Orlando with passion, shuddering at the thought of his narrow escape, looking once more at his arms to be sure he wasn't bitten.

"You'd feel it by now," said Bob. "LaVon says it's a dangerous spider with a fast-acting poison."

"Why in the name of God would anyone want to have a poison spider for a pet?"

"They're interestin," snapped LaVon, descending now from the porch with the tarantula's old home.

The tarantula greeted LaVon with upraised and threatening front legs, the other six slightly tensed as though to spring. "Poor thing," said LaVon. "She's dehydrated, I can tell," and she worked the atomizer, letting the soothing moisture fall on the tarantula. Suddenly, as though recognizing a haven, Tonya rushed into the box and LaVon clapped on the lid. She looked at Orlando. "Whyn't you get in your Porch and beat it off my property?" she suggested.

"Nothing could give me greater pleasure, you old bitch," said Orlando, suiting the action to the words. Bob was not sorry to see his old friend go. Prison had shaped him, as so many others, for the worse.

Down at the jail Sheriff Hugh Dough was taunting Coolbroth Fronk, who sat fuming in one of the two cells.

"So how come they named you Coolbroth? Why not Hotstew?"

"It's Irish. It was my great-granduncle's name."

"Hell it is. Sounds Lithuanian to me. Or Chinese. Tagalog or Fuegian."

"Dammit, I told you it's Irish."

"Don't swear at me, boy, or you're likely a be feelin depressed in a little while. And there's another thing I want a know. There's a kind a story goin around about you and why you got tossed out a Texas Tech."

"I didn't get tossed out."

"The way we heard it you was doin somethin pretty unusual to a bull they keep there on the experimental farm. They say you was pokin him up the ass with a piece a pipe. And the college wouldn't stand for such a perversion thing. Now, just between us, what was you tryin a do to that bull? Are you queer or what?"

"You are a dirty-minded old goat. Anybody in this place is queer it's you. I'll tell you but I know damn well you ain't got the brain a understand it. O.K. I am *not* tossed out a school. I'm on a break, workin on a project. And it wasn't a bull. It was a hog. Not that anything to do with art will mean much to you, but I'm a artist. A sculptor. Workin on a project—*Clichés of Disbelief.* You ever hear the expression 'In a pig's ass'?"

The sheriff nodded. "My sister collects stamps," he said, that being the only connection between the Dough family and art that he could conjure.

"Well, then, I am workin on a sculpture a the inside of a pig's ass. And I got a blue moon lined up, a tintype with nothin on it—*Not on Your Tintype*—and a lot more. It's a kind a conceptual art. Now, what about my phone calls? Don't I get a couple phone calls?"

"You get one and you already had it when you called your mama a hour ago. Guess she's not in no hurry to get you out." The sheriff gave Coolbroth one of his hard stares. "I heard a few things about your other misdeeds too."

"What other misdeeds? And I don't think parking a bicycle on the sidewalk is a 'misdeed.'"

"Well, it is. In Woolybucket. No, the misdeed I'm thinkin about is what you done with Dawn Crouch." He put his face near Coolbroth's and hissed, "It was *you* knocked her up, wasn't it? It's *you* goin a be the unnamed daddy."

"I want a see a lawyer," said Coolbroth, whose face was red with anger.

"Well, why didn't you say so right off," said the

sheriff. "I would a made a call *immediately*." He went out to his office and Coolbroth could hear his voice rising and falling as he spoke on the telephone. After a long time the front door opened and Coolbroth heard the sheriff laughing with someone. Footsteps came down the corridor and an elderly man with a fleshy nose shambled past without looking at him, turned, walked past again and went up front. Again he heard the sheriff laugh, the front door open and close. The sheriff came to Coolbroth's cell.

"You notice that fella?"

"Yeah, so what?"

"Well, that was a lawyer and you seen him. Lights out. You just ooze off to sleep now and have some sweet dreams a big-assed hogs and nameless little babies starvin a death because their daddies don't give a shit and let's not hear any more out a *you*."

Sheriff Hugh Dough flicked the light switch and twilight descended, though outside in the free blue air it was still two hours before sunset.

26

BROTHER MESQUITE

The day before he left for Denver Bob went to the Old Dog for a blowout steak and potato dinner, for he feared Uncle Tam's vegetarian leanings, imagining a platter of shredded cabbage ringed with boiled parsnips. He opened the café door at 1:30, when most of the regulars had already eaten and left, threw his cap on the corner table at the front tucked behind a jog in the wall but where he'd still have a good view of the traffic (the local habit of watching trucks and cars had overtaken him), speared a steak from the big bowl, now nearly empty, and Cy already beginning to cut up the leftover meat for the next day's beef hash. The potatoes were gone, chopped into tiny squares for the hash.

"I'll throw a new one in the microwave for you," said Cy. "About all that damn thing is good for, heatin coffee and cookin taters. I already put the sour cream and butter in the icebox, so you'll have to haul it out. You want a salad, there's about a cup's worth a coleslaw. That enough? Got plenty a parsnips. Plenty a onion pie, what they used a call 'quiche,' which the guys here would not eat if I called it that, but if I say 'onion pie' they like it. It's the word 'pie.' If I said 'shit pie,' they'd eat it. And, matter a fact, I put in double the onions the regular recipe, so it ain't the same thing anyhow. There's some cherry cobbler left. The butterball dumplins is all gone. Here comes Brother Mesquite, suppose he'll want some too. Why can't you fellers get in here at noon when it's all hot and good?"

As Bob was loading his plate Brother Mesquite, cassock hitched up, boots muddy, came in rubbing his hands and looking around the empty room.

"Looks like we beat the rush," he said to Bob. Cy snorted and muttered something under his breath.

"I hope I didn't hear that," said Brother Mesquite, spearing the ultimate steak and going in heavily for the onion pie.

"I got a joke I been savin up for you, Brother Mesquite," said Cy. "I'll have a coffee with you in a little bit."

"Mind if I sit with you?" Brother Mesquite asked Bob. "Just say, you want some privacy."

"No, sit down, sit down," said Bob, moving into the corner and waving at the chair across from him.

"Oh dear Lord, it feels good a sit down on somethin that don't move," said Brother Mesquite, from whose person emanated a powerful smell of horse. A briar hung from his hat brim. "I been a-horseback since daylight checkin fence. Plus I got the toothache again. We got some fence line we never put in long enough posts and those old buffs get to leanin and scratchin on them and they'll work right up out a the ground, the wire starts to sag and pretty soon she's on the ground and your stock is headin over the waterfall." He began to clean his fingernails with a handsome knife.

"Is that a rosewood handle?" asked Bob.

"Lignum vitae. Lee Reeves over in Shattuck made it. 'Made for the hand, not the eye,' he says, but what he comes up with is mighty easy to look at. You ought a get one."

"You use different fencing than for cows?"

"Oh yes. Bigger, longer posts, not so many cross fences since buffs don't graze like cows—cows are selective. They'll eat all the cream-puff grasses and plants so you have to keep moving them after a few days to another pasture unless you like to see bare dirt. Now the buffs, they evolved on the plains with the plants—the two grew up together, they *belong* together in this place, this landscape. The bison and the native plant species have a *relationship*. Your cow is out a place here and that's why they are so much work. You've got a keep them fed with food they like, you've got a give them water—those thousands a windmills, this and that. The buff rustles for hisself. He'll walk a long way for water, or find little seeps and springs you didn't even know was there and, if he has to, he'll dig a seep out with his hoof. Or if it's winter he'll eat snow. For all I know, maybe he licks the frost off fence wire. The bison is self-reliant and belongs in this country. The cow, bred to be placid and sluggish and easy to handle, is a interloper. For instance, you know how cows in a blizzard move with their rumps to the wind?"

Bob nodded, for he too had moved with his rump to the wind. But his mind was on the self-reliant buffalo. He imagined himself dying of thirst, clawing into the earth with his fingernails, going for the water below.

"Well, your buff don't do that. They head *into* the storm, so they get out a the bad weather quicker. Poor old cow moves with it, stays in the bad weather movin along with the storm until she drops dead or comes up against a fence and there she freezes. Another thing is there was some old wallers on the ranch, just little hollers, not used for a hunderd twenty years. We put our buffs out and in two weeks they'd found all those old wallers their ancestors made and took them over for theirselves. Anyway, we took out most a the cross fences that was on the old ranch and now we got three thousand-acre pastures and a couple five hunderds. Tell you what, you want to get a idea of what this country looked like a hunderd fifty years ago, come pay us a visit at the Triple Cross. You can see a long way and never get a fence in your eye."

"I'd like to but I've got to go up to Denver in the morning for a couple days. Maybe when I come back. *If* I come back."

"Your return in doubt?"

"Yeah. I think I'm in trouble with my boss. See,

I'm not what I said I was at first. They told me to lie about what I was doing here and I guess I picked the wrong lie because I just got in deeper and deeper and it's my fault some people got the wrong idea."

"Why don't you tell me about it," said Brother Mesquite, in a quiet voice, the first indication Bob had seen that he was anything but a bison-crazed rancher. "I'll get the dessert. You want coffee a go with your cherry cobbler? I'm goin a call the dentist. This tooth is murder."

He made the call, was back in a few minutes, slid a plate of cream-covered cherry cobbler across the table.

"Well, thanks," said Bob, gazing out the window at a pickup truck he thought he recognized. It must have just been through the car wash, for it was dotted with water drops. The driver, Francis Scott Keister, jumped out, jammed his hat on tighter against the wind and ran around the truck to the passenger door.

"Oh no," said Bob. "That guy hates my guts."

"What, old Francis? What did you do to him?"

"I don't know. He's just suspicious of me being here."

"With just cause?"

"Yeah. I prevaricated about what I was doing here and he smelled a rat."

A second person got out of Francis Scott Keister's truck, came with him toward the café, her long blond hair tangling in the wind.

"My God," said Bob, "that's Evelyn Chine."

"I don't believe I know her," said Brother Mesquite.

But when Francis Scott Keister and Evelyn Chine came in they did not glance at the corner table, walked straight to the back booth. Bob could not see them, and could only catch a few floating phrases and single words.

Cy said, ". . . that's left is this onion pie and some coleslaw. I can quick cook you up a steak—the grill's still hot. Or make a cold—"

"Ham sandwich good enough for me," said Keister. "That good enough for you, Evvie? You got coffee, Cy?"

"I'd *love* a ham sandwich," said Global Pork Rind's top site scout.

"Plenty coffee."

Their voices dropped to a murmur.

"Well," said Brother Mesquite, "how did it happen that things got so complicated for you?"

"It started," said Bob, "when Mr. Cluke told me I had to make up a cover story because people down here are hostile to hog farms. 'Not In My Back Yard,' and all that. And then LaVon Fronk just pinned me up against the wall about what I was doing here before I could think up something good and I said the first things that came into my head. And I could see she didn't believe me, so I thought up the luxury retirement place thing. And I still think it's not a bad idea. There's some beautiful country here. I been thinking I'd ask Mr. Cluke if Global Pork wouldn't set up a real estate development branch. When I am in Denver next week I'm going to ask him about the chance of that."

"You know, Bob, maybe you should not have taken a job that asks you to lie about what you are doin. There sure must be jobs out there that would let you be honest about the work. It sounds to me as if this Cluke bird must feel in his heart that his company is doing something morally wrong if he asks you to invent a 'cover story.' Is this job, this work, something you feel valuable and worthy?"

"God, no! I hate all this skulking around. I just took it because it was a job. I don't actually *know* what I want to do. My uncle, who raised me, runs a kind of secondhand shop and I don't want to do that. About the only thing that really interests me is like— history? History of the Santa Fe Trail." And he told him about his pleasant hours with Lieutenant Abert's account and his desire to retrace that 1845 path to see what the lieutenant had seen. "And books. I really like books."

"I didn't know what I wanted a do either," said Brother Mesquite, "at your age. I knew I liked animals—grew up on a panhandle ranch, youngest a six boys. Pretty religious family. I liked math and photography and I thought I would be happy workin as a missionary or teachin somewhere. So I tried teachin. I was terrible at it—didn't have what they call 'people skills.' And the missionary thing faded pretty quickly—that takes *advanced* people skills. I always seemed to end up in cities—I was in *New York City,* can you believe it, for six months—helpin with shelters and soup kitchens and findin a place for the homeless to sleep, honorable work, but I couldn't quit thinkin about the panhandle. Finally, when I was thirty, thirty-one, I figured that the contemplative life with its daily rituals and habits—no pun intended— was right for me. Simplicity, moderation, stability, prayer, work, responsibility and study. And when I found the Triple Cross right here in my home coun- try, I was deeply moved and grateful. You want more coffee?"

"Yeah," said Bob, half rising, but Brother Mesquite was out of his chair and off with the cups. When he came back he had two raised doughnuts as well. No wonder his teeth ached, Bob thought.

"Cy had these extra. Anyway, after a few years the abbot and the brothers listened a my arguments for a bison operation on the monastic lands. There's monasteries raise cattle but this is the only bison ranch. It took a couple years a research and discus- sion before we got it worked out. We started small with four heifers and a young bull and now we run almost three hundred bison. It's helped the monastery define itself. Before the bison we had a organic veg- etable seed operation, mostly plants suited to the southern plains, and we still do that, but the physical work a the bison ranch is good for us. We've learned from these animals—about their ways, about ourselves, about what suits this region a the earth. The monastery is a happy and productive place. And I am happy. Couldn't ask for much more from life."

"But don't you feel bad when the truck comes to haul your animals to the slaughterhouse?"

"No truck comes for that purpose. We raise breedin stock."

"Goddammit, Cy, this coffee's got a fly in it!" came an angry voice from the back.

"I can make you another pot, Francis."

"Forget it, we'll go down the old ladies' tearoom and get some. They make damn good coffee and you could learn something from them about desserts—get off your pineapple kick."

There was a clatter of dishes and the ring of coin and Francis Scott Keister, his right hand in the small of Evelyn Chine's back, walked to the front door without looking at Bob and Brother Mesquite. As the two got in Keister's truck Bob was astonished to see them go into a kissing clinch.

"Oh Lord," said Brother Mesquite, who was also watching.

"I thought she was interested in his ranch for a hog farm," said Bob.

"Why would *she* be interested in hog farms?"

"She's doing the same thing I'm doing and for the same company. Scouting hog farm sites for Global Pork Rind. This is part of my problem. She's competition. She's hogging my territory. Literally."

Cy came to their table with a cup of coffee from the

flyblown pot for himself. He sank tiredly into a chair.

"Sure hope Tazzy Keister don't know her husband's takin up with that girl. Bold as brass about it, too. Settin back there feelin each other up and all. Maybe him and Tazzy broke up. But I doubt it. Tazzy dotes on him. And they got that boy. It's not the first time Francis Scott Keister has fooled around. But never with one as short as that one is. You know how it is when you see a great big fella with a little bitty woman, right away you start stickin them together in your mind, tryin to figure out how they do it."

Brother Mesquite cleared his throat.

"Excuse me, Brother Mesquite, must be your hat got me to thinkin you was just another salty old cowhand."

"What was that joke you were going to tell me?"

"Oh yeah. Well, a cowboy walks into a bar, the place is almost empty, and he orders a beer. The bartender brings it to him and the cowboy says, 'Where is everbody?'

"The bartender says, 'Gone to the hangin.'

"The cowboy says 'Hangin? Who are they hangin?'

"'Brown Paper Pete,' says the bartender.

"'That is a unusual name,' says the cowboy.

"'Tell you what,' says the bartender. 'Call him that because he wears a brown paper hat, brown paper shirt, brown paper trousers, brown paper boots.'

"'Dang!' says the cowboy. 'That's weird. What are they hangin him for?'

"'Rustlin,' says the bartender."

Brother Mesquite groaned and Bob laughed. Cy looked at Bob.

"You know, Bob, Brother Mesquite here is about the best damn heeler in the panhandle."

Bob, who thought a heeler was a type of hound dog, nodded and kept his mouth shut.

"Best heeler I or anybody ever seen. He's just a ropin son of a gun. Fast? Oh yes."

Brother Mesquite, who had blushed a terrible purple, got up.

"I'm goin," he said, jamming his hat on. "The joke was bad enough, but this's worse."

"Modest, too," said Cy. "Can't stand a be praised a his face."

Outside, in the street, a dusty beige sedan drove slowly past, the driver staring at the Old Dog.

"That," said Cy, "is Tazzy Keister and I bet she is lookin for Francis Scott and that girl."

27

TRIP TO DENVER

Bob had been thinking off and on about going up to Denver for a weekend to see Uncle Tam and perhaps a real estate developer, but the latest letter from Ribeye Cluke made the trip a necessity.

Bob Dollar.
   I had quite a talk with your sheriff this morning. It was <u>NOT NECESSARY</u> for you to try and gain entry to a rival hog unit. What is involved in production is UNIMPORTANT TO YOUR JOB as a site scout. YOU are on my WATCH-OUT list.
   Maybe you don't realize that every Global Pork Rind site scout can get plenty of business <u>IF HE OR SHE WILL ONLY TRY</u>! I thought we had a go-getter in you, Mr. Dollar, but it seems I am being proved wrong. You have been on GPR's payroll for three months now and have not clinched a SINGLE piece of property. I explained last week why it was important for you to line up some solid sales. I am being queried by Bill Ragsdale from the Tokyo Head

Office as to why we are not seeing more locations established in the Texas and Oklahoma panhandles. The pork market is on fire, with the highest prices pork producers have seen in years. I explained to you that the panhandles were <u>prime territory</u> for hog farms. Neither you nor we can afford to wait—to dilly-dally along—to sit idly by and hope for the best. We've GOT to have those sites. SPEED—SPEED—and more SPEED is the order of the day. Nothing, absolutely nothing, must be permitted to slow down the tempo of hog farm site establishment. That is why YOU are so important in the scheme of things. Mr. Dollar, you have an important job to do, you have shouldered an important responsibility. That job, that responsibility, that DUTY is to cinch hog farm sites and pronto! Grab your pencil and start doing your part <u>RIGHT NOW!</u> Get in gear, Bob Dollar!

Mr. Ragsdale will be in Denver next Monday for several meetings. Your presence is requested. Please report to my office at 8 a.m. next Monday. <u>WITHOUT FAIL!</u>

Resenting the peremptory tone of the letter, Bob thought that on the way north he would treat himself to a few hours' vacation. If he left Thursday that would give him time to visit the quarry and get up to Denver by nightfall, spend two days with Uncle Tam and then tackle Ribeye Cluke. He would detour a little and visit the Alibates flint quarries, for he had seen a few of the multicolored arrowheads at the Tornado & Ball Point Pen Museum in Cowboy Rose, and was curious about the place, especially as Lieutenant Abert, without knowing what use the Indians made of the flint, had written on September 11, 1845, "Our last day's travel led us over a plain strewed with agates, colored with stripes of rose and blue, and with colors resulting from their admixture. They were coarse and of little value, but so numerous that we gave the place the name of Agate bluffs."

The night before he packed up all his belongings, not sure he would be coming back. There was a real chance Ribeye Cluke would fire him. When he told that to LaVon she reminded him in a mock-scolding voice that the Barbwire Festival was coming up in late June and he just had to be there, fired or not.

In truth he wanted to go but said only, "We'll see."

Lying in bed in the bunkhouse for perhaps the last time, listening to coyote harmony, he worked out a plan to explain the benefits of a real estate sideline for GPR. If Global Pork Rind had a real estate division, he would say, he could scout for hog farms and development properties at the same time. He imagined Ribeye Cluke and the unknown Mr. Ragsdale slapping their foreheads and crying, "Great Scott! What a totally brilliant idea!" He also imagined Ribeye saying, "You're fired!"

In the morning as he came onto the porch with his

suitcase his eye caught for the fiftieth time the shadowy shape in the shoulder-high grass of the fallow pasture. It was probably a shrub or particularly heavy clump of grass, he told himself, but maybe a weird anthill or another of the moldering carved figures that stood behind the bunkhouse. It was now or never to find out what it was. He set down the suitcase, climbed over the barbwire fence and walked slowly forward, listening for warning rattles, hoping all the silent snakes lived in California. In the field he passed a few metal stakes that had once carried barbwire, a fence that had divided the pasture. As he came closer to the shape he could see it was something other than a bush.

He parted the last stalks of grass and looked on the bizarre sight of an entire deer skeleton impaled on a metal fence stake, the head missing, the stake straight through the center of the chest. The curved ribs were cold grey with hard shreds of flesh on them. Dried sinew still held the bones together. At first he thought it must be the remnants of some ghastly ritual, but after staring at it from all sides he decided that it was the evidence of a freak accident, that the deer, bounding through the tall grass, had not seen the concealed metal stake and had, by pure bad luck, come down full force on it, impaled and killed, to hang like a grisly scarecrow until weather separated the bones and beetles chewed them to dust. Shaken and a little queasy, he went back to the porch, took up his suitcase, got in the Saturn and drove away.

But he could not get the skeleton out of his thoughts. He imagined himself the deer bounding through the tall grass. Maybe it was night, the first shot of moonlight paling the sky, metallizing the grass stems and seed heads. In such a glinting world how easy not to see the lethal spear in the tall stalks, and then the violent, piercing shock, a few seconds of instinctive jerking while the moon dims and goes out for good. Or maybe he is running in panic, chased by dogs, great leaping bounds that carry him high in the air, twenty feet and more in each spring, well able to clear the spike if it had been seen, but, bad luck, crashing down on it full force, there to hang, impaled, dying slowly while the dogs tore at him, to rot and shrivel under the morning sun.

At the National Monument office in Fritch he asked for directions to the quarries.

"You have to go with a guide. There's a group going at noon," said the tall brunette behind the counter. "You can go with them. Cal Wollner's leading it. You all meet down by the ranger station in half an hour."

Bob looked at his watch. It was quarter to eleven, and he had planned to be back on the road by 11:30. He would not be able to reach Denver before midnight if he also stopped at Autograph Rock near Boise City and went on to Bent's Fort in homage to Lieutenant Abert. Perhaps he would save the rock and the fort for the return trip—if there was a return trip.

The tour guide, Cal Wollner, came in and said, "Everbody ready? Wear your hat, it's hot out there. Don't want any sunstrokes."

It was a fair crowd that followed Wollner up the steep path. Every few hundred feet they escaped the burning sun under roofed, open-air shelters populated by overbearing yellowjackets where Wollner talked about the Indian groups, settlements, trade, migration, war. Lake Meredith lay below, deep blue. "Any questions?"

"I wonder," said Bob, "if the name Alibates is the Indian word for flint?"

Wollner smiled. "Nope. Name of a old cowboy who owned the property back in the nineteenth century. Allie, Mr. Allie Bates." But he could not tell Bob who the flint quarry Indians were.

At the top they saw dozens of small pits where the Indians had broken out the valuable flint. There were many small pieces lying on the ground, purple, white, pale blue, some mottled, others striped. Bob saw a beautiful piece of reddish purple diagonally striped with dusky blue. He wanted it very badly and when the guide went on ahead with the group following, he stooped down and pretended to tie his shoe, seized the piece and put it in his pocket. It was warm and greasy to the touch. In a few minutes he took it out and dropped it on the ground, caught Wollner's eye watching him. Wollner nodded.

"Don't even think about it," he said, unsmiling.

On the way down, the guide stopped to point out the obvious.

"There's Lake Meredith," he said. The dull blue sheet of water was corrugated with ridges like speed bumps.

"It's so *big,*" said one of the women.

"Yes. And that's only the top of it," said Wollner. "When they built the dam and she filled up, everbody in Amarilla and Borger come rushin down with their new boats a try her out. It was a nightmare. Most a them, livin here in the panhandle, never seen more water than a stock tank could hold and they had no idea how the wind could work up the old H_2O. They capsized, tipped over, swamped, drowned, smashed into each other. A deadly water circus."

From Stinnet Bob drove north, crossed the state line and, making his way through Guymon's confusing streets looking for 64 north and west, managed to get on 54 south heading for Goodwell. By the time he corrected his mistake he had crossed the dry Beaver River and was on a dirt road in an oil and gas field, surrounded by nodding jack pumps. The arid bed of the Beaver River depressed him. He knew it had once been a lively major stream called the North Canadian, with a sheltered valley that attracted ranchers and settlers. But early in the twentieth century the herd law that said ranchers must fence in their animals closed the open range, and the confined cattle trampled the grassy verges of the river as they congregated to drink. The banks of the Beaver began to erode and sand washed down into the bed. Within the decade the Beaver was dying and finally stopped flowing except in heavy rains, leaving a gentle dip in the landscape marking its old course, as though a large finger had traced over the prairie, its last trickles of water impounded as the Optima Game Refuge at the side of a highway.

He came out on 64 and turned left toward Boise City. Just outside the town stood an elderly Indian with his clothes and belongings in a maroon Neiman Marcus sack. Although he had not stuck out his thumb Bob knew he was hitchhiking and stopped for him.

"I'm going to Denver. Where you headed?"

"Trinidad. My daughter lives in Trinidad. Colorado."

"Well, that's on the way. Hop in."

The old boy, he thought, was as able to hop as he was to fly. Slowly and awkwardly he creaked into the seat, held his sack on his lap. Bob pulled out onto the highway.

"So you are going to visit your daughter."

"Not visit. Move in with her."

There was a long silence during which Bob saw himself sitting on Uncle Tam's doorstep.

"Where are you from?"

"Oklahoma."

Bob tried to keep irritation out of his voice. "Well,

I guessed that. Pick you up in Oklahoma, Oklahoma is the Indian state, that's what I guessed. What tribe?" Hoping that somehow the man was a Cheyenne and he could talk a little about Lieutenant Abert. But there was no answer and when he glanced over he saw the old man's eyes were closed, though he doubted he was asleep. Bob, somewhat annoyed, as he had expected conversation in return for the ride, drove on, the telephone poles striking across the plain near the road, the wires rising and falling in long swoops. He was in sand sage and dune country, among the wild plums and skunkbrush and occasional clumps of bluestem. There was no traffic and the country gave him a lonely feeling of dust and burned ground. The dry bed of the Beaver, slowly filling in, depressed him. It was impossible not to think of blowing dust gradually covering everything, the fine dirt settling in layers, the thickening layers compacting and hardening and still the wind carrying more every day, every year, filling footprints and ditches and arid streambeds, drifting over rocks, covering the bones of dinosaurs, the houses of men, the trails and roads, building up inch by inch, foot by foot, millennium after millennium, the multiple pasts of the scarred landscape gone and forgotten.

Mile by mile they moved into mesa country and the sandy land shrubs gave way to piñon pine, juniper and hackberry, to cholla and scrub oak. He was in the short grass country now and sure the old Indian was feigning sleep.

Just outside Trinidad the old man straightened up and peered out the window.

"Most there, ain't we?"

"Yeah," said Bob shortly, still sore that he'd had to drive in lonely silence for hours.

"I'm movin in with my daughter," said the old boy.

"You said that. When I picked you up. Nice you got family."

"She got a good job, nurse job. Her and her husband make a lot. Big house. I can have my own room, my own bathroom. They got no kids."

"You'll be company for each other," said Bob. Unless, he thought, you fall asleep at the dinner table or during the evening television, in which case you'll be no company at all.

"My son-in-law is learnin the medicine ways. I will teach him."

"What's that—'medicine ways'?"

"Ceremonies, dances," the man said vaguely, gesturing toward the horizon.

Suddenly he sat up and peered west beyond the streaming fences.

"Next exit," he said. "About a mile west."

Dutifully Bob turned off the interstate and got on Route 12. They moved west, but after a mile the old man said nothing.

"Coming up pretty soon?" asked Bob.

"Yes, pretty soon," the man said.

Bob drove. After another mile or two he increased

his speed and was soon flying along at sixty-five, the miles gliding under the tires. The old man studied the landscape and said nothing.

"How much farther is it?" asked Bob. "I thought it was only a mile off the throughway. I've got to get to Denver, you know."

"Yes," said the man. "I think we pass it a long time ago."

"For God's sake, why didn't you say something?"

"I don't know," said the man.

With a squeal of tires Bob made a U-turn. The speedometer crept toward eighty.

"Now you tell me when we are getting close," he said.

"I never been there," said the old man. "It's one a these road."

"'One a these road'? That's interesting. Couldn't be more than fifty of them branching off this one. What's the name of the road?"

"I don't know. I forgot my daughter's letter."

Now Bob saw he was in for trouble. The old boy had no idea where he was going and the letter with the address probably had the telephone number as well.

"Do you have your daughter's telephone number?"

"No. Wouldn't do no good. She's at work."

"Do you know where she works?"

"She's a nurse."

"Yes, but that could mean a hospital, or physical therapy center, or nursing home, or private home or a dozen other places. We'll pull over at the next tele-

429

phone booth and check the directory. They might be listed." And so he stopped at the Huerfano convenience store with its row of bright gas pumps.

"No phone booth outside. Must be inside. What's your daughter's name?"

"Shirley."

"Shirley what?"

"Shirley Brassleg."

Bob went into the store and looked around for the telephone. He could see a pale rectangle on the wall next to the rest rooms where surely a telephone belonged.

"They took it out," said the obese woman behind the counter. "Last week."

"God's sake, how can I make a call?"

"Everbody's got the cell phones these days. Nobody needs the old pay phones."

"I need one. I got to look up where this woman lives. Got her father in my car. He was hitchhiking and I brought him up from Oklahoma. He doesn't know where she lives."

"What's her name?" The woman had a phone directory in her hand, her thumb ready to skiffle the pages.

Bob felt foolish saying the daughter's name. "Shirley Brassleg. She's Indian. He says she works as a nurse." He could not suppress his tone of disbelief and sarcasm.

"Is she in Trinidad?"

"Yes, that's what he says. And that she lives on a

road somewhere off this one. He lost her letter with the name of the road."

"There's no Brassleg listed here. You can try information," and she handed a cordless handset to him. But information had no Brassleg either.

"Thanks," he said and went back out to the car. The old Indian was gone. He looked up and down the highway, checked the men's room, went back into the store.

"Did that old fellow come in here?"

"Nobody since you."

"Well, he's disappeared."

"I thought you said he's a hitchhiker."

"He is."

"Then what do you care? Maybe he didn't like riding with you, took a chance to get away." Her expression showed she would not like riding with him either.

"I gave him a ride," he said, "he's my responsibility," and went back to the Saturn, started it and pulled out onto the highway. He thought that if he were a smoker he'd light one up now. He wished he had bought a candy bar back at the convenience store. He was really hungry and tired and his legs ached where the edge of the Saturn's seat cut into his thighs. As he neared I-25 he saw a familiar shambling figure: it was the aged Indian, hoofing along. With a groan of exasperation he stopped.

"How did you get down here?" he asked, his voice tight with irritation, despite trying to imagine what it was like to be an old Indian with all your possessions in a Neiman Marcus bag.

"Got a ride. Lady said my daughter don't live here. Lady been here all her life. White hair."

"So what is your plan now?"

"I don't know."

Bob expelled a deep breath. He was in it now. He thought of Brother Mesquite and something he had said about experiences that let us grow as human beings. Bob could feel himself shrinking smaller.

"Get in." He breathed deeply through his nostrils. "We know she's a nurse, right? We know she works, right? We just don't know where. So I suggest we go to the hospital in Trinidad and ask if she works there. And if she doesn't, then it makes sense to try the sheriff. Sheriffs know everybody. They have to," remembering Sheriff Hugh Dough. "How does that hit you?"

"O.K. It hits O.K." The old man put his head back and closed his eyes again.

Bob drove like a fool, whipping in and out of lanes, riding the bumper of an old pickup until the driver pulled onto the shoulder after a few miles of this harassment, then trapped behind a road hog semi, Bob wishing he did have a cell phone so he could call the number on the back in response to the perky question stenciled there: HOW'S MY DRIVING?

"Lousy," he snapped at the truck. To his passenger he said, "Old man, if we find your daughter—" but he didn't know what to say next.

• • •

432

The hospital in Trinidad was a low-slung, modest affair and Bob guessed they dealt heavily in rodeo and horse accidents as it was ranch country all around. They went inside together, Bob determined that the old man would ask the questions this time.

"Go ahead," said Bob. "Ask them at the desk about your daughter. If she works here."

The old man had barely taken three slow steps toward the receptionist behind glass when a heavy woman in a magenta sweater set, pushing a wheel-chaired man with a face like a creased paper bag, said "Father!" and turned sharply in his direction.

"Daughter," said the old man calmly. "I forgot your letter. We been looking."

She glanced at Bob, who shrugged.

"He was hitchhiking. Down in Oklahoma. And I was on my way to Denver."

"Yes. This man gave me a long ride. He helped me look for you."

"But Father, you didn't have to hitchhike. And what were you doing in Oklahoma? I sent you money for the bus." She turned to Bob and said, "He lives on the Pine Ridge Res."

"I lost that money. Who is this man in the wheel-chair? This is not your husband, is it?"

"No, no. This is Mr. Gunnel. I work at the Trinidad Golden Age Home, and Mr. Gunnel has to come here for his dialysis treatments. I brought him in. It is certainly a surprise to see you here." She turned to Bob Dollar. "Shirley Mason," she said.

433

"We were looking for Shirley Brassleg."

"I married Bob Mason. I *was* Shirley Brassleg. My father here is Moony Brassleg. It's nice of you to give him a ride and take such care to look for me. My husband and I ask you to dinner tonight. I am taking Mr. Gunnel back to the nursing home and then I'll go to our house. If you could bring Father out it would be terribly helpful. Here, I'll make you a map. We won't take no for an answer. Bob—that's my husband—got an elk and we're having a nice roast." She was already scratching lines on the back of a sheet of paper that proclaimed GET CONTROL OF YOUR BLAD-DER. She thrust the paper into his hand, told her father she would see him later and hurried toward the exit, pushing Mr. Gunnel at speeds he had not experienced for years.

"That was lucky," said Bob. He would have to call Uncle Tam and tell him he'd be very late. He wished Shirley Mason had taken her father with her. He looked at the old Indian. He was carefully unwrapping a red lollipop he had selected from the paper bucket on the reception desk. When he felt Bob's eye on him he started a little, turned back to the bucket and chose a green lollipop, handed it to Bob.

"Thanks," said Bob, looking at the map. Yes, the Masons' house was on Boncarbo Road off Highway 12.

"That's not her husband," the old man said, licking the candy, "she says."

• • •

After a considerable search he found a pay phone at the end of a waxy-floored corridor and put in a collect call to Uncle Tam and explained the situation.

"Elk roast? See if they'll give you a little slice to bring home. I never tasted elk."

"You could if you go to that damn Buckhorn restaurant with the horrible waiters."

"Too expensive."

"What happened to the vegetarian thing?"

"Nothing. I still eat vegetables. But I'm not a fanatic. Not when it comes to elk."

Following the map they turned off Route 12 onto the Boncarbo Road, then onto a smaller and dustier road labeled Mud Gate, and bumped up a long, washboard hill so badly ridged the car shuddered and hopped, dust seeped through invisible cracks. Shirley Mason's directions read "2 mi log house on left red door." It was a small house, far from the huge place Bob had expected from the old Indian's description, but Brassleg seemed pleased and said, "Ah."

They pulled up behind a green Bronco and got out. The metal hood of the Bronco was still hot and ticking as the metal cooled. Shirley Mason came out on the porch and helped her father up the steps.

"Do you have a suitcase?" she said. He shook his head. "You didn't bring anything?" He held up the Neiman Marcus bag. She held the door open for them and Bob stepped into a glorious aroma of roasting meat and potatoes, of garlicky dressing, of fresh-peeled peaches simmering in a kind of cinnamon-stick homemade chutney.

"This is my husband, Bob Mason," she said, leading them to a fat, humming man in the kitchen where a mesquite fire crackled on a raised hearth, two rocking chairs in front of it. Bob Mason came forward with his hand outstretched, smiling and nodding. He shook Bob's hand with his own damp, fat fingers, patted the old man's shoulder, sat them before the fire and poured them cups of fresh coffee.

"The roast ready in about thirty minutes, maybe a little longer," he said. To Bob he said, "I am an unemployed teacher, my wife works, I stay home and cook and clean. So, Father-in-law, tell us your adventures."

The old man grinned and waved at Bob Dollar. "He is my adventure. He drive me from Oklahoma to here even if I lost the letter with the address. He is a good man."

Bob blushed horribly, remembering his impatience, his anger, his irritation at the old man's silence and apparent stupidity.

Bob Mason beamed. "What a lucky day for you, Father-in-law. You could have been picked up by a robber or hate killer. You could have been kidnapped or pushed out on the roadside. But here you are, safe and at home." He got up to baste the elk, stopped short and looked at the old man again. He asked, his voice suddenly grave and serious, "Did you not bring your medicine bag?"

The old man half smiled, put his index finger to his

right temple, then pointed to the Neiman Marcus sack.

"Father," said Shirley Brassleg Mason, "I don't understand what you were doing in Oklahoma, but please come see your nice room. It's all ready for you. There is your own television set and a table for writing or drawing." She looked at Bob Dollar. "My father is well known for his skill in painting. Several museums have his work. Look, there over the fireplace is an example."

He saw a curious and disturbing painting, an empty field of yellow with two slender sticks near the lower right. He went closer and saw the sticks were arrows plunged into the earth, nearly buried to their feathered hafts as though they had been shot from a great height in the sky and had picked up speed as they fell. There was nothing more, yet the painting seemed full of meaning.

The elk roast was superb, rich and with a faint wild tang. There was a small dark object in the gravy Bob Mason ladled onto his plate, and he thought it was a peppercorn but Bob Mason called it a juniper berry. Old man Brassleg refused the potatoes and salad and ate only meat. Bob noticed that his son-in-law cut the choicest morsels for him and kept his plate heaped. It was incredible how much meat the old man could stow away.

"No wine, I'm afraid," said Bob Mason. "This is a teetotal household. I'm a recovering alcoholic."

During the dinner, the firelight flickering over the table and reflecting in the dark meat juice on the platter, Shirley asked Bob what he did and, feeling comfortable and among friends, he began to tell them everything, about Horace Greeley Junior University and Orlando and Mr. Cluke and LaVon and the tarantulas and double-dealing Evelyn Chine and his failed efforts to get Jim Skin to agree to sell his land, his unsureness of what he should do with his life. The old man looked up from his mound of meat.

"You, a rich white boy, eat good, drive a nice car, fancy clothes, expensive shoes, do not know where your life goes?"

"I'm not exactly rich. In fact we're poor. The car isn't my car and my uncle runs a kind of junk shop and that's where the shoes came from. I just don't know what possibilities are best for me. I mean, should I go back to school or what? I don't think I'm going to be a hog farm site scout much longer. I think Mr. Cluke is going to fire me."

"I heard the name Jim Skin," the old man said. "Big fool. He's part Cherokee and lies about it. His dad was half-Cherokee and *he* lied about it. The Skins are liars."

Bob could agree with him.

"But," said Brassleg, "there's ways to make even a liar get honest."

"I wish I knew those ways," said Bob.

"This not-knowing thing is a young man's question, to find out who and what and where. But you are lucky. There are chances for you, a white young man. How you like it on the reservation, forty to eighty-five percent unemployment, no jobs at all, no money to get out, no school, nothing but get drunk, make babies, use the ADC check for bottle? Young men there do not think, What am I going to be in my life? Answer: a drunk, die young and miserable, leave damaged chirdren behind. They think, How long will I live?"

Bob flushed with shame, for it did seem he was rich and awful.

"More elk, Father-in-law?" Bob Mason lifted a dripping slice on the serving fork. The tender meat swayed. But the old man had fixed on Bob.

"You will have to find your way alone. Maybe this uncle you speak of will help you."

"Maybe," said Bob, subdued and miserable.

The old man said to the ceiling, "Have pity. Help this poor man to lead a good life."

For Bob the pleasant evening had gone sour. As soon as he could he left. As he started the Saturn he saw a light come on in the old man's room, saw Shirley Mason turn on the television set and set the trembling images in motion.

28

USED BUT NOT ABUSED

It was after midnight when Bob walked into the little apartment above the shop. All was silent and unchanged, a few dishes in the drainer, the counter-tops clean and shining, the chairs neatly aligned around the table, a small stack of bills squared next to Uncle Tam's checkbook and pen, the honey bear bottle in the center. Bob looked inside the checkbook and saw the balance was $91.78. Unless the bills were minuscule none would be paid in full. In the refrigerator he saw bundles of carrots, two cabbages, rotting bananas, a plastic bag of kale and, next to some senescent apples, a bunch of leeks and a container of mushrooms. A plastic sack of salad greens proclaimed fourteen times that the leaves within were "Organic!" It looked unpromising until he saw the ball of pizza dough and a square of mozzarella. Uncle Tam must be planning a mushroom and onion pizza, Bob's favorite. Looking around the pokey kitchen he knew that if he were fired he could not come back and live with Uncle Tam.

He heard Uncle Tam's bedroom door open and turned to face his relative.

"Bob! I didn't hear you drive up. Want some decaf?"

"Sure." He examined his uncle critically. He had the same cat face as Bob, a genetic gift from Slavic ancestors unphotographed and long ago perished, their features persisting through the generations. Uncle Tam looked smaller, greyer, less able in some sad way. He had lost enough weight that his pajamas, printed with green moose, hung on him like old curtains.

"You still on the vegetarian kick?"

"I am. But carrots have lost their thrill. Now I'm trying the exotics—chayote, cactus leaves, persimmons. There's some new kiwis, real, real small and sweet, they don't have those hairy rinds. Smooth. They taste like grapes. Probably genetically modified. But there's times when I think about eating a whole standing rib roast by myself. The first slice would probably kill me. Anyway, I thought about making pizza. If it's not too late. If you got any appetite. How was the elk?"

"The elk was wonderful. I did bring you a slice. And pizza sounds good. For tomorrow, right? I'll help you make it. What's been going on in the neighborhood?"

"Oh, the big news is Dickie Van Hose, remember him? Ran the drugstore? Van Hose Pharmacy?" He had been fitting in the coffee filter while he talked and measuring the coffee and water.

"Sure. Fat kind of guy with big eyebrows. What happened to him?"

"He invested all his money with a brokerage firm

downtown. All tech stocks. And he took a bath. Lost everything, mortgaged the house, lost that, sold drugs under the counter, lost the store. He was wiped out. And apparently he got despondent. He killed his wife and the three kids, left a note saying he was sparing them pain, then he went to the broker's office, Handfull and Palp down on Lincoln. He shot five people in the office including the brokers. Then he went home and shot himself. In the note he said Handfull and Palp 'destroyed me with their merciless greed.'"

"God, that's lousy." He poured milk in his coffee, added a little honey from the honey bear bottle. "And what do you hear from Bromo these days?"

Uncle Tam looked at him until Bob began to feel uncomfortable.

"Do you know that's the first time you've ever asked about him?"

"Oh, come on!"

"Yes, it is. You never really got along with him. He thought you were smart, Bob, but that wasn't a compliment. The crossword puzzle thing upset him. All that vying over 'ibex' and 'aorta' and 'Ares' and 'Oona.'"

"There was always a pattern to them. You had to find the pattern. He thought it was only individual words and that loused him up. Anyway, I never asked about him because—well, *you* know."

"No, Bob, I don't know. What do you mean?"

"Nothing. It's just—you're right, we never got

along. He—I always thought he resented me. Like jealousy."

There was a long silence.

"You're falling all over yourself. Well, anyway, I appreciate your asking. *Wayne* is doing very well in New York. He's been taking classes in design and the history of furniture for the last few years. Mornings he works at a classy antique store in the World Trade Center, down on a lower level. It's a beautiful shop, he says. I forget the name. He invited me to come there for a visit at the end of the summer. And he wants to come back here for Thanksgiving or Christmas, some holiday. He sent you another book—if I can find where I put it. It might be in my office downstairs."

"How's business, the shop?"

"So-so. This isn't really a very good location. I'm sorely tempted to get rid of everything except the Art Plastic. Start over somewhere else."

"I wish I could," said Bob. "I kind of hate this hog site job. I think it would be fun to have a little bookstore somewhere."

"That's how I started out," his uncle said. "It just grew into all-around junk. I still got most of the books in boxes in the storage space. Anyway, let's change the subject," he muttered. "Got something I want to show you." He left the kitchen and went downstairs to the shop. Bob poured more coffee into the familiar old Toby mugs. When his uncle came back he was carrying a Bible and Bob felt his heart sink. No doubt the vegetarian diet had stirred some dormant religious volcano in Uncle Tam and the lava would start to flow in a minute. But Uncle Tam passed him the Bible and told him to look in the map envelope inside the back cover. Bob withdrew the map and behind it saw a sheaf of hundred dollar bills. He counted them. There were twelve.

"What's this all about?" he said.

"Look at the back of the bills," said Uncle Tam. "You'll see."

One side of the third bill was covered with writing in red ink, very hard to read, but Bob made out most of it. It was a will.

I worked dam hard for this but have not got children or airs of any kind so this is for you, who-ever comes into posesion of this Holy Book, you are my lawful air, god bless.

It was signed "Floyd Lollar, Colorado Spgs 9–30–56."

"So," said Uncle Tam. "It made me think about my situation here. I've about decided to put the shop up for sale, find a new location."

"My God, that's a big step. Like move to New York? Take a vacation or do something you like?"

"No. New York is not a good place for me. And sometimes it's not a question of doing what you like. I know your generation puts a lot of value on that, but for most of us it's a matter of doing the best we can with what we've got and who we are."

"I know, I know," said Bob, bracing for the responsibility lecture. But it did not come. To fill the awkward silence he began to describe the brooch Freda Beautyrooms had worn at the quilting bee, sketching it out on the back of an envelope. Uncle Tam smote his brow with the heel of his hand and moaned.

"Why not here? Why Texas?"

29

RIBEYE CLUKE'S OFFICE

Bob slept in his old bed and in the morning he walked down to the bakery and bought brioche and Danish pastries and jelly doughnuts and both papers. He would look for an apartment near a bakery if he moved back to Denver. He and Uncle Tam sat companionably dunking pastries in their coffee and reading bits of news to each other.

"That brooch you described to me last night, it might be French—anyway European. The French took plastic quite seriously and made some beautiful jewelry. I'm guessing it might be a French Art Deco piece from the twenties—the pearlized celluloid and those rhinestone zigzags. See if you can't buy it for me."

"I'll try," said Bob. "But she's rich and headstrong and bold. Quite a few of the others at that quilting bee had nice things too," and he tried to draw the pendant necklace he remembered seeing around Rella Nooncaster's neck, saying, "This is nile green, this is black."

"Oh my," said Uncle Tam. "How I wish I could make her an offer. I wish you'd try for me."

"I will," said Bob.

"I found a few things myself while you were gone," said his uncle. "A pair of Beth Levine acrylic shoes. And I got my eye on some crazy flatware from the thirties, yellow with red polka dots. Trouble is the owner wants four hundred dollars. If that Sweepstakes money comes through—"

"You could spend some of the Bible money."

"Oh yeah, I could, but—I might have to use it for something else." He was silent for a moment and then added in a rush, "I might take that trip to New York and see what Wayne is up to. Now, what do you say we go to the Mayan and catch a movie this afternoon?"

On Monday morning Bob luxuriated in the hot shower, though he missed having his coffee on the bunkhouse porch. He dressed in his good grey suit hanging in the closet, knotted the tie his mother had painted of the sinking *Titanic*. In the kitchen he opened the window near the table onto an exquisite early summer day, robins shouting their endless *"Shut up! Shut up!"* Uncle Tam came in saying "Top a the marnin to ye" in a stagey Irish brogue. At 7:30 Bob went downstairs to the Saturn and drove to the Denver offices of Global Pork Rind. He could have taken the bus but thought Mr. Cluke might ask him to turn in the Saturn's keys on the spot.

Mr. Ragsdale from the Tokyo office was an unusually good-looking human being. Although he was in his fifties his chiseled jaw and regular features, his broad shoulders and athletic frame, his supple movements, deep tan and manicured hands combined with the Armani suit to say, "Here is a man to whom all good things come," but Bob thought to himself, So how come you work for a pork company? In actuality he said "How do you do, sir?"

"Sit down, Bob," said Ribeye Cluke, pointing at the lime-green metallic-toned aluminum chair across from his desk. Mr. Ragsdale sat in a leather chair off to one side, a chair exactly like Ribeye's own. Bob thought that perhaps Global Pork Rind bought them in large lots for their executives.

"Well, sir, Bob," said Ribeye. "I wonder if you know how close you are to being let go?" He frowned at Bob.

"Yes sir, I had that feeling," said Bob. "But I really do have some good prospects lined up." And he told them about Tater Crouch and Jim Skin. "And Mr. Crouch, sir, asked me what kind of money we could offer for his place. Of course I couldn't give him a figure, but I'd like to be able to set up a time for the Money Offer Person to come down soon and look at it. I had him *right there* and I couldn't go any farther because I couldn't give him a figure. And I've been thinking, sir," he went on, "that there's a subsidiary business Global Pork Rind could develop." Bob launched into his argument for luxury home properties, describing the Beautyrooms ranch in some detail but omitting the price Waldo Beautyrooms had floated.

"Great Scott!" boomed Bill Ragsdale. "We've actually got a site scout who thinks!"

"He *is* smart, Mr. Ragsdale," said Ribeye Cluke in a fawning tone.

"It's common sense," said Bob, his heart beating.

"I'll discuss it with Mr. Goliath," said Ragsdale. "Who knows? He might like it. And it's true that handsome properties do come to the attention of site scouts, but until now they have all rejected them as too upscale—unfit for a hog farm—and that's been the end of the matter. Of course we have to consider the bottom line. Can you have upscale properties in a region where confined animal farm operations take place? And, of course, it would necessitate an extensive infusion of capital."

"Sir, actually it wouldn't. Site scouts see nice properties all the time doing their regular work. So there'd be no need for extra people or anything."

Mr. Ragsdale smiled knowingly and lowered his eyelids.

Ribeye Cluke picked up another thread. "Bob, about Mr. Crouch's property. We will get a Money Offer Person down there. In fact we have a very good site scout in the region already and she has just been promoted to money offer status. She could size the place up and give Mr. Crouch a figure."

"Please, Mr. Cluke, not Evelyn Chine."

"What! You've met Evelyn Chine?"

"Sir, she's been after my prospects all along. She's here, she's there, she's everywhere. She's tried to cut in on me several times. Mr. Cluke, I don't care for Evelyn Chine. Neither does Tater Crouch. He's one of them she's tried to get away from me. He told me he didn't like her and wouldn't sell to her. Now what is he going to think when I bring her in to make the money offer?"

"That's a good point, Bob. I'll see who else we've got in the region who could help you out. I'll let you know in a few days."

"Thank you. Anybody but Evelyn Chine. And she's having an affair with a local married man. She's a real snake."

"That is malicious gossip, Bob. We don't do that."

"Oh?" said Bob then, recklessly, "but it's all right to lie about what I'm doing down there, right?"

Ribeye Cluke gave Bob a terrible look. "Watch it, Bob. You are not out of the woods yet. We are going to give you one more month to make good. You will sew up two properties in that time or you are out on your bumpus. And I see, Bob"—his tone was menacing—"that you are still wearing those brown oxfords. Did I not tell you to wear cowboy boots?"

"Sir, I *do* wear them all the time, but today, being in Denver I thought I would wear these. They go better with my suit," said Bob. "Mr. Cluke, people complain about the smell. The hog farm smell. It's really pretty awful downwind."

"That's the country, Bob. That's rural life. Feedlots smell too. Stock smell is a natural accompaniment of living in the country. The panhandle—in fact everywhere we put our hog farms—is rural, low-population *country*. Anyway, only a very few supersensitive souls are bothered. Most people are not affected."

"Well, they say other things too. They say the animals are confined in those buildings, that they suffer and live unnatural lives."

Ribeye Cluke turned to Mr. Ragsdale. "I can't believe I am having this conversation. I believe Bob *wants* me to fire him." Then he switched back to Bob, speaking in a sarcastically patient voice as though to a mental deficient. "We don't think of hogs as 'animals,' Bob, not in the same way as cats and dogs and deer and squirrels. We say 'pork units.' What they are, Bob, is 'pork units'—a crop, like corn or beans." There followed a long lecture on free enterprise and the American Way, the importance of economic opportunity and the value of entrepreneurship to the general good and the well-being of America.

Bill Ragsdale spoke in his sonorous, well-modulated voice. "Not only America, Bob, but the *whole world.*"

"But people down there in the panhandle feel like if they own property they have some say in what happens on it and next to it."

"You will find, Bob, as you mature, that lip service to the rights of the property owner is just that—lip service. What rules the world is utility—general usefulness. What serves the greater good will prevail. You know that highway departments can take property against the 'owner's' will to widen the thoroughfare for the general good. It's a similar situation. And if it were put to a general vote, time and again it has been shown that the public supports such moves because they benefit the greater community."

Bob suddenly remembered Bromo reading a paragraph from his ongoing essay, "This Land Is NOT Your Land," describing democracy as the duped handmaid of utility. He opened his mouth to say something but both men stood up. It was over.

Ribeye Cluke nodded at Bob. "Go nail down some properties," he said.

"Good to meet you, Bob," said Mr. Ragsdale smoothly. He nodded toward Ribeye and added, "You're well-guided by Mr. Cluke," and Bob knew the man was not going to discuss a luxury house property subsidiary with Mr. Goliath, whoever that Pork Rind giant might be. Hog farms were for the general good.

30

QUICK CHANGE

On the return trip he spent Tuesday night in Grandma's Comfy Motel in La Junta, and though bone tired, turned on the television set hoping for a good movie. The selection was peculiar: *Brother, The Good Brother, The Brother-in-Law, Uncle Vladya's Brother.* He fell asleep watching two angry peasants shout at each other in Russian, too tired to read the subtitles.

He crossed the Texas line early Wednesday morning, moving past the square shapes of cows, heads down, always eating. The new book from Bromo lay on the seat beside him—*Broken Hand,* a biography of the mountain man Thomas Fitzpatrick, who had been with Abert on the trip across the panhandle. It was Broken Hand who had warned the lieutenant never to tie his mules to shrubbery.

The cropland lay spread out like viridian bolts of corduroy seamed with pale roads. Thinking of the Front Range that frilled Denver, such flatness struck him as an anomaly. His eye traveled over the fields. Houses looked as temporarily there as items on the grocery counter. He passed an abandoned farm familiar to him now from his travels. In back were a few old-fashioned pig huts, hemispheres of galvanized metal tipped and crushed in weedy corners, for no one raised backyard pigs now.

In Woolybucket again, he drove past the grain elevators, their roofs crowded with pigeons who, although they could not get at the rich abundance below, were irresistibly drawn to it. They could not get it, but it was there.

At noon he was back at the Busted Star. Nothing different, another terrifically hot day, the sun pounding the earth with its hammer, LaVon's car was parked in a scrap of shade curled like old shoe leather. He knocked on the kitchen door, then opened it and put his head in.

"LaVon? You here?"

She came out of her office space, holding a rolled-up paper, large enough to be the map of Texas.

"Well, Bob, I guess you did not get fired. But you have missed all the excitement," she said. "Anyway, welcome home."

"What did I miss? I drove through Woolybucket and it looked the same." He felt a stir at her use of the word "home," for it seemed maybe he was home, a feeling that had not come when he walked into Uncle Tam's place. He got a quick shot of Uncle Tam in the panhandle, but that image blacked out immediately.

"Hah. It's *all* different. There's so much goin on I can't hardly say. Freda Beautyrooms had a stroke Saturday mornin. She died. Well, she needed a go on.

QUICK CHANGE

Her son Waldo come up for a weekend visit and found her half under the bed. He thinks she was lookin for a slipper or a piece a jewelry. She had all that junk jewelry. I can't abide that stuff clankin and danglin. A woman in Amarilla I heard about wore these big dangly earrings and she was peelin potatoes at her sink one day and one a the earrings went into the disposal and threw up a little chunk and it went in her eye and blinded her. But Freda is sure goin a be missed. She was in everthing. She was the official head a the Barbwire Festival Committee. Course, old as she was, she didn't do much, just a position a honor, but they need somebody. On Sunday they called and asked me if I'd take over, seein the festival is so close. But it's more than just showin up on the day and smilin around and sayin hello, which is all Freda ever done. It's still a lot a work has to be done. Like put these posters up."

She unrolled a large four-color poster showing a dancing couple togged out in western dress with strands of antique barbwire emanating from a spinning roll beneath their feet.

WOOLYBUCKET BARBWIRE FESTIVAL
DANCE•BARBECUE•QUILT
RAFFLE•RODEO
COLLECTORS MART & EXCHANGE

She let it roll up again with a snap. "Waldo Beautyrooms come over here lookin for you. He wants a talk with you. He's back in Houston now—they had the funeral Monday—but he left a number for you to call him up. I didn't think you was comin back so I probly lost it somewhere in the mess a papers."

"That's O.K. I think I have it anyhow. It sounds like a pretty upsetting weekend."

"Oh, that's not all. There's more. Francis Scott Keister—he's a rancher, you probly don't know him—and some woman went to the Hi-Lo Motel in Liberal for hanky panky and Francis Scott's wife, Thomasina—they call her Tazzy—followed them and shot through the window five times. Francis Scott was killed dead and the woman is in the hospital over in Amarilla. They say she might not make it. And Tazzy is in the county jail. Her mother is takin care a the kids."

"Good Lord," said Bob. "By any chance was the woman with Francis Scott Keister named Evelyn Chine?"

"That's the name. She don't come from around here. I saved the copy of *The Bummer*. They put out a special edition. Here it is. Look at that. They got a picture a that darn snake-face sheriff on the front page draggin poor Tazzy to the county car. She didn't want a go. You can see she got her heels braced. They almost had a carry her, I heard. They say the woman was workin for one a them big hog farm corporations. That's why Tazzy Keister shot her—she'd got Francis Scott ready to throw up to the hog companies and sell out. A lot a people think Tazzy ought a have a medal.

And that's not all. Some lady over in Roberts County got attacked in her own home by a escaped convict. She'd left the door unlocked for her husband. She wasn't killed but she was—you know *what*."

While Bob read the shooting story LaVon reheated the coffee.

"Thing that worries me is that's two deaths. And they come in threes. So we don't know who is goin a be next. We don't know what more is goin a happen. Somethin else, Bob. See, I didn't know if you was comin back—you said you didn't think so and I didn't hear different. So Coolbroth has moved into the bunkhouse. He used a stay there before he went off to school, and he wanted to get back into the place and do his skolpin. He's got ambitions now. This whole thing with Tazzy has got him on fire. He's fightin the hog companies and got a bunch a people in on it, meetins ever night. 'Artists Against Hogs' they call themselves. But in case you *did* come back, I asked around and there's a lady over on the Coppedge Road will accommodate you. Mrs. Jaelene Shattle. They've got a nice house with a little apartment at the back— telphone, electric, telvision and—here's the best part—there's a whirlpool bath. Her mother used a stay there before she died. She had terrible artharitis and the whirlpool helped her. Jaelene only wants fifty a month, same as here, even with all those amenities. I can call her up right now and tell her you are on your way, if you want?"

"Thanks, LaVon. I appreciate your trouble. It

sounds great. But I'll sure miss the bunkhouse. Just where is Coppedge Road, anyway?" It sounded vaguely familiar, but in his wandering drives he couldn't recall that he had ever hit on it.

"It's over by Tater Crouch's ranch. About a mile west. You go over toward Tater's but bear left where his road forks off, keep on about two mile as the road winds around, and after you cross the bridge it's the white house on the right. You can't miss it."

It was not until he turned onto Coppedge Road that the location hit him. The big King Karolina hog farm that so affected Tater Crouch was on Coppedge Road. In fact, he realized with sinking heart, Jaelene Shattle's house was the place west of Tater Crouch and must be right beside the hog farm. No wonder the woman was only asking fifty a month. Then his spirits revived. Maybe she would sell out too. But in a few minutes his spirits sagged again. Maybe she wouldn't. Maybe he would never get a hog site sale clinched. Depression, like a smell of skunk, filled the car. He felt he wasn't going to fall into anything fortunate, not a hog farm sale, not a dimpled, curly-headed girl. He did not want to lie but seemed unable to stop doing so. Yet he could not just quit and go back to Denver and look for another lightbulb job. He had taken up a responsibility—to find sites for hog farms and persuade elderly farmers and ranchers to sell out their decades of labor to the silent rows of Hog World—and he would not put it aside. That would be too much like his parents dumping him and haring off to Alaska. The words "Hog World" floated past again and he imagined a hog theme park where the entrance gate was an enormous hog replica and cars drove between the massive pink legs, a Disneyland of pork where the rides would be replicas of giant boars or intelligent piglets, a petting sty where children could feed carrots and apples to real swine, a place where the food kiosks would offer barbecued ribs and Black Forest hams, smokehouse bacon, sausages dangling from a dark and smoky *wursthaus* ceiling.

Jaelene Shattle was fat and careworn, her forehead lined with strain, her fingers nervously plucking at lint on her sweater. He wondered how she could wear a sweater on such a hot day. As he stood on the front step waiting for her to ask him in he could see, out of the corner of his eye, the low, neat white buildings of the hog farm a quarter of a mile to the west. The smell was not noticeable, perhaps because the wind was out of the east.

"Yes," she said, "we *are* next to the hog farm, and to tell you the truth, I don't know what in the world we are goin a do. It's not so bad now but when the wind changes and they turn on the fans it is very bad. My husband suffers from it a good deal. In the house we have nine special air conditioners and six air purifiers runnin all the time, so it's not too awful, but outside, when the wind is right, your eyes just flame up and your throat hurts. That's why I only ask fifty dollars a month for the apartment. Otherwise it would be two hunderd. So if you can stand the hog farm it's a good deal. Do you have a tendency to asthma?"

"No," said Bob, thinking he would give the place a try. If he couldn't stand it, why, he'd move. "I'll give it a try," he said.

"About the phone, you just use it like it was your own and I'll go over the bill with you when it comes in. It's easier that way and saves you from havin to call GTE, maybe the mainest telephone company in Texas. You'll sit for an hour, maybe two, listenin a fool messages and ugly music before they give you a live person. It's easier this way."

The apartment was sunny, spotless and pleasant; there was a large carpeted bedroom with cream-colored walls, its frilly-curtained window looking out on the hog farm, a large comfortable living room with a television set, an antique rolltop desk, a red sofa with blue pillows and a private bathroom with the fabled whirlpool. The windows were fitted with hail screens. With the air purifier humming he could not smell the hog farm and began to think of it as a minor inconvenience whose deleterious character was much exaggerated. If Tater bought some air purifiers and air conditioners he might not be troubled. He put aside Lieutenant Abert, spent a pleasant evening watching television, and, after a luxurious session in the whirlpool, climbed into the pink-sheeted bed and slept.

In the morning he telephoned Ribeye Cluke, enjoying the convenience of not driving to the Old Dog to use the pay phone.

"Sir, I'm in new living quarters. I have a telephone now." And he gave the number. "I thought you would want to know that Evelyn Chine is bad hurt and in the hospital."

"Hurt by what?"

"By a bullet. Bullets. She was caught in a motel bed with a married man. The man's wife shot them both. The paper says she is in the medical center in Amarillo."

"I see." There was a long silence, then Mr. Cluke's voice swelled to command-giving mode. "Bob, I want you to go see Evelyn Chine and talk with her doctor, get a full report on her condition. Call me later with that information. She was close to finalizing a big deal with a rancher down there. Fellow named Keister. You may have to take that deal over if she is not up to working for a while."

"Mr. Cluke, you want *me* to go see her?"

"Certainly. And get flowers."

"Flowers? That could take some time. There's no flower shop here. It's a café now."

"The hospital, Bob. They have flower shops in hospitals."

"O.K., I'll do it. But I think you ought to know that

Mr. Keister is dead. He's the one she was in bed with."

"I see. That's certainly too bad. Perhaps the widow would be amenable to persuasion. You see if you can suss out the lay of the land. Bob, one other thing. Do you still want us to send down the Money Offer Person on Mr. Crouch's property?"

"Yes sir, I do, but he'd better call me first to let me know when he's coming. And not tomorrow because it's quite a drive to and back from Amarillo."

"It won't be a 'he,' Bob. All our Money Offer Persons are women. It soothes the rancher to have a woman offer him money and makes him inclined to take a little less. Mrs. Betty Doak will come down later this week. She'll call you."

It was going to be a busy day if he had to drive to Amarillo, buy flowers, visit and assess the condition of Evelyn Chine, stop at Tater Crouch's place and let him know the Money Offer Person was coming down, get in touch with Waldo Beautyrooms. He didn't think he had to scout out how Tazzy Keister felt about selling the ranch to a hog outfit. She had made her opinion clear with her fusillade. And Jim Skin was probably a lost cause, though he would try to catch him later in the week. He called Waldo first.

"Hello, Mr. Beautyrooms. I was sorry to hear about your mother. I was in Denver over the weekend and just got back. Yes. Well, I spoke to my superiors and while they have doubts about the panhandle as a locus for luxury homes— Then why did they send me down here? Actually they sent me to scout for hog farm sites—" He held the receiver away from his ear as Waldo Beautyrooms' outraged screeches punctuated the miles between Houston and Woolybucket. He tried to explain the situation.

"But Mr. Ragsdale from the Tokyo office was there and he's going to present the idea to the company president, Mr. Goliath, and get back to me. And the minute I hear from him—" But Waldo Beautyrooms had hung up.

Next, because it was on the way, he pulled into Tater Crouch's driveway, climbed up the porch steps and knocked. The housekeeper did not answer and finally he turned the knob and sidled in, calling, "Mr. Crouch? You home?" knowing he was, for the truck stood in the yard. Still, he was startled when the old man appeared in a nightgown, his hair scattered thinly about his pallid dome.

"Well," he said. "She's gone into town for groceries. Come in."

"Just stopped for a minute, Mr. Crouch, to let you know that they are sending someone down to make you an offer. Later this week. You know, I'm not at LaVon's now. I'm over here, staying at the Shattles' place. It's right next to the hog farm. LaVon's son, Coolbroth, moved into the Busted Star bunkhouse while I was gone."

"That hog farm stink will make you sick. Jerky Shattle's got terrible lung problems from it. I expect it'll kill him. Their little grandson can't even visit. He gets to havin convulsions when he smells that smell. They are suin the hog farm, you know. I don't guess you'll last there long."

"They've got all these air conditioners and air filters and such. Inside it's not bad. Course I only spent one night there."

"Last night was nothin. You wait, you'll smell it. *That's* the place you ought a buy. It's ruined."

"Anyway, I'll be back with the Money Offer Person. It's a lady, Mrs. Doak."

"What happened to that other one, the liar? I heard Tazzy Keister shot her up."

"I'm going over to Amarillo right now to visit her. They've got her at the medical center there."

Tater Crouch made a face and told Bob he'd be waiting for him.

Bob stopped at the Old Dog for an early lunch.

"Well, well, look who's here," said Cy. "Didn't think you was comin back. I got beef ragout today, sides a baked beans, tossed salad, pickled walnuts, rolls and apple pan dowdy for dessert. Help yourself."

Bob heaped his plate, sat in the booth where he had last seen Evelyn Chine and Francis Scott Keister.

"Suppose you heard about the goins-on—Freda Beautyrooms, and Francis Scott Keister and that girl that was here last week, and the sheriff's little problem."

"I didn't hear about the sheriff."

"Tazzy Keister busted both his arms resistin arrest. He was pushin her towards his car, didn't have cuffs on her, her bein a woman and all, and she gets his left arm and cranks it up behind his back. They said you could hear the bone snap across the street. Then she lets go a high kick—wearin her work shoes with the steel toe caps—and gets the other one. She started a run for it but one a the deputies, Haish Smith, tackled her and he sure enough put on some cuffs, but not before she give him a taste a her knee where it hurts the most. Can't really blame Francis Scott Keister for wantin more gentle female companionship. Sheriff, with them broke arms, he's had a get somebody drive him around, one a the dispatchers, and for all I know, help him with more personal affairs like passin water. Quite the time Tazzy give him. She's strong, you know, workin on the ranch all her life. A lot a panhandle women is as strong as the men."

"Maybe that's the third bad thing. LaVon says bad stuff comes in threes."

"She's right," said Cy. "But I don't think busted arms can stand up to death and killin. There'll be another passin."

The restaurant was still empty.

"Everybody gone to Brown Paper Pete's hanging?" said Bob. "It's kind of quiet here today."

Cy grimaced sourly. "It's that ladies' place with all them damn desserts. Their regular menu is just sandwiches and soup, but they make a hell of a lot of fancy desserts and it looks like that's what cowboys and rig workers want. I had a drop pineapple I got so many complaints except from Jim Skin. Told him he could go to the supermarket and buy hisself a case a canned pineapple but that don't appeal to him. Them Christian ladies, the old whores, they got pies, they got cream puffs, they put out chocolate eclairs and coffee cake. I wouldn't a thought ranch hands would have such a grasp on confectionery items but Ernie Chambers come in and told me if I didn't start makin crème brûlée he was takin his business over there. 'What about pork roast?' I says. 'I seen you eat six big slices roast pork and gravy. You won't get that over there. You on a diet for canned tomata soup and egg salad sandwich?' Course he couldn't answer me, all shamefaced and full a Peach Surprise. Jesus Christ, I just as soon put a funnel in my mouth and run against the wind."

"Don't you think the novelty will wear off?"

"Maybe. No pineapple today!" he bellowed at the front door and Bob turned to see Jim Skin.

"That's O.K.," Jim Skin said. "I kind a had enough pineapple. I kind a got a cravin for meat. What a you got?" He noticed Bob Dollar too late to retreat.

"Like a beef stew. It's pretty good." Cy turned to Bob again. "Anyway, I'm thinkin about stayin open at supper time, catch the supper crowd. If there is one. Won't know until I try. There's not a place open for supper for fifty miles. Course maybe there's not no one wants supper away from home for fifty miles."

Jim Skin got a plate and filled it, stacked four rolls

atop the food, looked around the empty room and finally came over to Bob's table. Unease exuded from him like the odor of some bitter aftershave lotion.

"How are you, Bob?" he said cautiously. "I heard you left this country."

"Not yet. Had to go up to Denver and report to the head office. You given any more thought to talking with Ace Crouch about selling your place?"

"Hell, Bob, I been meanin a get in touch with you on that. And like I said, I thought you'd left the country. Ace don't want a sell just now."

"I see," said Bob, mopping up his gravy with a roll, swallowing the last of his coffee and rising. "Got to go. See you, Cy," he called and left Jim Skin abruptly, intending his rude departure to sting, to give the message that he knew Jim Skin was a conniving liar flirting with a gas outfit.

The medical center parking lot at Amarillo was nearly full and Bob had to settle for a space in the most remote corner where the wind had swept in an assortment of candy wrappers and leaves. An empty oil can rolled restlessly.

At the receptionist's desk a glass vase of dusty silk flowers with frayed edges obscured a full view of a woman with breasts the size of deflated basketballs.

"Evelyn Chine? Up in ICU. Only family members permitted. Are you a relative?"

"Yes," Bob lied. "I'm her brother." And then, of course, he began to believe it.

"Uh-huh. Your mother and father are up there now with her."

"Mr. and Mrs. Chine?"

"Who else?"

"Well, I'm her *step*brother. From Mrs. Chine's first marriage. I'll wait until they come down. I don't want to interrupt."

The woman looked at him, curiosity and suspicion mingled in her face.

"Are you a newspaper reporter?" she asked suddenly.

"No! Good Lord, no. Have they been here?"

"You bet!" said the woman. "Don't look now but those people over by the window are *all* reporters. You'd think nobody in Texas ever got shot before, the way they are carryin on. The Chines should be down pretty soon. There's a ten-minute limit on visits to ICU patients."

Bob walked over to the tiny florist's shop and bought a single yellow rose and a Mylar balloon stamped with the face of a cartoon cat. As he came out of the shop he glanced toward the reporters—half a dozen middle-aged people slouched in chairs, paring their nails or talking on cell phones. He recognized Babe Vanderslice, the Woolybucket *Banner*'s crack newswoman, and hoped she didn't recognize him. But then, what if she did? He could be there for any reason, though the rose and balloon marked him as a visitor to a patient.

• • •

QUICK CHANGE

The elevator doors opened and a short couple came out, the man with a cliff of hair like Conway Twitty's, their expressions stolid and glum. The big-breasted receptionist caught Bob's eye and nodded.

He told his lie again at the nurses' station and was told that his "parents" had just left.

"You can stay only a few minutes, now," said a handsome, black-haired young nurse who looked like a flapper from the twenties. She had dimples, which pleased Bob.

Evelyn Chine, crowned with a bandage turban, lay unconscious in the hospital bed, her face horribly swollen, both eyes black, crusted blood in one ear. A huge battery of machines and devices counted her heartbeats, her respirations, measured her blood gases, charted her brain waves. For the first time he realized she had been shot in the head. A terrific feeling rolled over him. He had only seen Evelyn Chine as a competitor, but now, as she lay helpless and wounded, he imagined himself saving her from her own reckless nature that had got her onto this thin ledge of life. No longer did he think of himself as Evelyn Chine's half brother. Now he was her lover, her fiancé and, his imagination tumbling like the colored balls in a bingo cage, her honeymoon husband. He saw himself bound to Evelyn Chine, saw himself swearing an oath never to leave her, pushing her wheelchair, draping a cashmere shawl over her tiny shoulders. But then these images shifted and he saw himself trying to mount her flaccid body, moving the helpless arms and legs into exotic and shameful positions. He put the rose on the table beside her bed and wrote on the white card that dangled from the neck of the vase "All my love, Bob," kissed her swollen, fevered cheek and went out to the nurses' station.

"What are her chances?" he asked the flapper-nurse.

"That's her doctor—Dr. Brun," the nurse said, nodding at a tough-looking woman with a squashed nose, the white coat identifying her as a repairer of broken bodies. "You'll have to talk to her. Oh, Dr. Brun— here's Evelyn's brother wants a talk with you."

The doctor advanced on Bob, seized his hand and palped it sympathetically. Her breath puffed out in a miasmic stench and she looked at Bob with hard greenish eyes like unripe berries.

"I'm Evelyn's husband," he said, imagining Evelyn's father pushing her wheelchair down the aisle, the bride's head lolling. "How is she doing?"

"I just explained everthang to her parents. They didn't say she was merried."

"They don't know," said Bob simply. "It was a secret marriage."

"Ah—you know the circumstances a her anjuries?"

"Yes. Evelyn often goes to motels with married men. It's a problem we're working on. She's in a twelve-step program for it. She's been shot before by jealous wives, but never in the head. Usually they miss. We have a lot of hope she will get over this with love and attention."

The doctor took a deep breath as if to freshen her lungs with an infusion of oxygen.

"Are y'all a reporter?" she said.

"No," said Bob. "I'm in real estate."

"Oh yeah? Well, she sustained a very serious anjury. The bullet disintegrated and scattered fragments in part a her brain? It is safer leave them fragments in situ than try and remove em. What we are concerned with now is swellin a the brain. The hard bony skull got no room for expansion, and, if the swellin is profound, we may have to tike out a section a her skull."

"Oh yuck," said Bob, earning a freezing glance.

"It is a *temporary* removal. When the swellin subsides we replace the bone."

"Is she going to be all right?" asked Bob, playing the fool.

"Only tom will tell, Mr. Chan," said the doctor, rolling her eyes and pressing the retractable button of her click pen. "But as she's got this serious anjury you'd do well a prepare yourself for the worse, though we always hope for the best. It's in God's hand and all we can do is say our priors."

31

MRS. BETTY DOAK

Jaelene Shattle twisted her hands and creased her forehead.

"Oh, Mr. Dollar, some women have been calling you all afternoon. A Mrs. Betty Doak phoned twice and said to tell you she would meet you tomorrow noon at the Old Dog for lunch. You know, it's funny but I think I know her. I think she was Betty Cream. I think she went to the Wink school same as I did. My dad was in the oil boom down in Wink years ago. We just kept a-movin around. A year in Wink, a year in Midland, a year in Amarilla. And the other woman said she would call back this evening. She didn't leave her name. Did you notice how bad the smell is today?"

"Yes," said Bob. In truth the hog farm effluvia was ferocious, a palpable, heavy ammoniac stink that burned the eyes and throat. "Have you ever thought of selling?"

"Who on earth would buy this place situated where it is? Mercy!"

"Ah—I suppose a hog farm would buy it. You know Tater Crouch is thinking of selling."

"Oh no! Then we'd be sandwiched in between two hog farms? My husband couldn't stand it. He's in the hospital right this minute in respiratory distress."

"If you sold you could move somewhere else, somewhere there aren't any hog farms."

"Where might that be? In a city, I suppose. We're country people and we've been on this land for four generations. The city is not for us. We've been happy here and my husband has worked his heart out to keep this ranch in order. We can't even run cows on it anymore. The cows can't even stand it. Do you think it's right that some main-hearted corporation can buy up panhandle land and force out the local people? I don't know what we are goin a do. My husband says if he were a young man he'd set grass fires and burn them out. I do not know what we are goin a do. That state senator in Amarilla is no help at all. He's on the side a corporate hog outfits. The corporations got the politicians sewed up in Texas, top to bottom. And down in Austin the panhandle is far away and folks think it is a worthless place anyhow—they think it is perfect for hogs. Tonight we will suffer with that stench."

"You might talk to your husband and see how he feels about selling the place and moving to a different region. Maybe down around Austin? There's enough rich folks down there that they won't let the hog farms in. If you think you want to sell, let me know. I can put you in touch with a buyer."

"I'll mention it to him when I go see him tonight. In fact I'd better get goin now." And she gathered up the hot casserole, murmuring "chicken pot pie, one a his favorites," and went out the door.

In his room Bob pulled off his dank clothes and took a cool shower. It would be a fine evening on LaVon's bunkhouse porch—which he missed—watching the sunset sky burn up. He turned on the television set but every station was showing something stupid and he turned it off again, looked for Lieutenant Abert's account of his travels. He could not find it and wondered if it was in the car or if he had brought it to Denver and left it in his old room. He went outside and checked the car. The book was lying on the back floor with a lollipop stick stuck to it at a jaunty angle. The new book, *Broken Hand,* was still on the front seat. He brought them both inside. He could hear the telephone ringing inside and made a dash for it.

"Hello?" he said, panting.

"What ya doin?"

"Who is this?"

"Don't you reckanize my voice? It's Marisa. Your girlfriend? From Front Range High School?"

"Marisa. Where are you?" he asked with a depressed little laugh.

"In Denver. Visitin my folks. I got your number from your uncle. What are you doin in the Texas panhandle? Isn't it awful down there?"

"No, it's got its own style. There are a lot of nice things about it. And I'm in the hog business. What about you, Marisa? I thought you went off to college."

"I did. But I graduated. Now I'm in graduate school. My boyfriend is working for his law degree and I figured I might as well go ahead with what I was into."

"What is that?"

"Entity configuration."

"What is 'entity configuration'?"

"Oh, just about anything. A person's business profile or a website or a business plan or even financial investment chart. It's like taking something that is like ectoplasm and shaping it up into something tangible. You know, making something that's mixed up seem clear and understandable. So have you got a girlfriend now?"

"Yes. In fact, I'm married. My wife's name is Evelyn. She has curly black hair and dimples. She's a professional dancer. Right now she's in Kansas City, dancing."

"Married! You married? Oh my God! Your uncle didn't say a thing. I called you up because I thought we could get together again sometime and see how we like each other now. Of course I couldn't come down to the panhandle. But if you came up here we could get together. My parents still go to church on Sunday."

"So do I," said Bob, "with my wife," and gently replaced the receiver.

He read Lieutenant Abert's account until the letters on the page began to swim. It came to him that the black Colorado squirrels with tasseled ears were called Abert squirrels and wondered if there was a connection. So far he had noticed nothing about squirrels. Perhaps he would re-read with squirrels in mind.

The next morning the stench was worse than ever. He woke with a headache, his ears ringing, his red eyes itching. He felt dizzy and disoriented as though he were coming down with the flu. Only in the shower under the stream of shampoo-scented water could he get away from the smell. It permeated everything. His clothes reeked, his mouth seemed filled with manure and mud. He raced for the door, nearly colliding with Mrs. Shattle.

"Bob, I talked to my husband and he says sell! We want a sell out too if Tater is goin to. That was the only thing keepin us here. We didn't want a make things worse for Tater. But if he's goin a make things worse for us, why then, we'll sell. We'll move to Canada or Greenland, somewhere they never heard a hogs."

"O.K., good. I'll talk to you about this when I get back—sometime this afternoon. Can I pick up anything in town for you?"

"No, Bob. I'm goin a town myself, get away from the stench."

He drove to the Old Dog with the windows down, the hot air rushing in and flinging his hair around. Two miles from the hog farm he could breathe again. Never was air so sweet. He put up the windows and combed at his hair with his fingers, damning himself for never carrying a comb, until he remembered the snow brush in the trunk, pulled over to the side of the road and used the awkward object to smooth his hair.

"Hey, Bubba," said Cy when he came in. "We got fried catfish and corn bread today, steaks if you don't like fish, and turkey hash for them don't like steak neither."

"I'm waiting for somebody," said Bob.

"Not Jim Skin?"

"No."

"Brother Mesquite?"

"No. A lady I've never met. Mrs. Betty Doak."

"Betty Doak? I think I know her. Wasn't she Betty Cream? Had a daddy worked the oil rigs?"

"I'm not sure," said Bob. "She might be. Mrs. Shattle thought so. Maybe you'll recognize her when she comes in."

And half an hour later, when Bob was beginning to think Mrs. Betty Doak had stood him up, a two-tone Grand Cherokee parked out front and a rangy woman with a pompadour of curls, her lank frame a thinly padded skeleton inside the blue rayon pantsuit, took the steps to the Old Dog two at a time and came in.

She looked at Cy, she looked at Bob. She put her head back and laughed. "Cy Frease, so this is where you ended up. I thought it would be Huntsville."

"It almost was, Betty. But I dodged in time. You are lookin good. I thought it might be you. Livin up in Okie land these days?"

"Yes, I got a little house north a Beaver, part a my mother's family's old ranch. Just a few acres. She left it to me. My daddy never had a ranch or a house or nothin he could call his own. Had a good time, though. Made good money and spent it all."

"I heard that. I heard you was somewhere up there over the line."

"Well, when me and Richard Doak got a divorce we was livin in Wichita Falls and I figured I ought a get back to the panhandle, even if it was the Oklahoma handle. There's no place like home, you know."

"I know. That's right. It's been a long time since we was kids in Wink. That was a rough town."

"Yes, but didn't we have some good times? A hard life but a happy childhood."

"Maybe we can get you down here a little more often. By the way, this is your lunch date, Bob Dollar. We got fried catfish, steaks, turkey hash. Choose your poison."

"Hello, Bob. Good a meet you. Let's get some of Cy's grub. Sure smells good. I get tired a cookin for myself so it's a treat for me to eat out." She took the catfish and salad.

Bob helped himself to the same and they sat at the table near the window.

"I know of Tater Crouch, a course, but I never met him and I never seen his place. I know his brother, Ace, pretty well. I guess I'm surprised they want to sell. The Crouches been here a long time."

"The smell. He can't take it anymore. There's a

hog farm to the west and it gets pretty gamey. Tater's getting old enough now so he likes the idea of living in town. And there's a couple even closer to the hog farm over there than Tater is, the Shattle place. Mr. Shattle is pretty sick from the smell and apparently he wants to sell out too. So we might go there and see what kind of offer you can make for that place too."

"I think I know her. Wasn't she Jaelene Defoos?"

"I don't know. But she thinks she knows you. Said you were in school together in Wink years ago."

"Then it's her. How about that. Two old school-mates in one day. Wink to Woolybucket. I ought a come down here more often."

"Amen," said Cy, who was listening.

"Cy, you must a learned a cook from your mother. Didn't she cook at the Star Diner in Wink?"

"Yes, she did. She made more in tips than my daddy made drillin. What used a bother her was the sand and the wind. She said the wind would just blast that sand and wear her nylon stockins full a holes."

Buckskin Bill and Sorrel Bill came in, looked at Bob and Betty Doak, helped themselves to the fish, asked what was for dessert.

"I don't want any dessert," whispered Mrs. Betty Doak to Bob, scratching the fish bones to the rim of her plate. "Let's just get down the road and see if we can clinch the Bar Owl *and* Coppedge Road."

They split the bill and Bob held the door open for her.

"Thank you, kind sir," she said.

"You come on back soon, Betty, y'hear?" Cy fixed her with a look. "Or I'll have to come up to Beaver and look for you. You in the phone book?"

"Yes I am. You do that—come visit. See you later."

After a polite wrangle over which car to use, Bob agreed to the Grand Cherokee, got in, and Betty Doak drove them toward Coppedge Road.

In the Old Dog the phone rang and Cy answered it, his laconic "Yeah?" giving way to exclamations. "No! That right? All right, all right. Just left. No, I don't know. Thanks."

He came over to Buckskin and Sorrel, put his hands on the table and leaned in. "Dispatcher at the sheriff's office. Tazzy Keister escaped from the jail, got her gun back out a the sheriff's desk drawer and said she was goin a shoot ever hog farm person she could find. Bob is on her list. Near the top. Tazzy got one a them old dispatchers to the cell and choked her half to death, made her unlock the door. The damn sheriff stayed home today. Not feelin good with them arm casts. They say his sister come down a take care a him for a while."

"Where was Bob and Betty goin? We could call up and warn them."

"I don't know for sure. I don't eavesdrop."

"Hell you don't. Well, I guess we'll hear about it if they get shot."

•　　•　　•

Tater Crouch's driveway sported a big mud hole abreast of the old bunkhouse. Rain had hammered the panhandle on Saturday. Betty Doak looked at the building and said, "I bet those walls could tell some stories."

That reminded Bob that LaVon, in hundreds of hours of talking, had never told him what caused the heavy scars on her grandfather's back.

Betty Doak drew the Grand Cherokee up in front of the house and they got out. The hog farm stink was strong and she wrinkled her nose. The housekeeper, who must have been standing near the door, whisked it open. She smiled at Mrs. Doak, ignored Bob, pointed to the crowded living room where Tater Crouch sat in his wheelchair.

"Tater! Tater, they're here!"

"I know it. Didn't I see them drive up? Go cut that damn pie and bring us some."

"Mr. Crouch," said Bob. "This is Mrs. Betty Doak. She's the Money Offer Person."

Mrs. Doak extended her hand but the old man waved it away.

"It won't do me no good now. Ace, he don't want a sell."

"Oh no," said Bob. "Oh no. What is wrong with him?"

"There is nothin wrong with him. He is just tryin a save a piece a the panhandle. He don't think hogs belong here."

"But they are here already. Does he have some way to get rid of the ones already here?"

"You better ask him that." Tater's hands shook and his eyes slid around. He glanced at Bob, looked away. "He's the oldest. He's got the say-so."

Back in Betty Doak's SUV Bob put his head in his hands. There was no point in going on to the Shattles'. He was not suited for the hog farm game. He thought about hitchhiking across the country, finding himself a new place. He thought about going to Alaska but he no longer cared to find his parents. He had made his way without them. He had grown up. He wondered if it was too late to become a cowboy and felt it was, at least a hundred years too late. He needed a job, but not this one. He needed an apprenticeship to something—gunsmithing, surveying, photography. A feeling of discomfort rose in him as though he had swallowed grapes with carpet tacks at their centers.

"Hm," said Betty Doak. "What are you goin a do now?"

"I don't know. I suppose a last-ditch effort. Go see Ace Crouch and ask him what the hell he is doing saying no to everything. He seems to be at the bottom of every land deal that's fallen through. I don't understand why he's doing it. It would be good for Tater to get into town. The Shattles need to be rescued too. And Jim Skin is hard up and got this lousy land good for nothing else."

"Is that how you see it? You're rescuin folks?"

"Well, in a way."

"I imagine there's others see it different. Tell you what. You go talk with Ace Crouch, give me a call if you need me to come back down. You can call me directly, just skip the Denver office. Save time. Here's my number."

They drove in silence back to the Old Dog where Bob said goodbye, got out and went to the Saturn, sat for a few minutes composing his mind. He got out again, went into the Old Dog.

"Cy," he said. "You know where Ace Crouch lives? I got to go talk to him."

"You got to be careful, is what you got to do," said Cy. "Tazzy Keister's on the war path and you're her target. She's escaped and she's got her old hog leg back and she is after your blood. I was you, I'd get out a town. Sheriff's office says she stole the sheriff's car and that she's considered armed and dangerous."

Bob did not take this news seriously. He couldn't believe that any woman, even a Texas woman, would stalk him with a gun and hunt him down. "Yeah, thanks, but where does Ace Crouch live?"

"Bob, you got guts, I'll say that. Ace lives in Cowboy Rose, Kokernut Drive, little white house at the end with a ten-foot windmill on the lawn. Sign sayin Ace Windmills. His shop's out back. You can't miss it. Watch your step."

32

ACE IN THE HOLE

Cowboy Rose looked different now to Bob, more worn and shabbier, set in its own narrow-minded ways. Kokernut Drive was a short street of small houses near the railroad spur. Heat waves ran across the road like water. Ace Crouch's house was fronted by a scabby lawn crowded with broken windmill parts and stacks of sucker rod. The shed at the back was jammed with more metal, aged trucks parked alongside the building. He took a breath and walked to the door, knocked, waited for several minutes and knocked again. He heard hurried footsteps inside.

The door opened and a faded, elderly woman with a handsome face looked at him.

"Mrs. Crouch?" He could smell burned food, hear tinny television laughter.

"Yes."

"Is Mr. Crouch home? My name is Bob Dollar and I need to talk to him."

"Home? He's never home. And when he is he's asleep. He's out fixin a mill on Head's place, the old Cow Bones Ranch. You can find him out there. You know how to get there?"

"No, ma'am."

"Let me think a minute." She looked up at the ceiling. "Well, you drive west on the Screwbean Draw Road, know where that is? Good. Then you go until you come to the junction with 943, then I'm pretty sure you turn right, that's north, and go about three or four or five miles until you hit Peeler Flats Road. Let's see. You turn right on Peeler Flats and go another ten or twelve miles until you see a big ranch gate with five or six cow skulls nailed on it. That's the main entrance. But you don't want a go in there. You want the other entrance, the north entrance, so go past the main gate and bear right at Jimmy Rim Springs Road where Powper Lane cuts in. About three miles up Jimmy Rim there's the back turnoff onto the ranch, big green metal gate, and that's what you want. Ace is out in what they call the Black Draw pasture. You should be able a see his truck out there and a course you *will* see the mill. You want me to write that down for you?" she asked at his confused expression.

"Please, if you don't mind."

She scribbled sentences, crossed one out, wrote again and handed him the paper. "It might be you'll turn left at Peeler Flats."

When he read the directions in the car they did not seem to tally with what she had said.

An hour later he was lost in a tangle of pale dusty roads punctuated with an occasional yucca, clumps of little walnut and paper mulberry, roads with such names as Big Dry Lake and Tidyout. Mrs. Crouch's directions and his map were of no use, for nothing matched. The flatland had given way to a series of dips and hollows cut by a twisted stream. Formidable plum thickets guarded the water. At last he pulled over and sat, let the dust settle. In the distance he could hear the irregular beat of pump jacks.

The nameless stream, black and deep, ran under a concrete bridge and in the water floated a wood duck and her train of ducklings aligned as though tied to her by a string. He looked down the road, unsure even if he could find his way back to Woolybucket. After a few minutes he could see a plume of dust from an approaching vehicle. He got out, ready to flag it down and ask directions.

A pickup truck came rattling over the hill and plunged toward him. It slowed as it approached and stopped abreast of Bob. The driver was young with a big round face, heavy-jowled, clean-shaven, dark eyes fringed with ink-black lashes, a snub nose, red lips, so red Bob thought the man might have been eating beets. His dark hair stood up in a crest like that of a jay and was already receding at the temples, but that defect lent him an elusive charm. He was, thought Bob, one of those rare males whom the word "cute" fitted.

"Hidy," said the driver. "You O.K.? Or broke down?"

"Yeah, the car's O.K., but I'm kind of lost. I'm

looking for the north entrance to the Cow Bones Ranch. Not the main gate."

"O.K. You are about seven miles off. What you do is go ahead the way you are pointin and after two miles or so you'll come to the old schoolhouse on the right—that's where me and my friend live. Keep goin another mile and watch for the sign for Powper Lane? Go left on Powper Lane and keep goin straight until you hit Jimmy Rim Springs. Turn right. It's a couple a miles up the road there, a metal gate. There's a sign on the gate, but I don't know what it says. Never got that near. We're not exactly pals a Dick Head and his hands."

"What about Peeler Flats? I was told to take a turn at Peeler Flats."

"Peeler Flats? Never heard of it. Not around here."

"Thanks," said Bob, wondering. There was something a little odd about the encounter. But he started the Saturn and pulled out, watching the fellow's pickup disappear in its own dust.

He found Powper Lane and Jimmy Rim Springs Road and, finally, a metal gate with a sign on it. The sign, though the letters were small, read NO TRESPASSING THIS MEANS YOU and the gate was locked. His choices were three. He could drive back to the main gate and go to the ranch house and say he was looking for Ace Crouch and could they please let him in, or he could park the Saturn, climb over the gate and walk in, or he could give up and go back to the Shattle place, call Ribeye Cluke and tell him the bad news.

THAT OLD ACE IN THE HOLE

Without really thinking about it he found himself climbing over the gate, his Global Pork Rind folders in one hand, walking down the caliche ranch road with floating blooms of white prickly poppy lighting the way. How far could it be to the windmill? A mile? He walked on. And on. After an hour and twenty minutes he was streaming with sweat, his pores clogged with dust. There was no shade, just the brutal sun and its killing rays. He was more thirsty than he had ever been in his life and he had forgotten his sunglasses so the white dust before him danced with red and green spots. He tried to make a hat with the pages from his brochures but the sheets were too small and slick, and they fell apart within minutes. There were some weak vines at the edge of the road and he was about to gather them and twine them into a leafy hat when he remembered the old lady's quilting bee story about the dancing girls and the poison oak. He was not sure what poison oak looked like but undoubtedly, the way his luck had been running, this must be it. He scrutinized the roadside for safer hat materials, stopped and gathered a mass of bluestem grass, which he tried to weave into something that would shade his burning face and head, but he didn't have the knack and the stems fell apart like the jackstraws they were. At last he took his shirt off and draped it over his head, feeling the vicious heat sting and burn his arms and bare torso. Now he knew why men wore undershirts—they could save themselves from sunstroke. Inspiration struck. He might not wear

488

an undershirt but there were his shorts. He would take them off, work a few twigs into them for a frame, and voilà!—a hat.

He had gotten as far as taking off his pants and shorts when he became aware of hammering hooves and turned to see a horseman galloping toward him on the road. There was no time to dress completely again, but he had pulled his underdrawers more or less on when the horseman pulled up. A very old man whose skull showed boldly through his meager flesh glared down at him.

"What are you doin on my ranch? Can't you read? Big sign says no trespassers?"

"Yes sir. Are you Mr. Richard Head?" He could not bring himself to say Dick Head.

"I am. And who the hell are you? And why are you paradin your bare ass on my road? You with them fairies in the old schoolhouse?"

"No sir. My name is Bob Dollar, sir. I am looking for Ace Crouch. His wife said he was working out here today. The gate was locked so I thought I'd walk in. And I got so hot I thought I'd try to make a hat out of my underwear."

"Well, of all the damn fool things. Why didn't you come up to the house and ask instead a wanderin around like a crazy man? You keep on long enough you'll find him if he don't find you first on his way home."

"How much farther is it—sir?"

"About eleven more mile. You keep rattlin your

hocks you might make it by supper time. If you don't suffer heatstroke," he added, looking at Bob's fiery face. "What kind a hat did you think you could make out a underwear, somethin like Lawrence of Arabia?"

"I don't know. I was just getting ready to start. Making them. It."

"Well. Here's what I'll do. You set down and cool off. Give me your keys and I'll ride back to the gate and git your car, tie up my horse and drive in this far. Then you can drive me back down a my horse at the gate and make the choice a gettin the hell out a here and seein Ace at home this evenin, or you can go ahead and drive out to the well and catch him there. He's got his own key to the gate. He can let you out again."

"Thank you, Mr. Head. I appreciate your kindness."

"I don't relish a corpse on my ranch road." And the old man turned his horse and rode off smartly, sitting as straight as a pipe.

An hour later Bob, in the Saturn with the air-conditioning cranked full on, saw the windmill in the distance and the big square truck parked beside it. The sun, now low in the sky, glinted on the mill's turning wheel. As he drew closer he made out the figure of a man on the top platform. The man was watching him, that much he could tell.

"Mr. Crouch?" Bob squinted up at the figure on the

windmill. The sun was behind him, throwing him into black silhouette.

"Call me Ace." The voice was unexpectedly deep and the tone was one of amusement. "Well, here you are, Bob Dollar, doin your thing for Global Pork Rind."

"Yes sir."

"Climb on up, Bob. I got some ice tea up here and you look like you could use it."

Bob began to climb the skinny metal ladder. He was a third of the way up when Ace spoke again. "Better hold the side rails, not clutch on the rungs. Rungs been known a let go but the rails is strong as a wet dog."

Bob climbed on, not looking at the ground below, gripping the rough, hot metal. As he climbed higher he felt a sweet breeze. He could hear the wheel above him sighing, hear the clank of the sucker rod rising and dropping, the rhythmic spurt of water into the tank. At the top he crawled onto the platform and, not daring to stand up, crept across to where Ace Crouch sat comfortably beside a bucket, a rope for lowering and raising it tied to the handle, a jar of tea nestled in the half-melted ice. He passed the jar to Bob as soon as he eased into a sitting position on the edge of the platform.

"My God," said Bob, taking in the view across miles and miles of prairie, white grain elevators rising in the distance. Despite the heat haze and the quivering mirage that made the main road look as if it were underwater, he could see thirty miles. For several minutes neither said anything, Bob enjoying the delicious air, the coldness of the tea, Ace thinking his own thoughts.

Finally the old man spoke.

"Why'd you come out here, Bob?" he said, a hard edge to his voice.

"O.K.," said Bob. "I'm here because I don't understand why you keep telling people not to sell to me. That land of Jim Skin's is worthless." He sounded querulous and whiny to himself. "And how about your brother's place? The smell is already so bad he can't enjoy life and he says he would like to move into Woolybucket. He says he would *like* to sell. Then there's the Shattles. They want to sell too, but because *you* said no, *Tater* said no and *they* said no. It's like you have a hold over all these people and they can't think or speak for themselves."

The old man pulled a cigarette from his shirt pocket and lit it. The wind carried the acrid smell of the match and then the smoke to Bob. Ace Crouch did not speak.

"So," said Bob. "What was I supposed to do, come to you first? Like on bended knee asking some warlord for permission to cross the country?"

Ace Crouch laughed a little but said nothing.

"Don't you think your brother would be happier in town?"

The old man stubbed out the barely smoked cigarette, tore the butt open with his thumbnail, scattered the tobacco to the wind and rolled the paper into a tiny pellet, which he flicked away.

"What do you see out there, Bob?" His arm swept the horizon where a few small clouds cooked like dumplings in the simmering sky. "Tell me what you see."

Bob saw he was being set up. "Barbwire fences, the road with some trucks on it and a gate. The railroad and two sets of grain elevators, suppose one is in Woolybucket. Pump jacks."

There was a long silence that stretched out and continued. Ace Crouch pulled out and lit another cigarette.

"I see more. I see home," he said. And when Bob craned his neck and peered in the direction of Cowboy Rose, the old man said, "Not *that* home. My home country, the place my people has lived in for a hunderd twenty-odd years from the canyonlands to the hills. You know, the Jones and Plummer Trail went right through here, right under the goddamn windmill we're settin on. You can see its trace."

"Mr. Crouch, I think of those times too. I think about Lieutenant Abert coming into this country in 1845 and exploring the Canadian River for the first time, and all that he saw." As he said this he half sensed that what he wanted was to *be* Lieutenant Abert traveling through the unmarred plains, not a callow salesman exhorting old people to give up their properties.

"This is a unique part a North America. A lot a good men and women struggled a make their homes in this hard old panhandle." Ace's face was as creased as dried mud, the old eyes slitted, peering into the haze.

Bob fidgeted. "The ladies at LaVon's quilting bee told me about the old days—melons and cowboys and oil booms—I could see how it was. That old panhandle homey kind of life."

"You don't hardly know a thing about this place. You think it's just a place. It's more than that. It's people's lives, it's the history of the country. We lived through the droughts that come and we seen the Depression and the dust storms blowin up black as the smoke from a oil fire. We seen cowboy firin squads shootin half-starved thirsty cattle by the thousand. Yes, that's who had a do it, the men who took care a cows all their lives was the ones had a shoot them too. And there was many a tough saddlebum turned his head away."

"That was almost seventy years ago, sir."

But Ace had the bit in his teeth. "Ever year a few more sell out to the corporations. Ever man for hisself. It's mostly the younger ones wants the money as they don't intend a live here. They got their hunderd reasons for it. I happen a feel we should stick together on this one and tell the hog farm corporations to go pound sand."

He picked up the tea jar and drank, passed it to Bob. "All we got is the land and the Ogallala and they are ruinin both. So that would be my answer to Global Pork Rind. *Go pound sand.* When you come here, Bob, why everbody thought you was a shinin light when you talked about puttin the land to use for nice houses, nature estates and all. It seemed like you was bringing in a kind a value-added situation."

"But Ace, we can't live in the past. And you can't bring it back. Don't people have a right to make up their own minds where and how they want to live their lives? Probably in forty or fifty years there'll be something else that pushes out the hog farms and somebody else will say how sad it is, how the panhandle hog heritage is being lost."

"Somethin else like what, use the panhandle for a atomic testin ground? And you sure don't need a tell me about change. A lifetime windmillin. It's like Brother Mesquite says: 'Things are as the windmill to the wind, constantly changin, makin a response.' But what things change *into* is somethin else. Just one or two people can stand up and fight back."

"I don't agree with that, sir. Ace. Look at the Indians. *They* fought back and you see what happened to them. They had something other people wanted. Same thing here. You got something the hog corporations want and they will get it."

"Not as long as I'm around. You know, your luxury home idea was pretty good. It could work if there wasn't no hog farms around. Maybe not just places for rich folks, but somethin more moderate. Not luxury homes but decent houses and room for decent people who got some respect for the land. I think you had the germ of a good idea there. Like to talk more about that to you."

"Frankly, sir, Ace, I think the hog farms are here for good. Maybe that's the future of the panhandle—people will move out and turn it all over to the hog farms and feedlots. Intensive stock-raising. It could be the best thing."

"Best thing for who? And would you be proud a be part a that? Here, have some more ice tea."

Bob sighed. "Well, best thing for the general good." He was getting nowhere. The man was hung up on the past. Ace passed the jug of iced tea to Bob and talked on.

"Bob, everbody here knows a few things about swine. Some still do raise them on a small scale. Phil Bule raises beeler pork, no antibiotics, no growth stimulants or hormones, and it's the best you ever eat. His pigs live outside and they can go in the sun or the shade as they want. The skin on factory hogs is as thin as tissue paper. Try to get em in the truck, just touch em and they bleed. An some a those hogs is so weighty their legs snap like sticks. Pigs twitch their head and rub themselves raw on pen wire. Of all the creatures' lives on God's earth, for downright pure-dee hell the life of a hog farm pig has got a be the worst." He crushed his cigarette butt against the tower's steel frame. "The whole thing is ugly and unnatural and I'm against it. And you should be too."

"I don't know what I'm against," mumbled Bob. "And I don't see what's wrong with adapting to change. There's plenty of people here who don't object to having corporate agriculture in their county. And they don't mind the lagoons, either."

"For Christ's sake, don't call them 'lagoons.' A lagoon is a beautiful pool a water set off from the sea. Anyway, here's the Canadian River valley, a small piece a the world, got its own cultural ways grew out a the place. It's a rural ideal, you might say. But a outside force can break it up. And then you git anger and resentment because what made the place special and good to people is wrecked. And that's where we are now, in shadowland."

"Mr. Crouch—Ace—it seems to me that windmills did a share of breaking things up too. I mean, you could say that windmills were a kind of anticommunity technology—every man for himself instead of water co-ops. So what you've done all *your* life has been against the panhandle too. How is that different than a businessman trying to make a living in large-scale stock raising?"

"You should a been a lawyer, Bob. It takes us back around the circle. There are so many people in the world now that there is not enough elbow room. Doesn't your rural resident born here have a right a live here? More right than a absentee corporate hog farmer to ruin the place?"

"Why should being born in a place give you more rights than anybody else? I've never understood that. It's like Francis Scott Keister going around with his bumper sticker, 'Texas Native.' I mean, so what?"

"It's historical and psychological rights. Hell, it's

gettin to sunset and we're at loggerheads. Time to git down and head out."

Nimbly Ace Crouch stood up, stretched, lowered the bucket of ice and tea to the ground, then went quickly down the ladder, half sliding. Bob followed cautiously and slowly, gripping the side rails. At the bottom the old man said only, "Follow me and I'll unlock the gate for you."

At the highway Ace Crouch opened the gate, drove through and parked his rig, held the gate open for Bob. Bob stopped outside the gate as well and, while Ace relocked the gate, tried to continue his argument.

"I mean, is it fair for your brother to suffer out there when he could be in town enjoying life? And what about the Shattles? Mr. Shattle is sick from the fumes. They need to sell those properties. And—"

"Son, Tater and me is movin toward death. We're in the years when we meet our fate instead a dodgin and twistin in the long game that nobody can win. We sorted it out, Tater and me, that we got a obligation to the panhandle. I'm the oldest one. I got the responsibility. And the power. Tater and me won't sell nothin to no hog corporation. You lose. But remember, you can't win em all."

"*All!?* I haven't won any."

Ace Crouch got in his truck. He nodded once and drove away.

Bob, who had never been a villain before, smarted with resentment. But he was afraid of losing the way again, so followed the old man's taillights.

33

FAILURE

As Bob drove into Woolybucket, tired and blue, for it had been a day strewn with the sandburs of defeat, he noticed that the lights were on in the Old Dog and people moving about inside, then remembered Cy's intention of staying open late to catch something he called "the supper trade" to combat the losses from the Christian competition. A bowl of chile would cheer him up. Maybe Brother Mesquite would be there, although he didn't see the monk's old pickup. He parked in front of the café and went in.

LaVon Fronk sat in one of the booths, a plate of pork chop bones and bread crusts before her.

"Well, Bob, just the one I was hopin a see. Come in on purpose, find out if you was around. Called Jae-lene and she said you been out all day. I got a favor to ask."

"I didn't ever expect to see *you* here," he said. "I thought you swore never to eat here."

"Coolbroth wanted a eat here but he gobbled and run off to one a his meetins. I have to say, Cy's a pretty good cook. What I wanted a ask you was if you would sit in the quilt raffle booth for a hour tomorrow at the Barbwar Festival. I got everthing covered except from two to three o'clock. Coolbroth won't do it. It's just sellin raffle tickets. The drawin is at five."

"Well, I guess I could. If it's just an hour."

"It is. At three o'clock it's"—and she consulted a list she pulled from her purse—"Mrs. Herwig. You remember Mrs. Herwig. Or somebody else. You know, Bob, there is some folks mighty mad at you for trying to git their land away for hog farms. Even Freda Beautyrooms' son there, that Waldo, he took a half-page ad in *The Bummer* sayin nobody should sell to you, you misrepresented yourself."

"I never wanted Freda Beautyrooms' place for a hog farm. He got it all wrong. I thought it would be a great location for the luxury houses."

"Oh yes, all surrounded by hog farms, stinkin to the north, south, east and west? He says you're not connected with any real estate firm. This's good pork," she said, gnawing on a bone.

"Probably from one of the terrible hog farms."

"No, Cy Frease gets his pork from Phil Bule. I asked him."

Bob heaved a sigh. "Anyway, nobody is selling to me. It's finished. I'm going to call Global Pork Rind Monday morning and tell them I couldn't make any sales."

"I don't understand how come you care so much about that company. Do you have stock in it? Are you related to the Pork Rind people?"

"No. It's just I took on a job and I wanted to—I

don't care anything about Global Pork Rind, but I think it's important to finish what you start."

"If you don't care, then quit makin a fuss."

"LaVon, I have a responsibility. You know my folks abandoned me. I don't want to be like them. I don't want to just walk out with the job unfinished."

"I don't see there's any kind a 'finish' to a job buyin hog farm sites. People change jobs all the time. It's not anything *like* your folks runnin off. Find somethin else to do. There's work out there for smart young men. That reminds me, Jaelene telephoned a tell you if I seen you that you had a bunch a calls today, urgent calls."

Bob continued to argue. "But what about those people who were going to sell their places? I mean, they are on the spot now. Sure, *I* can go off and find another job, but what about Tater Crouch? He's got to smell that stink forever. And the Shattles. Even Jim Skin, who could use the money for that old worn-out land."

"Don't lose sleep over it. Tell you something, all a them people *is* sellin their land, but not to you. There's another buyer."

"What, Evelyn Chine? She's hurt bad and not likely to be in her job again."

"No, not her. Ace. Ace Crouch is buyin it all. In fact, he bought the hog farm next a the Shattles and now he's tearin down the hog houses, just smashin away. The hogs all got trucked off this afternoon."

"Ace? Ace Crouch? But he's poor. He couldn't buy

a hog farm. Or all these ranches. I just talked with him this afternoon and he never said a word about buying the hog farm."

"He's not talkative, like Tater is. Anyway, you ought a go ask Tater. Seems Ace had a few surprises up his sleeve for Tater and everbody else."

"By God, I will," said Bob, who was puzzled and angry. He got up.

"Bob, don't you want supper?" called Cy from the stove. "You don't want the pork chops, there's spaghetti and meatballs."

"No time," and he rushed out the door.

He parked in Tater's front yard, leapt up the porch steps and opened the door without knocking. The old man was sipping from a tumbler of whiskey and watching television, *Sex in the City.* He looked up, gestured at the overcostumed actors.

"Don't seem like we're on the same planet."

"Tater," Bob said. "Tater, what is going on? What are you all doing to me? Will somebody please let me in on the secret? Your brother Ace chewed my ear off all afternoon about pioneers and moral geography."

"Bob, nobody's doin nothin to you. Ace laid it all out to me and he's the oldest. He got me to see that while we last we must not give up the panhandle to you or nobody. This is our place, and we are goin a hang on to it. Nobody is sellin a ranch to a hog farm from here on out."

"But how? First of all people here are too independent. They won't cooperate. Seems to me panhandle people would rather ruin themselves than work together. And Ace can't buy all these places. It would take millions and millions. You told me yourself he doesn't have a pot to piss in."

"I was wrong about that. He's got solid gold pots with diamonds around the edge. That old Dutchman he used a be windmill partners with left him everthing. He didn't say nothin because it's took a year for the money to get untied. He thought the lawyers might get it all. But they didn't, he got it. *Hunderds* and hunderds a millions. Ace is too rich to stand. He is a petrodollar billionaire. And see, him and Coolbroth Fronk and LaVon and the Shattles and Brother Mesquite and me and a bunch a other people is with him. He's got it in mind a buy up all the farms and ranches and the hog places he can, and politicians, too, if that's what it takes to git them on our side. We're goin a take down fences and open her back up, run bison in the panhandle. Brother Mesquite's goin a help with it. We got them Poppers comin down a talk at the church next Thursday. They're already doin this kind a thing in the Dakotas. Why not the panhandle? There's even a buffalo market now that Ted Turner's openin up them bison burger stands. Things is goin a change."

"I'll believe it when I see it," said Bob, turning on his heel and leaving. He left the door open as a sign of displeasure.

• • •

The wind was wrong and the stink of hogs more powerful than ever as Bob drove up to the Shattles' house. He supposed, if they really had moved out the hogs, that it was the festering lagoon—manure pit— that continued to waft its abominable odors over the prairie.

"Hello, Bob," called Jaelene Shattle. "Did you hear the news? Ace Crouch bought the hog farm and moved out all the hogs today. Next week they are goin a pump the lagoon into big septic trucks and take the stuff to Nevada. Should take it to Warshinton. Give the stink to the government."

"So you don't have to sell your place."

"Oh, we *are* goin a sell it. Tater, too. Ace is behind a big consortium, the Panhandle Bison Range. Buffalo, prairie dogs, prairie chickens, native grass, antelopes, all that kind a thing, somethin like a nature preserve. And he figures people will want a have houses near the nature preserve, see the buffalo and all. Sort of what you was sayin back when you was lookin for luxury house sites. Waldo Beautyrooms is goin a sell the Axe-Head Ranch to them."

"This is just talk," said Bob. "It can't work."

"We know it's goin a be hard work, takin back the panhandle from the corporations, but what else can we do? Give up and die? That reminds me, you had telephone calls today. Here, I wrote everthing down."

Bob looked at the sheet of paper: Abner Chine, urgent, with a Kansas area code number; Uncle Tam, urgent, with the shop number; Brother Mesquite, urgent, with the monastery number. He called Mr. Chine first.

"Oh, Mr. Dollar, I'm glad you reached me. Mrs. Chine and I want to talk to you about Evelyn. Her doctor seems to think that you and Evelyn are—married? Would that be so? Evelyn said nothing to us about it and in light of her situation—the doctor thinks she will be spending many months, even years, in therapy and will need constant care, so if she is married we need to know about it, as much for the insurance situation as anything else. Her employer says she did not incur the injury in the line of work so we are left holding the bag, so to speak."

"I'm sorry, Mr. Chine, that was a misunderstanding, entirely my fault. Evelyn and I are not married. I said that so I could get to see her. I'm sorry, sir, I didn't mean to cause a problem. Actually, I think she *was* injured in the line of work. Evelyn had an unorthodox but effective approach to sales."

"That could help our case, Mr. Dollar. Would you be willing to talk with Mrs. Chine and I about that?"

"Certainly," said Bob. "I expect to be driving up to Denver on Monday. Will you still be in Amarillo? I could go that way."

"We'll meet you there, Bob. How about two o'clock at the hospital? And you can see Evelyn. She's conscious now but they say it will be a long haul for her. It would do her good to see you. Even if she don't recognize you."

•   •   •

505

He called Uncle Tam at the apartment, for it was dinnertime and his uncle would be scraping carrots and chopping leeks.

"Hi, Uncle Tam. It's me."

"Bob, thank God. I was worried. There was a piece in the *Post* today. Front page. There was a shooting at Global Pork Rind yesterday afternoon. Wait a minute, I've got it right here. 'An unnamed woman, thought to be a disgruntled employee, entered a meeting room at Global Pork Rind and opened fire on four executives, killing one and severely wounding another. Mr. Quantum Goliath of Tokyo, the president of GPR, was at the meeting. The three survivors were taken to Denver General Hospital. The names of the deceased and injured were not given pending notification of next of kin. The woman is in custody.' I was going to listen to the eleven o'clock news and see what they'd found out."

"My God," said Bob. "They don't say who got killed?"

"Nope. 'Pending notification.'"

"I think I can guess who the woman is. There's a very angry wife from down here whose husband was planning to sell out their ranch to Global Pork Rind and he was having an affair with a GPR saleswoman too. Tazzy Keister. She shot her husband and the saleswoman and then escaped from the local jail. She was on the warpath, declared war on hog farm companies."

"Bob, you are in dangerous work."

"I was, Uncle Tam. But I'm out of it. I'm a failure. I couldn't even make one sale. I've abdicated my responsibility. I guess I'm like my dad."

"Whew. I am so damn glad you are safe. So you failed to buy up people's farms and ranches for hog facilities. Is that such a terrible thing? Come on home and we'll spread the whole thing on the table and take a look at it."

"I will come back next week. I promised to help at the big Barbwire Festival tomorrow. And all Sunday there will be cleaning up to do. I want to say goodbye to a few people here. They have a plan to get around the hog farm thing. So next week I'll turn in the car and talk with Mr. Cluke, tell him I quit."

"He might be one of the ones that was shot up at that meeting."

"He might. If you hear anything, let me know." He thought his twenty-five years of life were like a slag heap of mine tailings that had yielded only a few specks of gold. But when he said this to Uncle Tam, instead of sympathy or some unclelike bit of advice his relative howled with laughter.

"How small are those specks of gold, Bob? About the size of pepper specks? Or fly specks? Bigger than a grain of salt?"

"See if I tell *you* anything again," said Bob and hung up.

The last phone call, to the monastery, got him a

recorded message. "Good evening, You have reached the Triple Cross Monastery. We are unable to take your call now as we are at compline. Please leave a message after the tone or call again in the morning after lauds."

34

BARBWIRE

The telephone rang at sunup and Bob staggered out of bed, stepped on something extremely sharp and painful, hopped to the phone and picked up to hear Jaelene Shattle saying sleepily, "Who? Oh, Bob, he's still asleep. Can I take—"

"I'm here, Jaelene," he broke in.

A hearty male Texas voice boomed back. "Well, Bob, good mornin! It's a beauty. Look out your window and rejoice."

"Brother Mesquite?" He examined the sole of his foot, removed a goathead that had struck deep. How had it got into the house?

"Right. A beautiful day. Cool now, but she'll warm up. Sorry I missed you last night. Wonderin if you were takin in the Barbwire Festival today?"

"Yes. I promised LaVon I would sell raffle tickets in the quilt booth for an hour this afternoon."

"Good. I'll just look for you. What time will you be holdin down the raffle fort?"

"Two to three. But I'll probably go over there this morning and look around. I've never been to a Barbwire Festival before."

"It's quite the big affair. Woolybucket's day in the sun. Don't miss the rodeo. Yours truly is ropin. With Brother Hesychast."

"I would not want to miss that," said Bob. "When does it start?"

"Rodeo starts at noon. Look forward to seein you, Bob. I need a talk to you about something. Connected with Ace Crouch's project. You heard about that, right?"

"Yeah," said Bob, letting a little bitterness creep into his voice, looking out the window at the brilliant sky streaked with crimson and gold.

He showered (still a luxury after the sponge baths of the Busted Star bunkhouse days) and dressed first in shorts and sleeveless shirt, for he thought it would be hot, but when he looked in the mirror it struck him as an un-Texas costume. And there was the rodeo and the blazing sun—no doubt people would dress western. He put on jeans and a long-sleeved shirt, tugged on the never-yet-worn cowboy boots Mr. Cluke had told him were vital to success in the panhandle. Maybe that had been his problem, the wrong footgear. He looked in the mirror and was not displeased until he thought about Uncle Tam's account of the Global Pork Rind shooting. He would call LaVon and let her know. For once *he* would have the news. But when he tried her line it was busy.

Downstairs Jaelene, prodding a pot of grits, told him to sit down and have breakfast. She poured a mug of coffee, cracked two eggs into a buttered pan and shook pepper over them.

"You want orange juice, Bob?"

"I'd like a little. Can I help?" For some reason he held back from telling Jaelene about the shooting.

"Sure enough. You can butter the toast when it pops up. Most people don't have grits *and* toast, but Mr. Shattle insisted when we got married and it's kind of a habit now. There's jam in the refrigerator. Butter's right here."

There was jam and more jam. The Shattles had sweet teeth for sure, he thought as he plucked out jellies, jams, fruit curds and something called Blueberry Tiger.

Jaelene Shattle refilled their coffee cups, slid the eggs, flanked with sideburns of buttered grits, onto plates and sat down opposite him. He must be in Mr. Shattle's chair, he thought, spreading the Blueberry Tiger on his toast. He was surprised by the odd combination of chile, bourbon and blueberry.

"How is Mr. Shattle doing this week?" He wondered who at Global Pork Rind had died.

"Good. You know, I told him about Ace's plan and that they moved the hogs out and was goin a drain the lagoon and fill it up with dirt next week and that poor man, he just broke down and wept. It's been awful hard on him. He said, 'You tell Ace I'll buy all the buffalo I can afford.' I doubt he knows how much they cost. Not like cows! He'll be home soon as they pump that old lagoon out and it starts a sweeten up."

• • •

The air outside was lukewarm, the sky as unmarked with weather trouble as a sheet of blue paper. As he drove toward Woolybucket over a road the color of crushed almonds he realized he felt extremely well, free of the press of hog farm site finagling, ready for a day of pleasure. The temperature heated up as he drove. By the time he got to Woolybucket the bank thermometer read 94 degrees. In Woolybucket it seemed everyone felt as he did, for people were jovial and laughing, nearly everyone dressed in jeans, long-sleeved shirts and cowboy boots except for a few tourists in shorts, their legs already red. He did not have a hat and set out to find one in the dozens of kiosks and booths standing along Main Street. The town was transformed. Crews must have worked all night to get the stands and platforms and booths ready. The stage, with a sign wreathed in barbwire nailed across the front, was at the end of the street:

STREET DANCE 8 PM
PANHANDLE PINTOS
with
FRANKIE McWHORTER

Already crowds were moving along the street, clustering around the booths, breathing in the delicious smell of roasting meat and mesquite smoke. The thermometer climbed to 104 degrees, a heat almost as pleasurable in its intensity as a mouthful of cognac.

512

BARBWIRE

The barbwire kiosks drew heavy crowds, rashy and sweat-spangled, fanning themselves with rodeo programs and souvenir fans that read WOOLYBUCKET BARBWIRE FESTIVAL. The town was packed with collectors of barbwire, crowding the dealer kiosks that offered eighteen-inch strands of antique Crandel's Twist Link, Miles' Open Diamond Point and the like. A slight breeze from the northeast came up and someone said, "She's drawin moisture," pointing to the west, where Bob saw a dryline of thunderheads. The lawn around the courthouse seemed intensely tan.

Beyond the barbwire booths stood the sign booth, which featured designs and trinkets made of rusted wire. Bob, sweating heavily, bought a windmill for himself, and for Uncle Tam a barbwire owl as a curiosity. Behind the counter a rough-skinned man with narrow and slanting blue eyes under bushy brows, in jeans and a leather vest, armpit hair shooting out in pale bunches, told Bob he could make any name or design he wanted, even obscenities and rudeness, and send it in two weeks. Bob ordered a sign for LaVon's kitchen that would spell out VIVE LA FRANCE! He ordered another for the Shattles: WE ♥ CLEAN AIR.

He passed a heap of hide rugs and a display of huge curved longhorns ready for mounting on a Cadillac hood or the living room wall. There were booths for candy floss, snake cakes, bratwurst, Australian rain slickers and kitchen gadgets, pony-hide briefcases, bolo ties, leather and wool chaps. One boot shop carried hats and boots and Bob tried on summer straws until he settled on a Resistol poly-hemp with a hand-rolled brim, a Calgary crease and a black cord band. In the mirror he looked like a real Texan.

He continued his wander down the street in the shade of the hat, wondering why he had not bought one before now, passed bad cowboy art featuring lurid sunsets and rearing horses. People kept looking at the sky which had begun to cloud over. The bank thermometer had inched up to 107 degrees. The kitchen-gadget barkers shouted and waved multi-bladed implements. A few customers stood around the weather station and tornado warning systems booth.

"Keep that thing turned on," said Hen Page to the salesman, gesturing at the sky. Beyond it was the bison burger barbecue grill manned by Cy Frease, with Coolbroth Fronk putting the meat and fixings in buns and making change. Bob bought two with onions and salsa, ate them as he strolled.

He came to a gap in the booths, and in this open space sat Rope Butt in a saddle resting on an oversize sawhorse. From this perch he recited cowboy poetry on request for $2.50 a poem. Bob purchased a long comic recitation of Rope's own composition, "How to Make a Bridle," at a cost of five dollars, for it was, said Rope Butt, twice the length of a regular poem and had some bawdy lines for which there was usually an extra charge. When the recitation began to draw a small crowd Rope waved them away, declaring it was a private performance for a paying customer.

After the poem Bob paused to watch two arm wrestlers, both dripping sweat, the champion a huge cowhand from Goodwell, Oklahoma, who had so far defeated all challengers. Their fleshy arms made sucking sounds where their skins touched. There was a burst of applause from the stage as Buckskin Bill, chairman of the Barbwire Queen judges, announced the winner—Moxie Slauter, the oldest girl of Advance Slauter, a peaches-and-cream beauty with humidity-straggled maroon hair. Bob noted that she had double dimples and deserved to win.

At 11:45, in the liquid heat, he walked out to the rodeo arena at the north end of the main street, a place of steel and wood corrals he had seen fifty times deserted and forlorn, the air pale yellow with suspended dust. Now the place thrummed with diesel pickups and stock trucks, early comers already filling the spectator bleachers, horses and bulls and calves in the stock pens. The thunderheads loomed, the darkling plain flat beneath its indigo bulk. The entrance-way flew a banner announcing the 68th Woolybucket Ranch Rodeo. Barkers hawked cotton candy and cold drinks. He bought a ticket and went to the stands, picking out an aisle seat. The front row was taken up by eight assorted men, whom Bob guessed to be the monks from the Triple Cross, for they were dressed in chinos and short-sleeved shirts while the lay

Woolybucket audience wore jeans and cowboy boots. Tourists wore shorts and T-shirts. The smell of food was everywhere. A turkey leg vendor roamed the aisles selling the hot meat, followed by the taco man, the barbecue rib man and the popcorn lady, then the stringy youth with a pierced cardboard tray holding towering cones of cotton candy, to Bob's mind the second vilest confection on the planet, first place going to the candy apple. In the crowd Bob thought he saw the nurse with the flapper hair and dimpled cheeks, but when she turned he saw it was another woman. Perhaps he could see the nurse again when he met with the Chines at the hospital. Behind him someone said, "Fixin a have us a storm."

The inner wall of the arena and the fronts of the chutes were plastered with advertisements for local businesses. Many of the contestants were riding their shy ranch horses up and down in the arena to get them used to the crowd and the space. Brother Mesquite was with them, on his paint horse, Tic-Tac, a name the abbot had protested as unspiritual, but Brother Mesquite had grown up with horses named Tic-Tac and planned never to let the name fade.

Bob had been to many rodeos, but never a ranch rodeo. He knew some events were different. His program told him that the competitors were restricted to cowboys who worked local ranches, no professionals allowed. Three of the traditional events had been dropped—bull riding, which Bob regretted, and barrel racing, cause for rejoicing. The unfamiliar events were four-man penning, old-timer's bronc riding, double mugging, a feed sack race, a cutting horse contest and, as the last event, wild cow milking.

At noon on the dot the rodeo commenced, and Bob, surrounded by turkey leg munchers and squalling babies, stood with the rest of the crowd and took off his hat to the words of "The Cowboy's Prayer" intoned by Rope Butt. The line of thunderheads flickered with lightning but seemed no closer. The northeast breeze freshened and people sighed with pleasure. As the crowd sat down the Grand Parade began, composed of scout troops and the children of local business owners in gaudy costumes and waving advertising flags on horses groomed to spectacular showiness, their polished hooves gleaming, brushed haunches a-shine, manes plaited in intricate designs that would excite envy in an Afro-American beauty shop. The announcer, up in his high booth, was Warnell Pue, an Old Dog regular, and he was drunk, cracking jokes about the clowns (clothed in women's dresses chopped short at midthigh), mixing up names and even events. The contestants clustered with others from their ranches, stood leaning on the arena rails, alternately watching the action and the sky.

"Start with bronc ridin, ride as ride can, reglar saddle, first man out is Dalton Booklung of the Dirty Socks outfit over in Clayton, New Mexico, come all this way for the event. What? What?" He leaned down to someone shouting at him from the ground.

"O.K., little mistake there, not Dalton Booklung but

his brother Raine Booklung, still the Dirty Socks, Raine Booklung ridin Cap'n Crunch. This here is a mean bronc. He has put a man in the hospital already this year—he's in rooms 101 and 102."

Bob recognized Raine Booklung as the shirtless man from the barbwire sign booth. His long hair hung to the middle of his back. His wet arms gleamed. He stood on a rail of the chute pen while his brother and friends held a weasel-headed horse, suddenly dropped into the saddle like a sack of cement, the gate flew open, the horse twisted and reared, put his head down and his heels high and threw Raine Booklung into the dirt.

"One down. Guess that hurt, didn't it, Dalton?" called the announcer. "Little mistake, lemme see, the horse was not Cap'n Crunch but Devil's Avocado—no, Devil's *Advocate*." The cowboy, frosted with dust and manure, limped toward his friends and a bottle.

The bucking broncs won the day, defeating all of the cowboys, who included Dalton Booklung, announced, to applause, as "Doggone Booklung."

The team penning was next, an unfamiliar event to Bob. At the far end of the arena a small herd of calves with numbers on their sides milled about while half a dozen men set up a portable pen in the foreground. One man laid a chalk line in the dirt and four mounted cowboys from the Banjo-B Ranch entered the arena. One, with a red warlord mustache whose ends hung down on his chest, rode into the herd and began cutting out his three calves and driving them across the chalk line. The other men, without crossing the chalk line, tried to keep the calves from rejoining the herd but one small and agile calf broke away and raced back to the herd, and by the time the first rider cut him out again all three animals had fractiously gone in different directions. Only one calf was penned. One of the mother cows broke loose from somewhere and cantered into the arena.

"Better luck next year, boys," called the announcer. "Now we'll have some double muggin." The cow ran up and down, bawling for her calf. Warnell Pue's voice rang out.

"She's a mean old cow, she'll crawl and she'll bawl, she'll slink through the weeds like a reptile, goddammit. She'll horn you and ruin your business. Now we'll have some double muggin."

There were cries of protest that four teams had not yet competed in the penning, but Warnell Pue shouted back at them, "Well hell, better luck next year, boys, anyhow," and once more announced the double mugging contest. There was general confusion until two of the rejected cowboys climbed up into the announcer's booth and bodily removed Warnell. He was replaced by Advance Slauter, who mumbled about his lack of experience and said he didn't know any clown jokes, though he immediately tried to tell one, a long, involved story that brought in battle-axe mothers-in-law, a scolding wife, a smart dog, a mean bull and a talking horse, all to no point until the crowd groaned.

"All right, then, let's have the rest a the pennin. Heeeeere's the Wall Street Ranch boys. Better get on it, them cattle is mighty restless."

The team roping brought the crowd to its feet. The first pair out was Charles Grapewine and Shug Capps of the Diamond Bar. Grapewine, the header, tagged the corriente right in front of the gate and led it away in an L-bend. Capps caught the heels in a clean, traditional throw.

"Eleven seconds!" bellowed Advance Slauter as the timekeeper held up his stopwatch. None of the following ropers came close to that time. Bob saw Brother Mesquite outside the arena talking earnestly with his partner. Both men bowed their heads and mumbled together. Bob thought they might be saying prayers. Indeed, so often had Bob seen prayer and signs of the cross at rodeos that the entire event seemed one of religious ritual, requests to God for favor and thanks for victories. Brother Hesychast glanced at the sky and seemed to pinch the air in his fingers, rubbing it as though to gauge the humidity. The line of thunderheads was noticeably more distant and the northeast breeze cooled the plain. Maybe, Bob thought, there would not be a storm. After a brief discussion both men went to their bags and took out different ropes, but Bob saw Brother Mesquite change again, putting the new rope back and taking out the first—or a third—in its place.

The Triple Cross team was the last up. Brother Hesychast was on a tough-looking little blood bay quarter horse, rather thick in the leg, thought Bob, and Brother Mesquite on Tic-Tac. Both men wore their cassocks hitched up at the waist and crosses glittered on their chests. The horses wore overreach and splint boots to protect their legs, not common for ranch mounts, who generally had to take their chances.

Brother Hesychast atop his horse waited rigidly in the box and stared at some distant point in the arena. Brother Mesquite's eyes glittered like those of a cat who sees the mouse. The signal came, the steer burst out of the box and Brother Hesychast stood in his stirrups and rode, came up on the animal's left side, his rope twirling, the little blood bay rating the steer and then a smooth catch and the dally. The steer was fresh and lively and Brother Hesychast had to take hold strongly and turn him left across the arena. The steer was moving fast. As it turned Brother Mesquite bore down, in roping position, feeding the loop and then he tossed, roping the animal's heels out of the air, bringing the crowd shouting to its feet.

"Six one!" screamed Slauter. "Out a the air! How's that for a panhandle cowhand? That's National Finals stuff that we just seen. Goddammit, you won't see prettier ropin nowhere. Let's hear it for the Triple Cross boys." Bob shouted until his throat was raw.

The remaining events seemed tame despite the madness of the wild cow milking contest, wily old range cows cornered by three-man teams, who tried to squeeze a few drops of milk into a small bottle. Several cowboys limped from the field of battle, chased by the conquering cow. Wardell Pue, some-where in the crowd, began to call, "She's a mean old heifer . . ."

The Wall Street Ranch won the penning, the cow milking and the feed sack race and took overall honors for the day—three hundred dollars for the team, a saddle blanket for every competitor and the Woolybucket Ranch Rodeo cup, a real silver cup engraved with the names of the winning ranches going back to 1933, the second year of the rodeo. Brothers Mesquite and Hesychast each received a belt buckle and a pair of spurs made by esteemed local smiths, Brother Mesquite coming away with a set from Kevin Burns of Spearman, and Brother Hesychast a pair from Shamrock's Pat Vaughn.

Bob lunched a second time on a third bison burger, washed it down with black coffee and, for dessert, enjoyed two snake cakes, leaning forward to keep the powdered sugar off his shirt, when Sheriff Hugh Dough, both arms in casts and in company with his sister Opal, came up beside him.

"You got a call from your uncle. I told him I would pass along the message. It's about that shoot-out in Denver that Tazzy was involved in. Tazzy Keister? Your uncle said a tell you that the dead man is a Mr. Quantum Goliath. He is the president a Global Pork Rind. Tazzy went up there lookin for *you,* Bob Dollar. She went to the bunkhouse on the Busted Star first. LaVon saw her truck peelin out. You're lucky you was stayin at the Shattles'. Anyway, they got her now, she's in custody."

"What will they do to her? What about the son? Does LaVon know about the shooting?"

"Tazzy will have to stand trial. The kid is with his grandmaw. I expect he gets old enough he'll do like most Texas boys don't know what to do—join the navy. Yes, LaVon knows about the shootin. She listens a the police calls on her shortwave. She called me about seeing Tazzy in her truck the other day. You can't beat LaVon on news."

"Come on, Hugh, let's us git some a that barbecue," said Opal Head. "I'll feed it to you."

"All right, but first I got a go to the little boy's room. Let's go around by the jail a minute."

A little before two Bob strolled toward the quilt raffle booth, but while still at a distance, came onto a church jumble sale presided over by Janine Huske. That lady sat under a white canvas awning, her flushed face protected from the sun by a white lace hat trimmed with faux forget-me-nots.

"Hello, Bob Dollar," she called. "Want a do your Christmas shoppin early? We've got everthing from pot holders to doorstops. How about a nice jade elephant from Burma?"

Bob came over and shook her hand, glanced at the wares spread out on a table made of planks and sawhorses. It was a mish-mash of *Reader's Digest* books, gewgaws and paperweights. He caught his breath when he saw a wooden bureau drawer overflowing with costume jewelry, all of Bakelite and celluloid and other polymers he could not identify. The fabulous brooch he remembered from the quilting bee lay in sight. Janine Huske, following his eyes, said, "That's all Freda Beautyrooms' stuff. I thought it was kind a heartless a her son just a dump it like that—that's the way he brought it over, all higgledy-piggledy in that drawer—but that's what happened. Some of it's right pretty. Out a style now and all plastic. I would a arranged the nicer pieces but there's no room," waving at the stained ashtrays and yellowed boudoir lamps that took pride of place.

Bob picked up a green pearlescent key ring shaped like a tiny suitcase and centered with a Scottie dog cartouche. There were big chunky elasticized bracelets in dozens of colors. Some, with colored spots and ovals, he thought were special but did not know the name for them. There was a transparent yellow hinged bracelet with red geometric shapes superimposed on it, another black carved-hinge bracelet set with faux pearls. A tangle of earrings in extraordinary shapes had sunk to the bottom of the drawer, where they formed a mat of interlinked findings and fasteners.

"How much for the whole drawer?" asked Bob, trying to keep his voice steady.

"Oh, well, I don't know. They told me to sell each

piece for a dollar. But so far nobody's bought hardly nothin except LaVon found a red Eiffel Tower pin and she bought that. Tell you what, I'll go ask Rella Nooncaster. She's in charge. She's just over at the raffle booth." She pointed at the woman peering at her watch and looking around. Bob caught her eye and waved, pointed at his wrist to show he needed a minute. "If you don't mind waiting a minute I'll be right back."

"That's fine. Would you tell Mrs. Nooncaster that I'll be there as soon as we finish up? I promised I'd tend the raffle booth for an hour. That's where I was going when you caught me."

"Oh, well, I'm sure she'll make you a good price since you're helpin out." And she took up her purse and trotted toward the raffle booth. Bob unearthed a pin in the form of a black Bakelite bar with tiny brass cooking implements suspended from it. Uncle Tam would pass out when he saw this.

"She said how about twenty dollars for the whole shootin match?" Janine Huske's voice had the timbre of one bringing good news.

"Done," said Bob, foraging in his wallet. He handed her the bill, took up the heavy drawer and headed for the raffle booth.

"Here you are," said Rella Nooncaster. "I won't ask what you're goin a do with all that old jewelry. You must have a girlfriend somewhere? Or maybe it's for your mother or grandmother?"

"It's for my uncle," said Bob, pleased by the woman's face, the stage for a series of conflicting expressions.

"Takes all kinds. Anyway, here's what you do. Fill out the raffle tickets in two places, one for the buyer, one for the drawin. Five dollars a ticket. Give the pink one to the buyer, the white ones go in this box. And here's the money box. Whatever you do, don't leave the booth because both the money box and the quilt are valuable. Somebody will be here at three to take over. And thanks, Bob, for helpin out."

Sales were slow and Bob wished he had brought along Lieutenant Abert or *Broken Hand*. He began to pick out pieces from the jewelry drawer and rub them, sniffing for the phenol smell of Bakelite. A fat man with a paper sack of barbwire lengths and a bulky cylinder under his arm came up and looked at the quilt, which hung behind Bob.

"That's really something. That is a pretty piece of work. I'm an antique dealer from Charleston, South Carolina. I would surely love to buy that quilt. How much?"

"It's not for sale," said Bob. "It's a raffle. Five dollars a ticket and they have the drawing at five over at the bandstand."

"Well, let's us get whoever made it make another one for me. I'd pay"—and he paused, squinting judiciously at the quilt—"I'd pay two hundred dollars for one just like it."

"It's a whole lot of women make it, work on it for a year," said Bob. "Then it's raffled off. They only make one a year. These quilts bring thousands of dollars."

"All right, I'll take fifty tickets," said the fat man, peeling bills from the wad in his hand.

Bob's heart sank. He would be filling in the man's name and address for hours.

"What is your name, sir?" hoping for something short and quick.

"Hubbel D. Stocking. Address is Ye Quaint Antiques, 1371A Magnolia Boulevard South, Charleston, South Carolina."

"It may take me some time, Mr. Stocking, before I can fill out all your tickets. Would you like to come back for them in half an hour?" He was writing as rapidly as possible and had, in three minutes, filled out seven tickets.

"No. I'll set right here and wait. Tired of walking anyway. Brought my crossword puzzles, see?" and he pulled out a book of what Bob recognized as the easiest puzzles, insultingly simple, calling for such words as "cat," "here," "bell" and, for the big one, something like "Fourth of July." The cylinder under the man's arm turned into a folding chair and in a few moments the antique dealer was comfortably seated and filling in the empty squares of his puzzle.

At quarter of three, when Bob had written thirty-two of the fifty tickets, Brother Mesquite came up and said, "I'll take a couple, Bob. You got a minute?"

527

"Not really. I've got to fill out eighteen more for Mr. Stocking here and then I can do yours." His fingers cramped painfully.

"Tell you what, Bob, I'll give you a hand," and Brother Mesquite seized some tickets and began filling in *Hubbel D. Stocking, 1371A Magnolia Boulevard.*

"There you go," said Bob to the fat man, handing him the stack of pink tickets, turning back to Brother Mesquite. "That was beautiful heeling, Brother Mesquite. You could turn professional."

"I already got a profession, Bob. Pretty content the way things are. Got me a nice buckle and some beaut spurs, too," and he showed off the saucer-size buckle, which read

Champion
2000 Team Roping
Woolybucket 68th Barbwire Festival

Bob started to write "Brother Mesquite" on the raffle tickets.

"Whoa! I want my mother's name on the ticket," he said. "Write 'Laura Moody.' If it should win it goes to her." He hauled up his cassock and fished out ten dollars.

"Isn't that thing hot?" asked Bob, gesturing at the cassock.

"You wouldn't believe how hot. But it makes a nice statement, I think. After a rodeo we do usually

get a few boys wantin a know more about bein a
monk *and* a bison man. Anyway, Bob, I want a ask
you somethin. I guess you are headin out pretty soon,
right? Seein that the hog farm site business is not
doin too good?"

"I suppose so," said Bob. "In a few days."

"Well, you didn't buy many hog sites and you riled
some folks, but you also made a good impression on
some. Showed you had grit. Stuck with it even when
it got ugly. Ace is wonderin if you'd like a job workin
for us."

"Ace! For who? The monastery? Doing what?"

"No, for Prairie Restoration Homesteads. Sort a
what you was talkin about all the while—house sites.
Only not particularly for rich folks, not that luxury
estate thing. Soon as we get the hog farms cleared out
and the bison range established, Ace is thinkin there
would be people want a live where they can see bison
and watch the prairie come back. It would be like kind
a prairie restoration homesteads. Maybe one house per
square mile. Or maybe the houses clustered and the
rest empty. Wants to call them that—Prairie Restoration Homesteads. He's sort a talked to the Nature
Advocacy and the Wildlife Coalition and they think
there's somethin in it. If it looks like it's goin a take
off, they'll maybe come in with him. Each one a the
home sites would have a covenant—the buyer would
have to agree to maintain habitat for prairie species—
prairie dogs and burrowin owls, prairie chickens,
antelope or Baird's sparrow, the ferruginous hawk or

native prairie plants or whatever. Did you know there used a be black-footed ferrets here? And big old cougars and wolves and such? Ace wants a reintroduce the ferrets. Ace thinks there's people out there would be proud a get into such a way a livin, kind of a experiment in community habitat restoration. So he wonders if you'd like doin that kind a thing?"

"What kind of thing?" asked Bob.

"Why, sellin the homestead sites. Talkin a people about them. Like I just explained." He looked at Bob as at an idiot.

"I don't know," said Bob. "I *sort* of been thinking about going back to school. Learning about history, the Santa Fe Trail, learning Spanish, learn how to ride. Maybe start a small bookstore." He stopped, blushing and wordless.

"A bookstore! Never was a place needed one more. Woolybucket needs a bookstore bad," said Brother Mesquite. "I can teach you how to ride. Bunch a people can teach you Spanish. And the Santa Fe Trail is not far away. And you could still help with the prairie homesteads. Seems like you belong in Woolybucket, Bob. Tell you what, why don't you think it all over and get back to Ace or me in the next day or so?"

"I am," said Bob. "I am thinking it over." Brother Mesquite punched him on the shoulder and strode away, spurs jingling. The thunderstorm dryline had nearly dispersed, blown apart by the brisk wind that now sent paper and dust flying.

"Oh, Bob!"

He looked up at LaVon, who seemed coming apart in all directions, her face flushed, her hands full of papers, her lipstick a crooked smear as one who swipes it on without benefit of a mirror.

"LaVon. I tried to call you this morning, tell you about the shooting. But the sheriff says you already know."

"Yes, and it's terrible but it's the third death. At least we don't have that hangin over us. At least none a us knew the fella got shot."

"I knew him," Bob said. "He was the president of Global Pork Rind. He was my boss's boss."

"It's a tragedy. And poor Tazzy. And poor Francis Scott Keister."

"And their poor son," said Bob, hoping the boy had an uncle.

LaVon looked suitably tragic for a few more seconds, then said, "How'd you do? Sell any tickets?"

"I sold sixty," said Bob. "Fifty to one guy, that big man over there eating snake cakes."

"Oh Bob, didn't they tell you? The limit is ten tickets to any one person. Oh dear. The odds are very good now that that man will win the quilt and for a relative pittance."

"How many tickets have been sold in all?"

"I'm not sure. Over a thousand, I think."

Bob thought quickly. "His chances aren't that overwhelming. Fifty out of a thousand means the odds are one out of a hundred. Not that great. Just stir the names up well. Plus, whoever does win it gets it for a pittance anyway. I don't see the problem."

"I guess you are right. And in a few hours it will all be over and we can get back to our normal lives, whatever they are. I wanted a tell you, Bob, that Coolbroth is movin back into the house, to his grain-daddy's room. He says he can't do without the telephone since he got into this thing with Ace and them. So the bunkhouse is empty . . ."

Suddenly Brother Mesquite was at his shoulder again, whispering intensely.

"I'm serious, Bob. You think *hard* about it. I believe a bookstore would help everbody out. And Ace's is a noble project," and he was gone again.

"Well," said LaVon, "I better be getting back to headquarters. Give me your raffle tickets and I'll put them in with the others. It's a hour and a half until the drawin. I hope that big man don't win. He's not from around here."

"Don't let the wind get those tickets—they'll fly to Oklahoma. I suppose I've got to be getting along myself," said Bob.

But as he pushed through the crowd, walking along the sidewalk behind the street kiosks, he doubted Ace's plan could work. People did not want Baird's sparrow, they wanted bacon on their plates. He felt sorry for Brother Mesquite, for Ace, for the Shattles and Tater Crouch, even for Coolbroth Fronk. Their naïveté sparked his pity. He wanted to tell them that nothing worked out for the best, that ruined places could not be restored, that some aquifers could not recharge. They were all, except for Coolbroth, older than he was, Tater and Ace by many decades. How could they be so hopeful? How could they believe that prairie dogs would tame the urge to pump, to plow and crop, to build low white bunkers with giant fans and stinking lagoons? It was as unlikely as Evelyn Chine leaping from her hospital bed and roller-skating down the hall, as sad and hopeless as a snot-nose kid checking the mailbox for a letter with an Alaska postmark.

What would become of the panhandles, a region like a rug jerked back and forth, marked and trodden, spilled on, worn and discolored? Would everyone move to the edges and leave a huge center milling with bison? Would the buffalo be able to paw their way to water when the Ogallala was piped down to San Antonio? More likely, Ace would fail, for even he could not afford to buy up the entire top of Texas, and Habakuk van Melkebeek's money, from the bowels of the panhandle itself, would have been wasted. Then the place would turn into a massive hog farm, millions of hog bunkers and scummy lagoons spread across the old plain, waiting for what would come next. Would he be watching from Denver or would he somehow still be in Woolybucket dodging hail and eating cabbage pie at the Old Dog? But maybe Ace was right and this was the beginning of something huge.

In his mind's eye he saw the panhandle earth

immemorially used and tumbled by probing grass roots, the cutting hooves of bison, scratchings of ancient turkeys, horses shod and unshod pounding along, the cut of iron-rimmed wheels, the slicing plow and pulverizing harrow, drumming hail, the vast scuffings of trailed cattle herds, the gouge of drill bits and scrape of bulldozers, inundations of chemicals. What was left was a kind of worn, neutral stuff, a brownish dust possessing only utility. This ghost ground, ephemeral yet enduring, was what it came down to.

He passed the Old Dog as he walked. A sign in the window read CLOSED TODAY FOR BOBWIRE. He would miss Cy's cooking. He came abreast the old lawyer's office. There was a sign in that window as well, FOR RENT, and a telephone number. He stopped, pressed his face to the window.

He gazed into a high bare room with a stained hardwood floor. The walls were lined with empty bookshelves, floor to ceiling. The thin crack of an idea opened in his imagination. There was a small table and a wooden chair at the back, a box of papers. A door ajar showed another room with part of a tall window visible. He felt the wind pulling his hair. From the bandstand came the sound of a fiddle limbering up, ready to claw through the old tunes. He wanted time to stop, just for a few days, an hour. He needed to sort things out. But of course nothing stopped nor slowed, the minutes tumbling down, the day moving to a close, everything up in the air. He felt for his pen, found it and wrote the telephone number on the palm of his hand.

He would go back to Denver but not for long. LaVon owed him the story behind the photograph showing the deep scars on her grandfather's back.

AUTHOR'S NOTE

There are no counties named Woolybucket or Slick-fork in the panhandle country. The towns of Teemu, Cowboy Rose, Struggle, Woolybucket and Twospot are invented. The characters are not based on real people except in a remote way, as composites of human behavior, with some physical descriptions based on old photographs. Some anecdotes and incidents have been extrapolated from historical records and regional histories.

The costume notes of the 1884 leap-year party on page 154 are taken from William Curry Holden's *A Ranching Saga, the Lives of Williams Electious Halsell and Ewing Halsell* (San Antonio, Texas: Trinity University Press, 1976), vol. I, pp. 172–74.

Uncle Tam's comment on page 39 on humankind's inadvertent selection of rattleless rattlesnakes comes from Barry Lopez.

The lyrics on page 378 are from "A Perfect Day to Chase Tornadoes" by Mike Pratt and Jim White.

I know of no real Global Pork Rind Corporation nor any Barbwire Festival nor any monastic bison ranch. On the other hand, Bent's Fort is real, the names of many real panhandle towns are used here and the real James Abert spent many years in the service of the Topographical Corps.

ABOUT THE AUTHOR

Annie Proulx won the Pulitzer Prize for Fiction, the National Book Award for Fiction, and the *Irish Times* International Fiction Prize for *The Shipping News*. She is the author of two other novels, *Postcards,* winner of the PEN/Faulkner Award and the *Chicago Tribune*'s Heartland Prize, and *Accordion Crimes.* She has also written two collections of short stories, *Heart Songs and Other Stories* and *Close Range.* She has won two O. Henry Prizes for her stories. In 2001, *The Shipping News* was made into a major motion picture. Annie Proulx lives in Wyoming and Newfoundland.